The Pomegranate Gate

Also by Ariel Kaplan

Grendel's Guide to Love and War

We Regret to Inform You

We Are the Perfect Girl

The Mirror Realm Cycle

The Pomegranate Gate

The Republic of Salt

The Pomegranate Gate

ARIEL KAPLAN

an imprint of Kensington Publishing Corp.
erewhonbooks.com

Content notice: *The Pomegranate Gate* contains depictions of antisemitism, assault, murder, and torture.

EREWHON BOOKS are published by:

Kensington Publishing Corp.
900 Third Avenue
New York, NY 10022
erewhonbooks.com

All Kensington titles, imprints, and distributed lines are available at special quantity discounts for bulk purchases for sales promotions, premiums, fundraising, educational, or institutional use.

Special book excerpts or customized printings can also be created to fit specific needs. For details, write or phone the office of the Kensington sales manager: Kensington Publishing Corp., 900 Third Avenue, New York, NY 10022, attn: Sales Department; phone 1-800-221-2647.

ISBN 978-1-64566-094-1 (trade paperback)

First Erewhon hardcover printing: September 2023

First Erewhon trade paperback printing: September 2024

10 9 8 7 6 5 4 3 2 1

Printed in the United States of America

Library of Congress Control Number: 2023935301(hardcover)

Electronic edition: ISBN 78-1-64566-075-0

Edited by Sarah T. Guan. Permission to reproduce the cover design is granted by Rebellion Publishing Ltd. Book design by Cassandra Farrin and Kelsy Thompson. Map illustration by Serena Malyon. Pomegranate blossoms © Adobe Stock/natality. Hamsa © Adobe Stock/La Cassette Bleue. Azulejos tiles © Shutterstock/PK55. Author photograph by Ash Photography.

For my father,
Jonathan Daniel Kaplan

Can you see what I see, friend?
The sky is like a garden bed.
The stars are flowers blooming there,
watered by a pool, the moon.

—Solomon ibn Gabirol
(trans. Raymond P. Scheindlin)

Come with me, let's spend a night in the country,
my friend, you intimate of heaven's stars
for winter's finally over—you can hear
the doves and swallows chattering.
We'll lounge beneath the pomegranate trees,
palm trees, apple trees,
everything lovely and leafy,
stroll among the vines, and look with pleasure
at all those splendid faces,
in a palace loftier than everything around it,
built of noble stones,
solid, resting on thick foundations,
with walls like towers fortified,
set upon a flat place, plains all around it
splendid to look at from within its courts.
Chambers well-constructed, all adorned with carvings,
open-work and closed-work,
paving of alabaster, paving of marble,
gates so many, I cannot even count them!

—Solomon ibn Gabirol
(trans. Raymond P. Scheindlin)

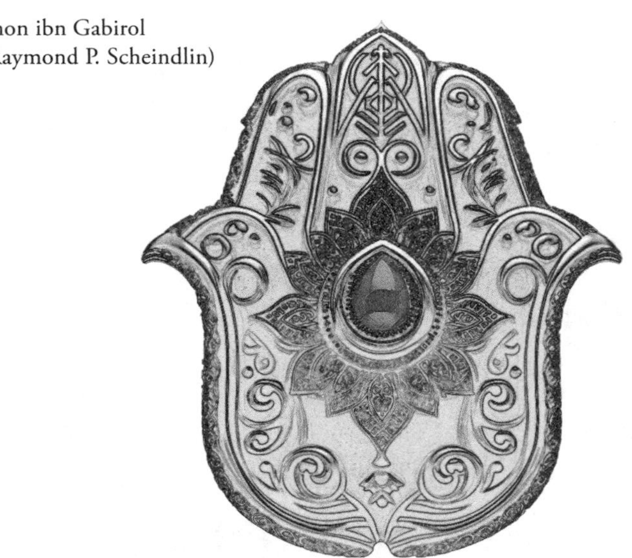

KINGDOM OF BARDENAS

KINGDOM OF SEFARAD

KINGDOM OF PETGAL

MANSANAR

LABRA

PENGOA

QORBA

SAVIRRA

RIMON

ELIOSSANA

MELEQA

MERJA

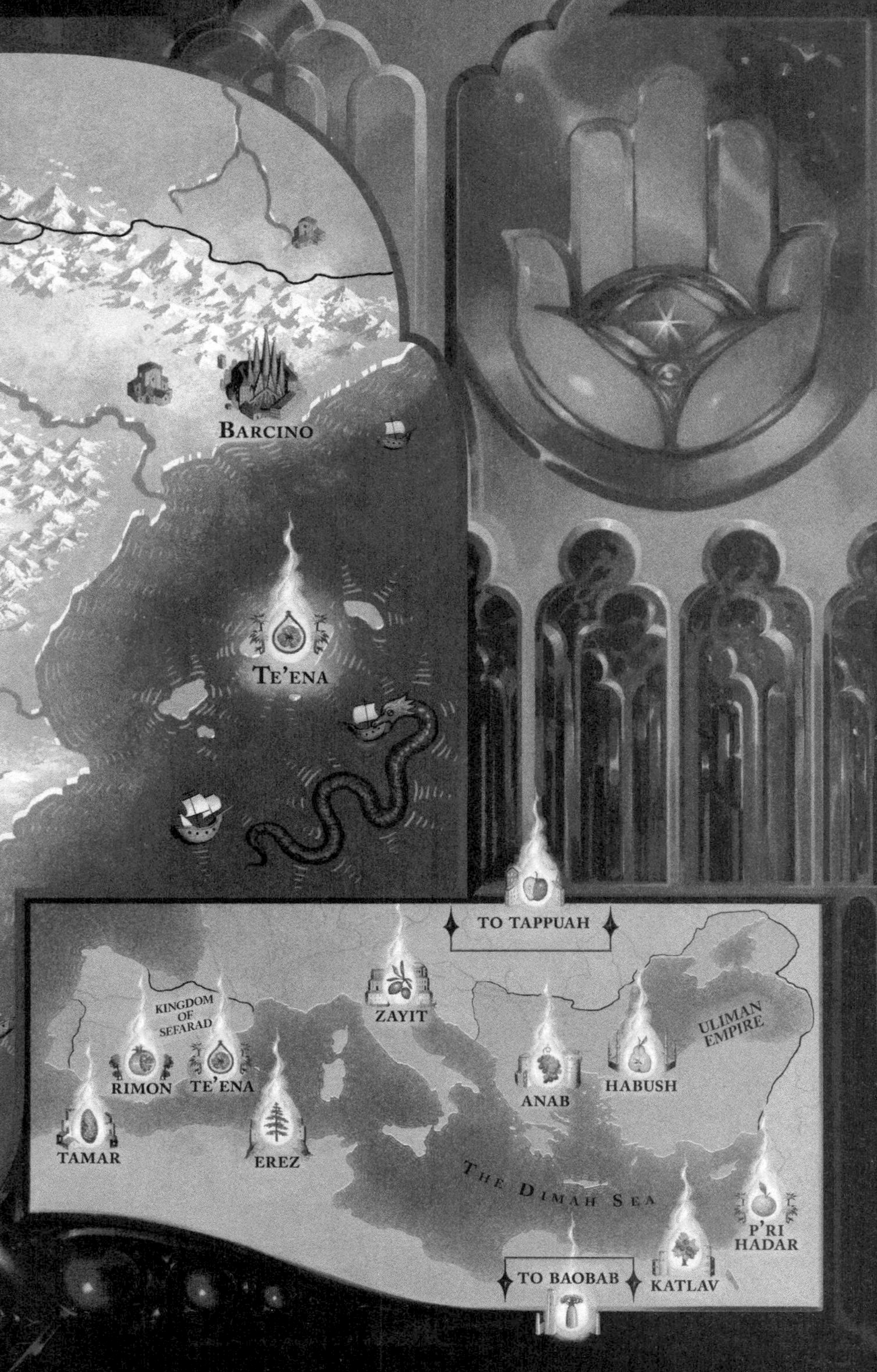

Barcino
Te'ena
To Tappuah
Kingdom of Sefarad
Zayit
Uliman Empire
Rimon
Te'ena
Tamar
Erez
Anab
Habush
The Dimah Sea
P'ri Hadar
To Baobab
Katlav

Dramatis Personae

FROM THE MORTAL WORLD

Toba Peres: A young woman from Rimon, known alternatively for speaking several languages and her sickly constitution.

Naftaly Cresques: A young man from Rimon, the latest in a long line of tailors. A bad one. Has visions and strange dreams that his father has forbidden him to discuss.

Abrafim Cresques: Naftaly's father, a tailor. Like Naftaly, he has strange dreams.

Elena Peres/Elena bat Beladen: Toba's grandmother. Has several sidelines she's used to keep the family afloat after Alasar lost his position at court.

Alasar Peres: Toba's grandfather, a former translator for the Emir of Rimon.

Penina Peres: Toba's mother, deceased.

The Old Woman: A beggar on the streets of Rimon, originally from Savirra. Her real name is unknown.

Salomon Machorro: A fabric merchant from the town of Eliossana; changed the family name to deSantos after being forced to convert. Has three children: Isidro, Antonio, and Katarina.

Mosse deLeon: Elena's brother, a banker living in Pengoa.

The Conde of Lobata: A Petgalese nobleman.

Dawid ben Aron: A half-Mazik from Luz.

Tamar of Luz: A human in Luz, friend of Marah.

FROM THE MAZIK WORLD

Asmel b'Asmoda (known in the dream-world as Adon Sof'rim): An astronomer and minor Rimoni Adon.

Marah: Founder of ha-Moh'to, former envoy to mortal Luz. Asmel's wife, Barsilay's aunt. Presumably deceased.

Barsilay b'Droer: Member of ha-Moh'to, originally from Luz. At one point a medical student.

Rafeq of Katlav: Expert on demons, member of ha-Moh'to, currently imprisoned.

Tarses b'Shemhazai: Member of ha-Moh'to, confidant of Marah. Originally from Luz.

Tsidon b'Noem: Also known as the red Mazik. A Rimoni with ties to La Cacería.

Relam b'Gidon: The illegitimate King of Rimon. Has three sons.

Odem b'Relam: The Crown Prince of Rimon; Asmel's friend.

Ardón b'Relam: The second-eldest prince of Rimon.

The Infanta Oneca: The Infanta of Rimon, cousin to the king.

LA CACERÍA

The Caçador: Founder and head of La Cacería.

The Courser: The Caçador's personal aide-de-camp. One of his three main lieutenants.

The Lymer: The Caçador's lieutenant. Commands the Hounds and Alaunts, responsible for work in Rimon and in the dream-world.

The Peregrine: The Caçador's lieutenant. Commands the Falcons, responsible for work abroad consisting mainly of espionage and assassinations.

Atalef: A demon with Mazik magic created by Rafeq of Katlav. Currently enslaved to the Caçador.

Geographical Locations

IN SEFARAD

Rimon: City-state in southern Sefarad.

Merja: Port city closest to Rimon.

Mount Sebah: The highest peak in Rimon, very near the Rimon Gate.

Guadalraman: The river running through Rimon.

Meleqa: Formerly Arab city near to Rimon, fell in a siege some years prior to the conquest of Rimon.

Qorba: City near Rimon. Original home of Elena's family.

Barcino: Northern port city in Sefarad on the Dimah Sea.

Savirra: Former residence of the Old Woman, home to a massive pogrom some years prior.

Mansanar: The capital of the northern kingdom.

Eliossana: Pueblo where the Machorros live.

OTHER LOCATIONS

Petgal: Country that shares the peninsula with Sefarad.

Pengoa: The port capital of Petgal, home of Mosse deLeon.

Labra: University town near Pengoa.

The Dimah Sea (the Sea of Tears): The sea that arose after the fall of Luz, between Sefarad in the west and P'ri Hadar in the east.

The Uliman Empire: A great multi-ethnic empire in the east, its capital is the gate city of Habush.

THE GATE CITIES

Luz: Legendary lost city, known as the location at which Jacob saw angels climbing a ladder to and from heaven, as well as the mythical source of tekhelet dye. The former seat of the Mazik Empire.

P'ri Hadar: The great city of the east, its queen is the oldest living Mazik.

Baobab: The most southern gate city, notable, like Tappuah, because of its great distance from the sea. On the mortal side, an important trade hub.

Katlav: On the southeast side of the Dimah Sea, an important center for education.

Erez: A city to the south of the Dimah Sea. Famous for its natural beauty and for being surrounded on three sides by a steep gorge, making it a natural fortress.

Tamar: A city to the south the Dimah Sea. In close proximity to Rimon; however the two cities are separated by the strait, so travel between them is limited in the Mazik world. An important producer of lentils.

Rimon: The great city of the west. After the fall of Luz, it suffered a series of bloody coups d'état that led to the rise of King Relam and La Cacería.

Te'ena: Made an island in the fall of Luz. Located roughly midway between Rimon and Zayit.

Zayit: North of the Dimah Sea, an important port city on the human side known in particular for its prominence in the salt trade. After the fall of Luz, Zayit became the wealthiest of all Mazik cities because of its continued trade with mortals, which was discouraged or forbidden elsewhere.

Tappuah: The city of the north; because of its distance from the other gate cities, Mazik residents are relatively isolated.

Anab: An important trade city in the Uliman Empire.

Habush: The capital of the Uliman Empire, in the east.

ONE

NAFTALY WAS DREAMING again, in that strange dream-landscape where the stars whirled overhead like snow on the wind and the people he met all had square-pupiled eyes.

They were all strangers to him, the square-eyed people he dreamed of—all save one: his father. In Naftaly's dreams, his father's eyes were odd, too, though waking they were wholly ordinary. Naftaly did not know if his own dreaming face had the square-pupiled eyes as well, having never come upon a mirror in his dreams, but he assumed so. He wondered how that looked, if it made him seem strange, or handsome, or hideous. No one ever remarked on it. His eyes, awake, were the same dark brown as his father's, round-pupiled and not particularly interesting.

In this dream, he'd come across his father eating oranges while sitting on a bridge Naftaly did not recognize, spanning what he supposed was meant to be the Guadalraman. They sat on the wall together, watching a swath of people traveling from one side of the river to the other, across the bridge which was lit at intervals with lights that seemed to burn without flame. It was a busy night, Naftaly thought. Probably he was dreaming of the end of a market day, though the people had no goods. He thought his subconscious could have come up with more interesting details: bolts of cloth or jugs of oil, or perhaps some sweets.

Naftaly was a tailor, son of a tailor, son of the same, though the elder Cresqueses had been at least passably good at their trade. The latest son was somewhat lacking in his ability to perform basic tasks, such as sewing in a straight line. His father insisted he would improve.

It did not seem to matter much to the trajectory of his life that he had not done so.

Everything was very settled on that score. Naftaly would take over his father's business, and with a great deal of luck he would not run it into the ground. He would greet his neighbors every morning, all of whom knew him from early childhood as a man of limited utility, but who would bring him work, anyway, because that was what one did with one's neighbor's mostly useless son. It was already too late for him to find another trade and, truthfully, he wasn't sure he'd be any better at something else. He had few friends, because he was too acutely aware of how much he was tolerated for his father's sake, and because he did not know what to talk about with other men his age, nearly all of whom were married. He was not especially devout, nor was he keen on drinking and brothels. What he wanted, more than anything, was to be a help to his parents rather than a hindrance, but he'd failed rather spectacularly in that regard.

He would keep Shabbat and the festivals, and run his shop until he couldn't any longer, and like this he would grow old.

Very occasionally, he would think about some alternative path he might have chosen, if he'd insisted when his father had denied him the opportunity to train with someone else. He imagined himself a very good trader of oil, traveling all the way to the sea, with so much spare money that the neighbors would admire him and come to him for help—and he *would* help. In this other reality, Naftaly was the greatest philanthropist Rimon had ever seen. Men would take his hand in thanks, and he would smile and say something like: "I'm so pleased to have been able to serve you."

He tried to quash such thoughts, but it was easy to daydream when sewing a hem in a poorly lit room. Perhaps this was why he was such a bad tailor. Better not to wonder about that.

On the bridge, Naftaly vaguely wondered where his father had gotten the oranges.

His father was slim, as was he, neither particularly tall nor particularly short; if either of them had a notable feature, it was their shared inability to grow much in the way of a beard. He offered one of the oranges to Naftaly, who took it with a nod of thanks. He did not say, *Thank you, Father*, because his father had told him long ago that one should never give up one's name in a dream.

"Not even to you?" he'd asked.

"Not to anyone," his father had said. "Never say your name, or mine, or even call me 'Father' out loud."

Naftaly didn't know if other people had these sorts of rules; if they nearly always dreamt of strangers who were never to learn their names. But occasionally when his friends or schoolmates mentioned their dreams, it seemed like theirs were different. They dreamt of pretty girls. Naftaly had never dreamt of a pretty girl.

He ate his dream-orange in silence. Finally, his father said, "They're in a state today."

"A state?" Naftaly asked. His father nodded toward the people rushing across the bridge. They did seem to be in a hurry.

"What's wrong?"

"Not sure," he said. "But something is happening, or is about to."

From the crowd on the bridge, he heard a whisper that rose up like a hiss: *La Cacería.*

"La Cacería?" Naftaly asked his father. He'd never dreamt of a hunt before; it made no sense for anyone to be hunting in the city, in any case. Did they think a buck was about to run across the bridge?

His father dropped his dream-orange and grasped him by both shoulders. "Wake up," he said. "Wake up now."

"What? How?"

The sound of hoofbeats came loud and fast, and two men rode in overland and blocked the far end of the bridge, bringing the crowd to a halt. Both tall: one dark, one with hair that looked dark at first glance but shone red when the starlight hit it. Both were dressed in dark blue. "No one move," the red man said.

Naftaly's father grabbed hold of Naftaly's ear and twisted it. "Wake up!" he ordered.

In his bed, Naftaly sat up with a start. He reached for his ear and found it still tender, then swung his legs over the side of the bed and made his way downstairs to find his father in the kitchen pouring a cup of wine with shaking hands.

"Father," he said.

"Naftaly," his father replied. The two never spoke of their shared dreams. Abrafim Cresques, in fact, denied them so often that Naftaly had for a long time thought they were merely an invention of his own imagination.

"Father," he said. "Please."

His father set down the wine, still half-full, saying, "Don't sleep again tonight."

\+ + + + + + +

IN TOBA'S GRANDFATHER'S bookcase, there was a map, rolled up, that stretched from Pengoa on one end all the way to P'ri Hadar on the other. When her grandfather's students were elsewhere, when she was done with her chores and no one was around to see, she liked to unroll it on the long study table and admire it. It had been inked by a master, with details so small you had to put your nose to it to see them all: imagined beasts at the far end of the sea; a cap of snow on Mount Sebah; impossibly tiny ships in the harbor at Merja.

That day, however, the students were there, arguing in hushed tones about the interpretation of one law or another, and how the Rambam said one thing and the Ramban another, yet Moses de León has said some third thing, but possibly (or probably) they were all three wrong. Toba wasn't particularly interested in this argument, which she thought had to do with how hungry one had to be before it was permissible to eat locusts.

If you were hungry enough to be seriously considering it, Toba thought, you ought to just eat them. Fortunately, Toba had never been that hungry. She'd never seen a locust, but she'd heard them described and they sounded vile, with the creeping and the swarming and all those extraneous legs. Anyway, they weren't supposed to be arguing about this at all. They were meant to be translating some mathematical text from Arabic into Latin, but the dryness of the work seemed to be too much for them, and arguing about locusts was more amusing. "Point of clarity," one of the young men put in, "are the locusts crawling or jumping?"

They were in higher spirits than usual. Rimon had suffered for two years under a siege from the northern queen, before the Emir of Rimon had surrendered the city at the beginning of winter and gone into exile across the sea. The government had changed, and the city had held its collective breath, but so far, the only significant day-to-day difference was that they were no longer eating the dregs of months-old rationed wheat. The city had fallen back into its old rhythm. In the Muslim quarter, the call to prayer came its usual five times a day. In the Jewish quarter, the shops closed down on Friday evenings. Except now, in the Christian quarter, a bell had been installed in the church, which rang, Toba thought, rather more than was strictly necessary. Still, the inhabitants went about their usual business of life, keeping the occasional wary eye on the workings of the new order. The Muslims had been promised immunity, and the Jews, too. The wind blew from a new direction, but still, the sun rose and set, as it had always done.

While the young men neglected their work and Toba's grandfather snoozed in his northern-style armchair (*the greatest thing ever to come out of the north*, he often said), Toba holed up in a corner with the map spread out across his personal desk. Toba traced the outline of the continents with her eyes. So many cities. There were so many cities. Where would she go, if she were to go somewhere? It was a game her grandmother had played with her since she was small. *Of course we are safe*, she would say. *But if you had to flee, where would you go?*

The north was full of barbarians, at least until you got to the lands of the Burgers. Then of course there was the issue that some king or other was expelling the Jews every few years, once they discovered that confiscating their property was a useful way to enrich the royal coffers. Petgal, in the west, had so far managed to avoid such behavior, but then you lived with the sea at your back, and that itself made Toba nervous. The south looked slightly more promising, but only just. East was surely better, with the ancient city of P'ri Hadar or the great port of Anab. Farther still were the silk road and the spice ports, where a traveling merchant might have a use for a wife who could write in five languages—even one without a womanly figure or much skill in housekeeping.

The door flew open, and the boys at the table jumped. Toba's hand flew to her throat; sometimes, when she was surprised, she had the instinct to shout, though she never had. The man who'd burst in was Reuven haLevi, a friend of her grandfather's.

Reuven cast his eyes around the room at the frightened faces of the young men, most of them too young even to have a beard, and Toba's blinking grandfather, who was too weary even to stand up.

"What's happened?" Toba's grandfather asked in a sleepy rasp; the voice of a man who had seen many things happen, and was not about to get out of his chair for one more.

One of the boys vacated his spot at the low study table and Reuven collapsed in his place on the floor. "I can't even say, every person in the street has heard a different rumor. Either we're going to be fed to the lions or driven into the sea, I don't know."

"There aren't any lions in Sefarad," Toba pointed out from her corner.

"Well, it'll be the sea, then," the man said with a wan smile. "I was trying to get to the Nagid's to learn the truth of the matter, but half the quarter is in the streets."

The boys pushed up from the floor then, and out through the courtyard, opening the gate out onto the street, which was indeed full of people and a great deal of noise. Several of the people were weeping. All were making haste toward the house of the Nagid; a throng of people, men and women both. No children, though. Those must have been left at home, which meant that whatever was happening, it wasn't entirely safe in the streets.

Toba's grandfather said, "Toba, go find your grandmother before this grows any worse."

Elena was visiting a neighbor a few streets away; her penmanship was so fine she was often called up to write letters for people; even, sometimes, for the rabbi himself. "Go," he said.

Toba hastened through the door and out onto the street.

From the other direction came a woman wailing openly, her mouth agape as if it were locked that way, in a permanent howl.

Toba picked up her pace, wishing that she could move with some legitimate haste. It would be good, right now, to be able to do more than walk.

It was one of the peculiar things about Toba, and there were several: Toba could walk, but she could not run; she could talk, but she could not shout; and she could write faster—with either hand—than she could speak. If she moved at more than a brisk pace, she would find herself splayed on the ground; jumping, likewise, was impossible for her. And if she tried to raise her voice, it was as if a hand were constricting her throat, and it would be several long moments before she could breathe again. The writing was less of a trouble, though it had vexed her grandfather's students when she was younger, particularly when she'd flaunted her talent of writing with both hands at once, a gift her grandfather had warned her to conceal.

Odd things, all of these, and then one more: while Toba slept, she could not dream.

As a child, she'd been the object of torment. The other children had conspired to make her run—by stealing her toys and then fleeing—and then laughed while she fell. Or they'd pulled her arms behind her back until she was forced to call for help, and laughed when she'd collapsed, breathless on the ground.

She hadn't much cared for other children.

Her grandfather had taken pity on her, and so, instead of playing with the neighbors, she'd spent most of her early days assisting him, sitting in with his students. At first, they'd been charmed by the tiny girl who learned as quickly as they did, but as she became a woman, they'd become less easy with her. Her grandfather had expected marriage proposals; for a scholar, a wife literate in five languages was a boon in free labor, but he hadn't considered that this was only for a *wealthy* scholar. For a poor one, well, he would need someone to manage a household, and Toba wasn't much good at that sort of thing. She was too quiet, too peculiar, too weak. Food often tasted poorly to her, and she ate little as a consequence. She'd been a sickly child, and now she'd become a sickly woman, more than ten years past marriageable age.

Still, she hurried as fast as her sickly legs would carry her; too fast, in fact, and she found herself sprawled on the ground. She instinctively curled in on herself, expecting to be trampled by hundreds of feet, but felt a pair of hands on her shoulders instead.

"Get up," said the voice associated with the hands. "You're going to be crushed."

Trembling, she got to her feet. A young man was in front of her blocking the path of the people who would have stepped on her; no easy feat, since he wasn't especially large himself. "Are you all right?" he asked.

She didn't recognize him, which wasn't a surprise; Toba rarely went out, and unless he trained with her grandfather Toba was unlikely to have seen him. "I'm fine," she said. "I'm going to get my grandmother," she added, though he hadn't asked that.

"Can you get there on your own?"

"I think so," she said. He nodded and was gone, and she started to cross the plaça to find her grandmother.

TWO

THE PLAÇA WAS entirely filled with bodies, and most of them were dead.

That was Naftaly's first impression. He reeled and nearly fell, then he blinked the image away. They were not bodies. They were people, living people, swarming the square, all talking at once. He knew why; he'd already heard the bitter choice that had been laid at the feet of his kinfolk . . . stay and convert, or leave. And not just leave, but leave everything.

People were weeping, and not only the women. Men sobbed openly. Those, he knew, would be the ones who were planning their own exiles. Those who had already decided to stay could not be so bold as to weep in public.

As he crossed the square, the people persisted in morphing into bodies in his eyes. "Not now," he whispered. "Not now." But Naftaly Cresques was a bit touched, and always had been. He saw things, generally *unpleasant* things, and it was not simply a matter of willing the visions away, he had to wait for them to pass. Right now, they did not seem to feel like passing. The fact that he hadn't slept well the night before was probably not helping.

He felt himself collide with someone, and that seemed to be enough to quiet his mind, and his vision snapped back to reality. A girl. He'd bumped into a girl, who responded by smacking face-first into the ground.

He hadn't bumped her hard, but she was so slightly built a child could have knocked her over. As he bent to help her get up he realized it was Toba Peres, with her uncovered hair braided like a crown around her head. He didn't know her, not really, but he did know her history—dead mother, absent father, raised by her grandfather, who had once served the Emir of Rimon and had a small fortune until he lost it, though *how* he'd lost it was the subject of a great deal of speculation. The pendant that she wore around her neck had come askew, and she straightened it before moving on. It was a hamsa, a palm, with the largest sapphire Naftaly had ever laid eyes on set in the center. It didn't square with the tales of Alasar Peres's lost fortune, that pendant, unless he'd spent everything on a gem for his housebound granddaughter.

Then again, maybe it was just a piece of blue glass. In either case, the granddaughter in question got to her feet, Naftaly made sure she was well, and she spared him the quickest of glances before ricocheting off in a different direction. He wondered where she was going, since the Pereses lived on the other side of the quarter. But he had to get home himself, so he shoved his way through the crowd, grateful the people around him were living this time, and made his way back to his house, above his family's tiny shop on the other side of the plaça. When he got there, he found the door barred.

He banged on it for a few minutes before the housekeeper answered. She was pale and trembling.

"You've heard," he said, and she nodded. She was probably hoping the Cresqueses would choose conversion, because she'd worked for the family twenty years and would lose her post otherwise. But Naftaly knew his father, and it was an unlikely choice. The Cresqueses didn't have much in the way of property to worry about losing if they left, and Naftaly's father was devout besides. His mother, oftentimes the dissenting voice in the house, had died last year, and Abrafim Cresques had lost much use for the outside world afterward, reducing his spheres to work, prayer, and mounting frustration at his son's ineptness with a needle and thread.

Naftaly's father was upstairs in his small bedroom, and he called Naftaly in. "I need to tell you something important."

He looked very tired, probably because he hadn't slept, either.

Naftaly hoped it might be something about the dream-world, but when he entered the room he saw that his father was holding a book. It was small, thick, and obviously old—whatever title might have been on the cover had long ago worn away. The entire volume was encircled by a tape which seemed to be holding it closed. "What is that?" he asked.

"Only a book," his father said, handing it over. Naftaly took it from him; the cover was ancient-looking and the pages within were yellowed indeed.

"Why is it sealed?" Naftaly asked, fingering the tape.

"Don't open it," his father snapped.

Naftaly looked up at his father's pale face. "Why?"

"No one must ever read it," he said, taking the book back. "It's sealed to prevent someone reading it accidentally."

Naftaly was not sure how someone could accidentally read a book, but his father continued: "It's a curse. An ancient curse, my father told me, and his father before him. I'm showing it to you because you must know that no matter what happens, we must not lose this book." With his heel, he pressed on one of the floorboards, lifting the other side. He then tucked the book underneath.

"A curse? Why do *we* have it? Why not destroy it?" Naftaly asked, because such an object didn't seem like it should belong to a tailor.

"It's been passed down," he said. "No one can remember where it came from, but it's been ours for ten generations at least, and we're charged to keep it safe and hidden. It isn't possible to destroy it."

"Have you tried?"

"Stop asking questions."

"Is it—" Naftaly began, and then stopped. He tried again: "Does it have to do with the dream-world?"

Turning to go downstairs, Naftaly's father said, "There is no dream-world."

\+ + + + + +

THAT NIGHT, NAFTALY dreamt of the bridge again, only this time there were no people at all, not even his father. He walked to the opposite end, and found himself in the terraced city where he usually dreamed, still wondering where everyone was; he'd never before dreamt of a world where he was the sole inhabitant. Toward the outskirts, he found himself walking through streets lined with small houses.

Hoofbeats. He heard hoofbeats again, coming from farther within the city. He looked for an alley to step into, and found none, and then a door opened just ahead of him and a tall man, black-haired and wearing a brocade coat, stepped out and hissed at him, "Get inside," and, when Naftaly failed to move, the man stepped out farther, grabbed him by the collar, and pulled him in.

"What can you be thinking?" he asked, slamming the door shut. "To be outside now?"

"I'm looking for—someone," Naftaly said, managing to stop himself before mentioning his father.

"Pray he's inside, somewhere," the other man said.

"What is happening?" Naftaly asked. This was, he thought, the first time he'd managed to speak to one of these dream-people. His father was nearly always with him, and had counselled him to avoid the other people in his dreams at all costs. He'd certainly never been alone with one before.

He bore a passing resemblance to the man he'd seen on the bridge: the man in blue, with deep red hair. But this man's hair was black, he was lankier, the bones in his face sharper. Besides that, his eyes were doubly strange; not only square, but with irises the color of sunset. He couldn't recall ever having seen such eyes before, even here. The orange-eyed man replied, "La Cacería has sniffed someone out; I don't know who."

Naftaly wanted to ask the meaning of any part of that statement and did not dare, lest he expose himself as some sort of outsider. This man assumed Naftaly understood the nature of this dream place and what happened here, and he was not sure what would happen if he revealed his ignorance. It occurred to Naftaly that this might well be a real person, who in a few hours would wake, just as Naftaly would, and go about his normal day.

Outside, the horses raced past. The other man still had Naftaly pinned between himself and the door. Naftaly closed his eyes until the hoofbeats receded, then opened them to find the other man, still too close, regarding him calmly. He said, "How is it I don't know you?"

Naftaly said, honestly, "I don't know."

The other man looked like he would have said more, but then muttered, "Damnation," and vanished, leaving Naftaly alone in the house, too afraid to go back out, until dawn came and he woke, and discovered that Abrafim Cresques had died in his sleep.

✦ ✦ ✦

TOBA'S GRANDPARENTS SEEMED unable to come to an agreement about what to do next.

Alasar Peres had been a translator in the court of the Emir Muhammed VI—father of the emir who had surrendered Rimon to the north—until arthritis had claimed his hands. Now he taught languages in his home to students hoping to make their way to the university. Toba's grandmother said he'd spent too much time among scholars and it had turned his brain to mush. He was, she said, too optimistic for his own good.

"We're staying," Alasar said one evening. It was late, and he and Elena were sitting at the table lit with a pair of oil lamps; ostensibly, he was reading and she was mending a stocking, but in reality both of them were mostly staring into empty space. "We'll convert, in public," he went on. "What we do at home is our business."

"Are you mad? We can't risk that!" Elena said. "If they come for Toba—"

Toba, who had been translating a bit of Ovid from Latin into Arabic to settle her nerves, looked up at the mention of her name. Alasar gave his wife a quelling look.

"Nobody's coming for Toba," he said. "Be quiet."

"We're leaving," she said. "Toba and I. You can stay here by yourself if you want. But we are going."

"You can't leave on your own," he said.

"Try to stop me."

Alasar's hoary eyebrows roused themselves, but he made no answer, and Elena sighed. "Alasar, please. How many times do you need to be proved wrong?"

He rubbed at his eyes. "They aren't letting people take money out of the country."

Toba leaned forward. She hadn't heard this part. Elena said, "What?"

"It's in the edict. No money. No gold. No jewels."

"The crown is seizing it?" Elena asked.

"Yes! Do you understand? If we go, we lose everything we have left."

"Yes," Elena said. "But we live."

"We can live—"

"Here," she finished for him. "I know what you're thinking, you old fool. We'll live here, until someone decides they want what little you have and starts tapping on the shoulder of the Inquisition. You'll be up in smoke in a week."

"What do you think will happen to us if we leave? I'm an old man. You expect me to build a life from nothing? Here, we have a home. I have a reputation, and I can teach anyone who would learn from me."

"We can go to my brother's," she said. "In Pengoa. He'll take us in. He has space."

"I have no interest in spending my waning years as your brother's dependent," he said.

"Alasar," she murmured. "If they take Toba . . ." and then she moved to whispers. Alasar's head bent to listen, his eyes closed. After some time, Elena stopped talking, and they just sat, staring at the table. Finally, Alasar said, "Very well."

Toba waited for more of this conversation to unfold, or to be included in it, somehow. When neither occurred, she slipped out of the room and into the courtyard, carefully stepping over the cracked stones in the center that had broken apart in some earthquake long before Toba's memory. She picked an orange from the tree nearest the gate and weighed it in her hands, looking up to the sky, where the moon was full and seemed very, very close.

She leaned against the gate and looked out at the rows of houses up and down the street, most of which were still burning lamps themselves. Likely every family in the quarter was having some version of the conversation she'd just overheard, though she wondered about her grandmother's special concern for herself. It seemed odd to her that anyone should think that Toba was in more danger than her grandparents. Toba had no money to steal. She had no friends to inform on her, and she seldom went out enough to attract the attention of . . . well, of anyone, to be honest. She was, she thought, as safe from public scrutiny as possible. Except for her grandfather's students, few people knew much about her at all, and she thought it unlikely that those young would-be scholars could make their way into the pockets of the Inquisition.

So why was her grandmother so worried about her, particularly?

Likely she was just being overprotective. Elena seemed to run that way naturally, probably as the result of losing her only daughter in childbirth. And it had been such a strange death, people used to tell Toba, before Elena could chase them away. Penina had been strong, sturdy, and rarely ill; the last person on earth anyone would suspect could die bearing a child. If it could happen to her, said the neighbors, it could certainly happen to anyone—but Toba, for certain, should never marry, because if Penina had died in her childbed, little, sickly Toba had no chance at all. Clearly, they said, she must take after her father. The slime. Whomever he was.

Toba's parents had been married in Meleqa. He'd been a merchant, and after Penina had died he'd left Toba in the care of her grandparents and gone back to Anab.

It was no wonder Toba had developed a terror of childbirth, and in her heart, she hoped her grandparents would live forever, and she'd never be forced to marry at all. She could stay at her grandfather's side, translating Ovid and Ibn Sina, forever and ever.

To the south, a light streaked the sky.

Toba squinted to get a better view . . . it must be a falling star, she thought, except in Toba's experience falling stars did not travel that way. She'd seen one or two sitting outside with her grandfather on warm nights, trying to cool off before bed. Their trails were usually horizontal, or diagonal. This shooting trail was exactly perpendicular to the horizon. And it had appeared to be traveling upward from the ground.

Shooting stars, Toba thought, did not go up.

She decided to get her grandfather and show him, but before she could, the trail had faded as if it had never existed.

Toba put a piece of orange in her mouth, only then realizing when her mouth filled with bitterness that it was still completely green.

APRIL WAS COMING to a close, and Naftaly was wandering the streets alone, at night.

This was not a habit of his generally, but ever since the edict and his father's death Naftaly's visions had grown worse both in frequency and intensity, and he found that if he kept moving he seemed more able to shake them off. It was the grief, he told himself, though he struggled to call it that. He did not feel sadness so much as numbness. He missed his father, he'd loved his father. But his father had always held him in an infuriating spot that somehow managed to be both suffocatingly close and at arm's length. *Keep to the house,* had been his father's refrain, *take over the family business—because I don't believe you can succeed in anything else—but never ask about your dreams or visions or what any of it means.*

His visions were at their worst when he was alone and indoors; at least outside there was the chance that something might jar him out of them. So far, he thought he'd kept his neighbors from realizing how badly he was afflicted. The last thing Naftaly wanted was for someone to a call a physician, who would probably sedate him with poppies, or the rabbi who might call him possessed. He was fine, the great majority of the time. He was not mad. He just occasionally . . . saw things. Things that weren't, in the most technical sense, real.

Naftaly supposed that probably many people saw things that weren't real, and had elected never to bring it up, which is what Naftaly's father had instructed him to do back when he'd mentioned it as a boy.

It had been a vision of ships, the countryside turned to seawater so real he could smell it. He'd been on board some large sailing vessel, and the rolling of the waves had rendered him nauseated and retching. When he'd come out of it, after perhaps thirty seconds, he'd told his father.

"Runs in the family," he'd replied over the top of a pair of trousers he'd been stitching. "Don't tell anyone."

This seemed to be his father's answer to most of Naftaly's difficulties.

The worst problem with these visions was that whenever Naftaly saw something odd, he had trouble telling whether it was real or a figment of his mind. So when he was wandering the quarter under the full moon and saw what appeared to be a falling star shoot up from the ground somewhere outside the city, his first thought was, *I hope this doesn't grow worse.*

He waited for it to morph into a monster that ate the moon, or to see a phantom city in the mountains, which he now saw fairly regularly. But when nothing more appeared after a few seconds, he began to wonder if it was real after all, some strange phenomenon of the night sky. He wished, not for the first time, that he'd been afforded the opportunity to study, to make his way to the university instead of preparing to take over his father's tailoring business. Perhaps then he would have known what that light shooting up from the ground might be.

But that was not to be. The afterimage of the star faded, and Naftaly decided to return home, only to find himself plagued by the worst headache of his life, a pain that started behind his left eye and radiated outward, as if there were something embedded there trying to escape.

Naftaly lurched sideways, a hand over the offending eye, and vomited, and then passed out in the street.

He woke the next morning, victim to the end of a woman's broom. "Wake up," she said. "Drunk thing, spending the night in my doorway. Go home."

He sat up. The pain was gone, but he felt weak, as if he'd been sick. "I'm not drunk," he said. "I'm ill."

"Be ill at home," she said, prodding him again with the broom.

"I'm going," he said, getting up. "You can put your weapon away."

"I'll show you a weapon," she said, and hit him soundly over the head, leaving him with a mouthful of bristles.

When he arrived home, sometime later, he found the door bashed in.

THREE

THE DETRITUS THAT was left of the Cresques family belongings was scattered in the street . . . this seemed to consist mainly of random bits of fabric, though from this distance Naftaly couldn't tell if these were the remains of his family's clothing or his father's work at various stages of completion, left unfinished with his death. A wooden spoon lay just inside the threshold, the handle broken into splinters, making Naftaly wonder what nightmare might be inside. The street itself was deserted, as if everyone had barred themselves inside their houses.

An old woman grabbed his arm just as he decided to go inside. "Don't," she said. Naftaly recognized her as the ancient widow who came by occasionally looking for alms. He wasn't sure where she'd come from, but for most of Naftaly's life she'd been something of a fixture in this part of the quarter, and she ate at Naftaly's table and slept by the fire once or twice a month. Naftaly supposed she had rounds she made, to lessen the imposition when she knocked on the door and asked for a meal.

"What happened?"

"I'm not sure they've all gone," she said in hushed tones. "There were a number of them; I couldn't tell if they all left, at the end."

"Who?" he asked. "Who did this?" He almost expected her to say *demons*. Or even *Maziks*, the way she was holding his arm, her knuckles white through her papery skin. Old women were often frightened of boogeymen and old tales. Particularly those, like this one, who lived a hair's breadth from starvation and exposure. The real fears intermingled with the invented ones, until it was hard to keep them straight.

But she simply said, "Bandits. Thieves, opportunists, I don't know. The door wasn't barred. That's how they got in."

The door hadn't been barred because Naftaly hadn't been home to bar it. The housekeeper only worked a few hours a week, now—he had nearly no income with which to pay her, beyond a few outstanding debts left to his father—and she would have gone home long before dark.

"They were drunk," she went on. "Very drunk, and looking for treasure. It was only a few hours ago."

It had been dark a few hours ago. What had she been doing on the streets in the middle of the night? Either she had nowhere to stay, or she'd decided the street was safer. She stared at Naftaly as if daring him to ask.

"We have no treasure," he said, though she must have known that. "We have nothing; why would they pick a tailor's house?"

"It was a group of peasants," she said. "They were drunk on alcohol and their own freedom."

"Freedom?"

"To take what they wanted. The other houses were locked tight. And the richer ones have guards posted, besides. I can't think why you'd leave your home undefended right now."

Naftaly's head still ached. He said, "It wasn't intentional." He listened for any sound from within but heard nothing. "I don't think anyone's still there," he said. "I'm going inside."

"Here," she said, pulling a paring knife from within some hidden pocket of her skirts. "Take this."

He stared at it incredulously. "You have a knife?"

"Yes, I have a knife!" When he made no move to take it, she said, "Do you want me to carry it?"

He took it from her. "I'll carry it," he said, though he hardly knew what he'd do with it against a band of drunken farmers. The blade was only the length of his finger. It was suitable for boning a chicken, perhaps, not for cutting down burly men. Still, he was surprised when she made to follow him inside.

The house had been ransacked. There had been little of value to begin with, but anything remotely useful—anything metal, for instance—had been taken, and anything small enough to carry was gone. Anything too large had been smashed. There was truly nothing left; even the small pantry was stripped bare, leaving nothing more than a few dried beans that had spilled their sack. Naftaly no longer owned so much as a turnip.

Naftaly picked through a few shards of broken pottery. He wondered if there was any point in cleaning up the house. He didn't own it, anyway. May as well leave the mess to the landlord to deal with.

"Why bother breaking what they didn't want?" he muttered.

"They didn't seem particularly intelligent," she said. "Or kind. So there's that."

"You're lucky they didn't see you," he said.

"I'm too old to bother with," she said. "And I don't exactly look as if I might have swallowed a diamond, do I?"

"No," he agreed, because she did look somewhat the worse for wear. She was a beggar, she never looked *good*, exactly, but the folk of the quarter always made sure she had enough; she had passable clothes to wear, decent food to eat, and a safe place to sleep. Right then, she didn't look as if she'd washed recently.

"The conversos won't be seen helping me unless I convert as well," she explained. "I've had a bit of a time."

"Well, what are you planning to do?"

She picked up a stool, only to discover it was missing a leg. She let it clatter back to the floor and sat on the edge of the hearth instead. "I've heard there's a fund for those who want to leave but lack the means."

"A fund?"

"So I'm told. They'd send you, too, if you asked; you had little enough to begin with."

He nodded. "Where will you go?"

She sighed. "Twenty years ago, I would have gone to Anab, but now, it seems far. But I've heard there's a group chartering a ship from Merja. They're headed to Pengoa."

"To Pengoa? Why not make the journey overland?"

"It would take weeks," she said. "Of hard riding or walking. And the countryside has more peasants than the sea has pirates."

Naftaly pondered this. He knew nothing of Pengoa, besides the fact that the Inquisition had not managed to make inroads with its king. On the other hand, if he stayed, he had nothing except his weak skills. Perhaps in Pengoa he could find some tailor in need of an assistant to cut his cloth or sew his hems, enough to garner a wage he might live on. "This chartered ship," he said, "do you know who arranged it?"

"It was Isaach Burgos," she said, and he nodded: Of course. The oil merchant; Naftaly felt a pang. It was he, when Naftaly had been small, who had liked the look of him and offered him an apprenticeship, lacking a son of his own, but Abrafim had elected to keep Naftaly at home instead. What a missed opportunity that had been. There was money in fat.

"Shall we go now?" she asked.

He would have said yes, and left right then, only some thread of memory snagged at him as they crossed the threshold. "Wait," he said.

"You want to bring some broken furniture along?"

But Naftaly had remembered the one item of potential value that was removed from plain view. Leaving the old woman outside, he went up to his parents' small bedroom, moved aside a section of torn mattress, and pressed on the loose floorboard with a toe.

The book was still inside. Secreting it within his coat, he went off to see Isaach Burgos.

✦ ✦ ✦

THE COURSER OF Rimon tied her hair off her neck and into a braid that she wrapped around her head, holding it with silver pins made from the bones of her enemies.

The Caçador disapproved of her hairpins. They were overkill, he'd said. A true force in the world need not be so obvious. If you had an enemy, he often told her, you simply made him disappear, and never spoke of him again. That action alone was all the message necessary to quell one's foes.

As her commander, he'd always been impatient with her, but lately it had grown worse. She was never subtle enough, never clever enough. Occasionally she killed people he wanted kept alive, but there was always a reason for it. Sometimes men were more delicate than they looked. It was hard to gauge the difference between maiming and killing, especially when you were in a hurry, and the Caçador often had her rushing these days.

It was a trial, he'd told her, of immortality: one made plans that took centuries, even millennia to come to fruition, and then everything came due at the same moment. The Mazik King, rumor whispered, was growing weary. Changes were afoot in mortal Rimon. And this meant, by the strange power of the Mirror, that Mazik Rimon was on the cusp of a new age. All this together meant the Caçador must act now or not at all, before the turning of the world occurred without his input. The next age, he was determined, would bear his fingerprints on both sides of the Mirror, in both Rimons, and beyond.

And so, some months before, he'd gone to the Inquisitor of mortal Sefarad, and he'd made a deal: He would give the Inquisitor the words he'd need to convince the Queen to expel her Jewish citizens. The Inquisition would remand all stolen Jewish assets—money, gold, property—save one: the Caçador would receive every confiscated book.

This must have seemed to the Inquisitor like an excellent deal: What use did he have for those books? None, save fuel for a bonfire. At any rate, the Caçador knew what the Inquisitor did not: the Inquisitor was about to get what he wanted even without help. In some other version of history, in fact, he already had. It was a peculiar gift of this particular Mazik, that he could see the infinite dimensions of time. In some other realm, the Inquisitor had accomplished his goals. In another, the Inquisitor had gone further and made himself king. In still another, he'd found himself beaten to death by his own mob. The Caçador had shared these visions with the Courser in a dream some time ago. He liked to make sure his subordinates did not forget the extent of his abilities.

In this reality, however, the Inquisitor was still on the cusp of getting his way. And when he did, the book he sought would certainly be burned. That was what the Caçador was trying to prevent.

Already, the Queen, the church, the peasantry were lined up in perfect order; the Inquisitor only needed to nudge them with a finger and they'd all accede to his plans. He didn't need the Inquisitor. But the Caçador was good at convincing people that they did.

The Inquisitor had agreed to the deal, but there was one further stipulation: The Caçador was leaving behind his personal emissary, the Courser herself, to ensure the bargain was kept to the letter. One book, the Caçador had told the Inquisitor, kept back or burned, and the deal was void. The Courser would kill him.

The Inquisitor had not been nearly worried enough about this possibility, but the Caçador had. "Do not," he had told her, "kill him without my express order."

The Courser had not answered quick enough, and he'd been very displeased. "Answer when I speak, Courser," he'd said.

He hadn't asked a question, and she hadn't realized a direct order—*Don't kill him of your own volition*—required a reply, since it was not as if she could do other than obey him.

"Yes, sir," she'd said, which had only irritated him further. What he wanted, she knew, was more than obedience: he wanted her to anticipate his orders, and when she did not, he was frustrated. He wanted a

Courser whose mind worked like his, and hers did not. She was a blunt instrument, where he wanted a scalpel.

She kept her position for one reason only: she was not fully Mazik, which meant she could work in the mortal realm other than beneath a full moon. It was, he told her, her only gift, and he ought to know, too, since it was he who had raised her.

He'd taken her from the arms of the midwife—already dead by this point—and looked down into the Courser's eyes. She'd already said her name, and he'd repeated it back to her; she hated the sound of it on his lips, and then he'd said, "Say this, or I shall kill you: I give to you my entire will, for as long as I shall live, by my own name." And she'd already seen what he'd done to the two women in the room, both the midwife and her mother. She did not want to go the same way, so she'd said it, and he'd smiled; the first of his smiles she'd earned. He'd taken the small knife from the midwife's apron and said, "Rejoice, small one," and he'd cut the cord still jutting from her tiny abdomen. "You are to be the left hand of the new age."

She hadn't understood, and her tiny mouth had turned to a frown.

"You will understand," he'd said. "Soon enough." And he'd wrapped her in the swaddling clothes the midwife had prepared, and he'd taken her from her mother's house, and she'd never seen any of her mother's people again. For three days, he'd doted upon her day and night, and then on the fourth day, he'd presented her with a pail of water and said, "Change it to milk, or you will starve."

She hadn't known how, and she'd wept, and she'd starved, until her ribs had stuck out through her once-plump flesh, and she'd thought she would die. But on the twelfth day, she'd turned the water to milk, and he'd smiled again. "Good," he'd said, and then said her name again, and she'd shuddered.

She'd since learned not to shudder. Her face betrayed nothing: not when she was hurt, not when she'd hurt someone else, which was something she did often. The Courser was well aware that the Caçador had honed her very deliberately into his sharp-edged tool; she was no fool and she knew what she was and what she'd been made for. The Caçador's purpose was to make her his weapon. Her own purpose was simply to live, a desperate desire that rendered her clarity of will unusual, even as a child.

It served her well as Courser. The Caçador—the man and the Caçador, the founder and lord of La Cacería, were one and the same . . . there was no replacing him. His lieutenants, however, were eminently replaceable—especially his Courser, who existed only to do the Caçador's bidding and had no subordinates of her own. The two other factions within La Cacería—the Hounds, led by the Lymer, in charge of Rimon and the dream-world, and the Falcons, led by the Peregrine and responsible for missions abroad—were where La Cacería held most of its power. If the Courser had commanded some soldiers of her own, she might have felt more secure, but she had no one but herself.

At the moment, she was working as a glorified courier, which did not suit her at all. The Inquisitor had his men seize load after load of books; they were sent back to him in Mansanar, and then she took possession of them and transferred them through the gate. She'd pointed out that this would be an easier process if she were to go through the dratted books herself; then she wouldn't have to move them, if only the Caçador would tell her what she was actually looking for. He'd simply stared at her, not answering, and then dismissed her.

So she sat in the midst of towering piles of books stolen at the border, and picked up the topmost volume and skimmed it, and saw that it was the ledger from some business or other, and slammed it back down, because it was worthless: they were all likely worthless, but she was stuck here, and she hated it. The Inquisitor's men had been told to obey her, but they cast glances at her she did not like, and she could not even kill them, because she'd been ordered not to. They were angry, too—the sheer volume of additional labor created by the collection of books had meant a halt to autos-da-fé in the capital, and their chief enjoyment seemed to be burning people for no particular reason, and the lack of it meant they were casting about elsewhere for amusement.

She heard a fight erupt down the hallway: the room she was in was full, so they'd started piling the books in another, and it was from there that she heard the sounds of shouts and blows. Making her way into the chamber, she found two of the Inquisitor's men throttling each other over a book that had fallen on the ground between them. Without a word, she approached and picked it up. The two men stopped their argument and watched her open it.

The pages had been hollowed out, the book itself made into a box, and within the space inside there was a small tangle of jewelry: a few silver chains and a brooch set with an opal. Nothing terribly valuable; probably the contents of some housewife's jewel-box, who had gambled on hiding her things in a book and lost because she hadn't known of the ban. Holding the snarl of items in one hand, the Courser said, "Nothing here belongs to either of you; why should you bother to fight over it?"

"The *books* belong to the Conde," one of the men put forth, the Conde being how they referred to the Caçador, whom none of them had ever seen. "Nothing else."

She put the jewels back into the book and snapped it shut. "There is no distinction made between the books and their contents," she said. "Follow your orders."

These men knew her, so they dropped their heads. The one who'd spoken muttered, "Yes, Lady."

She would have gone then; would have, but then it occurred to her she'd expected more of an argument. The Caçador hadn't mentioned a possibility of the books containing things apart from paper and ink; the case *could* be made that anything odd within them belonged to the Inquisition and not to the Conde. That no one had made that case seemed suspicious. She said, "Were there any more like this?"

The men fixed their eyes on their own boots and made no answer. There: one of them flicked his eyes toward his companion's. That was enough. "Show me," she said sourly.

The man in question scowled.

"It will go better for you if I don't need to ask again," she said.

Squaring his shoulders, he led her to the back of the room, where a table held a half-dozen volumes. "Only these," he said, and she went and flipped the covers open and found the first five empty.

"What was in these?" she asked quietly.

"Coins," he said. "They were divided by the men who found them. Do you want me to find out who?"

"No," she said. "Order twenty lashes for the entire regiment." He flinched, but did not argue. She opened the last book and found a glass phial stopped with a cork.

"What is this?" she asked, removing the cork and smelling a thick liquid she could not identify.

"Amapola," he said. "I don't know why it was hidden: there's no ban on medicines. But there's enough there to knock out every man in the regiment for a week."

She looked at the phial in her hand. "It brings sleep?"

"It's meant to relieve pain," he said. "Or so I've been told."

The soldier of the Inquisition was still waiting on her orders; she could hear him shifting his weight from one foot to the other, eager to be away from her. She weighed the bottle in her hand. She wondered, in her tired mind, if that much amapola could put a dozen men out for a week, what it would do to her, drunk all at once. If she would sleep for some extended time. If she would wake, after. She put the bottle back inside the book and closed it.

"I'll put this aside," she said. "If the bottle breaks, it might spoil the other books. Tell me if you find more."

"As you say," the man said, and left.

FOUR

THE PERESES LEFT Rimon under the cover of night.

The first reason for this was that they hoped to cover a great deal of ground very quickly, and traveling when it was cooler meant they would require fewer stops to water the horses. The second, and most compelling reason, was that they hoped to be spared either a gauntlet of peasants as they left town, or a gauntlet of thieves. Already rumors were swirling that the Jews were swallowing jewels to smuggle them out of the country, and a sharp knife in the belly of a passing refugee might result in wealth beyond imagining.

As a point in fact, Toba did have the remains of the Peres fortune on her person, in the form of two items sewn into her dress. The first of these was her grandmother's wedding ring, a castle ring made from silver, which she'd forced Toba to take somewhat against her will, to barter for help if she ever required it. The second was Toba's amulet.

It was a permanent fixture around Toba's neck; she had been ordered never to take it off. The amulet was a hamsa with a blue stone in the center; through the stone, if you looked very carefully, you could see a second, smaller stone within it in the shape of a starburst. Behind the stone, within the hamsa, there was a small scroll with some prayer written on it.

It had been in their family, her grandmother told her, fourteen generations, made as a remedy for some forebear who'd been cursed in some way, and given to Toba to counter her sickly nature. She'd asked her grandmother if she was cursed, too, and Elena had said not; it was only to ward off evil that might seek her out for her delicateness, but she'd looked as if she hadn't quite believed what she was saying. Toba was not inclined to believe in curses, but she knew there was something wrong with her, and perhaps that was it—what other explanation could there be for why she must never take it off? Toba wore it to bathe, she wore it to sleep. Her grandmother had explained that she would not be allowed to take it out of the country, and so she'd hidden it in the bodice lining of Toba's dress, over her heart.

Those who were traveling met outside the city gates, slipping out quietly to avoid attention. Once assembled, they began the trip south.

Two hours out of Rimon, the wolves began to howl.

There were two groups among the small caravan: the carts, which held the refugees' belongings, the elderly, and the children; and behind them, those who were able to walk.

Toba was among those on foot, though Elena had tried to argue a space for her in a cart, because of her sickly nature.

"She can't possibly walk all that way!" Elena had argued. "Look at her!"

But Toba had insisted, because she'd known that if she rode someone else would have to walk in her place, a child or a wizened grandfather, and she could not bear it.

So Toba walked, while her grandparents rode in a cart. And she walked slowly, because really, Toba was just as sickly as her grandmother had said.

In the distance, the wolves howled again. "They won't approach us," said a man walking nearby, to his wife and not to Toba. "There are too many of us by far."

That sounded a bit like something Toba's grandfather might say, right before her grandmother called him an old fool. Toba tried unsuccessfully to quicken her pace, then gave up when her lungs began to call a warning wheeze. Thinking a different tack might better serve, she made her way to the edge of the caravan of foot traffic, where at least she might not have to worry so much about impeding the rest of them.

Around her, her neighbors began to sing a lament.

Toba listened quietly as they sang about exile and Babylon and rivers of tears. At the third refrain, she began to whisper along with the voices around her, and feeling buoyed by emotion, raised her voice to sing with them.

Too much. She felt an invisible hand around her throat, and doubled over, gasping, tears stinging her eyes. People began to push past her, and she staggered sideways to get out of the way.

She felt herself going faint, and pushed herself farther from the margins of the caravan, off the side of the road itself, drawing one great breath, and then another.

The tingling in her fingers and toes subsided. She laid a hand against her heart, where her amulet was sewn into her dress, and tried not to panic.

Only then, she felt a hand on her arm, and a pinch in the middle of her back, which Toba recognized a moment later as the point of a blade.

✦ ✦ ✦

THE OLD WOMAN applied a pincer grip to Naftaly's elbow.

"Ouch," he said.

She squeezed harder.

"Would you stop?" he said. "I'm walking as slowly as I can already. And trim your nails when you can."

"That man," the old woman hissed into his ear. "You see that man ahead?" She nodded at a man picking his way through the throng of people ahead of them.

"He's too old to be beardless," the woman said.

This was true; he looked at least forty, and his face was shaven. He was dressed like a Rimoni with the same green woolen cap that Naftaly himself wore; the people of Rimon all dressed more or less the same, class and income were more significant than background: they all dressed in the Arab style, with long tunics and covered heads. This man, however, looked like he was in a costume, and not a very good one, either, like he'd stolen clothes sewn for a smaller man.

"What is he doing?"

She turned him a withering look. "Perhaps he thinks this is a party, and he's only here for the food."

Naftaly watched the man make his way through the crowd, and then saw his target . . . a young woman near the edge, who had stopped moving and seemed to be having some sort of a breathing crisis. Naftaly couldn't see who it might be from this distance, but watched as the man took hold of her arm and forced her farther from the road. Naftaly waited for someone closer to do something, to help, but it was dark and the girl made no noise of complaint. If the old woman hadn't pointed out the situation, he might have missed it, too—a small woman in a dark dress on a dark night.

"Why isn't she crying out?" the old woman said.

"Stop!" Naftaly called, but the people were singing, and children were crying, and the horses and wagons were noisy on the road. By then the man was already dragging the girl into the woods, and there was no one near enough to help, even if they had heard. "There's a thief!" he cried—hoping *thief* was the right word—but there was too much sound to hear one person. Leaving the old woman behind, he took off after them into the woods.

+ + + + + +

THERE ARE FEW instances in most people's day-to-day lives that call for either running or screaming. Perhaps, Toba thought, if she'd married and had children, she might have had a need to shout at them or chase after them, and in that case, maybe she would have had to address this problem earlier. But Toba had no husband to harangue or children to scold, so the first time her handicap became a situation of life or death occurred as she found herself forced away from her neighbors at the point of a knife.

She hoped, for a brief moment, that someone would notice, but no one did, likely because it was dark, or because everyone was focused on their own families, or the song they were singing, or because Toba could only make her complaints heard in a normal tone of voice or risk another breathing crisis, which she knew she could not do.

"Let me go," she said, making her voice as firm as she dared. "I have nothing you want."

The thief made no answer, but continued dragging her farther from the road and into the hills. Dried-out branches of chaparral caught on the hem of her dress, and she struggled to plant her feet in the dirt, only to slide in the dust. Ahead of them, a line of pines blocked the moon and scented the air. The man carried her through the tree line and flung her to the ground.

This, Toba knew, was not good at all.

"Give me everything you have," he ordered. "Or I'll slit your throat."

Her hand went automatically to her neck. The ground underneath her was damp, which Toba vaguely thought was odd, because it had not rained for ages. "I don't have anything," she said.

"I know you have a jewel worth more than your life," he said.

"I have no jewel," she said smoothly, because while Toba couldn't shout she could definitely lie. "If I did, it'd be taken from me at the border. You must know the law."

"I saw you," he said, "in the city, the day of the edict. I know who you are, with your giant sapphire, I won't believe you've left it." His hands were suddenly on her, searching. "Where is it? Hand it over."

Toba decided to see whether she could kick. It turned out that she could, and the man fell back, clutching his jaw. Her foot smarted in her boot.

"You will be sorry," he said, "that you did that."

Toba searched the ground for the knife; the man had been pawing her with both hands, so he must have set it down somewhere. Unable to find it, she took hold of a rock instead, scrambling to her feet and clutching it in her right hand and wondering if her best bet were to throw it or wait until he came closer and try to bash his brains in. If she threw, she risked missing. But if she waited, she risked being stabbed.

"It's a bad idea," she told the man, "to attack someone who cannot run away."

He snickered. "If you fancy yourself dangerous, you're about to find otherwise."

Unfortunately for Toba, that was probably true. She weighed the rock in her hand. She wished she'd spent more time in the kitchen and less with books; then she might have more strength in her arms. She decided she couldn't risk him coming closer. She threw the rock.

Her aim, at least, was good. It hit him squarely in the temple. But it was only hard enough to leave a scuff and make him angrier. He advanced, saying, "This will go quicker once you're dead." In the distance, there was a howl, then two, then three.

Toba backed away, hands instinctively raised, and the man grabbed her wrist, and a second set of howls answered the first. "Damnation," he said, because *these* howls weren't in the distance. They were close enough to raise the hairs on the back of Toba's neck. He let go of her arm and turned, knife in hand to face an entire pack of Sefardi wolves—nearly as large as pack-ponies, gray-brown fur hackled and lips pulled back over their teeth.

Toba took a step backward, and then another. She edged away as slowly, as gently, as her catlike feet would allow. The thief, only a tall man's length away, was not similarly careful. He turned and ran.

When the wolves charged, they took him down from behind. He did not scream.

Toba decided the best course of action would be to slip away before they remembered there had been two people there instead of one, and she continued to back away on silent feet. The sounds of crunching and gore turned her stomach, but she didn't dare turn her back.

Her foot, stepping back again, missed the ground, and she found herself sliding belly-first down a steep hill, on fallen pine needles, and then on fallen leaves.

She hadn't realized they'd been on the crest of a ridge, and she tumbled most of the way down before she caught herself on the root of a tree—some deciduous monstrosity which looked several hundred years old. They were too high in the hills for such a tree, but when she looked around, she saw that it was only one of many.

Unfortunately, she'd gone in the wrong direction. The road was on the other side of the wood; she was getting farther and farther from her grandparents, but she couldn't well go back the other way. Right now her priority was not being eaten, so she got up and stumbled the rest of the way down the hillside.

The valley below her appeared to be glowing.

It was the moonlight, she decided. The moon was full, the second in the month, which her grandfather had told her was rare.

She had no plan beyond escape as she continued. Perhaps, she thought, she could hide until the sun came up, and then double back; the caravan would be long gone, but at least on the road she had the hope of finding help. Perhaps she could use her grandmother's ring to pay for a ride to Merja. Or perhaps her grandparents would realize she'd been left behind and come back to look for her.

In the woods. In a ravine.

That seemed unlikely. Still, lost in the woods was better than being *eaten* in the woods.

Behind her, she heard growls. Toba turned slowly and saw the pale yellow eyes of half a dozen wolves.

She shielded her face with her arms and prayed. Mostly she prayed it would be quick.

A man's voice sounded in the dark, barking orders in a language Toba didn't know. She looked up quickly to see a man with straight silver hair to the middle of his back, beardless face pale in the darkness, dressed entirely in charcoal gray, from cloak to boots. Before him, the wolves recoiled, ears pinned, tails dropped. In a swift motion, he drew his leg back and kicked the one nearest him with the flat of his boot; yelping, the entire pack turned and fled.

The man saw Toba, his eyes skating over her, but said nothing and continued walking, as if the wolves had only managed to get in his way and he'd had no interest in walking around them.

"Wait," she tried to call, but her voice died.

He wasn't alone, she realized: there was a second man, olive-skinned rather than fair like his companion, his black hair pulled to the back of his head in a knot, his face as clean-shaven as the other man's. He was dressed in the same style, but seemed younger—it was hard to say without more light. The two men exchanged a glance, a nod, and then walked on together. Toba watched them walk on into the valley. Behind her was the road, and the pack of wolves.

Toba rose on her quivering legs and followed the men.

The two made their way down into the valley, through the thick trees that seemed to be growing into one organism; the ground was more root than dirt. On the other side was a grove of trees heavy with red fruit. Peering through the darkness, Toba saw they were pomegranates—hundreds of pomegranate trees, the ground under them covered with moss, heavy with dew in the cold night air. In the center of a grove, a sliver of light ran from the middle of the trees up into the sky.

This, she knew, was the falling star she'd seen from her courtyard. Creeping closer, she watched as the two men walked between the trees, and then directly into the sliver of light and then there must have been some trick of her eyes, because Toba could no longer see them. The wind picked up the leaves, leaving the air rustling like a crackling fire, and she heard the phantom sound of her name, but there was no one there to call it.

Toba wanted to go back to the road, but not as much as she wanted to live. So she followed the men into the light.

FIVE

NAFTALY TRIED TO catalog the events of the past evening, mostly to see at what point things had started to lean toward the improbable. This was a technique he used from time to time, to try to understand the precise moment he'd begun hallucinating because otherwise, later, he would not know how many of his memories were dependable.

Here is what he knew to be true: When he'd followed the girl off the road, she'd been held captive by a villain. And when he'd finally come close enough to help—close enough to see that the girl was Toba Peres—the villain had been attacked by wolves. He was fairly sure of both of these points, though the bit with the wolves did seem like the sort of figment his mind was likely to conjure.

After that, Naftaly was not entirely sure what was real and what was not.

Apparently, the thief had been eaten. Apparently, Toba had fallen down a ravine, and apparently there had been two very strange men, one of whom had called off the wolves, and apparently, they had disappeared into a beam of light, and Toba had gone with them. He remembered calling out to her, through the trees. He remembered her not hearing. He'd been too far off. Or else he hadn't really called her after all—only one of the men, the dark one, had looked back then, just for a moment. And he'd looked, in that moment, like the man from Naftaly's dream—the tall man with the orange eyes.

Probably this indicated that he'd been addled by then, and everything seemed a bit muddled anyway, because after all this had occurred, after he had himself approached the beam of light, Naftaly had fainted.

He'd woken parched with thirst in the pomegranate grove, the light gone, and the only thing he had to be grateful for was that he hadn't been eaten in his unconscious state. He'd managed to stagger back through the wood in the direction of the road, only to collapse again once he got there.

When he woke the second time, he was being nudged in the ribs by someone's foot.

He groaned and put a hand up to block the light. It was very bright—no longer near dawn at all.

"Wake up."

"I'm not well," he replied. He lowered his hand enough to determine the identity of his conversational partner who was, as he'd suspected, the old woman again. Why hadn't she gone on with the rest of the caravan?

"Listen, do you do this often? I wouldn't have agreed to travel with you if I'd known you were prone to this sort of thing."

He slowly sat up, rubbing his temples. In his mind's eye, Toba Peres disappeared into a sliver of light. He definitely wasn't well.

"What sort of thing is that?" he asked flatly.

"Fits," she said. "This isn't a good time to develop a nervous condition."

"Why are you here?" he asked. "Why didn't you continue on?"

"Well, you bolted off the road! So I followed you into those dratted woods, but I couldn't find you, and when I came out again, the caravan was gone and I was . . . here."

Naftaly looked around again. He hadn't gotten a terrific look at the road before he'd run after Toba last night—it had been too dark, and he'd been distracted—but it was true that this did not look like the road several hours out of Rimon.

"Did we come out on the wrong side?" he asked, knowing it was a foolish question. There was no wrong side to the wilderness; either you came out on the side of the road, or you were in the mountains.

"I don't know where we are," she said. "I thought perhaps I'd come out farther down, but I only walked several minutes. I marked the spot and tried backtracking a bit, but that didn't look familiar either, so I came back." She indicated a nearby pile of pebbles made in the shape of an *X*.

Naftaly prodded his temple again to make sure he was really awake. It throbbed under his finger, which meant he probably was.

"I suppose we have more pressing problems, anyway," she went on. "Where is the girl?"

The girl. He said, "I don't know."

"You don't know? Was she murdered? Or eaten? I heard wolves, that's why I came back to the road."

"I don't know," he said again. So the wolves, at least, had been real. "I lost sight of her."

"You," she said, "are lying. And you aren't very good at it."

When he didn't answer, she said, "I'm very good at sussing out lies, you know. *I don't have any money. I'm completely out of bread. The space by my hearth is filled with aggressive cats.* I can tell when it's nonsense. I know you know where the girl went, so just tell me. I can bear it." She squared her shoulders. "Was she eaten?"

Naftaly scanned the length of the road, hoping someone might come along with a skin of water, at least.

"Well?" she said.

"I was useless," he said. "There was a thief, but before I could confront him, he was attacked."

"By the girl?"

"By the wolves. And then she was attacked."

"By the thief?"

"No, he was dead by then. By the wolves again, and then there were two other men."

"More thieves?"

"I'm not sure about that. One of them frightened the wolves away, and I called to Toba but she didn't hear me, and she followed them into . . . something."

"A house? A cave?"

"No, it was more like . . . a light."

"A light. She went into a light?"

"That's the part I'm not clear on. And then I fainted. And then I woke and came back here."

"And fainted again."

Naftaly stewed a bit in his own failure. Every young man, Naftaly supposed, imagined he could be heroic if only the circumstances presented themselves. Here, the circumstances had been perfect: a girl, threatened three times over. And Naftaly's greatest contribution had been to run into the woods and faint. Eventually, he said, "Well, yes."

"Hmm."

"Do . . . do you think we should go look for her?"

"Oh, no, I don't think there's a point, do you?" She gazed back into the trees, as if she might see something there. "She followed a pair of strange men into the wood."

"Into a light."

"A light in the wood. Either she's dead or she wishes she was, I expect."

"Have you ever been told," he said, "that you're excessively fatalistic?"

"Oh, then, by all means, let's go after her. With any luck, you'll land on her next time you keel over, if I don't die of old age first." She stood up, brushing dust from her skirts. "We should pick a direction and start walking before the day grows hotter. Any ideas?"

Naftaly could see nothing in any direction . . . only the mountains behind them and the strange trees. "We seem to be in the middle of nowhere."

"We can't have gone far enough to be in the middle of nowhere. There must be a pueblo nearby. Get up."

He did, slowly, carefully, because his head still ached. "I don't think she's dead," he said. "I think she's . . . elsewhere."

He thought of the man's eyes again, and his silver hair, and his lineless face. Logically, it was most probably a vision. But it didn't *feel* like a vision. It felt real. And the man felt like one of his dream companions, odd-eyed and oddly ageless.

But his current companion ignored him. "This road appears to run south," she said. "If we keep walking, we'll either find a village, or someone leaving the city will come upon us, and perhaps we can barter for a ride in a cart. With any luck, we'll still get to Merja."

"But, Toba—"

"Even if you knew where she was, which you don't, what are you going to do against two men, who may well be armed?"

He puzzled over that.

"Hashem have mercy, you're a fool. How is it you're still alive? Listen, we can't rescue the girl. We don't know where she is. We don't know who she's with. We have no resources—"

"Few resources—"

"*Very* few resources, you're ill, and I'm ancient." She started down the road. "We keep going. The best we can do is to look after ourselves, and get to Pengoa as quickly as possible."

"You speak like you have something grand to do there," he said.

"I have nothing grand to do anywhere," she said. "My life has three purposes: to find enough food, to sleep someplace warm, and not to die at the hands of the Inquisition."

Naftaly meant to remark on the patheticness of the life she'd laid out for herself, but it really wasn't so different than his own life's trajectory. "Is there truly nothing more you wish for?"

The old woman thought it over. "I would like my own bed." She turned back to him. "If you aim for simple pleasures, boy, you are far less disappointed when your life turns into nothing much. Now move your feet."

Naftaly was not happy with this plan, but he had nothing better. His head still aching, he followed the old woman south.

\+ + + + + + +

PASSING THROUGH THE light left Toba with a strange, unwholesome sensation, as if she'd passed through a curtain of cold water, but somehow been left dry on the other side. It had been dark for a moment, and then she was through, and it seemed as if she'd simply walked from one part of the valley to another . . . the landscape was the same, the sky looked the same, even the pomegranate trees appeared to be the same, down to the arrangement of their branches. Only now she could see the men again, and she followed as fast as she was able, wishing she could call them back. If they could just escort her to the road, this misadventure would be over. The light was beginning to shift, as dawn broke before them. They were walking west, and the rising sun as it peeked over the horizon shone into her eyes.

That part was very wrong. She'd lived near these mountains all her life, and she was quite sure they loomed from the east, and that was not where the sun was beginning to ascend.

She glanced down at her feet as she picked her way across the landscape, and then stepped firmly into a person.

Toba looked up and realized she'd walked directly into the man with the silver hair. Only he'd been several hundred feet ahead of her only a moment ago, and she'd never seen him so much as turn around.

He was definitely, solidly there, however. So tall she only came up to his sternum, with sharply cut features wearing an expression that was alarmingly blank, like he'd schooled all of the emotion right out of his face.

She could not tell how old he was. His face was completely unlined, yet his hair was perfectly silver, and something about him seemed old indeed.

His eyes were the most alarming thing about him; his irises were too large, far too large, and his pupils were square—rather, they were rectangular, like a goat's. They were blue, and the whites of his eyes, too, were not truly white but a pale blue themselves, like the sky after a hard rain.

"Your eyes," she said.

He startled then. "My eyes?" he said, as if there was nothing odd about them at all.

"I'm sorry," she said. She knew, at that moment, that she'd made a terrible mistake.

She'd followed a pair of Maziks.

That was the only explanation. She tried to remember if her grandmother had ever told her what to do if she ever met a Mazik, but no one sensible actually *believed* in Maziks, and she'd never been particularly interested in fairy stories. She liked reading her grandfather's books better, of philosophy and law and mathematics, and they never gave the rules for making conversation with inhuman spirits. *Never trust a man you meet under a full moon*; that was what her grandmother used to say when Toba was small, but that was the extent of what she'd told her about such creatures.

But these Maziks had saved her life. Even if Toba wasn't sure that had been precisely intentional.

"How did you come to be here?" the Mazik demanded.

"I . . . I followed you."

"Through the gate?"

"The gate?" she breathed.

He exchanged a glance with the second Mazik, who had come to stand nearby. His hair was dark—glossy black, darker even than

Toba's—but his eyes were even odder, not only square, but the gold of a sunset. Unlike his companion, however, his face was not blank. It was bemused. "Well," he told the first Mazik. "This is a problem."

The first Mazik turned away.

"What do you suggest we do with her?" the dark-haired Mazik called after him.

Toba shivered. That wasn't promising at all. But he didn't sound particularly homicidal. He seemed more annoyed than anything.

"Judge for yourself," the first Mazik said, slipping the satchel off his shoulder and handing it to his companion. "I have things to do." And he walked away from them, head held high, hair shining in the too-bright light.

"Judge for myself," the second muttered, adjusting the satchel to hang behind his back. "How very helpful." Toba could not say why she felt that he was the younger of the pair, but it was a strong impression. Turning to Toba, he said, "I don't suppose you'd be decent enough not to bleed on me if I cut off your head?"

"No," she said quickly. "I'll make it a point to bleed out all over your lovely boots. It will be horrible. Gore, everywhere."

He sighed. Under the rising sun, the charcoal of his clothes was fading away to a green the color of a peacock's tail, and he patted his sleeves as if hoping to expedite the change. "Of course," he muttered. "And then I'd be left to deal with your oozing corpse." He started walking. When Toba failed to follow, he called back, "Are you coming?"

The silver-haired Mazik was out of view, leaving only the darker man behind, before Toba could reply. "Why should I follow you? You've just considered killing me."

"I didn't kill you," he said. "Are you hoping for a better offer? Because you won't get one. You can't go back through the gate, not until the next moon. And if you go wandering around by yourself, someone *will* cut your head off, whether you threaten to bleed on his boots or not."

Toba pondered this. "I see," she said.

"I'm so glad you understand," he said. "Let's get started."

"No," she told his retreating back. "I mean, I understand that you want me to go with you because you're worried I'll be caught by someone else, and that person might find out I followed you, and there must be some penalty for that."

He stopped walking and cast an eye over his shoulder. "If I were so worried about that, why wouldn't I have killed you in the first place?"

"What is in your satchel?"

"Amusing girl," the Mazik said, turning to face her. "That isn't any of your business."

She planted her feet and said, "Is it heads?"

The Mazik stared at her. Finally, he said, "Did you just ask me if I'm carrying a parcel of severed heads?"

"Yes," she said. "Or fingers. Or toes. Or ears, I don't know."

"You have the most ghastly imagination. Where did you come from?"

"I want to know what sort of man you are before I follow you home," she said. "What were you doing before, on the other side of the gate?"

"You think we were collecting trophies?" He held up the satchel with one hand. "You'll note there's no blood."

"I think you're perfectly capable of creating a satchel—"

"That would not leak viscera. I can't believe I'm having this conversation. Fine. Feast your eyes, then." He reached into the bag and pulled out the contents. "Are you satisfied?"

It was a book, very old; from this distance, she could not read the full title, but she caught the word *history*. She held out her hands for it.

"Oh," he said, "I think not." He slid the book back into the bag. "Not that you could likely read it. Now, can we go before someone else comes upon this ridiculous discussion and ends us both?"

Toba considered a moment: it seemed to her that a Mazik with a sack of books was probably less dangerous than one without. "Fine," she said, before adding, "I can read it. I can read five languages."

Here the outer edge of the Mazik's eyebrow lifted slightly, before he turned and continued on, leaving Toba scrambling to keep up. They crested the hill, and below them was a city.

It did not sit in the valley, as Rimon did, but in the hills above—a white terraced city that caught the light of the sun and mirrored it back, forcing Toba to shade her eyes. "Are we going there?" she asked.

"No. Adon Asmel doesn't live in the city." He grasped her by the shoulders and turned her forty-five degrees in in the other direction. His hands, through her dress, were like flames, and she flinched. "We're going there."

In the distance, there was a white-stone alcalá and two towers spanning either edge of the front wall, but unmarked by any sort of banner. It was difficult to make out from the distance, but the sides seemed to come out at odd angles, and Toba suspected that from a bird's perspective it would show itself to have six sides. There seemed to be nothing else in the area; no estates, no other buildings at all.

Toba turned back to the city. It was small, she thought, smaller than Rimon, and sat on the hillside, like a terraced garden, while the valley below was strangely empty. Her eye drew a boundary around the town, following the crenulated wall that demarked the edge of the city. She counted four gates, which seemed to correspond to the cardinal directions. The road they were on would lead, eventually, to the gate at the southern entrance.

"When we arrive," she said, once his hands were no longer on her shoulders, "what will happen?"

"Well," he said airily, "I suppose I shall have to find something useful for you to do.

SIX

SEVERAL HOURS LATER, Naftaly and the old woman came to a fork in the road. Naftaly, blessed with a young man's eyes, stood on a tree stump for a better vantage point and scanned the horizon. "Left is the continuation of the main road," he said. "Right looks like it leads to a pueblo."

"Does it look familiar at all?"

He looked again. It was not a tiny village; it was a town, big enough to have a wall. "I'm going to climb up for a better view," he said, indicating a nearby tree that had several thick branches.

"Is that wise?" the old woman said. "If you faint again, you'll fall out."

"I'm fine," he said, jumping to catch the lowest branch, then pulling himself up to sit. "It's nothing to worry about."

"Going into a dead faint at random intervals seems fairly worrisome to me. Have you always been this way, or has it developed recently?"

He said, "I've always been this way. It's not much worse than it's always been." He got his feet under him and stood, clutching the branch above him. He did not know why he felt like confiding his condition to the old woman, but if they were to travel together, he supposed she must know why he occasionally collapsed or became alarmed for no reason. His father had ordered him never to tell anyone, but his silence hadn't been much use to him up to now. If she knew, this old woman, she might be able to keep him safe during one of his episodes. Her alternative was to be alone in the wilderness, and he did not think she would choose that. "You see, I sometimes see . . . other things, than what are in front of my eyes."

The old woman began to emit a bitter, slightly hysterical laugh.

Naftaly almost lost his balance. "Could you not—"

"What a thing," she said, "I really am cursed."

"It's got nothing to do with you!"

She went on as if he hadn't spoken. "Three husbands, one worse than the last. So I vow, *I vow*, never to marry again." She ran her eyes up and down his skinny frame above her in the tree. "And so I hitch my wagon to a boy, and he turns out to be mad."

"I'm not mad," he said. "And you aren't hitched to me."

"I should have let them burn me in Savirra," she muttered. "Would have saved me so much running around." She sighed and rubbed a knot out of her neck. "Anything else I should know? You have fits and see things."

"That's about the sum of it, yes."

She sighed again. "Well, you seem harmless, I suppose there's that."

Naftaly looked out at the town again, but now there were pines blocking his way, and he decided to go up one more branch. After a moment, the old woman said, "I don't suppose there's a chance you ever see anything useful?"

"Oh," he said. "And now you're interested."

"It's a reasonable question!"

He looked down at her, which was a mistake. The ground swam a bit, and he clutched the trunk; he hadn't meant to go so high.

"So do you?" she asked.

"No," he said. "Not really. Lately it's . . . dead people. I see a lot of dead people."

"Well, that's charming."

"Mmm." He looked out again. It was a lovely little town, surrounded by a white wall. He could see the gate from his vantage, and barely made out people coming and going: women trailing small children, horses, wagons.

It was a familiar little town. On the eastern side, he could see a whitewashed building with horseshoe-topped pillars in front, which he recognized as a synagogue.

Only this town was something like twenty miles west of where they should have been.

"You're scowling," the old woman called to him.

"This is Eliossana," he said.

"No," she said. "It can't be."

He began to climb down. "It is," he said into the trunk as he felt his way back down with his feet. "My father used to buy cloth there. I went with him several times. There used to be a draper"—he climbed down another branch—"he bought up cheap cloth in Meleqa and sold it in the Rimon market." He jumped down to the ground. "Salomon Machorro, I think his name was."

Since Naftaly was not much for the technical aspects of tailoring, his father had hoped he would be better at the business side of things; interfacing with fabric merchants and keeping up with the latest styles, and for a time, it seemed like Naftaly might be not entirely hopeless. But then the siege had come, cutting them off from anything outside of Rimon, and his education had come to an end almost as soon as it had begun.

The old woman did not look pleased.

"What is it? You know him?"

"No," she said. "It's just that Eliossana is nearly as close to Meleqa as to Rimon."

Naftaly frowned, trying to remember the discussions he'd heard about the progression of the war. Meleqa had fallen two years prior, before Rimon had come under siege. If Eliossana had fallen with Meleqa, it would have been under northern rule for the past two years, in which case Salomon might well have packed up and left. Someone more worldly than Naftaly would surely have known the fate of the smaller towns in the area, but Naftaly mostly kept to his own house, and his father didn't like to discuss the happenings of the greater world. Now Naftaly was in it, and he hardly knew how it operated.

"Do you think it fell with Meleqa?"

The old woman threw up a hand. "That's just it, I don't know," she said. "I beg for my bread; I wasn't exactly keeping up with the details of the war. Had your father spoken to his friend since the siege ended?"

"I'm not sure," he said. "I don't think so. Still, even if it fell, he may still be here. And even if he's not, there may be someone else who can help us get to Merja."

The old woman said, "I'm not sure that's our aim any longer. If we're so far west, we won't make it to Merja before the ship sails. And we haven't enough money to book a second passage."

That had occurred to Naftaly, too. "Perhaps," he said, "perhaps they'll realize we're missing, and they'll leave word for us in Merja. Perhaps they'll leave enough money for us to make the voyage later."

The old woman didn't point out this seemed unlikely.

Naftaly said, "Let's see if we can find Salomon Machorro."

\+ + + + + +

NAFTALY AND THE old woman made their way through the serpentine lanes of Eliossana. He could no longer remember how to find the house of his father's draper, but he had fairly clear memories of the synagogue, which had been endowed by the merchants of the little town some two hundred years prior. It was bigger and fancier than one would expect in a town so small, the façade anchored by horseshoe-topped pillars; he'd been told it had been modeled after a synagogue in some northern city. "I believe it was this way," he said. "But I can't swear to it."

"How long ago was it you were here?" asked the old woman, as they picked their way through the cobbled streets. The town had been rich, once, but now it was falling into disrepair, and the road was pocked with holes. Holes and animal droppings.

Naftaly hoped they were animal droppings. It was hard to remember the way when he had to pay so much attention to what he might be stepping in.

"It was before the war," he said. "I was a boy."

"You're still a boy."

"I'm as close to thirty as I am to twenty," he said.

Ignoring this, she asked, "Does the town look the same?"

"No," he said sourly. "It doesn't."

For one thing, they'd just passed a tavern that Naftaly had no memory of. And while he hardly expected to recognize anyone from a few visits eight or ten years before, he had yet to see a single man with a covered head.

"There," he said, pointing. "That's the synagogue."

There was a small white building ahead, fitted with peaked windows along the front to welcome the light. As a boy, Naftaly had thought it must be one of the loveliest buildings in Sefarad, the face carved like a single piece of elaborate lace. "We should go inside," he said. "There must be someone there who can help us."

The old woman caught his arm tightly. "Wait," she said.

"What? Why?" Naftaly turned to look at her, just as, from within the synagogue, a bell chimed, twice, and then twice more: a synagogue no longer. It had been made over into a church.

Naftaly felt a wave of dread pass through him. "But where are all the Jews?" he whispered. "They can't have all gone, can they?"

"If they converted the synagogue there must be no one left," she said. "Either they fled, they were killed, or they converted. In any case, there's no help for us here."

"Wait," he said. "There's something posted on the doorway there. I'd like to see what it says."

"It can't say anything helpful to us."

"I'd still like to know," he said. "Can you go look? You're inconspicuous."

"You can't possibly think anyone ever took the time to teach me to read."

"Fine," he said, straightening his tunic. He stalked closer to the door, stopping just close enough to read what was written there.

He did not need to read far. It was an Edict of Grace.

The forced converts of Eliossana would have a month to confess their Judaizing and receive some sort of penance. After that, they would be at the mercy of the Inquisition. They would take testimony from everyone in town, looking for people who bathed on Fridays, or took the veins out of their meat, or never bought pork in the market.

Something like this had happened in every town outside of Rimon itself over the past years, since the Queen had brought the Inquisition to Sefarad. It had happened in Barcino, where Naftaly's mother's people were from. An uncle—a convert who had walked into the Church with open arms and a desire for more opportunities than his heritage allowed—had run afoul of them some time ago, in a year prior to Naftaly's remembering. But his mother told the story: he confessed, and the Inquisition accepted his confession, and then they'd sentenced him to ten years rowing a galley. And so instead of perishing quickly at the stake, he'd gone slowly in the hold of a ship.

But his mother had told Naftaly: her uncle had been sincere in his conversion—he'd cut ties with the family after—and his confession had been made under torture. And they'd killed him anyway. "Never forget it," she had said. "They claim interest in your heart, but all they really care about is your blood."

Naftaly returned to the old woman and whispered in her ear.

Here was the issue: the Inquisition could not touch them, not until August, anyway, but it meant that any conversos living in Eliossana would be hard-pressed to help them, which might lead to prison, torture, public burning, or all three.

However, that it was here did give a clue what had happened to everyone. "If the Inquisition is here," he said slowly, "there must be conversos. If all the Jews had died or fled, they wouldn't bother. Salomon Machorro might still be here. They could be anusim."

"If he is here," she said, "do you really think he'll help us with the Inquisition looking over his shoulder?"

"He might," he said.

"Not if he wants to live," she said. "We should go back to the road, follow the caravan."

"All the way to Merja? On foot? With no food or water?"

The old woman had no answer to that. The men in the tavern were watching them warily. It was early, Naftaly thought, for there to be so many men drinking wine.

The old woman said, "We should get off the street. Or at least keep moving."

Naftaly had inadvertently met the eyes of a man watching them from the tavern, who responded with an obscene gesture. The old woman took his arm meaningfully and began pulling him back up the road.

+ + + + + + +

TOBA FOLLOWED THE Mazik toward the alcalá, out of view of the city the Mazik told her was also called Rimon, straddling a river that was also called the Guadalraman, in the shadow of a mountain that was also called Sebah.

As they drew closer, she could see that the alcalá was not one large building but several smaller ones. In the front there was a wall with a gate in the center, and through this was a courtyard housing a garden filled with trees and flowers and ornamental greenery of strange types Toba did not know, with leaves shaped like fans, like hearts, like the faces of foxes. Every tree bore fruit: oranges, figs—which should not have been in season—pomegranates, apples, and some orange-and-red fruits that were shaped like raspberries but were the size of melons. In the center there was a tiled fountain, a circle set inside a hexagon set inside a starburst. On the other side of the garden was a set of broad, white steps, leading up to a dais, and then, behind this, a building with a dozen or more arched doorways.

"This is the public garden," the Mazik said. "You may make use of it. Adon Asmel's private garden is in the inner courtyard; keep out of that while you're here."

Toba was still struggling to keep up. The Mazik climbed the stairs to the dais, turning when he saw Toba was still on the other side of the fountain. "Can't you go faster than this?"

"I'm afraid not," she said.

"Is there something wrong with you?" he asked.

Shrugging helplessly, she said, "Yes."

Looking thoroughly exasperated, he crooked a finger at her. She felt a pulling sensation, and then found herself at his side, on top of the dais, struggling to keep her balance. He turned and kept walking, entering the building and turning to the left, leaving her struggling to catch up again.

"The kitchen," he said, "is back the other way, not that you'll need to go there. Asmel's private apartments are along the western wall; don't go there either."

"Where *should* I go?" she asked.

He stopped in front of a room with a great wooden door. It was, Toba realized, the only door she'd seen so far; all of the rooms seemed open to the gardens, as if the building itself were only a latticed shell meant to demarcate spaces and offer a roof. The heavy wooden door was completely mismatched with the rest of it.

"Here," he said, pulling the door open and walking inside.

It was a library. The wall that contained the doorway was lined with shelves, as was the wall on Toba's right. The wall opposite her contained an open window that looked out over the garden they'd walked through, and above that was a line of colored-glass windows depicting intricate geometric shapes that cast multicolored sunbeams on the floor. She could not see the fourth wall; concealing it was a labyrinth of shelves, set so closely she could not say how long the room continued in that direction. The area before her was an open space, taken up partly by a large table made of the same wood as the door. The Mazik disappeared into the maze of shelves, but kept up his talking.

"Which five?" he asked.

"I beg your pardon?"

"Which five languages, girl, or was that an idle boast?"

Toba had paused to examine the contents of a shelf—a mistake, as now there were two paths through the books, and she wasn't certain which one he'd taken. "Hebrew, La'az Sefaradi, Latin, Zayeti, and Arabic. Do I go right or left?"

"I'll start you on a translation," he said, his voice coming from the left. Toba followed it but found herself in a cubby of books, so she turned and tried the other direction. "Though I expect you're too slow to finish it before the next moon. You've gone the wrong way again; you just passed me."

"I'm very quick," she said.

She heard a small snort. "All evidence to the contrary," he muttered from somewhere ahead. It was dim amid the shelves; the light from the window barely reached here, and the strange sconces on the walls—which housed stones instead of candles—did not reach this far. Toba's eyes had never been very good, and she had to steady herself on a shelf when her toe caught on the uneven floor. She came around a corner and saw the Mazik before a cubby in the shelf-labyrinth. He hadn't heard her approach, and from within his satchel he pulled out the book she'd seen before, and then a second. He frowned at the shelves for a moment before sliding both volumes into an empty spot between two others.

“I read faster than I walk,” she said, and he turned sharply, frowning.

After a beat, he said, “Let’s hope so.” He turned to a nearby shelf and pulled out another book, holding it out to Toba.

She took it, reading the cover. It was a book she knew.

“You’ve seen this before?” he asked, reading her expression.

“Yes,” she said. “Once or twice. This is a translation, though.”

“Is it? Fine. I’d like a copy in Latin and one in Arabic.”

Toba hesitated before asking, "You want me to translate the Hebrew translation back into Arabic?”

The Mazik looked a little consternated, as if he hadn’t realized that was quite what he was asking, but said, “Just—yes. That’s what I want.” He brushed past her and she followed him through the shelves, back to the main gallery. Indicating the table, he said, “You may work here,” and then turned to leave.

“Paper,” she blurted.

“What?”

“I’ll need paper,” she said. “Or parchment, if that’s what you use here. But the work will take four times as long on parchment, so I hope it’s paper.”

“Ah,” he said. He doubled back and smacked a palm down on the table. Underneath appeared a stack of perfectly formed leaves of paper. “That’s all, then?”

“Ink? And a pen?”

He shook his head, feigning—she thought—annoyance, but managed to summon ink and a trio of pens, seemingly out of the surface of the table. “Is there anything *else*?” he asked.

Toba pondered this. What if he disbelieved her? What if this was some trick to prove she’d only made up her skills, to keep herself alive, and when he found out, he’d do something dreadful? “I can really do this,” she said.

“I’m sure you can.”

“I’m not lying to you.”

"I have not implied thinking so."

"Would you like a demonstration?"

"No."

But Toba was providing one anyway. She'd opened the book in front of her and transcribed the first line. Only she'd decided to ignore her grandfather's warning, and she wrote with both pens; the Latin with her right and the Arabic with her left.

The Mazik drew back in shock. "How are you doing this? And why?"

The why, obviously, was to prove her usefulness. As to the how, she said, "It's easier for me this way. I only have to parse the meaning of each phrase once."

He asked, "Can many mortals write with both hands at once?"

She said, honestly, "I don't know. But you see, I really can do your work. You don't have to worry."

"I wasn't—"

"What should I do when I've finished? Should I find you?"

"Me?" he asked, as if such a thing had never occurred to him, that he might ever see her again.

"Him, then?" she asked, indicating what she thought was the direction of the door.

"Adon Asmel? Why would he want to see you?"

"To review my progress?"

He laughed. "Little one," he said. "Do not find yourself seeking approval from Asmel. You won't get it." Looking a bit disconcerted, he waved an arm and manifested what Toba could only describe as a shadow, saying, "Here. If you must have someone to bring you paper and ink and to yammer away at, you can have this."

Toba looked at the shadow. "Is it—" she said. "What is it?"

"A servant," he said.

She peered at it closely; she could see the stone wall behind it as clearly as if she were looking through a glass of water. "Is it some different sort of Mazik?"

He scoffed. "It's only a figment I've created. A shade." To the shade, he said, "If she asks for ink or pen or paper, you may provide it, but nothing more."

Hesitantly, Toba got up and approached the shade. It felt neither hot nor cold, and she leaned closer to see if it had a smell: it did not. "What shall I call him?" she asked hesitantly.

"Call it? It has no name. It's simply a shade, it has no will. It will do what I've asked, that's all."

"It can make paper from nothing. So it has magic?"

"I made it," he said, "so it has a fraction of mine. It will be able to meet your needs."

"Thank you," she said, uncertainly; to the shade, she said, "Can you speak?"

"That it cannot do," he said, and turned his back on her. "*If* you finish, you may leave your work on the table."

"And if I don't?" she asked his back.

"You just keep speaking, don't you? If you don't finish, then leave whatever you have done here."

"I mean," she said, "what will happen to me?"

He looked at her incredulously. "Oh, all right. I shall unhinge my jaw like a serpent and swallow you whole. May I take my leave now?"

She gasped. And then he really did leave.

Toba went to the large window and looked out at the garden and realized that in a place so large, she'd only seen one person. Where were the servants—or were there only these shades? For that matter, where were the other Maziks? She looked back toward the shade the Mazik had left her, who only hovered in the corner and looked like nothing much. If only it could talk, somehow, as she had so many questions.

Someone was maintaining all this, unless it was being done by magic. But if they could maintain an estate by magic, why would they possibly need her to translate a three-hundred-year-old book? Returning to the table, she looked down at the first line she'd translated; she'd never read the *Guide for the Perplexed*, but she'd scanned the first few pages more than once over her grandfather's shoulder. This appeared to be the same text. It looked old, though. As if, rather than having been printed from a block, it had been written by hand. The pages were going very yellow.

She wondered what other books she'd find in the Mazik's library.

She wondered how many of them were Mazik books . . . books she'd never have another chance to read.

Putting the *Guide* aside, she went to the nearest shelf, scanning to see how the books were organized, by author or language or date, but there was no making sense of it; it was as if they'd all been grouped according to when they'd been acquired, or else simply at random.

Reminding herself that she was not here to be the Mazik's librarian, she sat down in the surprisingly comfortable chair to translate the Rambam.

Seven

ELENA PERES'S MIND was a clockwork.

That was what her husband often told her; he'd seen an example of something he called a mechanical timepiece at court, some gift to the Emir of Rimon from some Burgundian prince. Alasar had explained that the inside of the clock contained a spring and some assortment of gears: it needed to be wound once daily to generate the tension it required to function.

Elena had asked her husband to draw her a picture of the inner workings of the device, but of course one could not simply disembowel an item belonging to the Emir, even if he'd had access. So she'd tried to design one herself, using the vague explanations offered by her husband, until she'd reluctantly admitted defeat: she could not, she decided, replicate the timepiece without seeing it first. Shortly thereafter she'd found herself expecting a child—her only child, as she would sadly learn—and applied that same detailed dedication to understanding the inner workings of the small creature that Hashem had put in her care.

Her husband depended on her for her clockwork mind; she saw details that others missed, and operated with a logic that often eluded him. When he read, he frequently mired himself in the prose, stopping to wonder why a writer had used one word, one metaphor, instead of another, losing himself in hidden meanings Elena thought were less the result of authorial intent and more the product of Alasar's own esoteric thought patterns. Elena, conversely, had little use for words, seeing only the ideas beneath them, and could point out exactly why one idea worked and another did not. The truth was, Elena often thought, that Alasar should have been a poet, and Elena should have been a rabbi. But things being as they were, Alasar was a translator and Elena was his wife.

It was not a bad life, however. She had a husband who respected her. She'd had a child she'd loved.

And then that child had died.

\+ + + + + + +

AS THE CARAVAN moved down the serpentine road of the mountain, the moon loomed overhead. It seemed too close to Elena—it made her uneasy. Her own mother had taught her to fear a full moon, passing on some bit of homespun advice she'd learned from her own mother and back so many generations: *Never trust a man you meet under a full moon.*

The caravan arrived at an inn near Almeria just as the sun was getting low, as planned—they'd written nearly twenty letters, making sure they would have someplace to stop on their journey so they would not have to sleep unguarded in a field somewhere, and this particular inn, owned, Elena knew, by a converso family, had agreed to a night's lodging in exchange for only mildly usurious rates. Their belongings would be guarded overnight, and they would have use of his rooms and his dining room, which meant most of their party would enjoy sleeping on the floor, though Elena supposed that was better than sleeping outside.

It was only once they arrived and she went through their party that she realized Toba was no longer among them. She'd done her best to keep her eyes on Toba from the cart where she rode with Alasar, but it had been dark and Toba was slow, always. She'd asked the cart to stop, to let her walk along with her granddaughter, but Alasar had talked her out of it. "What good will it do her for you to lame yourself?" he'd asked, which was ridiculous because Elena was as hearty as anyone, even at her age, but she had been too tired to argue. And she'd stayed in the cart, and now Toba was gone.

Feeling a rising panic, Elena and Alasar spoke to every person, asking after her. But no one remembered having seen the girl since they left Rimon.

She was not the only one unaccounted for, either: the Cresques boy had likewise gone missing. This changed things in the minds of the rest of the group, who decided, rather quickly, that the pair had run off to convert and then marry.

Elena insisted this was nonsense. "She doesn't know the man!" she insisted. "He's never even been to the house!"

But someone remembered seeing them in the plaça together, and Naftaly had held his hands on Toba's shoulders in a rather intimate gesture. Elena balked at the idea, but it was easier for the others to believe they'd eloped, because it meant there was nothing more to be done. They were lost to them, by their own choice. It was too bad, but they could hardly drag the pair out of the country, particularly if they'd already accepted baptism.

"This is ridiculous," Elena told her husband. "If the tailor's boy wanted Toba, he would have come and asked after her. She must have fallen on the road, you know how she is. We'll have to go back for her."

Alasar agreed that it was odd, but there was no way to go back except on foot; they had half a share of a cart, and no other means of transportation. He tried to hire a horse at the inn, but no one would give him one for the little money he had.

They were too old to make the journey on foot, Alasar so arthritic he could barely walk more than twenty paces at once, and Elena deaf in one ear, and who knew where Toba even was? Elena wept, while Alasar begged the party to turn back.

But no one agreed. The risk of falling behind, of missing the transport they'd already paid for, was too great. "What can we do?" Alasar said. "We can't simply leave her."

Elena bit her lip and said nothing while the bowl of soup in front of her went cold. Then, as they were finishing their meal, the friar arrived.

He was alone, Elena noted with some comfort, and had not arrived at the head of a column of men bearing torches. She tried to guess his order from his clothes, but there weren't many such men in Rimon. At any rate, he seemed to be there only to preach, to beg them to reconsider for the sake of their souls, not to force them at the end of a pike. He gave an impassioned speech, he shouted, he wept, and the innkeeper looked more and more uncomfortable, making Elena wonder about the sincerity of his own conversion. The friar railed until his voice wore out from overuse, and then he slumped back to the innkeeper's own bedchamber to sleep off his ecstatic—if rather useless—ministry. The party drooped with exhaustion once he was gone; they'd already gone a night without sleep. While the rest laid down on pallets of blankets and little else, Elena went outside for some air, and to think.

The friar had arrived on an old donkey, swaybacked but sturdy-looking. Elena patted the animal's nose and she snorted. The moon, waning now but only barely, lit the courtyard. *Mama*, she thought, *you would not have left Toba behind.*

She needed paper, and she needed ink, and she had neither.

Taking a smooth stone off the ground, she sat down and made a map in the dust, with Rimon on one end and the inn on the other and the road sketched between. The stone was soft, and with the edge of her thumbnail she carefully made the impressions of the letters spelling *Toba bat Penina*.

She tore a strip of cloth from the bottom hem of her skirt and tied a loop around the stone, then spat on the stone three times, then swung it in a circle over the map she'd drawn on the ground.

Nothing occurred. No pull, at all, in any direction.

She widened the map, adding Meleqa to the west and Merja itself, and still, there was nothing. Untying the rock, Elena threw it aside, scowling at the dirt in front of her.

She couldn't simply have vanished.

Actually, her mother's voice told her, she *could* have vanished.

She took a second rock.

This one was harder than the first, and she found she could not score it with her nail. Taking a small knife out of her satchel, she scratched *Naftaly ben Abrafim*. And she tied that rock to the strip of cloth, and swung it in a circle.

It landed on the ground with a small thump.

But it was in the wrong spot; too far west, and too far south, and they had not even come through Eliossana. Retying it again, she made another circle in the air, and again, it came down with a plop directly on the spot where she knew Eliossana to be.

Putting the stone in her bag along with the knife, she rose. She went to the railing where they'd tied their horses, having not had enough room for all of them in the inn's small stable, and she untied them one by one. It would slow the caravan, she knew, perhaps long enough for a single rider, and then, hopefully, two, to ride out and then return again. It was a risk: that she'd be caught, that she might be left behind, that she might make the rest of her people too late to Merja, but she took comfort in knowing she was only doing what her own mother would have done in her place. She looked again, to make sure there was no candle still lit inside the inn. She whispered some very old words to the friar's donkey, which made the animal's ears prick and her nose sniff the air. And then she climbed on her back and rode away, muttering a series of numbers best known only to some creatures that live in the deep sea, to the rhythm of the donkey's hoofbeats.

Eight

TOBA WORKED ON the Rambam text until her eyes began to give out; not long, since she hadn't slept the night before. She would have tried to push through, but her penmanship was suffering—particularly in the Arabic—and she didn't think the Mazik would appreciate a sloppy translation. As it grew dark, the round stones set in the walls began to glow, winking on one by one.

Leaving her work and the shade behind, she decided to find a room with a bed. Resting one of the light-stones from the wall on the palm of her hand, she went out into the corridor and tried to remember which side of the alcalá was west so she could avoid accidentally stumbling into Asmel's private rooms.

Most of the rooms she did find were completely empty, as if the alcalá had once been inhabited by a large number of people who had since abandoned it. The walls were a very old, beige stone, and the floors were wood that was worn in the center, as if many centuries of feet had all trod the same path. She began to despair of finding a bed, and hoped she might at least find a blanket, or a tapestry, or something she could lie on to soften the floor, as her feet began to drag with exhaustion.

She came upon another set of wooden doors, made to match those in the library, set in an arched doorway. They were notable because most of the rooms had no doors, and also because this set of doors was cracked. A fissure ran horizontally across at the level of Toba's shoulder; she traced it with a finger and found its edges smooth. Pushing the door open, she half expected a second library, but while this room was vast—the curved exterior wall made it seem like a semicircle—it was entirely full of furniture that appeared to have been smashed, dragged inside, and then left to rot. The small part of the floor that was uncovered had been coated with a layer of dust so thick her boots left small footprints in it, as if it were snow. She picked her way through the mess, coming up with the leg from a broken chair or bench, and then the torn-off front cover of a book, written in Hebrew of all things, called *A History of the Common Demon* by someone called Rafeq of Katlav. She turned it over in her hands; what was left of the binding was singed. It was an odd enough object that she'd just decided to take it with her when she saw, in the detritus, something covered with cloth. Moving an upside-down table from on top of it, she saw that it was a cushion large enough to recline on; she could see others peeking out from within the mess. She gave it a hard tug and managed to get it out of the midden, and then gave it a thump with her palm, only to be rewarded with a plume of dust that made her cough her throat raw.

Dragging it on the ground behind her, with the front cover of *A History of the Common Demon* in her pocket, she continued down the hallway. She had two criteria for a bedchamber: it needed to have a door she could shut, and it needed enough floor space for her to be able to lie down. She'd just started to think about dragging her cushion back to the library when she came around a sharp corner and found a set of stone steps leading to a second floor. At the top of these was another door—small, this time, and on the other side was a room ten paces across, with a large window looking out into darkness and only a marginal amount of dust on the bare floor.

It was a good room, she thought, right at the top of the stairs, because she would be able to hear anyone coming. She tipped the top half of the cushion out the window and beat it a few times, releasing as much dust as she was able, before flinging it down on the floor, flopping down on top of it, and falling immediately asleep.

\+ \+ \+ \+ \+ \+

SHE WOKE TO the too-bright sun streaming in through the open window on a breeze that smelled like orange blossoms. Straightening her dress as best she could, she went to the window and looked out over a garden that was not the one she'd come through yesterday.

It must have been Asmel's private garden, she decided, and then worried that gazing at it might also be some kind of trespass, though the other Mazik hadn't said so. This was smaller than the garden in the main courtyard, but grander, with a fountain that sent a spray ten feet into the air, which Toba could hear from inside her room, and she wondered that she hadn't noticed the sound the night before. Several stone benches seemed to grow out of the ground, and in every corner stood an orange tree in full flower, while songbirds called from their branches.

She saw no sign of Asmel there. She wondered where he was. Probably a Mazik lord did not work for a living; she wondered what he did with his time, when he wasn't traipsing off to the mortal world in search of old books.

In the light of day, Toba could see soot marks on the walls, as if there had been a fire in the room at some point, but it must have been ages ago because she could detect no burnt scent anywhere. She wondered what had burned there, because there was no sign of so much as a rug or curtain or stick of furniture. If something had burned, shouldn't there have been ashes? And if the ashes had been cleaned, why were the soot marks left on the walls? It made no sense. She swiped a finger against the wall and brought it to her nose . . . it had no smell, but left a black mark on her finger that she rubbed off on her already-filthy dress. She perused the perimeter of the room, and then noticed there was a single stone in the wall without soot, as if it had either been cleaned off or had not stuck there in the first place. Feeling a strange compulsion, she reached out a finger and tapped the stone, only to have it vanish at her touch.

Toba jerked her hand back, expecting some disaster, but when none came she peered into what was a hidden space inside the wall. Inside, she could see a stack of papers.

Enough morning light came into the room that she could see the pages were written in Hebrew. Carefully, she reached in and pulled out the stack of papers. As soon as she touched them, they crumbled to dust.

She jerked her hand back, feeling as if she'd committed a murder. It was a genizah, it must have been, and she'd just destroyed whatever was in it. She put her hand, covered in the dust of the pages she'd ruined, to her lips before looking back into the space. Two pages remained; underneath them was a book. She did not dare disturb either.

It seemed strange, yet again, that she'd only seen human writing in this place, in the library and in the genizah (Was it a genizah? Toba could only guess). Toba wondered again if there were any Mazik books in the library. She wondered what language the Maziks spoke among themselves, or what sort of letters they would use in a book, or if she could read them.

She also wondered if there was food somewhere, because she hadn't eaten in over a day.

Her amulet was still stitched inside the lining of her bodice, barely cool against her ribs, and she missed the weight of it around her neck, the familiar ice of it on her skin. Having nothing at hand to tear the stitches that held it in place, she tore them out by hand before slipping the chain over her head and then, in case one of the Maziks took a liking to it, tucked it back down the front of her dress, tapping her fingers against it until it cooled her skin beneath.

Remembering that the Mazik had made some vague mention of a kitchen, she decided to go in search of it, picking her way down the steep staircase and back past the rows of unused rooms. The place must have once been occupied by many more people than one lord and his vassal, or whatever the younger man was to Adon Asmel. He could well be his son, Toba supposed. She'd have no way to know.

Long past the library she found a room she thought might be a kitchen, only because there were a great number of metal platters and bowls stored on a table along with cabinets that appeared to be some sort of a pantry. There was, however, no oven, no place for a fire, and no other way to cook.

She began opening and closing cabinets, unearthing a great deal of blown glass and some cutlery, but found no food at all until she went into a cabinet in the corner, in which there lay a burlap sack containing several pounds of dried lentils.

That was all. The sum total of the food stores of the entire alcalá amounted to lentils. And she had no way to cook lentils. She was going to starve. She had no way, even, to find the Mazik and remind him she needed to eat regularly, which he might not know. Did a Mazik eat proper food? Perhaps he ate babies, or fire, or nothing at all.

Then she remembered: there were fruit trees in the garden. She grabbed a few handfuls of the dried lentils, wrapping them in her handkerchief, and went out to the courtyard.

She left her handkerchief to soak at the corner of the fountain and plucked three apples, sitting down at the edge of the water to eat them one after the other. Hopefully the lentils would be soft enough to eat by evening, even if she could not cook them. She looked down at the leftover apple cores and wondered what to do with them; the garden was too well-kept to simply leave them. She wiped apple juice from the corner of her mouth and decided to go off to find the library again when suddenly Adon Asmel was directly in front of her. He did not look pleased.

"You have eaten the fruit," he said. "Why would you do such a thing?"

Her first reaction was terror; he seemed taller, somehow, in his anger, and while he was not precisely a broad man, he dwarfed Toba.

She wondered about the punishment for eating a Mazik's enchanted apples. Death, most likely. By beheading, which seemed like a favorite. Toba wondered—and not for the first time, if she was honest—what it might feel like to be beheaded, if there were a moment during which her severed head might still be conscious. She hoped not. She'd not like to be aware of her own decapitation.

It struck her that *decapitation* was a curious word, because it implied that her consciousness resided in her body, and her head was an organ that might or might not be lost, when really, it should be the other way around; it wasn't that her head could be cut off, but her body from her head, where her mind lived. She didn't think there was a word for this. It troubled her.

"I think," she told Adon Asmel, "that *decapitated* makes no sense. It should be *decuerpitated*."

His mouth opened a bit, as if he were unsure how to respond to this bit of inanity, because he was only interested in the fate of his magic fruit, not in her linguisto-philosophical breakdown of the manner of her impending death.

She decided to try to keep her dignity in her last moments. She would not blubber, or fall at his feet. He glared down at her, his impatience doubling because she wasn't answering his accusations. She presented an apple core to him in what she knew to be a childish gesture, as if offering her refuse would somehow make up for her transgression. "I'm ... I'm sorry?" she said. Childish, again, making it a question. "I was hungry, and I could find nothing else, besides lentils."

"Lentils," he repeated flatly, and then muttered, "Barsilay," in a tone that indicated it was either the name of the other Mazik, or else some sort of Mazik curse.

With trembling hands, she took the packet of lentils out of the fountain. "They were all that was in the kitchen," she said. "And I could find no way to cook them—"

He took the handkerchief from her and opened it, removing three lentils and placing them on the edge of the fountain, on top of a green leaf that looked like the face of a cat. Passing a hand over them, they were changed to a round of bread and a block of white cheese, the leaf grown to the size of a plate.

"Thank you," Toba said. Asmel held out an impatient hand. Not knowing what he wanted, she tore off half the bread and offered it, but he shook his head and pointed toward the apple cores she'd left by the edge of the fountain. She put them into his open palm together with the one she'd tried to offer him earlier, where he closed his fist around them, opening his hand again to reveal several small seeds. Inclining his head toward the tree she'd picked the apples from, he said, "Plant them among the roots. And don't touch the fruit again."

Toba saw that the tree she'd taken the apples from was already beginning to sicken and drop leaves that had suddenly gone yellow and brown. "I'm sorry," she said, "I didn't know."

She turned back to ask him how to get more food later, but he'd already gone. She sat down and began to gnaw at the bread, finding it sweet and delicious. *I'm sorry?* she repeated inwardly, *I'm sorry?* like a daft bird, repeating words that held no intrinsic meaning. She was a fool. A tiny, inarticulate fool.

But, she told herself, reaching for the cheese, at least she was a fool with her head still attached. Or her body, depending on how one looked at it. She was alone, trapped in the Mazik realm with no hope of rescue, no money, no friends. But she was capitated—could one be capitated? Perhaps it would be simpler to say her neck was unsevered—and she had food, at least for the moment, and she had books to read: three of the necessary conditions for a reasonable existence. Minor triumphs, her grandfather had once told her, when she'd spent an hour on a single sentence of Ibn Hansa, were still triumphs, and should be treasured accordingly.

+ + · + + + +

NAFTALY AND THE old woman found themselves walking back toward the road while having a running argument, the argument being whether they were more likely to die traveling alone to Merja with no food, or more likely to die when the inhabitants of Eliossana decided to kill them. The old woman had taken the second position, pointing out that while the Inquisition had no interest in a pair of unconverted Jews, the townspeople, who appeared to be underworked and fairly inebriated, might.

"It's you I'm looking out for," the old woman said. "They won't bother with me; I'm so old I'm nearly invisible."

"You sound pleased by that."

"Oh, it's a gift, I assure you. My point is, if we stay here you are likely to find a knife sticking out of your gut at some point. This whole place has gone wrong."

"We just need to find Salomon," he said. "Even if he's converted, I'm sure he'll at least help us get to Merja."

"You're forgetting that he may very well be dead."

"You have no reason to believe he's dead."

"You have no reason to believe he isn't."

"There's no point continuing this discussion until we've—" Naftaly trailed off and frowned at the road: he heard something. A horse, he thought, but far off, and he focused on it until he caught sight of a rider coming around the bend from the south: a person riding a rather moth-eaten donkey. His eyes scanned up to the rider.

"Are you listening?" the old woman said. "Or are you having another fit?"

He said, "That's Elena Peres coming up the road."

She cuffed him on the back of the head. "Stop that," she said.

"Damn it," he said. "What is wrong with you?"

"Can't you turn it off for a bit?"

"This isn't a vision," he insisted. "That is Elena Peres."

"Right," she said. "Alone, on a horse, twenty miles from where she should be."

"I think it's a donkey," he said, squinting.

"Elena Peres is halfway to Merja, and I can't believe she's ever ridden a donkey in her life."

Elena Peres was close enough now to see their faces, and she drew rein and looked down at them from the bit of height she gained from her donkey-back perch and her own large frame. Then she flung herself down from her saddle in such a rush that she landed half on top of Naftaly, who tried to catch her but got kicked in the chest for his trouble.

"You," she said, clutching his shoulders. "It's you."

Naftaly could not think why Elena Peres should be so emotional to see him, but she went on, "Is Toba with you? Are you married?"

Naftaly and the old woman exchanged a glance over Elena's shoulder as he tried, and failed, to set her back on her feet. "I . . . no," he said. "We aren't *married*."

"No? But she must be with you?"

When Naftaly failed to answer, she said, her voice rising, "Have you *seen* her, at least?"

Naftaly tried to determine the gentlest way to tell an old woman that her grandchild had disappeared into the wilderness with two strange men. From behind Elena, the old woman said, "The wolves did not eat her. I would lead with that bit."

Nine

"WE'LL HAVE TO ride to Merja," the old woman said.

"Three people on a donkey?" Naftaly said. He'd explained, as best he could, what had happened to Toba. Elena had seemed oddly unsurprised; probably that was a product of age. At a certain point, Naftaly guessed, you'd seen the world turned absurdly upside-down often enough there was nothing left to shock you. "How do you expect that to work?"

"We can't stay in Eliossana," the old woman said, ignoring the logistics of her proposal, "it isn't safe here."

"No," Elena said. "I'm sorry—what is your name?"

Naftaly startled a little, because he did not know, either. The old woman said, "What?"

"What do you want me to call you?" When the old woman said, "I don't care what you call me," Elena turned to Naftaly and asked, "Fine—what do *you* call her?" and when Naftaly only looked confused, she added, "Do you not think old women have names? That they fade away like the color in our hair?"

"Don't fuss at him," the old woman said. "Everyone who ever used my name is dead. I don't much care for it anymore."

"Then am I supposed to just call you *old woman*?"

The old woman shrugged. Moving on, Elena said, "As you like. The point is that Toba might yet return. If the boy can find the spot again, she might come back the way she went. We must stay until the next full moon."

"The next full moon? You want us to stay here *a month*?" the old woman asked.

"If she's gone where I think," Elena said slowly, "that may be the only time she can return."

"Where is it you think she's gone?" asked Naftaly.

"There will be no ship for us in a month," the old woman said. "And what of your husband? Is he not also alone?"

"No," she said. "He is not." Turning to Naftaly, she said, "Can you find the place again?"

"Where . . ." he began, stopped, and began again. "Where do you think Toba is?"

Elena made a gesture that might have been meant to ward off the evil eye. She said, "Elsewhere. Can you find it again?"

Elsewhere was no answer at all, but it seemed all she was content to give at the moment. "There was a wood there," he said, "and a valley, I think we would see it coming up the road in daylight. It was an odd place; there were no great trees before or after."

The old woman muttered a curse.

"Then it's decided," Elena said. "We'll find your draper, we'll stay here until the next full moon, and then we'll go to find Toba."

"No one's decided that at all," the old woman protested.

"There's no point rushing to Merja now anyway," Elena said. "We can't possibly make the ship now."

"The ship is one problem," the old woman said, "but there's one other thing the boy's forgotten to mention." The old woman pointed out, prodding Naftaly with her bony finger. "The Inquisition is here. It's a fairly critical issue."

Elena said, "Damn them." Turning to Naftaly, she said, "Listen, we'll never make it to Merja without help; we're too far away. We could sell the donkey, but it wouldn't be enough to get us to Merja *and* on a ship. We need to find someone willing to help, and there's a chance you have a friend here. We'll go look for him, but remember: if Salomon

Machorro lives, it won't be his name any longer. And we'd best not walk into the middle of town asking for him by his real name."

"What do you suggest?" Naftaly asked. "All I recall of him was that he was unusually tall and had two sons and a daughter with a lisp."

"Then we'll ask for a fabric merchant," Elena said. "With three children. And hope it's the right one."

\+ \+ \+

DECIDING THE TAVERN was a likelier bet than the church, they headed back in that direction. Inside, Naftaly found himself the object of many glares, and carefully adjusted his tzitzit to make sure it was under his tunic. He took a coin Elena had given him and set it gingerly on the bar. The men around him were mainly drinking port, so he asked for that, too, his eyes stinging as he sipped at it. The barman scowled at him. "This is an odd place for the likes of you."

Naftaly rubbed at the scruff on his chin that steadfastly refused to turn itself into a reasonable beard. "I'm only passing through," he said.

"You ought to pass faster," the barman replied.

"I'm afraid I'm traveling on foot," Naftaly said, a little more stiffly than he'd intended. "It's a bit slow."

"I wager I could find you a seat in a cart. For enough silver."

Naftaly tightened his grip around his port; the barman wasn't being helpful, precisely, he was being opportunistic, but at least he wasn't chasing Naftaly out of the bar with a knife. Someone who profited off the misfortunes of others might only be a hair's breadth better than the person causing them, but at least the opportunist wouldn't harm you for nothing. He tucked the knowledge away for later use. "I'm afraid," he said, "I'm a bit short on funds at the moment. I'm actually here to collect a debt, if you could point me in the right direction."

The man poured another mug of port and handed it to a sullen boy who reached for it over Naftaly's shoulder.

"I'm looking for a fabric merchant," Naftaly went on. "One who used to do business in Rimon."

"A name," the barman said, "would be helpful."

"I'm afraid I don't recall it," Naftaly said. "He had two sons and a daughter who ought to be grown by now."

The barman eyed him suspiciously. Naftaly added, as an afterthought, "He owes my father a great sum of money and I intend to collect it."

"The man owes your father a great sum of money, and you don't recall his name?" Those within hearing distance laughed. "And what do you intend to do with a great sum of money, in any case? You can't take it with you."

Naftaly leaned in a little closer. "What I intend to do with it is my own business. And I'm afraid if he hears I'm asking for him directly, he'll find some way to avoid me." The barkeep spat into the woodchips littering the floor.

"You likely want Alfonso deSantos," he said. "Only he died last year."

Naftaly felt a great weight descend upon him. "And his heirs?" he asked quietly. "Perhaps I might go to them."

"He has a son," the barman said. "He still sells cloth." And then he described, with some pleasure, how Naftaly could find his house. "When you collect," he said, "come and find me, and I'll secure you passage wherever you're going. Only three hundred milliarès."

Naftaly's entire life was not worth three hundred milliarès, and the man smiled, revealing a set of teeth too fine for a tavernkeeper.

"I may also have a donkey to sell. She's quite sturdy."

The barman said, "I can offer you one hundred milliarès, sight unseen."

"One hundred!"

Naftaly departed, leaving most of his drink unfinished.

The old woman and Elena were huddled in an alley the next street over.

"Well?" Elena asked.

"Well, he's dead. But I have directions to his son's house. And a lead on a ride in a cart, if only we can come up with three hundred milliarès."

The old woman laughed shrilly.

Elena said, "When?"

"I didn't actually agree to that," Naftaly said, turning the corner while the women followed. "The Machorros might help us, but not to the tune of three hundred milliarès, and that was only for me. And don't ask how much he offered for the donkey, you won't like it."

Elena said, "Hm."

They walked the rest of the way quickly; the Machorro—the deSantos—house was not far from the center of town, and it didn't take long before they came to a house with a wrought-iron gate in the front, its bars twisted in the shape of a lion.

Hanging from the wall, next to the front door, was a ceramic Madonna, with downcast blue eyes that seemed to weep. She was still glossy, as if she'd been painted only recently.

"Perhaps we should go," Elena said.

"Wait," the old woman said, approaching the statue and running her eyes over it. She ran her hands over the statue's feet.

"What are you doing?" Naftaly demanded.

"Looking," she said. Her improbably nimble fingers found a seam behind the Madonna's right ankle and she opened it. Inside, there was a scroll the size of a fava bean. The old woman turned to make sure the others saw it was a mezuzah, and then closed the foot again. "They'll help us," she said firmly.

"How did you know to look in the foot?" Elena asked.

"It's always in the foot," she said.

+ + + + + +

THE SHADE WATCHED over Toba as she slept.

She was not particularly grateful for this. After Asmel had caught her eating fruit in the garden, he must have had some words with Barsilay, because he'd expanded the shade's abilities to be better able to provide for her needs. (Toba had said, "Did it not occur to you I would need to eat?" and Barsilay had said, "It was *one day*, you little wretch, no one starves that fast.")

Toba had never considered herself particularly gregarious . . . she was happiest reading a book next to her grandfather, who would also be reading a book, in companionable silence. But her brief time in the Mazik realm, with only the wispy shade for company, had left her eager for more solid companionship. Before Barsilay had left again, she'd stopped him with a litany of questions, beginning with, "How many of the books on those shelves were written by Maziks?"

He'd said, "None."

"None!"

"This is a library of human books."

"Then where are the Mazik books?"

He'd only said, "Elsewhere."

"Can I see them?"

"No."

Toba had pursed her mouth in disappointment. She'd wanted, very badly, to see a Mazik book. But if they were really elsewhere, perhaps she could go and find them once Barsilay left her alone again. Where did he go, she wondered? Perhaps he had a family who needed him at home. She asked, "Do Maziks marry?"

He laughed. "Yes, of course, when we choose."

"But you have no wife?"

He smirked. "I have no interest in such a thing."

"And Adon Asmel?"

His smile vanished. "What use could you possibly have for such information?"

"None, I suppose, I was only curious. It seems an awfully grand house for a lord and his . . ."

"Heir," he said.

"His son?"

"Not quite," he said.

"So Asmel has no sons?"

"You enjoy digging, don't you? No, he hasn't any children."

"But he *had* a wife."

"I never said that."

"You implied it when you told me he had no children, but declined to speak about a wife. Either he has a wife and she's hidden away somewhere, or he had one and she's left him, or he had one and she's died."

Barsilay screwed up his face in frustration. "You are going to cause me no end of trouble."

"I suppose I could go looking for her," she said.

He sighed. "Don't bother. You'd be looking for a woman more than a few years in the grave." When Toba opened her mouth to ask more, he said, "Now, that's enough, little inquisitor." He rose from the chair, which blinked out of existence, and left, leaving her with only the shade for company again.

As much as she appreciated the food and extra ink that appeared whenever she asked, or the bath, or the clean clothes—which were finer than anything she'd ever owned—the shade gave her a creeping sort of feeling, like she was being helped by a large insect. Perhaps it was because it had no face. Before she'd gone to bed, she'd tried draping a blanket over the dratted thing, but then the blanket had gone straight through to the floor. She'd considered asking the creature to turn its back, but it didn't precisely *have* a back. So she asked it to extinguish the lights and pretended not to know it was there, while it hovered in the vicinity of her feet all night.

When she woke, the shade had taken it upon itself to straighten the room, and was laying out her clothes for the day and pouring water into a basin that had appeared from nowhere. She wondered if she could ask it to stop, or if it were obeying some higher orders from Barsilay concerning what she could and could not actually tell it to do. She'd asked it to help her find the Mazik books, and it had merely hovered uncertainly before her, eventually disappearing and then reappearing with the skull of some unidentifiable animal. Toba assumed this was Barsilay's idea of a joke.

Climbing out of her bed, she looked out the window at Asmel's garden to see that Asmel himself was present within it, seated on one of the stone benches that appeared to have grown up out of the ground near the fountain. The birds in the orange trees were singing, and after watching a moment, Toba realized they were singing to Asmel, and that Asmel was not alone. A second man—not Barsilay, but some other splendid Mazik, darker-skinned and dressed head-to-foot in embroidered purple—was pacing between the orange trees; gesturing in circles as if he were trying to puzzle something out. He was speaking, Toba could see that much, but she was too far away to hear him. Asmel, for his part, did not seem to be responding. He sat straight as a statue on the bench with his hair bright in the sunlight, and Toba thought he was the most beautiful thing she had ever seen, and also the saddest. He held his left hand in front of him, palm up, and Toba saw that it was marked with a symbol; in the bright morning light it appeared deep blue, and it covered most of his hand. He clenched and unclenched it a few times before fisting it and pressing it against his forehead. The second man did not seem to have noticed any of this, and continued his inaudible monologue, tugging absently at his ear.

Toba could not put her finger on why Asmel struck her as so unbearably sad. His face had not changed from its usual impassive state, but there was something about his eyes, like a tragedy was playing out behind them. One of the birds, some tiny, perfectly blue creature, landed on Asmel's lap, and he lifted a careful finger and stroked it twice before setting his hand back on the bench. The other man was growing frustrated, and his voice, which had been low, grew louder. "Do you hear what I am telling you? If you marry her, she can press for a pardon. You can redeem your name, Asmel; I need you positioned to help me when the time comes."

"You ask a great deal," Asmel said.

"I offer more. You don't have to like the woman. Just give her what she needs and be the ally you've promised." He lowered himself so that he and Asmel were on a level, and said, "The rumors are true. The King grows weary, and my brother is making questionable friends."

Toba let out a breath. Asmel's eyes jerked to her window, and she saw his mouth twitch into a scowl, just barely. He rose from the bench, spoke a few words in the other man's ear, and then watched as the second man strode from the garden. Once he was gone, Asmel crooked his finger as Barsilay had done and Toba found herself standing before him.

The songbirds left in a flurry of dismayed cries and flaps of tiny wings.

"I believe you were told this garden is private," he snapped. "That prohibition referred to your eyes as well as your person."

"I'm sorry," she said. She could see that the marking on his left palm was mirrored on the right, a character of some kind, or a letter in a language she did not know. She didn't dare ask the significance. Maybe it helped him to do magic, though she hadn't noticed such markings on Barsilay.

"You seem inordinately fond of apologies. Each time I see you you're offering them like sweets to a spoiled child."

"Would you prefer I didn't?"

"I would prefer you did as asked in the first place," he replied tightly.

"I did not realize that chamber looked out over this garden when I chose it," she said, resisting the urge to ask who the other Mazik had been, or why he'd been making a speech while Asmel sat like a stump, or where he'd gone. "I will move my things to another, if you wish. Or cover the window."

But Asmel made no indication he'd heard either of her suggestions. Instead, he said, "Barsilay tells me he's set you to translating one of my books."

"Yes," she said, wondering at the change of subject. Perhaps Asmel cared less about her transgression than he'd let on. It occurred to her, briefly, that he'd only used it as an excuse to call her down. "I've been making good progress, if you—"

"I don't wish to see," he said. He turned his strange, sad eyes on her. "What have you to go back to, in the mortal realm?"

He means to keep me, she thought. *I'll be translating his library until I die.* She said, "My grandparents."

"Is that all?" he asked.

"Yes," she said. "We're . . . forgive me, but I don't know what you know about the state of things in Sefarad at the moment."

"Everything," he said. "That is why I asked. You have no home to return to?"

Toba felt a rather acute pang at that statement. Part of her felt that the expulsion was all some sort of misunderstanding, that the Queen would wake up in a day or a week and wonder where all the Jews had wandered off to, and then they would all go home and back to their lives.

"Nothing beside my grandmother and grandfather," she said. "And since I came here, I'm not sure how to find them again."

"That would be no trouble," he said. Toba felt herself begin to hope he was telling the truth.

"You would return me?"

"Of course," he said. "You are hardly a prisoner; I have no use for you." He nearly smiled. "My nephew set you that assignment to keep you from wandering, I have no need for translations."

Toba scowled at her feet.

He added, "If you're thinking of stopping the work, I'd advise that you don't. You agreed to do it."

A bird began to sing again, from within the orange tree, some melody that was more than normal birdsong. "What happens if I do stop the work?"

"You'll be in Barsilay's debt until he releases you." He rose from the bench. "The two of you made a verbal contract."

Toba thought what that might mean. If she and Barsilay had made a contract, that meant he considered her . . . maybe not an equal, but at least a person significant enough to enter into legal arrangements. She said, "Who is the arbiter of contracts here?"

"You would rather not know, I think," he said. "If you are considering bringing a suit against Barsilay in a Mazik court, I would advise against it in the strongest terms."

"Because they'd decapitate me on sight."

He made that same thinned smile again—Toba realized this was probably as close to expressing mirth as Asmel got. He said, "I thought you'd decided the term was *decuerpitate*, but yes, you are correct, you wouldn't live long enough to argue your case, even if you were in the right."

She crossed her arms. The sun was growing warm overhead. She said, "I am not pleased with the terms of my contract with Barsilay."

"Your pleasure is of no concern," he said. "You already agreed to it."

"I didn't know I could negotiate," she said. "Or that I was agreeing to a contract! How was I to know I was in a position to have legal status here?"

His near-smile slipped. "Barsilay's agreement with you was entirely fair."

Toba paused and looked back toward her window in the alcalá. "He's your heir as well as your nephew?"

Asmel did not like this question, but he said, "He is."

"Well, then, your heir has demanded a great deal of my own labor without payment."

"Your board," he said, "is your payment. Your *life* is your payment."

"My board, which he tried to deny me, as that should have included food from the outset. And my life, which I shall not have at the end of this, under Barsilay's terms. You plan to return me through the gate, where I will be alone without a coin to my name. I'll starve within a week, and even if I don't, you've indicated you're fully aware of my status in Sefarad. By Barsilay's terms, I either make myself an apostate or walk into the sea, if I haven't died of exposure first." She gestured at the alcalá behind them. "And you clearly have the funds to pay me for my work. Your refusal is downright parsimonious. And dishonorable."

He narrowed his strange eyes. "You blame me, but I am no party to your agreement. Your quarrel is with Barsilay."

"Barsilay," she replied, "is your heir, so his contracts are, by default, also yours."

He glared at her, as angry as a cat on the receiving end of a pail of cold water, wishing, Toba guessed, that he'd murdered her when he'd had the chance. He couldn't now, though, because doing so would violate her contract with Barsilay.

"I demand payment," she said. "From you, as Barsilay's superior." At his quelling glare, she said, "That look won't work. I don't need you to like me. I need you to pay me."

"I've already told you, I have no need for your labor," he said. "Barsilay's contract was offered out of pity—you have no value to either of us."

"A false pity that leaves me dead," she said. "And if you seek to shame me for arguing for my own life, you're wasting your time."

"Fine," he said. "I will make you an agreement of my own, but I shall ask more of you than Barsilay did. Here are my terms: If you manage to keep yourself hidden, if no one but Barsilay or myself sees you until the next full moon, and you swear an oath never to speak of this place to anyone, to any person, any creature, living or dead, dreaming or awake, I will return you through the gate with enough silver to earn passage anywhere." Seeing her rising objection, he added, "*Enchanted* silver that you will be able to hide from whomever you chose. Do you agree?"

She had not expected the terms to be so much in her favor directly out of the gate, and Toba wondered what he was leaving unsaid. It was an awfully high price for keeping her mouth shut. "You make it sound very simple," she said. "All I do is keep quiet?"

"*Hidden* and quiet. Do you agree?" he repeated.

"If I fail," she said, "what will happen?"

"Are you planning to fail?"

"I want to understand the terms I'm agreeing to."

He huffed out a short breath. "On the first part," he said, "if anyone sees you, you'll be killed, but I expect you already understood that. On the second, if you tell anyone about this place, well. I can't say what would happen, so I won't speculate. *Do you agree*?"

"How much silver?" she asked.

"You can't be serious," he said. "I'm offering you treasure for practically nothing."

"I want to understand—"

"The terms," he sighed. "Teach me to be kind. I'll give you a piece of enchanted silver for every page you translate." He held out his hand, showing what looked like a milliarè, to illustrate the exact size of the coin he was offering. "If you think you'll get better terms from any other Mazik, you are very much mistaken."

It was a good deal. A very good deal. She knew how much translation was worth even to those who valued it, and it was not this, and

Asmel did not even want her finished pages. It seemed too good to be true, so it likely was, unless the price of Asmel's pity was higher than she'd realized.

"Still you hesitate," he said. "You needn't agree. You still have your bargain with Barsilay, and I've already said I'll return you through the gate at the appointed time." He stood. "I shall take my leave now; I have other things to do than argue with an ungrateful twig of a mortal whose greed outsizes even her own tongue."

She opened her mouth to argue that it wasn't greed to want to survive, and then bit back the answer, because he'd already offered her survival twice over. To him, she noted, she probably did seem greedy in not accepting a bargain that seemed, on glances both first and second, to benefit her a great deal and him not at all. "Very well," she said. "I agree."

"Fine," he replied. "Now keep away from the windows." And he made a shooing motion with his hand, and she found herself back in her bedroom.

A piece of silver for every page. It was not a fortune, precisely—*Guide for the Perplexed* was not a long book—but it would be enough to bribe or barter her way to Pengoa, with a bit left over, and the silver would be masked, so she could take it with her.

If she considered her grandparents' house to be her home, wherever that might be, she could go home again. Toba would sit at a long table with her grandfather again, and help her grandmother with the chores, and it would be like it was before. Only, perhaps, better, because this time she would have a purse full of enchanted silver to buy whatever books or foods or trinkets anyone liked. She would have restored the Peres fortune, and all for a month's translation, something she enjoyed anyway. She would make it to Pengoa, triumphant and rich. She would only be a little late.

Toba made her way back to the library and set herself to work.

TEN

IN THE MACHORROS' sitting room, Naftaly sipped a cup of watered wine and made brief eye contact with Elena. The old woman had already slugged hers down and was starting to doze in her chair.

"How much should we tell him, do you think?" Naftaly said.

"The minimum would be best for all of us," she said. "He doesn't need to know anything about Toba's disappearance with the Inquisition around. We need lodging for a month, and passage south, if he can manage it: that's all."

"What reason are we giving for staying an entire month?" Naftaly whispered, but by then a man and woman near to Naftaly's age had entered the room, and they did not look pleased to see them. Naftaly rose. "Sir," he said hesitantly, because he did not recognize the man or the woman he presumed to be his wife at all, "I'm not sure if you'll recall me."

"Oh, I remember you, you're the son of that tailor." Turning to the woman on his left, he said, "My sister was rather sweet on you once."

The sister in question went quite red in the face. As did Naftaly. "You'll excuse me for forgetting your name," the man went on. "It's been some time."

"I'm Naftaly Cresques," he said. "I'm afraid I don't recall yours, either, Señor Machorro."

"It's deSantos now," he said. "Please. I'm Antonio; my sister is Katarina." Naftaly watched him take in his appearance and his companions'. "Excuse me, but are you accepting baptism or leaving? I can't think what would have brought you here."

"We were passing through to Merja," he said.

Antonio frowned. "This town doesn't fall between Rimon and Merja."

"We got a bit turned around," Naftaly said. "And separated from our caravan."

"By twenty miles?"

Naftaly did not know how to explain the fifty miles. Elena said, "I'm afraid my mother is too frail to continue the journey for now." She patted the old woman's shoulder, and she did her best to look feeble, which was not difficult since she was already mostly asleep. "We're hoping with a bit of time she might recover her strength. I'm afraid if we move her too quickly, it might be the end for her."

"You ought to leave her," Antonio said, which caused the old woman to rouse herself. To her, he said, "You should accept baptism, it's all that's left to save you."

"Not," she said, sitting up a bit, "likely."

"It needn't be sincere," he said. "Let them pour some water over your head, come home, wash it off, and live your life."

"If it were that simple," Elena said, "why is the Inquisition here?"

Antonio gave no answer.

"You're worried," she said. "Are you under suspicion already?"

"I'm not," he insisted. "Why would I be? I eat a side of bacon in public every Saturday. I'm only worried now because you lot are here. You're rather . . ." He waved a hand at them: their clothing, Naftaly's Rimoni-style head covering, his sidelocks. "Obvious. I'd rather not be seen consorting with you by my neighbors." He passed a hand over his face, muttering, "You had to show up here *now*."

"We don't particularly want to attract attention, either," Naftaly said. "But we have no one else to ask for help."

Katarina tugged on her brother's sleeve and the two stepped out of the room with a nod.

"We're fucked," the old woman said.

"We should come up with an alternate plan," Naftaly said.

But Antonio had come back into the room by then. "Very well," he said. "Here is what I can offer you: lodging for a month and passage south. But in exchange you must make yourselves less conspicuous."

"How?" Naftaly said suspiciously.

"Shave your face. Cut your hair. Uncover your head. And if you want my help, you'll go by some other name until you leave Eliossana."

"I was always partial to Fernando," the old woman mused.

"Not that one," Elena snapped. "We'll call you Santiago." To Antonio, she said, "We agree."

NAFTALY DREAMED HIMSELF in a grand building full of striped columns.

Each column was topped with an arch the shape of a horseshoe. The arches went on in all directions as far as he could see, with no sign of exterior walls or windows or daylight. He felt dizzy and a little ill, and could see no sign of anyone else, so he decided to pick a direction and walk, in the hopes he might find his way outside. Why it was so important to see the sky he could not say, but he felt stifled, like he was being crushed by lack of air and sun. He figured straight ahead was as good a direction as any and began to walk.

The arches—and the columns that supported them—were staggered, so walking in a straight line was impossible. He weaved his way through, going under a right-hand archway, then a left, and so on, hoping he was going more or less in one direction.

He walked faster, then faster, then he was running, but every spot in the place looked exactly like every other spot, and when he looked back he didn't seem to have moved at all.

Naftaly began to panic.

Remembering his father's trick, he grabbed the underside of his own arm and pinched, hard, but did not wake. He began to run again, stumbling between the columns, until at long last he saw someone ahead.

It was the man with the orange eyes, he thought with some relief, and then realized he was wrong. It was the man he'd seen on horseback, on the bridge, his red-black hair loose down his back. This time, his hair was tied in a braid, but there was no mistaking it was the same person. He remembered his father had feared whoever this was. He willed himself to wake, and didn't.

"Hello," the man said. "Are you lost?"

"Is there a way out?" Naftaly asked, hesitantly.

"Of course," the man said, "if you tell me your name."

"My name?"

The man smiled. His face, Naftaly thought, was very beautiful, despite his eyes. His irises, around his square pupils, were a vivid blue that seemed overly bright for the dim light inside whatever building this was. "How can I help you when I don't know who you are?" he asked.

Naftaly knew better, but he was desperate to get out. He said, "I'm called Yeshua."

The man cocked his head to one side like a bird. "Why are you lying to me?"

"I'm not," Naftaly said. "Please, can't you show me the way out?"

"Very well," he said. "Give me your hand."

Somewhat reluctantly, Naftaly held out his hand. Before he could pull it back, the other man took it between his fingers and kissed it, causing a searing, white-hot pain to break out on the back of Naftaly's hand, and Naftaly to cry out and fall to his knees, and then wake.

Naftaly sat up, cradling his right hand against his chest. The old woman leaned over him, shaking his shoulders and ordering him to wake. "What the devil is wrong with you?" she asked, while he gasped and then broke out in a sob, and then another. She'd lit a candle and the entire room was bathed in dim yellow light.

She looked down at his hand and swore. "Now how," she said, "did you manage that in your sleep?"

On the back of Naftaly's hand, which last night had been smooth and healthy, there was a blistering burn in the shape of a kiss.

He made an experimental fist and winced at the pain of it. "I don't know," he said.

"This is a bad business," the old woman said. "I don't like anything that's happened since we came here. We ought to leave."

"But Toba—"

"You don't honestly think we're ever going to see that girl again," she said. "Elena Peres is delusional if she really thinks so. I'm telling you, if we stay here, it will go badly for us."

"But Antonio said he'd help us—"

"I don't like that, either! He *should* have thrown us out! He *shouldn't* be willing to risk his family for us."

"Perhaps he has a kinder heart than you do," Naftaly said.

"I doubt it. Listen, tomorrow morning, we go back to that barman and ask him for space in his cart."

"We haven't any money!"

"We'll get some," she said. "Somehow. Or we'll negotiate. Did you even try to get the price down?"

Naftaly had not; he had no idea how to barter in such a situation. She said, "I'll help you. Will you go with me to talk to him?"

"But even if we did somehow get the price down and come up with enough money to pay him, Elena's set on staying to wait for Toba."

“If Elena Peres wants to die here, more power to her. I won't. I suggest you don't, either. Think about it, while you're nursing whatever abomination has happened to your hand.”

Naftaly did think about it, while he went down to the kitchen to find a jug of cool water to run over his hand. Abandoning Toba and Elena seemed wrong, but he couldn't help but suspect the old woman was correct in her assessment.

But the next morning, the old woman had become ill and could barely make it through breakfast without falling asleep, and then she'd spent the rest of the day in her bed. Traveling with her was unimaginable. Leaving meant abandoning not two people but three.

Eleven

A FEW DAYS later, Toba was in the library—she'd come to think of it as *her* library—when Barsilay appeared rather suddenly. He had an unfortunate habit of turning up without making a noise, which she suspected he did because he enjoyed making her jump. Perched in his hand was a tray of food, which he slid onto the table. "I hear you're making a supreme nuisance of yourself."

"Did Asmel say that?"

"Did Asmel . . . ! You interrupted his audience with Prince Odem, I'm surprised you're still alive, you fool. What can you have been thinking?"

"I was only looking out the window."

"Ah," he said, "that's right, you took the chamber at the top of the stairs—you know that room was infested with demons last year." He gave an exaggerated shudder. "All those arms. All those *claws*. Took me weeks to get them all out. Kept coming back."

"Demons!"

"They don't cause much trouble beyond the mess, don't worry. Well, I guess they cause trouble for mortals, but I'm sure they won't come back to that room while you're in it. There were only six or seven, anyway."

Toba looked sourly at the food. "You could switch rooms if you're concerned," he suggested.

"No, I like that room, and I think you're toying with me."

Barsilay laughed. "Just eat your lunch and keep your eyes on your work. Every time you annoy Asmel I have to hear about it, and he's ornery enough even without you underfoot."

Toba reached out and picked up a bowl of stew—he'd brought two bowls of something with eggplant. "Was this lentils?"

"Of course," he said. "Everything's lentils, at the start. They're easy to grow and easy to transport, and changing one food to another's easy as anything."

Toba had to admire the efficiency, as she stirred the contents of the bowl, churning up some almonds with the eggplant. Did he change each individual ingredient, or the whole thing at once? It seemed awfully complicated, but she supposed it didn't matter much, so long as she had something to eat. "Do you want to see the parts of the translation I've finished so far?" she asked.

"Not remotely," he said.

"Then . . . do you want some of this stew?"

Barsilay made an agreeable face and took the other bowl.

Toba ate a few bites in silence. The food here was awfully good. Her grandmother's meals often tasted unpleasantly salty, even when she swore she was leaving it out. But the meals Barsilay made always tasted almost sweet. She wondered if it was some side effect of the magic he was using to make them, or something to do with the lentils he used.

"Barsilay," she said, testing the name to see if he'd mind the familiarity, and when he didn't, she asked, "What is this place?"

"What can you mean? What does it look like?"

"It looks like a castle."

"Then it must be," he said.

"But why is it all torn up inside?"

He turned a circle in the library, indicating the pristine shelves. "How is it torn up?"

"Not this room, but the rest. The rooms are either empty or full of soot and broken furniture."

"Housekeeping is dull," he said.

"So you just set fire to things when you don't want them anymore?"

"Don't you?" His eye twinkled. He was having her on, and he knew she was perfectly aware of it.

"I found this," she said, handing over the burned cover of *A History of the Common Demon* by Rafeq of Katlav, "in a pile filled with burned papers." He took the cover and crushed it into his hand, down into a single cinder, which he then blew in the direction of the window.

"I had no idea there was a Hebrew translation of that," he said. "Don't snoop anymore."

"It was a translation? Was it a Mazik book, originally?"

"Hush."

"Was this place a great library? Like in Katlav, but for Maziks?"

"No," he said. "It was not a great library, like in Katlav, and I heartily suggest you keep your eyes and your thoughts and your person behind that table until the next moon. There is nothing here that can interest you. It's just a lot of soot and broken furniture, as you've said." At that, he lifted his head and turned toward the window. After a moment Toba, too, heard a peculiar sound coming from outside. She straightened in her chair; first, she thought it might be Asmel's birds again, but then she realized it was music. Pushing her chair back, she went to look out the window; the library was high enough in the alcalá that she could see over the front wall out to the road she'd walked up her first day. Riding on this was what she first thought was a pageant wagon, but on second glance was clearly a silk tent being pulled by half a dozen matching gray horses.

Toba leaned out the window for a better look; the tent had six sides and was red as a glass of port; in front of it, on what Toba supposed was the base of the entire contraption, was a driver, but so far as Toba could tell he held no whip. From this distance, Toba could not quite make it out, but he seemed to be singing. To the horses.

The tent was suspended over the ground and had no wheels. She could not tell how it was attached to the golden platform, or to the horses.

Barsilay joined her in leaning out the window. "Ah," he said, rather bitterly. "Of all the pretentious things." His mouth was twisted a bit to the side in displeasure.

"Who is that?"

"The Infanta Oneca," he said. "Didn't I tell you she was coming?"

Toba's eyes went back to the strange conveyance out the window. "Must have slipped your mind," she said.

"Yes, I suppose so." He clapped her on the shoulder and she jumped a second time. "I suggest hiding."

"What?"

He rolled his eyes a bit. "She's here to press for a betrothal. It won't be a brief social call."

"An Infanta? Wants to marry one of you?"

Barsilay said, "Not me; Asmel. And it's like this: Asmel was widowed at the beginning of the age, and Oneca needs a match, and quickly—rumor has it the King wants her gone and is trying to pack her off to some backwater Adon in Anab. She's here to discuss terms before he can finalize the arrangement."

"She'd rather marry Asmel and become the lady of . . ." She trailed off and decided to let the insult remain implied rather than explicit: "*this*?"

"It would seem so."

"But why?"

Barsilay shrugged a lazy shoulder. "To spite the King, one would presume."

This made little sense to Toba; what princess would consent to marry the lord of a ruined castle for spite? But Toba did not expect to understand the ways of Maziks. Barsilay lay his finger across his chin as if he were considering his next words. "It would not be for the best if she found you here."

"Yes," she said, "I suppose finding a human loitering about might hurt Asmel's chances."

"Mmm," he replied, and then reached out and grabbed the back of Toba's dress, snatching her backward. In her ear, he murmured, "We don't need any of her retinue seeing you hanging out the window."

She glanced back down and saw that the tent-carriage had come unaccountably closer in the moment she'd looked away, almost as if it had jumped nearer the alcalá. Before, it had been several hundred yards off. Now, it was just in front of the gate.

Toba looked back at all her work scattered across the library table, arranged like a T with the Maimonides in the center, her notes below it, and her half-done translations to either side.

"Leave it," he said. "She won't come in here, and if she does, she won't pay it the least attention."

There was a banging on the gate, three ringing blows like the sound of a stone striking a bell. Toba said, "Who is going to let her in?"

"Damn it," he said, turning crisply on his heel and striding back toward the door. "I wasn't joking about hiding," he said.

"How long will she be here?" she called after him.

"No one knows!" he shouted from farther down the hall.

Toba gathered herself, decided to take the Maimonides with her so she'd at least have something to read while she was confined for Hashem knew how long, and then decided to leave it after all when she heard the gate creaking open. She bolted from the room, down the hallway and through the outer courtyard, where she saw Asmel, settled in one of the chairs across from the fountain, leaning a cheek against a hand and looking rather downtrodden. Around him were tables filled with food, and a few shades bustled about, doing some last-minute arranging of flowers.

It looked as if he were trying to impress his would-be bride. Only his face didn't match the intensity of the preparations at all.

Of course, that was how his face normally looked.

Toba's slippers slapped the white stones of the courtyard as she cut across to the part of the alcalá where she kept her small cell of a room, hurrying up the stairs and slamming the door behind her.

It was only then that she realized she was stuck there with nothing to do, and no way to tell what was happening elsewhere. She didn't even have a way to tell when the Infanta had gone, unless Barsilay remembered she existed and got her out. Her shade, which had somehow come into the room ahead of her, could not even be sent to spy since it couldn't speak.

From out in the courtyard, she could hear the faint strains of stringed instruments. Squatting down to peer out over the windowsill, she felt herself flung backward and felt a rush of cold air; when she got herself back up off the floor, the window had been bricked in.

The light-stones winked on, leaving only a dim light in the room. "Well," she told the shade. "I suppose it's just us."

The shade hovered uncertainly in the corner.

"It's a pity you can't speak," she said, sitting down heavily on the bed the shade had made from her dusty cushion. There was furniture now, at least; the shade had somehow produced a wooden trunk and a small table and chair. Looking up, she said, "Can you play chess?"

When it didn't answer, she tried again: "Will you make a chessboard?"

It did. Wondering what would happen, she nudged a pawn forward. The shade somehow caused a pawn to slide forward from the other side.

"At least that's something," she said, and moved her knight out.

WITH ALL THE things the Caçador had taught her, he had never told the Courser about what it meant to die. One death, he'd led her to believe, was like another: one minute you were there, and the next you were in the void in unbroken death, the most terrible fate a Mazik could meet. She'd felt the fear in her blood when he'd told her that, and he'd seen it.

"You have the void-terror," he'd said. "Good. We all share it. It will help keep you alive."

The horror of nonexistence was every Mazik's greatest fear, one so terrible that he might be unable to think on it at all, because too much consideration of it might lead to madness. Since Maziks did not die of old age or disease, he might well expect to avoid such a fate. The unbroken death, the Caçador had explained, when the Courser was young, was only achieved through violence. It was, he'd told her, her greatest weapon, that she might deal it out. But its overuse might also lead to her undoing—or, implicitly, the Caçador's—as a Mazik who fears unbroken death from his master or comrade is likely to turn on him. Never kill a Mazik, he'd told her, unless under a direct order, or unless there is unequivocally no other choice.

Only much later did the Courser learn that there was another way a Mazik could die: the dreaming death. If a Mazik died in her sleep, she simply remained in the dream-world: her body might cease, but the part of her that dreamed would continue, forever, in that place with the whirling stars. When a Mazik grew weary, when his mind was done with this life, he would eventually seek out such a death.

She'd found this in a book she'd taken off a man in Te'ena, before she'd burned his house; long ago, before she'd killed the previous Courser. The Caçador did not think she would read a book she found, which is exactly why she did it.

The book did not say how this could be done, if the weary Mazik would have a friend kill his body, or take poison, or simply will himself to it. She'd been angry about that. What was the point of telling her this with no instruction?

She'd killed the man in Te'ena in the plaça at noon, having followed him from his home. He'd known she was following him, and eventually he'd turned and said, "Are you waiting for an invitation?"

If she was, that was it. She'd set her right hand on his shoulder and made her left into a blade.

Usually she was not sent for assassinations abroad, that was the province of the Peregrine, but in this case the Caçador had had no choice: Te'ena had been made an island in the fall. The only way in was over the sea, a route impassable for a full Mazik because of the salt. The Maziks who lived in Te'ena had dwindled over the years, most choosing death over isolation. Her target was one of the few that remained.

She hadn't known why she was killing this particular man; he was a scholar, and old—one of the relics of the Second Age. He hadn't begged for his life. He'd only looked at her, golden eyes bright in the sun, and said: "Monarchy is Abomination."

She'd hesitated, then, and said, "What does that mean?"

"You tell your master that," he'd said. "From me. From the order of ha-Moh'to."

She'd cut off his head, and then gone to his house to search for her second target: a stone shaped like a starburst. The book on death had been on the table in his library, and she'd wondered if he'd foreseen his own, if that's why he'd been reading it. Or else, he'd known she was coming, and wanted her to find it.

The starburst wasn't there: she'd searched twice, then burned the place and searched the ashes.

She'd found one thing, though, that survived: a letter, sealed inside a bubble of magic that had made it impervious to flame. It looked like glass or a film of soap, but she'd struggled to burst it. When she'd finally managed it the bubble fizzled and blew away in the smoke, and she was left with a letter addressed to Asmel b'Asmoda. It contained only two lines: the first: *The rent remains*; and the second: *The Dimah Sea is rising.*

The rent, she did not understand. The Dimah Sea . . . she tapped the paper against her lip, wondering if she should give it to the Caçador. It wasn't what she'd been sent for, however. So she burned that, too.

+ + + + + +

TOBA LASTED IN her room until the next night, by which point she realized she could not stand to be confined any longer.

The worst of it was that she didn't even know whether the Infanta was still there. How long did it take to woo a Mazik lord? And it wasn't as if she could count on Barsilay to tell her these things. She might well be trapped in her room until the next full moon, which would render her forsworn to Barsilay, since she wouldn't have completed her work, and she'd barely have enough silver from Asmel to ride five miles in a chicken cart. She rubbed her thumb on the edge of her rook and checkmated the shade again, after which it helpfully reset the pieces.

She'd come to realize that the shade always played the same defense, and after losing the first three games she'd beaten it at increasingly short intervals. "You're actually not very good at this," she said, and of course, the shade said nothing. It had brought her a dinner of garlicky fava beans earlier, and she picked at an apple tart it had made for dessert. "Can you bring me things other than food?" she asked. "Real things, that you didn't conjure? Can you bring me the Rambam book from the library?" When it did nothing, she rephrased: "Bring me the Rambam book from the library."

Still nothing. "It would be easier if you could talk," she said. She scowled to herself. If the shade was some lesser version of Barsilay, it should be able to do most of what he could do, which meant it should be able to engage in snide conversation. Unless, that was, Barsilay had specifically given it orders not to. And if Barsilay had given it rules to follow, those rules must have loopholes. Laws always did.

"Bring me a pen and paper," she said. "And ink."

The shade did so. She dipped the pen in the ink and said, "Write down a list of the orders that Barsilay gave you."

The shade only quivered in response.

"So you can't write, either."

No reply, of course. She drummed her fingers against the chessboard. Her mind went to the books she'd gone through in the library: mainly, they were written in Hebrew or Greek or Arabic, with a few in Zayiti mixed in. She had not seen any in Latin, but the chances Barsilay did not know it, if he knew the others, seemed slim.

Could the shade write in a language Barsilay did not know? Would that fall outside of the rules he'd made?

No, that wasn't enough. She needed something that would not count as writing at all. She needed a script that Barsilay did not know.

That would seem to have left out nearly everything Toba knew. She weighed a pawn in her hand, and wondered what it had been in its life before it had been a chess piece. Did it come from nothing, or was the shade converting matter from one form to another? She looked up at the shade. "It doesn't have to be real," she said. No response. Time for an experiment. Taking the pen the shade had brought before, she held it out and said, "Draw me a circle."

It complied, drawing a circle the size of an orange, as perfectly round as if it had traced it. She'd found her loophole: Barsilay had ordered it not to write. He hadn't ordered it not to draw.

"You can use a pen," she said. "Let's have a lesson, then." She drew a smaller circle, next to the one the shade had drawn, and said, "This means *yes*," and then made a long dashed line. "And this is *no*. Remember that, and use those symbols when I ask you a question. Did Barsilay order you not to speak?"

The shade drew a circle.

Toba smiled.

"Did he order you not to help me with the translation, apart from giving me ink and paper?"

Another circle.

"Which included not moving or touching the books?"

Yet another.

Ah, all right. "I suppose you have a large number of rules to follow in regards to me," she said. "I'm guessing one of those is that you're not to let me leave the alcalá?"

Yes.

"Can *you* leave the alcalá?"

No.

"Hm," she said. "But perhaps you can go places I can't. I want you to go between here and the library and tell me if you see or hear anyone."

The shade set down the pen and silently slipped out the door. Toba peered into the dark hallway and counted the seconds until it returned, which it did a few minutes later.

"Does it appear to you that everyone's retired for the night?" she asked.

Taking up the pen again, it wrote, *Yes.*

"You neither saw nor heard anyone? Everything was quiet? All right then," she told her friend. "I'm going to collect my work." And she slipped down the steps toward the library, with the shade hovering at her heels.

She made her way down the corridor, ears straining to hear music or footsteps or anything that might indicate the presence of Maziks, but there wasn't so much as a whisper. When she came to the open door of the library, however, she hung back a moment.

Barsilay had said the Infanta would not go in there, and indeed, it was dark inside, except for the barest light that shone in from the waning moon coming through the window. Toba decided she would simply go in, claim her work, and take it all back to her room.

Toba crept inside, the shade still hovering behind her, smelling the comforting aroma of old books. She was almost to her table when she realized there was someone sitting in her chair, and that she was watching Toba sneak into the room. A tall woman, still as a statue, with a diadem of rubies across her dark hair and a flat expression. Her eyes took in Toba, and then she went back to the book in front of her, trailing a finger down the page as if she were finding her place.

Toba realized her mistake; she had asked the shade to check *between* her room and the library. She had not asked it to check *within* the library.

It was too late to go back out, so Toba bobbed a bow, and kept her eyes cast to the floor.

The woman's chin was resting on the back of one hand, and with the other, she lazily turned a page. She was reading the book, in the dark.

Toba waited a few moments, decided the Infanta was not going to acknowledge her, and began to back out of the library again.

A voice said, "Well, you aren't a shade, are you?"

Toba froze in slipping backward. She made no reply, but shook her head fractionally.

She heard the sound of another page turning. "I don't know why he collects all these," the Infanta said. "Do you?"

Again, Toba shook her head, her chin tucked against her chest.

"I thought Asmel kept no living servants, besides that irritating Luzite," she said, and then Toba heard the familiar thump of the book closing, and the squeak of a chair being pushed back. "Does he have a harem hidden somewhere, hm?"

Toba could feel her palms prickle, because with the book closed, there was nowhere for the Infanta's eyes to be besides on herself. She searched for something to say that would please her, divert her eyes from her. "I'm," she began, "no one of consequence."

"That much is obvious," she said. "Yet, here you are. In the middle of the night, no less, creeping about like a mistress. Or a thief. Are you a thief? Shall I cut off your hands?"

Toba was not sure which would play out worse for her: being thought Asmel's mistress or a criminal. She cast about for something that might sound pleasing. She could not be household help, because Maziks seemed to only use shades for that. A librarian? No, that might invite more questions about what the books were for, and she could not risk a prolonged discussion. "I'm neither of those," she whispered. "I'm—a crafter of baubles. He charged me to create something that might delight you. It was meant as a surprise; I'm sorry to have spoiled it."

"Baubles," the Infanta said. "*Really*."

In Toba's pocket, her grandmother's ring seemed a great weight. It was finely wrought, too fine, really, for a betrothal ring, but her grandfather had bought it off a trader in Meleqa some fifty years ago, thinking it would impress the daughter of a good family. A silver castle ring, the top featured a square tower with four smaller turrets and one in the center; it opened to reveal a hidden compartment, which contained a single white pearl. Apart from Toba's amulet, it was the only item of value the family had owned.

The ring had worked; Elena's family had been impressed. Toba hoped it might work again, though it pained her to give it up. Better than dying, she reminded herself, presenting it to the Infanta on her open palm, hoping her hand did not tremble too much.

The Infanta plucked the ring from Toba's palm and, through her eyelashes, Toba watched her inspect it before tossing it to the stone floor. "If Asmel hired you to create a love-token," she said, stepping closer, "then why did he turn down my offer of engagement?"

Toba startled. "I'm sure there's been a misunderstanding."

"*I don't wish to marry you* leaves little room for interpretation," the Infanta said. "I offered him the chance to join my house, a house of honor, forsake this rubbish heap, and he refused."

Toba hazarded a glance up at Oneca. "You asked him to give up the alcalá?"

The Infanta said, "Who are you really? His lover? You're so stunted I can hardly believe it."

"No," she said. "I'm just the jeweler."

"Lies," the Infanta said, and quick as a cat, reached out and grabbed Toba's chin in her hand. Her fingernails dug painfully into Toba's skin.

She tipped Toba's face up, and she had a glimpse of the Infanta's pale, ferocious beauty before she had the presence of mind to screw her eyes shut. "Are you the reason he's refused me?"

"No," Toba whispered.

"Look at me," the Infanta ordered.

Shaking, Toba said, "Adon Asmel ordered me not to look on you. It would be disrespectful of me to sully you with my inferior gaze, Infanta."

"Asmel! I outrank Asmel!" the Infanta hissed. "Which is why his refusal makes no sense, and I would know why. Look at me!" With her other hand, she struck Toba across the face. Toba would have reeled back, but her chin was held so tightly she found she could not move at all.

"Please," Toba said. "I am not worth your anger. I must do as he says."

The Infanta tsked. "I don't believe you're some little paramour of Asmel's: you're much too timid, and you're too homely to be one of Barsilay's. You must be something else. A secret child?"

Toba winced at the suggestion, but the Infanta went on. "No, I'd see some of him in you, and there's nothing. So tell me, little creature, what are you doing here, in this library, with these books?" Her breath was hot on Toba's cheek, she was so close. "What information is Asmel sharing with you, hm? Is he poking his way back into realms best left forgotten?"

"I'm not sure what you mean," Toba said.

"Open your eyes," the Infanta said softly. "Or I will pluck them from your skull."

For a moment, Toba actually considered whether this would be the better course of action, because being blinded would be terrible, but still a good deal better than being dead. But then Toba realized . . . the Infanta was completely sincere, and once she'd taken her eyes, she'd easily see the shape of Toba's pupils. If she was going to die, she might as well go all in one piece.

Toba blinked her eyes open and, her disguise gone, glared at the Infanta face-on in defiance.

The Infanta gave an expression of disgust and she dropped Toba's chin as if she'd discovered she was holding a bilge rat by the tail. "Filth," she spat.

Toba began backing rapidly away, driven by the instinct to escape. "I only wandered through," she said. "I'm not really here. That is, I'm here temporarily."

The Infanta advanced in a single step that was somehow many and took hold of Toba by the throat. "Tell me," she said. "What you are doing here. How many realms has Asmel shown you, other than his own?"

It was only the one hand on Toba's throat, but it was enough to cut off Toba's breath. She felt the rush of panic which always accompanied her loss of air, only this was far worse, because there was no convincing herself that this would end. She would die here, by the Infanta's brutally strong hand. Toba clawed at the woman's fingers, and then she remembered her amulet.

To ward off evil, her grandmother had told her. If a murderous Mazikess did not qualify, Toba was not sure what would. Still prying at the Infanta's fingers with her own right hand, with her left she reached down the front of her dress and grasped her amulet, thrusting it against the Infanta's arm.

"Get that thing away from me," the Infanta said; letting go of Toba's throat, she tore the amulet from around Toba's neck and flung it into the floor, where it landed with a crack that seemed to burst Toba's eardrums and tear at the backs of her eyes. Released, Toba fell to her knees and, as her lungs filled with air, for the first time in all her life, she began to scream.

She almost stopped herself as soon as she started, thinking *I can't do this*, but she *was* doing it. Toba was screaming, a sound Toba had never before made, and she found that she couldn't have stopped if she'd wanted to. The Infanta looked at her in horror, the sound growing louder with the seconds, a sound that pulsed inside Toba's bones, and then the beautiful lead-glass windows lining the wall shattered, raining down shards of colored glass over the Infanta and Toba both. The scream went on and on, until Toba found that her breath had run out and she fell back, clutching at her raw throat.

But the Infanta was looking at her differently now, wearing an expression Toba could not place. "Well, well," she said. "Whose child are you?"

Toba reached for the amulet, hoping it might work again, but it had cracked irreparably: the stone had skittered across the floor somewhere, and from inside the hamsa the scroll had fallen out and burned to ash.

A hand closed on the Infanta's shoulder, large, male, and Toba caught sight of blue eyes and silver hair as the wrath went out of Oneca and she collapsed on the floor at Toba's feet.

TWELVE

NAFTALY SHAVED THE smattering of scruff on his face and then trimmed the edges of his hair. He was sad to put away his clothing—made, of course, by his father—but it was travel-worn and torn in places from his adventure in the woods, and so he put on a new pair of northern-style trousers and a jacket with brass buttons. He was meant to stay indoors as much as possible, but the story he was instructed to tell anyone was that he was a distant cousin from Mansanar who was en route to Merja to scout out trading opportunities in Zayit.

Naftaly did not think he could play off this story, knowing nothing of trade and having never so much as visited Mansanar, but he'd decided it was in his best interest not to point this out. He picked at the hem of his coat and went into the sitting room to find Elena and the old woman sitting at the table together; Elena had a book in front of her and a pen, and the old woman was mostly unconscious in a chair nearby; whaever illness she'd contracted after their arrival at the deSantoses was not improving, and in the past few days she'd become quite addled.

"What are you doing?" he asked Elena, who had just added a digit to a column of zeroes.

"Taking precautions," she said.

"Against the Inquisition? It looks like you're rewriting Antonio's books."

"Only partly," Elena said. "Turns out the old man kept rather poor records in the year before he died. I'm trying to create something presentable in case someone asks to see it."

This made little sense to Naftaly; by the time the Inquisition was in possession of your books, you were no longer in a fit state to worry about what became of them. "You're entering false data?"

"Yes," she said, turning the page as he peered closer. She was increasing the expenses, by a great deal; adding digits to various columns which had previously been left blank, and thereby making the family business appear to be in some financial straits.

"I'm not sure I understand," Naftaly said. "Why would Antonio ask *you* to do this?"

"We owe him a favor," she said simply. "I told him I could keep the handwriting consistent."

"None of what you're saying makes sense," Naftaly said, but then Katarina came in, looking quite pale.

"Where is my brother?" she asked, but Antonio had already come in, drawn in by the sound of his sister's strained voice.

"What's happened?" he asked. He looked, Naftaly thought, exceedingly tired, like a man who'd been waiting for bad news, and here it came.

"The Inquisition arrested Maria Amalia," she told him.

Antonio glanced Elena's way before setting a hand on his sister's shoulder. "It will be fine," he said.

"It won't," she said. "It won't be fine."

"Who is Maria Amalia?" Elena asked.

"She was our parents' maid," she said. "Before they died. We pensioned her last year."

No one spoke for a while. Naftaly said, "Did she have any ill will against them?"

"No," she said. "But she wouldn't need to. She didn't go in to offer testimony, she was brought in for . . ." She hesitated. "Questioning."

An interesting euphemism. "Could she implicate you?" Naftaly asked.

"She could implicate our father," she said.

And the altered records began to make sense; she was helping them hide their money. If the old maid spoke against them—hardly unforgivable, under the circumstances—the following would happen in short order: they would exhume Salomon Machorro's remains, burn his bones, and seize his assets. Which begged the question: where *was* the money?

Elena said, "I don't think eating a side of bacon in public is going to help you."

+ + + + + +

ASMEL STARED DOWN at Toba in barely contained fury, over the prone body of the Infanta. "Damn it," he said. "Damn it all." Over his shoulder, he called Barsilay, who skidded into the room.

"What in damnation—" he started, seeing first the Infanta slumped on the floor, and then getting a look at Toba. "Oh, mother of monsters," he said.

Toba looked between the two men: Asmel enraged, Barsilay seemingly terrified, but she felt too strange to comment on their reactions. At first she thought she felt very ill, but after a few moments she realized that wasn't it . . . she actually felt *well*. "I don't understand," she said, in a voice stronger than the one that normally came from her throat. "What's happened?"

"Did you not know?" Asmel demanded. "Did you really not know?"

"Know *what*?" she asked. She crept on hands and knees to the spot where her amulet had fallen. The stone was intact; the rest cracked and burned. It no longer felt its usual cold against her fingers.

Asmel swore again, under his breath this time. "Did you speak to her? Did you say anything at all?"

"There wasn't much choice," Toba said helplessly.

He closed her eyes. "Of all the things. If you'd kept silent, I might have been able to erase her memory of you." To Barsilay, he said, "Take care of that." He indicated the Infanta. "Make sure she stays asleep."

"She *will* wake up at some point," Barsilay pointed out. "We can't kill her."

"Yes, I realize that," Asmel snapped. Lowering his voice, he said, "Odem says the King grows weary. This is not the time for mistakes."

Barsilay turned his eyes toward Toba. "We seem to have made one, anyway."

Indicating the Infanta, Asmel said, "Just keep her out as long as you can. I'll be there soon."

Barsilay gave a long-suffering sigh and lifted the Infanta into his arms, carrying her from the room. Asmel gripped Toba around her upper arm, dragging her to her feet. His hand held her much too tight.

"Wait," she said, but he only took her to the wall nearest the door, where the bookcases were lower. Probably something had hung there, once, but now from waist-height up was only bare wall.

He set his hand against the stone; it rippled like water and smoothed and reflected the room back at them: in it, she saw Asmel's face, the broken windows, and her own cowering form.

Asmel thrust her toward the looking glass. "Explain," he said.

She looked at her own reflection.

Square-pupiled eyes stared back at her, and she recoiled, then reached out to set her fingertips against the glass, seeing if it was some trick, a magic mirror. "I—I can't," she said. "What did she do to me? What did she do to my eyes?"

"She did nothing," he said. "Who are your parents?"

"My mother died giving birth to me. My father is a trader in Anab."

"So you've met him."

"Well," she said. "No."

"Of all the fool . . ." He shook his head. "And the amulet?"

Toba lifted it in both her hands, treasuring her broken heirloom. "My grandmother gave it to me. She told me I mustn't ever take it off."

"I'm sure she did," he said sourly. "Did she make it?"

"No," she said. "She inherited it." She held it out to him. "I still don't understand."

"Don't approach me with that *thing*," Asmel said sharply. "Your father was no trader. He wasn't even mortal. Your mother died birthing you because you aren't mortal, either."

She shrank back from him, and he began to pace. "The amulet," he said, "was used to bind you, to shrink you down into a mortal, to keep you weak and undetectable."

"Undetectable? By whom?"

"By the mortals and Maziks who would have killed you," he said. "How your grandmother got it or knew to give it to you is another story. A very interesting story, I'm sure."

"So you are saying my grandmother *knew*?"

"Oh, she absolutely knew. I suppose you should count yourself lucky. Most mortals, knowing what she did, would have strangled you in your cradle."

At that, Barsilay appeared in the doorway. "She's stirring," he said.

"I told you to keep her out!"

"I did try," he said.

Asmel turned his dark gaze to Toba. "Get to your room," he said. "Lock yourself in. And don't you dare open the door for anyone but me." He quit the room, his hair billowing behind him.

Toba looked helplessly at Barsilay. "He's so angry," she said. "Why is he so angry with me?"

"Because if she remembers you," Barsilay said, "we're *all* as good as dead." He turned to follow Asmel, throwing out, "I highly suggest you do as he says."

Toba made her way to the stairs to her tower as quickly as she was able, and once there, lifted her skirts and began to climb. Faster, she thought. She needed to go faster.

She realized she *could* go faster. She quickened her pace, and then again, and then again, waiting to fall. When she didn't, she thought, *I'm going to run.*

THIRTEEN

THE WANING MOON made Elena uneasy, as she counted the days until it would be full again. Too many. Toba had been gone too long, and would be gone longer still. She smiled grimly at the sky. This was the first time she'd ever *welcomed* a full moon.

She'd always believed her mother's maxims were nonsense: never trust a man you meet under a full moon, indeed. As if Elena would ever be traipsing around alone, at night, whether the moon was full or not. Probably it was a leftover piece of some wives' tale; her mother was always telling her to fear something or other: the evil eye, food that tasted like lentils even when it contained none, a horse with eyes like a goat's as if such a thing existed, meat with too little salt. So when she'd had her own daughter, she'd never bothered to teach her to look twice at a man you only saw under a full moon, a decision she'd come to bitterly regret.

Penina Peres had met the man at a moonlit wedding feast for the neighbor's daughter. The family was well-off enough to throw a grand party after, and it had spilled from their courtyard into the street. Elena hadn't seen him, not then, but those who were there said he was the handsomest man alive, with hair the color of flint and eyes like jet. Then at the next full moon he'd appeared in the Pereses's courtyard and enticed Penina outside to sit with him and gaze at the stars, and then at the third full moon he'd flattered his way into her bedroom.

All this Penina had confessed once her condition had become clear, and even then she insisted that he was returning to marry her. Alasar had nearly bankrupted himself, riding all the way to Meleqa and bribing the rabbi there for false marriage papers. The trader from Anab was a fiction from the moment Alasar and Elena invented his name.

And then Penina had died, giving birth to her enormous, square-pupiled baby.

Elena had given Penina an herb to bring the child forth early by several weeks, so big had she grown, but even then it had been too late. No one, the midwife included, had ever seen a newborn so large; the fact that Penina had managed to birth her at all was something of a miracle, though after she'd lost too much blood to survive. The midwife had wanted to kill the child on sight, and the Pereses had spent the other half of their fortune bribing her to give an oath she would tell no one. They'd hidden Toba away in back rooms of the house, her cries too loud to belong to a normal baby, and they'd worried.

At the next full moon, a man with flint-colored hair and eyes like jet had come to the house, asking, as if it were normal to pay calls in the dark of night, if he might see Penina.

Elena had startled back a bit, because she'd seen him before. It was only the once, but his was a face one did not forget, not least because it had not altered in more than twenty years.

She'd seen him in her mother's courtyard; she'd snuck out for some air, because it was so stifling hot in the house; it was August, and it hadn't rained in weeks. She was out in the garden when a gentleman came to the gate, asking if he might have a bucket of water for his horse. It was a strange request, to ask for water for a horse after sundown in the middle of the Judería, but she could see no harm, so she'd told him yes. Through the gate, he'd kissed her hand. And then her mother had come roaring out the front door and chased him off with a broom.

Elena had been mortified. "He only wanted to water his horse," she said. "There was no need to threaten him."

"You're a little fool," her mother had said, and then she'd been betrothed to Alasar the very same week.

It was the same man. Elena wondered if he recognized her. She didn't think so. Elena had been no great beauty even in her youth—too tall and stouter than was fashionable—and her hair had gone early to gray. She wished her mother had been there, with her broom.

She wished she had been there with a broom for her own daughter, who now lay dead.

Elena told him Penina had died, and then, though he hadn't asked, she told him that her child had died, too. It was the first great lie she'd ever had to tell.

He'd nodded solemnly. "I am sorry to hear it," he'd said, and then he'd gone.

At three months old, Toba walked.

At six months, she dressed herself, fed herself, and spoke as eloquently as a scholar.

At a year, she was strong enough to open the heavy wooden doors they used to keep her shut inside the nursery.

The first time Elena woke to Toba looking down on her in her bed, saying, "I built a fire to make cakes," she knew she was going to have to break her promise to her husband never to tell anyone. So she did what thousands of women had done in times of trial: she wrote to her mother.

The woman lived in Qorba with Elena's brother, quite a wizened thing by then, still spouting her old wives' tales, and Elena had to admit to her that her clockwork mind could not solve the problem that was her grandchild. She prayed that her mother wouldn't instruct her, as the midwife had, to kill her outright.

Instead, two weeks later her mother had arrived on her doorstep, leaning heavily on her chagrined son's arm. He, of course, knew nothing.

"Let me see the child," her mother had said.

Elena let her in. They'd moved from their home near the alcázar to a smaller one farther on the outskirts of the quarter, having spent their fortune first on their daughter's honor and then on their grandchild's life. After sending her brother away to find Alasar, they'd found Toba in a corner of the courtyard. She'd dug up piles of earth and mixed it into a thick mud, which she'd formed into the shapes of animals.

The animals were moving.

"The elephant," the child said happily, "and the lion are friends. But the bear is cruel so he can't play." With a pointed finger, she'd sent the bear to a spot under a bush, where he was made to sit and think about his actions.

Elena's mother regarded this without as much surprise as one would think, watching as Toba created another animal to play with the lion and the elephant.

"What is that one called?" Elena's mother asked, as the newest creation spread its wings and preened its mud feathers.

"That's a Ziz," Toba replied without looking up. "I will ride one when I'm older. She will be silver and I'll call her Leb."

Her mother had drawn Elena aside.

"Are you going to tell me to kill her?" Elena had asked unhappily.

"Hashem no," she'd said in horror. "Whatever else she might be, she's still Penina's. What do you know of the father?"

"I know nothing of him," she'd said. "He came here, only once, after she was born."

"And you sent him away?"

"I told him she'd died."

She nodded. "You were right to do that." Elena's mother reached into a pocket in her skirts and pulled out a handkerchief, unwrapping it to reveal a hamsa the size of a woman's fist, set in the center with the largest sapphire Elena had ever seen, not that she'd seen many.

"I've kept this hidden," she said. "Your father would have made me sell it, or your brothers would have, but I had a feeling." She pressed it into Elena's hand. The metal was cold as frost.

"I don't know where it came from," she said, "only that it was made for a girl-child and passed down. I don't even know when."

"A girl-child?" Elena repeated. She touched the gemstone with a finger. It made her uneasy, like it was sucking some thread of health out of her.

"Yes. A girl-child born with square eyes. The family wanted her killed, but her father sought out a tzaddik, and he blessed an amulet to bind down the child's Mazik-half, and she wore it until she died."

Elena did not ask if they were descended from the square-eyed woman—the woman who was half-Mazik—she knew that they were.

"Will it hurt her?" Elena asked.

"Yes," she said. "I believe it will. But what happens otherwise?"

What would happen, in short order, would be that Toba would find her way out of the courtyard and into the street. And that would be that.

Elena brought the amulet to Toba. "Dearest," she said. "Your great-grandmother has brought you a gift."

Toba eyed the amulet suspiciously. "I don't like it," she said. "It's a sickening thing."

The two women exchanged a glance. "Love," Elena said, "you must wear it."

The mud animals stopped playing and seemed to look up at the women. The elephant pawed the ground. Toba said, "No." Then, "If you try to make me, I'll run away."

Elena wanted to weep. She nodded at her mother. And she pinned Toba's arms to her sides.

Toba thrashed—she was already as strong as a seven-year-old. "Do it!" Elena ordered, and Elena's mother looped the amulet around Toba's neck. As it fell against her chest, she let out a scream Elena thought might shatter her very bones. Her mother grabbed Toba's legs, which were kicking wildly, but the scream went on, and the wall of the courtyard split asunder, a crack running up one side and across the cobbles to the opposite edge. The mud animals rushed at Elena, splattering themselves on her skirts, leaving her caked in dirt.

Then Toba's eyes rolled back and she lay still. Elena's mother fell back, clutching at her chest and struggling for breath.

"Are you well?" Elena asked.

"We'd better get her inside," was all she'd said.

They took her in and lay her on her bed. "Will she live?" Elena asked shakily.

"Yes," her mother said. "She'll live." She'd leaned over the child to check her ragged breathing. Satisfied, she'd turned to Elena and said, "You'd better clean yourself up before Alasar returns."

Elena had brushed at the mud on her skirts, but her mother shook her head and dabbed at Elena's neck with her handkerchief instead, coming away with a smear of blood. Elena's eardrum on that side had burst.

\+ \+ \+ \+ \+ \+

INSIDE THE DESANTOS house, Elena could see the light of a candle in the window of the room she knew belonged to Antonio. He would likely be reading through the false accounting log she'd been creating for him, in writing that first mimicked his father's and then his own, to hide the sudden disappearance of the deSantos family fortune.

The fortune which was largely buried in a chest under the courtyard, as ordered by Salomon Machorro when news of the fall of Meleqa had reached the pueblo, immediately before he dragged his entire family to the nearest church to accept baptism.

It had been a sound plan, and had saved all their lives, but then came the difficulty of getting the money back out again. First there was the problem of someone noticing them digging up the courtyard. Then came the problem of how a family of recent converts would go about making it safely out of the country with a chest full of silver.

And now the Inquisition was here.

Elena knew how slim their chances were, and the old woman did, too; Elena'd had to start dosing her with the amapola she kept on hand in case of an emergency with Toba, to keep her quiet. She'd have to start bringing her off the drug soon, and she suspected that was going to be an unpleasant process.

Elena turned her mind to the problems of her granddaughter in the land of the Maziks, and her husband halfway to Pengoa, and the treasure buried beneath the cobblestone courtyard, and the Inquisition, who would be coming, if not tomorrow, then someday soon. And when they did, they might notice that the mortar between the stones had been painted recently, and they would wonder why, and they would dig.

FOURTEEN

NAFTALY WAS STARTING to grow concerned about the old woman.

She'd been sleepy and incoherent for days; he'd wanted to call for a doctor, but Elena had convinced the deSantoses that it was simply the result of stress and travel on her old body. She insisted on keeping her confined to bed instead, regularly spooning soup into the old woman's half-conscious mouth to keep her strength up.

It did seem a little convenient to Naftaly, however, that she'd fallen ill just when they'd needed her feebleness as an excuse for their stay in Eliossana. He waited until Elena was occupied with Antonio and snuck into the room where the old woman slept.

"Are you legitimately ill?" he asked her, prodding at her shoulder. Her eyes fluttered open.

"'S you," she slurred, as if her tongue were too large for her mouth. His hopes fell; she was ill. Possibly she'd had a stroke, and that meant they wouldn't be able to take her to Merja, even two weeks from now. No one recovered from such a thing so quickly, if they recovered at all. Probably she would grow worse. Probably she would die from this.

"I'm here," he said in what he hoped was a comforting voice. "Are you in pain?"

"No," she said, struggling to sit up.

"You should lie still," he said, though he didn't know why. Wasn't this the usual advice for a sick person?

"No," she said. "No, help me." Naftaly slid an arm behind her back and pulled her to a sitting position, propping a pillow behind her back. Still, she listed sideways a little until her shoulder was leaning against him. She smelled strange, not of sickness, exactly, but not her normal old-woman smell, either. It was on her breath, he realized. But he couldn't place it.

"That woman," she said, and drew a great rattling breath, then coughed up some phlegm. "She's . . . she's putting something . . ." and here she began to slur her words so badly he could not make her out.

"What?" he asked. "What did you say?"

"That woman," she said. "That *woman*! It's . . ." and she extended a gnarled hand in the direction of the wooden chest at the foot of the bed.

Leaning her against the wall, he went to kneel in front of the chest, opening the iron clasp and propping the lid on his shoulder. Inside were only some folded items of clothing Katarina had given Elena; they were too large for the old woman, who'd been thin even before their misadventures. "It's just clothes," he said.

"No," she said. Her voice was a little clearer, like she was managing to rouse herself a little. "There's something else. Every time she gives me something to eat, she opens that chest first. There's something . . . I can taste it."

Naftaly ran his hands over each item of folded cloth, all the way to the bottom. "There's nothing here," he said, but he knew there was something odd on the old woman's breath, so he took each piece of clothing and unfolded it.

There, rolled inside a woolen skirt, was a glass bottle, half-full of some brownish tincture. He sat back on his heels with it. "I have it," he said, unstopping the bottle and taking a whiff. It was the same strange, sickly sweet smell he'd noticed on the old woman. He brought it close enough for her to see, and she took a whiff from the bottle before turning her head away.

"Break it," she said. "Break it before she can give me any more."

He started toward the window, meaning to throw it down onto the courtyard, but then stopped himself. "What if it's just some kind of medicine?" he asked. "It could be—"

"Fool of a boy," she said. "It's amapola, don't you know the smell?"

"How do you know the smell of amapola?"

Leaning hard on an elbow, she said, "I know a great many things. Break the bottle; I'm lucky she hasn't accidentally dosed me to death."

Naftaly smelled it again, though he honestly couldn't have said what it was. He was willing to take the old woman's word for it and break the bottle, but then he said, "What if she has more?"

"Another bottle?" she said.

"If I confront her," he said, "she'll say it's medicinal, whatever it is, and if she has more she might find a way to keep giving it to you." He tipped the contents of the bottle out the window. "I'll have to find something to replace it with. Then we'll confront her once you've recovered."

"What good will that do? We can't trust her."

But out the window, Elena had just appeared in the courtyard with Antonio, and they were pacing off an area near the southern wall. She was pointing at the ground and he was nodding. "What are they doing?" he muttered.

"I have to get out of here," the old woman said.

"You can't even walk yet."

There was a soft knock at the door, and Katarina put her face inside. "I heard your voice," she said to Naftaly. "Is everything all right?"

"Not remotely," the old woman said.

"What is your brother doing outside with Elena?" he asked. Katarina stepped into the room and came near the window. She watched silently for a moment as the pair seemed to be judging whether that part of the courtyard could be seen by the neighbor to the east.

"Do you know what today is?" she asked softly.

"No," Naftaly said. "What do you mean?"

"The Edict of Grace," she said, "ends today. It's the last day for us to come forward and confess without facing trial."

"But you're not going to," he said quickly. "You wouldn't do that."

"No," she said, dropping her voice. The pair outside spoke closely, Elena with a fair amount of energy. Antonio was scowling, either listening very hard or not liking whatever he was hearing. Katarina said, "You never asked what happened to my oldest brother. Isidro."

Naftaly glanced away from the scene in the courtyard. "I'm sorry," he said. "You never mentioned him. I assumed . . . I assumed he'd passed away."

"No," she said, as Elena knelt on the ground outside and ran her fingers along the mortar between the stones. What was she doing? "He's not dead." She looked back toward Naftaly. "Our father had a plan, before he died." She glanced back at the old woman, but she'd fallen asleep again.

"My father had two great treasures," Katarina went on. "His fortune, and his grandchildren. Isidro's children. He split them up. The grandchildren he sent away. But he thought they'd be at risk, traveling with a great sum of money, so the fortune he left here, until it was safe to retrieve it again."

"Only it never has been," Naftaly said. "It's buried in the garden—that's why you had Elena make the business look like it was failing. So if the Inquisition got hold of the books, they wouldn't know to look for the money."

"We were just going to straighten out the financial records in case anyone went sniffing around, and then wait for the Inquisition to leave again. But now they've taken Maria Amalia. If the Inquisition finds my father guilty—and they will—they'll seize the property. They're only waiting for the end of the grace period because they need to follow protocol. We need to find some way to take the money out of Eliossana before it's too late."

Naftaly felt inside his coat for the small book he kept close, his own heirloom. "It's nearly too late now," he said.

"I know," she said. "That's why we're retrieving it tonight."

\+ + + + + +

NAFTALY FOUND ELENA sometime later, hunched over a piece of paper, scribbling furiously.

"What are you doing?" he asked, a little hotly.

"Writing to my brother," she said. "In Pengoa."

He watched her a little incredulously for a moment, and then added, "I meant, what have you done to the old woman?"

"Done?" she said very flatly, like she was not even interested in selling the lie. "What can you mean?"

"I found the bottle," he said. "And she knew, already. I poured it out."

She looked at him quizzically. "I filled the bottle with watered rum. You've been dosing her with that since this morning," he explained.

"Damnation," she muttered, setting down her pen. "There'll be no controlling her now."

"Controlling her!"

"She was fixing to leave," she said. "She would have gotten herself killed out on the road alone, if I'd let her go." Over Naftaly's objection, she said, "I was protecting her from herself."

"I don't believe for an instant that's why you drugged her," he said. "You did it because if she'd left we'd have lost our cover. You needed her here, and sick, to explain why we needed a month's board."

Elena shrugged, a motion that reminded Naftaly of a bird settling its feathers. "But I don't understand why you've continued drugging her. You're helping the deSantoses with their books; they won't put us out."

Elena side-eyed him.

It was not an expression Naftaly cared for. What difference did it make to Elena if the deSantoses escaped with their silver? What Elena wanted was Toba.

"Why do you need her to remain ill?"

Slowly, she said, "It will aid in their escape."

"How?"

"The deSantoses have a great deal of hidden treasure that they can't safely transport. They need a way to conceal it."

"To conceal it—" Naftaly took a step back. "Hashem's sake. You can't mean to seal it inside her *corpse*?"

Now it was Elena's turn to gawp. "I am not a monster," she said. "No such thing."

But Naftaly suspected he was not so far off, because what Elena had already done had bordered on the monstrous. He knew little about the intricacies of amapola dosage, but he knew enough that too much—particularly in the system of an elderly woman, could easily be fatal. Risking the old woman's life so that she could search for Toba was terrible. Doing it for money was far worse. And he noted that she still wasn't volunteering how she'd planned to use the old woman to conceal the deSantos fortune.

"I thought all you cared about was rescuing Toba," he said.

"That is all I care about," she said. "But to rescue Toba I need funds. I *sold* Antonio this plan."

"Sold it?"

"And in exchange, he's giving me a tenth of his fortune. It will be enough to get all four of us to Merja, and then to Pengoa, and then to support Alasar once we're there. This benefits all of us, the old woman included. The deSantoses have offered us board and ground transportation; that's all. Unless we do better, we're still trapped here. I can think of no other way to get the money we need. Can you?" She sat back in her chair.

Naftaly could not. He might be able, with enough time, to earn enough with his shoddy tailoring for one passage on a cut-rate schooner, but even that seemed unlikely. "What is it you mean to do?" he asked.

"I wasn't going to kill her," she said, and strode toward the window. She was a tall woman, nearly as tall as Naftaly, and a third bigger around. It struck him that if it came time to overpower her, he wasn't at all sure he could. He hoped she didn't have a second bottle of amapola.

"I'm pleased to hear it," he said.

She went on, "There is only one thing the men of the Inquisition fear, and it isn't God."

Naftaly frowned. What did powerful men fear? More powerful men, he supposed. "The crown?"

"The Inquisition owns the crown, child."

"The Cardinals, then?" When Elena shook her head, he continued: "How should I know? A hot bath? Eggplant stew? The angel of death?" The truth dawned on him. "The angel of death. You want them to think she's diseased. With what? They won't believe it's plague this far in the hills."

Eyeing him, Elena carefully pushed up her sleeve, where the inside of her arm was covered in a spotted red rash. Naftaly stepped back with his arm over his mouth.

"It's dye," she said, showing him a small pot of burgundy fluid, which sat on the other side of her work-table. "I wanted to have a test patch, to see if it was convincing."

Naftaly had to admit that it was very convincing. He wasn't sure what disease it was meant to emulate, but it looked like one he didn't wish to contract. "It's meant to be a scarlet fever rash," she said. "It's a delicate balance. We need it to resemble something virulent enough for the guards at the gate to keep their distance, but benign enough that they won't insist on burning the body."

Naftaly gawped at her. "The body?"

"I only needed her unconscious," she said. "Not dead. Come here."

Naftaly stalked uneasily to the corner of the room, toward the table draped in a lace cloth. Elena removed the candlesticks on top and set them on the other table, and then removed the drape. Underneath was a coffin.

Naftaly half expected her to ask him to lie in it.

"Open it," she said. "You only need to slide the top down a bit, and then look inside."

He carefully pushed the top down a foot or thereabouts. Thankfully, it was empty.

"How does it seem to you?" she asked.

He couldn't imagine what she meant. "Are you asking me to comment on the craftsmanship?"

"Look closer."

He did. It looked like a pinewood coffin; the wood had been freshly cut and smelled pleasantly of trees. "It's a coffin," he said. "It's empty. I'm not sure what more you mean for me to notice."

"Knock," she said. "On the bottom."

Looking at Elena, he rapped his knuckles twice on the bottom of the coffin. The resulting sound was hollow.

"It's a false bottom," he said, in some surprise.

Coming to stand next to him, she slid the top back another few inches, showing him a few notches which appeared to be flaws in the wood. "It lifts out," she said. "The silver will be concealed within, until the deSantoses are safely away."

"You designed this?"

She nodded. "There's no way to detect it, unless one measures both the outside and the inside and compares the numbers."

"Which one is unlikely to do, with a body lying there," he said.

"It's a sound plan," she said.

"Not any longer. She won't agree to it, not after what you did."

"No," the old woman said from the doorway. "She won't." And she launched herself at Elena with a speed that Naftaly would never have expected.

✦ ✦ ✦

TOBA RAN, THE stairs a blur beneath her, as she flew up them, realizing, halfway, that the shade was keeping pace with her. How utterly useless it had been.

Of course, that had been mostly Toba's fault, assuming that the shade needed to do more than keep to the letter of her requests.

When she got to the top, she fell against the wall, panting. She'd run. And she'd stayed upright. Her heart was racing with the unaccustomed exertion as she hurried into her small room and forced the door shut.

There was no way to lock it. "Can you bar it somehow?" she asked the shade, but it made no move to do so. The only furniture in the room was the wooden trunk where she kept her clothes, and the bed. She suspected that neither would keep out the Infanta, but Barsilay thought it was important to follow Asmel's instructions, so she first pushed the bed—very laboriously—against the door, and then pushed the trunk against it. That done, she huddled under the window, shivering, when it occurred to her that the bedframe was solid wood, and she should not have been able to move it at all.

✦ ✦ ✦

IT WAS LATE that night when she heard booted footsteps outside her door. Without knocking, the door began to swing inward, immediately smacking against the side of the bed. "What the—" came the voice of Asmel. "Open the door this instant."

"You told me to bar it," Toba explained. "There's . . . there are some things in front . . ."

"*This* time you listen," he muttered. He began to force the door open, and the bed and chest began to slide, rather noisily, across the floor.

"If you just . . . wait . . ." she said, getting up to move the trunk, but Asmel had already opened the door half a foot and slid into the room. The shade cowered back into a shadow, rendering itself invisible.

"That wouldn't have kept her out," he said, regarding the misplaced furniture. He cast a glance toward where the shade was attempting to conceal itself in the corner, and flicked a hand at it, making a quick motion with his fingers. "Return to Barsilay, you useless thing."

The shade failed to disappear. Asmel scowled at it and repeated the gesture, but still it remained, which seemed to make him angrier. Turning back to Toba, he said, "She's asleep again. I've managed to erase most of her memory of you. She'll wake tomorrow morning with a great headache believing she took very ill while here and having no desire to marry me at all."

"Oh," she said. "I'm . . . I'm sorry." Then she remembered that Asmel had already declined the Infanta's marriage proposal, because she'd asked him to give up the alcalá. Though it made little sense . . . why would he turn down an offer of marriage to a princess to retain title to a ruined, empty shell?

"I am not," he said. "But the issue remains—she heard your voice, so she won't forget you. I've smudged things enough that she won't remember exactly what you told her, or what your eyes looked like, but she knows you're here, and there's nothing I can do about that."

He pushed his silver hair out of his face. "I've convinced her that you are my ward, sent from P'ri Hadar because your parents are dead."

"You don't look especially pleased by that."

"*You* should be pleased by that," he said. "What I ought to be doing is killing you."

She shrank back against the wall. Toba was aware, always, that Asmel was not human. His face was too smooth, his movements too perfect, his eyes too strange. But as he put his face very near hers, the reality of his difference seemed much more immediate. He was something very old, and very powerful. He walked on two legs and spoke her language, but they were not the same sort of being, not at all.

Except he was telling her that they were. She quailed against the cold stone wall; flinching from the heat that radiated from him. How much of that was temper Toba could not say.

"Stop regarding me that way and listen, because I haven't much time. Your conception was a violation of our law, as was my decision to bring you here. Now you've been seen. If you are found out, we're both dead, and Barsilay as well."

Toba opened her mouth, closed it, and tried again, her voice more squeak than it had ever been: "Couldn't you . . . couldn't you just put me back through the gate?"

"Your mortal half will keep you from dying when the moon sets, but without the amulet there is no way to conceal your magic. You would be sensed, and hunted, and killed, but not before you were tortured for information about who you were and who might have helped you." He stood up, giving her a breath of cooler air, and with a wave put the furniture in the room back to rights before he continued. "Our only chance is to keep you here and try to pass you off as a full Mazik. And I think that's damned unlikely to succeed. Most likely La Cacería will have us all drinking flames before the next moon no matter what we do."

Toba wondered at *La Cacería*. Asmel said, "La Cacería is an order that supports the King and ensures our citizens do not engage with ideas or activities that might tend to displace him. I believe you are familiar with the general features of such an order?"

She said, "Most unfortunately."

"Among other things," he continued, "La Cacería is charged with enforcing the ban on Maziks consorting with mortals. They are rather fond of fire." He leaned back from her, and his eyes went to the window, still bricked in. He held up a hand, dissolving the stones, and took a long breath of fresh air. "They are not well fond of me."

"Yet you live," she offered.

"Yes," he said tightly. "I live. Have you understood what I have told you?"

"I think so," she said. "Only, can you tell me, is it that I can't go home now, or ever?"

"Not ever," he said. "I'm sorry to say."

She turned it over in her mind, never seeing her grandparents again. It felt impossible, and as she prodded at the idea, she found herself rather numb. Toba had been so settled on the fantasy of joining them in Pengoa with her pockets full of silver, she could not see a way forward without that dream. She'd thought of it with every page she'd translated, keeping a tally in her mind of what she'd earned. Her grandmother would praise her to heaven when she found out the deal she'd made. Not ever? It couldn't be true. He was only angry, Toba told herself, and why not? The Infanta was horrible. Anyone would be angry, having to deal with a creature like that. He would recover his temper.

Her breath gave a little hitch, because if she needed this many words to convince herself, it was not a good argument.

Asmel hunched down so their eyes were level. "You're stunted, even for a human. That's likely the work of the amulet. And you may be clever among humans but here, you know nothing. But perhaps, *perhaps*, if I can bring you up to some very low standard, I can manage to keep us alive. If you give up any hope of ever living as a mortal again."

She exhaled slowly.

He glanced at the door behind him. "The Infanta should not see you again while she's here, and she'll be returning home in the morning. Stay hidden until then."

He drew himself back to his full height and made to leave. Toba said. "And what happens after that? After she leaves?"

Asmel said. "Well, if you're my ward, I'll have to present you at court."

"At court," she whispered.

"If you manage to survive the ten hours before the Infanta leaves, we'll discuss that. Right now, your only objective is not to leave this room for any reason. Until the sun sets tomorrow night, do not open this door again." He opened the door and exited. Toba sagged to the floor.

FIFTEEN

"DAMNED WITCH," THE old woman shrieked, trying to get her hands around Elena's throat. "You despicable, disgusting, foul-souled spawn of a snake!"

Elena had levered her arms between them and was holding the old woman off as she hissed, "I'll *kill* you."

Naftaly managed to insert himself between them. "Stop," he said. "Stop, both of you." To Elena, he said. "She's right, what you did was unforgivable." To the old woman, he simply said, "Don't kill her."

"Why not?" she snapped. "She'd easily enough have killed me."

"I know my business. The effects of the drug were temporary." Elena smirked at the old woman's vigorous state. "*Obviously*. The amount I gave you was miniscule."

"And what if I became accustomed to the drug, and wanted more?"

"We would have run out eventually," Elena said with a shrug. "We're out now, in any case."

The old woman threw up her hands and turned her attention back to Naftaly. "She's completely amoral! You think she wouldn't do the same to you if it suited her?"

"There was no real harm done," Elena insisted. "If I'd let you leave that first morning, you'd be dead of thirst on the road right now. Keeping you quiet saved your life—you weren't capable of making that journey on your own."

"You have no idea," the old woman said, "what I am capable of."

"Enough," Naftaly said. "Enough now; Elena, give me your word you have no more amapola."

"I have no more on hand," she said.

"Her word means nothing," the old woman said.

Naftaly searched between them. Of course, the old woman wasn't wrong, but on the other hand, he couldn't believe that Elena had meant any lasting harm. He said, "I'm choosing to believe you."

"Dear Lord," the old woman said. "You're an idiot." To Elena, she said, "I won't kill you now, only because I suspect this fool would be stuck dealing with the aftermath. But I am leaving this house, and you had better hope our paths never cross again." And she swept from the room.

"Wait," Naftaly called, chasing after her. "You can't mean to leave on your own."

"Come with me, then," she said. "You can't think you can trust that woman. And the deSantoses only care for their treasure; they'll toss you aside as soon as your part in this is over, rest assured."

"How can you know that?"

"I've seen their type before," she said. "Don't think they'll treat you as one of them: you aren't. Come with me. We can still get to Merja."

"We have *nothing*!"

"We have our wits," she said. She shook her head. "We have *my* wits. That wretch might succeed in getting the silver out from under the cobbles, but if she thinks she's getting a tenth of it she's a greater fool even than you."

"And what about Toba? Do you mean to abandon her, too?"

She barked out a laugh. "My boy," she said, "I like you. But with thoughts like that, you're as good as dead. Are you coming with me or not?"

Naftaly sighed. He'd followed her out into the courtyard and halfway to the gate. He couldn't say why he felt rescuing Toba was his particular responsibility, whether it was because he was the last one who'd seen her, or because he'd harbored illusions of being the hero the night she'd disappeared, only to have that fantasy dashed. But he wanted to save her, to feel that he was more than the poorly equipped, half-mad son of a tailor.

Except at present, he *was* only the poorly equipped, half-mad son of a tailor. He had no money, and no way to get any outside of Elena's scheme, and he didn't see how the old woman was going to be able to do any better. He wanted to be a hero, and perhaps that was absurd. But wanting not to die on the way to Merja was practical, no way around it, unless they planned to pay for a place in a cart with pretty words or eat Naftaly's pocket lint on the way. He said, "I can't leave. I'm sorry."

"Then I wish you well," she said. "For all the good it will do."

THE COURSER HAD been twelve years old when she'd assumed her position, which she'd done by killing her predecessor.

"When you're strong enough to kill her," the Caçador had said, when she'd been old enough to wield a weapon, "you may take her place."

Taking her place meant she could hold her own among La Cacería's foot soldiers, and it was for this reason alone she coveted the position. Three lieutenants presided over the Maziks in the order: the Peregrine, who presided over the Falconry; the Lymer, lord of the Hounds; and the Courser herself, who had no men to command but served as the Caçador's personal emissary. The previous Courser had been standoffish—she seldom acknowledged her, but she'd never been cruel. The Courser hadn't hated her.

The rest of them were another matter. The Falconry she worried little about: their work was almost exclusively abroad, and they were so secretive that it ill served their purpose to challenge or be cruel . . . if you were marked by the Peregrine you just died, probably without even knowing how. The hounds, though, parading in La Cacería blue, delighting in the fear that roiled in their wake—they were a hazard she could not dismiss. So when she'd had the opportunity to kill the previous Courser and take over her position, she'd done it, and she hadn't been sorry. Becoming the left hand of the Caçador provided her with security as much as power.

The next day she'd found herself in La Cacería's windowless headquarters in a room full of Alaunts. She hadn't known they were there; she was looking for the Caçador's offices, which moved at irregular intervals, and had been in that spot a few days prior. He'd neglected to tell her that he was shifting his chambers, or where the new ones would be located. Probably this was intentional.

The Alaunts sat around the edge of a long table, feasting: they'd killed earlier in the day, and were merry from it. The elite of all the Hounds, she knew well not to trust them. By all accounts, they were difficult to control, and she was barely more than a child. They'd looked up at her and smiled. They were armed, all of them, with sabers. One of them rose, wiping his mouth on his sleeve, and grinned at her approach.

"Well," the Alaunt said. "Courser. Congratulations on your appointment."

She didn't thank him. Better to speak as little as possible to men like this. She would have left, but that meant either turning her back, or backing out and showing that she feared them. She resolved, then, never to enter a room without knowing exactly who was inside.

"I hear you're a good bit swifter than your predecessor. Must be how you killed her, eh? Would you like to tell the tale?"

"No," she said.

The Alaunts chuckled. "Well," he went on. "At least your face matches your title. We won't forget what to call you, will we?" One of the men whinnied. It was undignified, even for an Alaunt. They were drunk. From the table, one of the men called, "May I have a ride, Courser, or are you for the Caçador's exclusive use?"

His head came off before he could register that her arm had become a blade; it rolled across the floor while the rest of his body sagged and then collapsed in unbroken death. The other Alaunts stared at her, openmouthed, at the blade at the end of her left hand. The one who had spoken first had leapt back in alarm.

They wondered, she knew, if it was painful; even the Alaunts were fearful of pain. It would never occur to them to change their own flesh to steel, to endure the sharp agony of it, and watching their mixture of horror and fascination, she realized that she must never be seen carrying a blade made from anything but herself.

It was a gamble, killing an Alaunt, because the Caçador had ordered her not to kill any Maziks unless she had no other choice, lest his own forces begin to turn on him. She reasoned that she *hadn't* any choice; either kill one now and live in uneasy truce with the rest, who might spare her some respect or at least a little fear now, or deal with the bunch of them later. She would let Tarses think her impulsive in her anger—it's what he believed of her anyway. And it was safer to let him think her incompetent than see that she carried a spark of defiance.

She returned her blade to a hand, which she used to pick up the Alaunt's severed head, its face frozen in mirth. He had not even had time to alter his expression.

Holding it by the hair, she let some of the gore drip to the floor before she turned it into an apple the color of the sun. She wiped it on her trousers. She ate it slowly, while the other Alaunts watched, wiping the juice onto her sleeve, savoring each bite, and when only the core was left, she tossed it to the man who'd called her horse-faced, saying, "Plant the seeds in the courtyard."

He looked slightly sick, but he complied, and in a few weeks when the fruit came she made sure every Alaunt ate it. Those who refused, she made it known, would join him in the courtyard, their own heads in the Courser's belly.

She rather hoped a few of them would take her up on it. It had been a good apple.

The Lymer had found her sometime later, his red-black hair an affectation the Courser despised. The commander of the Hounds, he was nominally in charge of the Alaunts—as much as anyone could claim to be—and she expected him to object to her killing one of them, or ask if their insolence truly merited unbroken death. But he'd hopped lightly up to the wall she'd sat on near her tree, and taken one of the apples, and wiped it on his sleeve, and eaten it. "Not bad," he'd said, giving her a charming smile. "Which one was this?"

"You expect me to remember their names?"

He'd laughed. It had been as false as his hair. "No, I suppose not."

She'd not answered. He'd licked his thumb and rubbed it at some invisible spot on her sleeve. "Blood," he'd said, only there'd been none.

"It's there," he said.

"Your eyes are not quite normal."

He'd grinned. "Neither are yours, Saber-arm," he'd said, and she'd gone cold. Taking her wrist, he turned it over, as if looking to see if there were still steel embedded in it. "Is there a trick to it?" he'd asked.

"No," she said. Then: "Only, you make the bone into the blade, and the flesh just falls away."

He'd released her arm. "That sounds dreadful."

She'd considered killing him then, because of the comment about her eyes, and because he'd touched her, and because she didn't like his face. It would have been easy, to do it. But then there would have been no one left to control the Alaunts but her, and that sounded tiresome indeed.

Also, the Lymer was old, and old Maziks knew things. Wetting her lips, she said, "What is ha-Moh'to?"

His brow had lifted, and his shoulders had tensed. Smoothly, he said, "Where did you hear that name?"

"From a target," she said.

"Ha-Moh'to," he said, "is a myth. An old myth. You needn't concern yourself with it."

"As you say," she said.

She moved to rise but found the Lymer gone from her side, and then he was behind her, his arm made into a blade of his own, held to her throat. Somehow, the apple he'd been holding had been thrown against the wall, where it dripped pulp down to the ground.

"Don't kill any more of them," he'd said in her ear. "They're miserable to train."

Her eyes had slid sideways to meet his; his own face was next to hers; he was not tall for a Mazik. He'd moved so quickly she had not even seen it happen.

"Left hand of the new age: Tarses may make you a queen, but your reign will not be here, and no Mazik will be your subject. Say we understand one another."

"We do," she'd replied, and he'd withdrawn his blade and gone, leaving her to tend the scratch along the side of her throat.

But she'd seen his face after he'd turned the blade back to bone, and she smiled. He had not expected it to hurt as much as it did. The Lymer, for all his speed and strength, could not bear pain. She would not forget the lesson.

\+ + + + + + +

TOBA FOUND THAT she could not sleep that night. For the first time in her life, she wasn't cold; she was blazing hot, and no matter how much clothing she removed—which wasn't much, with Barsilay's shade lurking nearby—she could not make herself comfortable.

The Infanta had left hours before: she'd seen her conveyance leave, and the shade had confirmed it. "Is it forbidden for me to sleep in the garden?" she asked the shade, who had taken to carrying a scrap of paper with it. It helpfully wrote *No*, so she put most of her dress back on and went back out into the front garden, where she splashed some of the cool water from the fountain onto her face and then lay down next to it, resting her elbows on the edge and letting the mist cool her. She wondered if all Maziks were so hot, and if she'd get used to it, and perhaps if Maziks slept less than other people, which was why she did not feel tired. She cast her face upward to catch the mist and looked at the vivid stars, and realized she did not recognize any of them—none at all. Whatever stars her grandparents might be under, they were not these. Her heart turned over with longing.

"Are they different stars?" she asked the shade, trying to distract herself from her melancholy. "Than the ones in the mortal realm?"

No.

"I need to teach you a larger vocabulary," she said. "You're of limited use this way."

Yes.

"Or I could just learn to read Mazik," she said. "Probably there are answers in Mazik books." She eyed the shade. "I suppose you still won't bring me any Mazik books."

No.

Well, that was that. The shade may have been of limited use, but at least it was efficient. Still, though, it would be helpful to have someone to talk to. Her grandmother, if she were there, would have some advice. Her grandfather could probably figure out how to read Mazik, if he had some books in front of him; he was clever that way. Leaning over the edge of the fountain, Toba trailed a hand in the water, where something nibbled at it. Sitting up again, she realized it was a golden fish. Had there always been fish in the fountain? She couldn't say with absolute certainty, but she didn't think there had been. She put her hand back in the water, and the fish rubbed its body against her like a cat. There were two, she saw: the second was white as a doe's tail. "Were there always fish here?" she asked the shade.

No.

Well, that was too vague a question to warrant a reasonable answer, anyway. "Were there fish here five minutes ago?"

No.

"Where did they come from?"

The shade flitted uncomfortably, as it always did when she asked a question it could not answer. "Never mind," she said. "Don't strain yourself."

But the shade was still shrinking into the night, and Toba saw that this was because Asmel was on the other side of the fountain, looking up at the stars with a blank expression.

"Did it go well with the Infanta?" she offered.

He looked at her sourly. "No, it did not go well," he said, then conceded, "It went as well as could be expected. She did not get her way. There will be hell to pay for that, some day."

"Why . . . why wouldn't you marry her?"

"That's none of your concern," he said.

"Pardon me, but I believe it is, given that I'm now a permanent resident."

He offered up an angry glare. Toba went back to stroking the fish. He said, "The terms she offered were not those I'd been led to expect."

"She asked you to give up your house and join hers, she said, and to give up the alcalá. You'll excuse me for saying it seems to me that you'd be getting the greater part of that bargain."

"Yes, I'm sure you think so." Asmel's expression broke. "There are fish in the fountain."

"They're very beautiful," Toba said. "And friendly. I didn't know fish could be friendly. See?" She put her hand in the water, and the large golden carp rubbed its scales against her.

Asmel reached into the water and pulled out the white fish, examining it with a frown while it gasped, its mouth and gills working the air in vain. "Stop," she said. "It can't breathe when you do that."

"Hush," he said.

"But it will die." Toba's chest began to ache, and the ache grew exponentially in the next few moments. "Put it back," she wheezed. "*Please* put it back."

Watching her carefully, he put the fish back in the water, where it immediately swam as far away as possible. Toba rubbed the soreness out of her ribs and drew a deep breath.

"That was an exceptionally dangerous thing to do," he said.

"I didn't do anything!"

Asmel went back to looking at the fish. Toba realized there were more of them now; the newest was blue. There were four altogether.

"I would stop that, if I were you," he said.

"Stop what?"

"Making new fish."

"I'm not making anything. I would know if I'd made fish," she countered.

"One would assume so. But you don't. Have you no idea how you created them?"

"I wasn't even thinking of fish! I only had my hand in the water and there they were."

"Give me your hand," he said. She tentatively put her right hand out, and he turned it palm-up. "Close your eyes, and think of a fish."

She did.

"Try again," he said.

She did.

He released her hand, and Toba opened her eyes. "Did something happen?"

"No. What were you thinking, when you first noticed them?"

She'd been thinking she wanted to talk to her grandparents, but she said, "Only that the stars were different than I'm used to and I wished the shade could talk. I can't see how that would create fish."

"It wouldn't," he said. He glanced at the pond again. "There are six now."

Toba said, "I feel ill."

He looked at her closely. "You're going to kill yourself if you don't stop."

"I would stop, if I knew how! How can I create fish from nothing?"

"You can't create fish from nothing," he said. "Those fish are part of you, the same as the shade is a part of Barsilay. You're snipping bits of yourself off."

"It isn't intentional!" She felt a rush of dizziness and slid down the fountain to the ground.

"Damn it all," he said. He knelt down and lifted Toba in his arms and started back indoors.

"What are you doing?" Toba croaked.

"Putting some distance between you and the water," he said, "until you can control yourself." With long strides, he carried her back inside, passing Barsilay, who was walking out with a platter of food.

"I was bringing her dinner," he said, and Toba dimly thought, *It's after midnight, you slime.* "What are you doing?"

"There are seven fish in the fountain," Asmel said over his shoulder. "Put them in a pail and bring them inside."

"*Fish*," Barsilay repeated. "What do you want with seven fish?"

Asmel turned to go down the hallway to his own rooms. "She's going to have to swallow them."

\+ + + + + + +

ELENA WAS PACING in the main room of the house, very angrily, when Naftaly went back inside, having watched the old woman disappear into the wider world. "Of all the selfish . . ." she muttered.

"She's gone," Naftaly said.

"What am I going to tell Antonio?"

"They'll have to try something else," he said. "Or just leave without the silver; they could do that, you know."

"Katarina wants to," she said. "But he won't leave without it, and the Inquisition will be coming soon, if I'm right."

"You seem very invested in this," he said.

"I'm very *invested* in being paid right now," she replied. "It was a sound plan. We would have called the doctor, he would have found a mendicant old woman with scarlet fever, and then we'd have had enough time to extract the silver and leave with the enriched coffin before anyone was the wiser, giving us enough funds to put us up at a nearby inn until the next moon and then get a ship to Pengoa."

"There seem to be a great number of variables in this plan," he said.

"It would have worked," she insisted. "I've played it out twelve different ways. And in each of them, it always works."

"And what if Toba doesn't come back? Have you played that version out?"

She frowned. After a moment, she just said, "It was a sound plan."

Naftaly followed her gaze out to the courtyard again. Finally, he said, "Then let's carry it out." He squared his shoulders in what he hoped was masculine resolve. "We don't need a real body for the coffin; the guards won't want to look at it too closely, if you tell them the person died of disease. You'll only need to show them the bottom few inches of the coffin if they ask to see inside. The legs, and the feet."

Elena's face went pensive. "You're proposing we fill it with a false body."

"It's simple enough," he said. "It will be a scarecrow, more or less; all that needs to look real is a pair of boots and some trousers. They won't want to see the face of a corpse."

"Clever," she said thoughtfully. "Perhaps I haven't given you enough credit. But how are you proposing we create a realistic body?"

"I'm a tailor," he said. "I'll sew you one."

SIXTEEN

TOBA FOUND HERSELF laid out on a couch in a large room she hadn't seen before—she realized this must be one of the rooms on the western side of the alcalá that Asmel kept to himself. Her vision swam a little around the edges. She'd never felt so ill, as if the strength had leeched out of her body, or wrung out like water from a sponge. She felt cold. And wet. She patted down her clothing to determine if she were wet in truth, but found herself bone-dry. In her peripheral vision, she caught a shimmer of phantom silver scales, then blue, then red, and found that closing her eyes did not stop the illusion.

Asmel was storming around the chamber, pulling books from shelves and slamming them down on the round wooden table in the center, books with writing on the covers that she could not read, set in silver and gold leaf.

Toba emitted a bubble of laughter. She'd found the Mazik books.

There were a great many of them, too, though many of the shelves held scrolls rather than bound books.

"Your fish," Barsilay said, dropping the bucket down on the table, which elicited a hiss from Asmel as he moved the books out of danger from the slopping water. "When did we get fish in that fountain?"

"They aren't real fish," Asmel said. "And we need to get them back into the girl. She can't stem the flow." He took the smallest of the fish, a silver one the size of Toba's thumb, between his thumb and forefinger and said, "Start with this one."

Toba said, "No."

Barsilay examined the contents of the pail and said, "Are they truly hers? They're very well done."

Approaching Toba, Asmel said, "You must do it." Over his shoulder, he added, "Hold her nose."

"Don't you dare," Toba said. "I'm not swallowing live fish."

"They aren't live fish!" Asmel said. "And if you don't, you'll be unconscious soon."

"We could slit your belly and shove them in directly," Barsilay suggested. "Does that sound better to you?"

It did not. Taking the goggle-eyed, suffocating fish from Asmel, Toba put it on the back of her tongue and gagged it down, panting and gasping and retching. Then she realized that was the smallest fish, and the largest was as long as her forearm.

"Well done," Barsilay said, as if praising a dog. "Only six more."

SOMETIME LATER, TOBA'S throat was aflame, but at least she no longer felt faint. She nursed a cup of spiced milk to settle her stomach, while Asmel pored through his books and Barsilay lounged across the foot of Toba's couch.

"That was exhausting," he said, staring up at the ceiling. "I am exhausted."

"Really," Toba said. "Are you?" To Asmel she said, "What are you reading?"

The room was a puzzle; she'd thought it was another library at first, with so many books and shelves, but while she rested on the couch she'd looked up and realized the entire structure was without a ceiling.

Not without a ceiling, she concluded after a few minutes. It was capped by an almost invisible glass dome; it might have been open to the night air, but Toba could see the outlines of a metal armature holding it together. She'd never seen the dome from outside, and she wondered if it had been made to be invisible, or if she'd simply never bothered to look closely enough. She should have been able to see the light-stones, though, shining in the sconces, with no roof to keep the light in. Unless Asmel had not lit them since she'd come, until now. The top of the dome created some sort of strange distortion that Toba took to be magic, until she realized, upon closer inspection, that it was a lens. Casting her eyes down to the floor, which, unlike the rest of the alcalá's, was smooth, she noticed a circle set into the stone in bright brass, that seemed to tick off intervals in short arcs.

She wondered again what sort of place the alcalá had been before it was ruined. Maybe Asmel was just one of those aristocrats who fancied himself a scholar because it made him look intelligent at parties. Only she could not imagine the man at a party.

Along with the books and scrolls, the shelves were filled with items made from metal and glass, some of which Toba recognized as astrolabes and some of which she could not identify at all. One appeared to be an hourglass on its side, with a metal disk set between the two halves, yet it contained no sand. If she'd had the energy to stand, she would have examined it more closely. What was the purpose of an hourglass without sand? Maybe Asmel magicked it in somehow. But what was the disc for?

"I'm trying to understand what happened," Asmel said, shutting the book. "But there's no understanding to be had here. I don't know why you can't feel what you're doing. I don't know what it means. I don't even know what kind of magic a half-Mazik is *supposed* to have, so I've no idea how to treat one when something goes wrong." To Barsilay, he said, "I don't suppose you know anything useful?"

He shook his head. "Perhaps if I'd studied longer it would have come up. Marah would have known."

Asmel said, "Everything of hers is long gone."

Toba sipped at her milk, tearing her eyes away from the hourglass, and from the circling stars overhead—the wrong stars—which left her dizzy if she looked at them too long. He went on: "I suppose it's a good sign that you have magic at all. If you can control it, it will make things easier for us in the long run."

"To pass me off?"

"Yes," he said. "Though first we'll have to get you to the point where you don't accidentally kill yourself."

"It's very unsafe to have seven defenseless incarnations of yourself swimming around," Barsilay said lazily. "If a hawk flew down and took one, say, it would be highly unpleasant."

"Would it kill me?" she asked.

Barsilay stretched his arms expansively, "We could try it and see, would you like that?" Asmel, who was shuffling books into stacks, narrowed his eyes a hair's breadth and said, "It would hurt, and badly, and you'd remember the pain for the rest of your life." He let out a heavy breath and flicked his eyes to Barsilay. "Put out some lentils."

Barsilay reluctantly got up from the divan and put a handful of lentils on the table from the pouch he wore at his hip. The thought of eating anything turned Toba's stomach. "I couldn't possibly," she said.

"You aren't going to eat them," Asmel said. "But now that we know you have magic, you're going to start learning to control it—I know you're tired," he added, over her objections, "but if we hadn't found you outside just now, you'd be dead. At the very least you need to learn how it feels to send your magic out, so that you know how to stop it. Come here."

Hesitantly, Toba got up from the divan and approached the table. The pail that had held her fish-selves was gone, but the wood still bore a wet ring she resisted the urge to wipe away. "If you can translate, you must have studied," he said.

"Yes, with my grandfather."

"This will be no different," he said. "I will demonstrate what you are to do, and then you will do it."

Toba did not answer, because she was trying to make out the writing on the Mazik books, which she itched to hold. The characters were blocked—it was like a very complicated Rashi—but there wasn't a single one she could understand. She wondered who had written them. She wondered how old they were.

"Some indication that you are listening would seem to be warranted," Asmel said testily.

"I heard you," Toba said, but this seemed to be the wrong answer because Barsilay burst into peals of laughter from the other side of the room. "I meant to say," she tried again, "that you may proceed in your lesson. I'm sure you'll be pleased with my efforts."

"Indeed," Asmel said with a lifted brow. "Let's hope so. We're going to start very simply."

"I'm sure that's not necessary."

"We're going to start very simply," he repeated. He took two lentils between thumb and forefinger, met her gaze, and set them in front of him. "Are you observing?" he said.

"I've already said so twice," she said.

He held his palm over one of the lentils, lifted it away, and it had been replaced with a small round of bread. Toba frowned; she'd already seen him do as much, and she'd seen Barsilay do as much, but there was no actual demonstration—from lentil to bread, he'd performed no visible labor. What was she supposed to emulate? He'd used no spell or motion.

"Proceed," he said.

"What?"

"You've just boasted about being a quick study. Proceed."

She took the remaining lentil and placed it in front of herself. "It might be helpful if you explained what you actually did."

Slowly, he replied, "I made bread."

"Yes, I saw that part," she said. "But you must have done"—here she gestured wildly—"*something*."

"Put out your hand," he said. She tentatively held it out, waiting. Perhaps he was going to give her a talisman, or something. Did he have such a thing? Perhaps he'd held it in his other hand, and she'd missed it.

With a sigh, he turned her hand palm down and set it over the lentil.

Oh.

"And now?" she asked.

From the divan, Barsilay called, "The only skill is in honing your intention. Your will is your magic. Think of bread."

"That's all?"

"A specific type of bread," Barsilay said.

Toba pictured the spiral loaves her grandmother made for the new year. She wasn't sure why it tasted better to her than the braided sort, but it did. She imagined a loaf with currants in it. Currants and perhaps a bit of honey.

Under her hand, there was only a lentil.

Several hours later, there was still only a lentil.

✦ ✦ ✦

NAFTALY WENT OUT that afternoon to speak to the barman about space in a wagon to Merja.

The trouble was that Elena had instructed him to book space for three people—himself, Elena, and Toba—which meant leaving the old woman behind. He was meant to negotiate the price down, somehow, which seemed unlikely, and arrange to pay only half up front in exchange for the donkey, which seemed equally unlikely.

He'd told Elena as much, but she'd insisted an opportunist wouldn't turn down money in hand when it was offered, so off he'd gone.

He was halfway there when he noticed a nun across the street. She was not the first he'd seen in town—there must have been a convent nearby, and it must have been some liberal order that sent its sisters on errands; he'd seen several pairs of them over the past few days. This nun, however, was highly notable, first because she was alone, and second because she was picking someone's pocket.

The nun looked rather familiar. He watched her quickly slide the man's purse into some hidden pocket of her habit. When the man turned around and saw the nun standing so close behind him, she crossed herself quickly and made prayer motions with her hands.

Approaching, Naftaly peered at the face under the habit. "Are you . . ." he said. "Why are you dressed like a nun?"

The old woman looked to make sure her mark was no longer within listening distance and replied, "That's a long story. Very complicated."

"You stole the habit," he offered.

"Well," she said. "That's the sum of it, yes."

"Where?"

"There's an abbey," she said. "Just outside the town. I thought this might be useful."

"You might have watched them for a bit before deciding to disguise yourself," he said. "You're not the least bit convincing."

"I am very convincing," she insisted hotly.

"You crossed yourself backwards," Naftaly told her. "You begin on the left side."

She frowned. "Is that so? I had no idea there was a pattern to it."

"You're going to get yourself killed doing this."

"I'm in less danger than you," she said. "Passing time with that madwoman. I've spent the entire afternoon longing for amapola. Even my toenails hurt. I feel dreadful."

"You seem to be getting around all right," he said. "Keeping yourself busy, with the stealing and the . . . the praying."

"If I can keep this up," she said, "I'll have enough to get a ship in Merja by early next week. It'd be faster work, but none of these people carry much coin on them." She fished the purse out of her skirts and peered inside. "That's just pathetic."

"Look, would you just come back with me?" he asked. "You're safer with us than out here on your own. Are you going to sleep on the street in your habit? You think no one will find that odd?"

She scowled.

"You hadn't thought of that, had you?"

"Perhaps I could stay in that church over there," she said. "If I ingratiate myself to the staff."

"The clergy. It's *the clergy*, not *the staff*."

"I could take you by the arm," she went on. "Right now, like so, and shout, *I've caught a Jew! I've caught a Jew!*"

"Keep your voice down! It doesn't work that way."

"Well, how does it work?"

"I've never been dredged up by the Inquisition," he said. "But I'm pretty sure they don't have roving bands of elderly nuns combing the countryside picking us off." He shook her off his arm. "Listen, I'm going to that barman to discuss arrangements to Merja. I told Elena—" here the old woman spat on the ground—"How charming of you. I told her I would make arrangements for three. I'll make them for four, and I'll find you again to tell you the time and place, but it won't be until after the moon. After tomorrow we'll be staying at the inn a half mile down the road toward Merja. You can find us there."

"After tomorrow? Are you still planning that madness with the coffin?"

"We are. It's a sound plan."

"And who did she convince to *lie* in the coffin?"

"No one," he said. "We're making a false corpse." When she looked at him incredulously, he said, "It only needs to be minimally convincing."

"Hashem's sake. You're going to try to sneak five pounds of silver past the Inquisition with a *minimally convincing* false corpse—do you hear what you are telling me?"

"It's a sound plan," he repeated. "The corpse is diseased—"

"You don't believe it's a sound plan for a minute! You need to start thinking for yourself, boy. Just because Elena Peres's voice is loudest doesn't mean it's right."

"So you would have me listen to you instead."

"I would have you listen to reason!"

He shook his head. "Your goal is only to preserve yourself."

"And hers is only to preserve her grandchild. What's yours?"

"To preserve as many people as possible," he said. "I want to save all four of us. And right now, Elena's plan is the only one that gives me a chance to do that. So I'll follow her lead for now, but not because I can't use my own mind."

He waited for the old woman to respond, but found her eyes had fallen on a half-drunk man wandering out of the tavern and staggering into the street.

"I'm sure that was very important," she said, patting Naftaly on the shoulder. "But duty calls, boy."

He watched her relieve the drunkard of his purse, and went off in search of the barman.

"A wagon to Merja, eh?" the barman asked. "For how many?"

Naftaly put his hand in his pocket, and realized that for all the old woman's protests, his one coin had miraculously become two. He said, "There will be four of us."

\+ + + + + + +

NAFTALY THOUGHT ELENA'S plan seemed sound enough, right up until he was stuffing wool into a pair of Antonio's trousers. He'd already done the boots; the coat was next, which he planned to stitch to the waist of the trousers to keep them from shifting inside the coffin.

He'd wrapped the wool around some metal weights Antonio used for dying to give the corpse proper heft, but as he worked, he began to wonder. What if the guards wanted to see more than the bottom half? The legs looked well enough, but no amount of tailoring could produce a realistic face. The longer he thought about his conversation with the old woman, the more he began to think she'd been entirely correct. The whole plan was ridiculous.

Elena came in and set a plate of food in front of him; meatballs, he saw, which he'd been smelling earlier; in all their preparations, he'd missed lunch. He stabbed his thumb with his needle and sat back, sticking the wound in his mouth.

"You should eat," she said. "You won't have another chance until we're at the inn."

"Hm," he said. "The inn." He took his thumb out of his mouth and finished sewing the coat over the trousers.

"What's wrong?"

"Well," he said. "As I've been constructing this, I keep thinking of all the things that could go wrong. What if the guards ask to see the entire corpse? The face won't pass muster, even in the dark."

"It will pass muster, if you'll try not to look so culpable." She took the sewing from his hands in order to finish it herself. Her stitches, he noted, were finer than his.

Naftaly slid the plate of food toward himself and speared a meatball, which was so heavily spiced with pepper it was difficult to get down. He found himself grimacing.

"I know," Elena agreed. "Katarina sent the maid home early, and she made these herself. She's still sweet on you, you know, and she'll have quite a dowry by tomorrow. I could put in a word for you with Antonio."

"I think Antonio has higher aspirations than to wed his only sister to the son of a tailor," he said. He reached for the watered wine Elena had brought up with the food and downed it quickly to wash away the taste of the meatballs. "I doubt he'd agree."

"Are you sweet on her too, then? She's not bad to look at, and she knows her way around a business better than her way around a meatball. It's not a bad match."

"I don't . . ." he said. "It hadn't occurred to me."

"No? You're long past old enough to marry; your father never had anyone in mind for you?"

"We never discussed it," he said. "My father was not prone . . . to discussions." If he were honest, the unspoken truth was that his father did not think Naftaly was capable of supporting dependents. It was because of the war, his father had put forth as an excuse, but since Naftaly had no interest in the intimate particulars of a marriage, he hadn't pressed the issue.

Naftaly blinked a few times—the room was listing, and he steeled himself: he would not have an episode in front of Elena.

"Antonio could certainly help you get situated in Zayit. Or you could join in his business, if you didn't wish to start your own . . . Are you all right?" she asked.

"Yes, of course," he said. He hadn't eaten in too long; surely that was making things worse. He downed another dreadful meatball. "There's only one thing we haven't discussed: who is Antonio claiming is in the coffin? Isn't the point that it's meant to be a family member?"

She sighed. "You're such a kind-hearted boy."

Naftaly realized he could no longer feel his toes, and his fingers, likewise, were going rapidly numb. Elena watched him carefully. "You wouldn't," he said. He lifted the wine and sniffed, looking for the scent of amapola, but there was nothing out of the ordinary. She watched him set the glass down.

"It wasn't in the wine," she said.

"What have you done?" he slurred, in dawning terror, as Elena came to her feet fast enough to keep him from falling out of his chair. "The plan . . . the plan . . ."

She laid a hand on his cheek. "Try not to worry," she said, then added, "If you find yourself vomiting later, try to turn your head to the side, if you can."

The room began to close up around him, and as he felt himself going under he saw Elena slide a pot of red dye toward herself, take a small brush, and begin to paint his hands.

SEVENTEEN

ACCORDING TO ASMEL, there were three feats of magic performed very easily by the smallest of Mazik children. The first of these was transforming lentils into bread. The second was changing the temperature of water. The third was changing the color of cloth.

Toba could do none of these. Her head ached from exertion, because for all Asmel claimed to be teaching her, he could not seem to offer any explanation as to how she was expected to do these things. He seemed to think it was meant to be an automatic process, and could not understand why, in Toba's case, it was not.

"Perhaps," Toba had said, "if we started with something easier."

"There *is* nothing easier," Asmel said. "What you did with the fish was already much more advanced than what I'm asking you to do. You only have to decide to do it with some reasonable amount of conviction."

"Try touching here," Barsilay said, tapping two fingers between his eyes. "It may help."

"That does nothing," Asmel said.

"It might! If she believed it did!"

Toba tried the technique. When it didn't help, she took the lentil and threw it out the window. Asmel said, "A tantrum *certainly* won't help."

Barsilay's boots came down to the floor with a *thunk* and he made a show of rising. "As amusing as this is, I'm going to retire for the evening. If I'm going to die, I may as leave a well-rested corpse." He waved at the shade and said, "I don't have enough energy to make another one of you. Come and draw me a bath." He strode toward the door. The shade made no move to follow.

"A bath in my rooms," he said. "Not here." When it still did not move, he clapped twice. It did not respond.

Barsilay gave the shade a dark look. Asmel said, "It failed to obey me as well. You must have corrupted it somehow."

"I haven't corrupted it!" Barsilay said, but made a dispelling gesture anyway, saying, "Enough of you," and then looked horrified when it failed to disappear.

Turning to Toba, he said, "What have you done to it?"

"I haven't done anything."

"You must have done something."

"It only does little chores for me and tells me things. How could I have altered it? You've seen I can't do magic. Clearly I haven't made it a fish."

"It tells you things . . ." Barsilay said. "That's not possible; it can't speak. I made sure of that."

"I know," she said. "That's why I gave it a pen. And some paper."

Barsilay put a hand to his temple. "You taught it to *write*?"

"Only a little!"

Underneath the window, Asmel's shoulders began to shake, and he laughed, long and hard. It was a bizarre reversal, Barsilay so angry and Asmel laughing. "What are you going to do now?" Asmel asked. "She doesn't even know what she's done."

"Well, I'm *sorry*," Toba said. "I had to communicate with it somehow. So you have a slightly more useful servant; I'd think you'd be thanking me. I've only improved it."

"When you taught it to write," Barsilay said, "you bound it to you. But it's still my magic that gives it life."

Toba looked to the shade; if it were possible for a shapeless dark mass to look bemused, this one did. Given a slip of paper, it would probably write, *Ha*.

"You've stolen yourself a servant that draws its power from Barsilay," Asmel said. "He can't even dispel the thing now."

Toba said, "Oh dear." Asmel laughed again. "Well, how do I release it, then?"

Sputtering, Barsilay said, "You just *do*."

Asmel came and stood before her. "There are gestures that will help you focus your intention," he said. He conjured up a piece of fruit and held it in his left hand; an illusion, she assumed, since he hadn't used a lentil. Then, with his right, he held a finger in front of his heart. "Focus on releasing the magic," he said, and the fruit disappeared.

Toba held her own finger in front of her heart and thought of releasing the shade. Unsurprisingly, nothing happened. She scowled and tried again.

"Turning yourself purple," Asmel said, "won't help. You aren't passing a stone."

Toba grumbled and tried again.

"Try harder, please," Barsilay said, but after a few more failed attempts, Asmel said, "Enough now. She can't do it yet."

Barsilay swiped a hand at the shade in fury, and it went straight through. "I'm sorry," Toba said. "I didn't do it on purpose."

"I don't forgive you," Barsilay replied, and stormed from the room.

Toba said, "How long is he likely to remain angry about this?"

Still amused, Asmel replied, "You've stolen his magic. Men have been ended over less."

When she put a hand to her belly, he added, "Don't worry. Barsilay's far too honorable to kill someone as defenseless as you are."

"What a comfort," she said.

\+ + + + + + +

ELENA'S PLAN WAS fairly simple. Its only downside was that it necessitated lying to its key player, because Elena did not think she could convince Naftaly to voluntarily lie silent in a coffin for the better part of a day.

She did feel badly about lying to the child, first about her possession of a second bottle of amapola, and then about the ridiculous business with a false corpse. Probably the boy would be extremely angry when he woke up. No matter, though. Elena was used to handling angry people. At least he'd be angry and fairly rich.

She finished applying the red dye to his face, creating an asymmetrical rash in multiple layers, and then rubbed salt on his lips to chap them. He did look dreadful. She wondered how long it would take the dye to wear off; she would have some explaining to do, when they got to the inn. Probably she would have to sneak him in through the back.

"Look," she told him, before they closed the coffin without hammering the nails all the way in, "I am sorry about this, but you'll thank me in the morning."

And Elena believed this, too. Or nearly did.

\+ \+ \+ \+ \+ \+

AT THE GATES of Eliossana, Elena found her group stopped by the guards. She'd expected this, and watched as Antonio paid the standard bribe. The soldiers looked a bit on the haggard side; she supposed they may have had a larger than normal number of people leaving town lately, what with the Inquisition breathing down the necks of a pueblo with a significant converso population. She peered at the horizon; the sun was just thinking of setting. She'd sedated Naftaly for what she'd hoped would be half a day, and they still had half of that time remaining.

The lead guard—who'd called Antonio by name—pocketed Antonio's money and eyed the coffin that was very prominently displayed in the back of the wagon. Katarina and some of the servants snuffled in false grief.

"Quite a set-up just to haul the dead," the guard said, patting one of the draft horses pulling the wagon. "Must have been a big fellow."

"It's not the weight so much as the distance," Antonio said. "We're taking him to my family plot in Meleqa."

"Meleqa," the guard said. "That is quite a way to take a body."

"It's what his mother wants," he replied. "She lives there and wants him close."

The guard knocked his fist again the coffin, making Elena flinch. "Didn't realize you had cousins there, deSantos."

"He was my mother's sister's boy," Antonio replied a little stiffly. Elena had quizzed him on all possible questions. His delivery was, unfortunately, rather lacking. She'd have thought he could tell better lies than this. There was an art to it that he lacked; you simply imagined a world in which the lie was true, and then imagined yourself living there, so you weren't so much lying as constructing a new reality and then telling the truth once you got there. It was a technique she'd had to learn when Toba was an infant, in order to keep her alive.

"Hm," said the guard. One of the other guards was hovering at his shoulder; nearby, some others wore the livery of the Inquisition. "I'll have to have a look, you understand. There's been a fair bit of smuggling going on since . . . those fellows showed up here."

"Smuggling of bodies?" Elena asked.

The guard eyed Elena, who stood a bit taller than him, and drew his mouth tight. He rapped his knuckles against the top of the coffin again. "Doesn't appear to be well nailed, does it?"

"Well," said Antonio. "It's not like we have to worry about him escaping."

Over his shoulder, the guard called to two others, "Let's get this over with, lads."

Katarina made a noise of protest, which Elena echoed. She'd assumed they would ask to see the body, and the silver was very well concealed. Still, though. If Naftaly chose now to snore, they'd have some quick explaining to do, and it wouldn't look well for them.

The two other guards pried off the lid, and they looked down at Naftaly's still face, stepping back quickly at the sight of his painted rash.

"What did you say he died of?"

"Scarlet fever. He had a heart ailment," Elena said, because she no longer trusted Antonio to lie for them. "It was too much for him." She let out a shuddered breath. "And him so young, it hit us frightfully hard." Turning away, she said, "I can't bear to look on him. Please let's give him his privacy now."

The guard nodded and they replaced the lid. "Make sure the nails are in all the way," he said. "Or the lid's likely to slide off on the road."

"That's not necessary," Antonio said, much too quickly. "His mother will want to see him."

"Then they can pry the nails out in Meleqa," he said, and Elena flinched as the guards hammered the nails back down one by one with the hilts of swords and the ends of cudgels.

They'd gone another thousand yards when, from within his coffin, Naftaly began to scream.

Eighteen

TOBA WAS FAMISHED, she was cross, and she was running out of paper.

She was in the library, translating the Rambam she'd nearly finished, and came to the realization that in a few minutes she'd have to stop, and that irritated her almost more than her empty belly.

She hated Maziks, all Maziks, and she didn't even care that she was one. She resolved to tell them so, the next time she saw one. *I despise you*, she would say. Too weak. *I detest you. You are a stain on the landscape of the world and ought to be wiped off.* Not a stain. *A blight*; that sounded firmer.

Then Barsilay appeared with a tray laden with a feast's worth of food—fowl, of some kind, and meatballs studded with fruit resting on beds of grape leaves and rice dyed gold with saffron—which he deposited on the table, his face smugness itself. She decided calling him a blight might be premature, as she ogled the tray with great feelings of lust. Asmel had ordered her to have no food until she could transform it herself, which she still had not done. In addition, he'd insisted she'd have no bath until she could conjure her own water. She could also have no paper, no ink, no fresh clothing, and no source of light if she wanted to work past sundown, and he'd stood and watched her repeat these instructions to the shade, so that it could not help her, either, though it continued its impotent hovering. "Do something useful," she'd told it earlier, "or go away." It had done neither; the only worthwhile thing it *had* done was to stand in front of the window to shade the sun from her eyes.

"There," Barsilay said. "That was heavy, I hope you appreciate it."

"But, Asmel . . ." she said slowly.

"Is being short-sighted. If you don't eat, you'll become even more frail than you already are. We should have started fattening you up days ago."

Still, she eyed the platter as if it might be a trap of some kind. Probably it was poisoned, or it would taste like fish, which she had vowed never to eat again. The feel of phantom scales still lingered at the back of her throat.

"Well?" he demanded. "That piece of work you wore around your neck did you no favors. You might still be made into a reasonable-sized person if we feed you enough."

Toba lay her hand against the spot where her amulet had long rested; it seemed to her that the skin there was still cool under her hand. Her fingers traveled upward to test the bruises the Infanta had left on her throat, but they had healed days ago. A gift, she supposed, of her Mazik blood. She stroked the spot where the Infanta's fingernail had scraped open the skin. "Barsilay," she said. "The Infanta said something, when she was about to murder me. She asked me how many realms Asmel had shown me, beside his own."

Barsilay stopped in the middle of scooping up a meatball with a leaf, dropping it back to the tray. "She asked you that?"

"Is that a shocking thing for her to have asked?"

"More than shocking," he said. "It's highly illegal, in the punishable-by-unbroken-death sense."

"You mean what she was implying, or that she asked the question at all?"

"Either," he said. "I can hardly believe she would ask you such a thing. She must truly have lost control of herself. Even a Cacería informant wouldn't ask that directly. I'd advise you to forget it."

"But why would she—"

"She was angry," he said. "People say foolish things when they're angry. Eat." He indicated the tray. "I don't want to have to warm it up again."

Toba leaned forward to catch the aroma. It did smell delicious. And not at all fishlike, though she realized it was the first food she'd been given that wasn't cheese or vegetables. "Is it kosher?" she wondered.

"It was never actually *alive*," he said. "And it takes a great deal more magic to make pheasant than cheese, so I hope you enjoy it. All of it." He tapped the edge of the tray with a long finger. "It won't be hot for long; I recommend starting."

"You expect me to eat the entire thing?"

He nodded crisply. "The entire thing, yes."

"I couldn't possibly."

"Oh, for heaven's sake . . ." He picked up a leg and took a large bite. "There. Now it's not the whole thing."

Giving in, she picked up a slice of what she suspected was meant to be pheasant breast and took a bite.

Definitely not fish. But also . . .

"Well?" he asked as she took far too long in chewing it. "What's wrong?"

She held up a finger while she chewed. "It's just. Well . . ."

"Well what?"

"It tastes like lentils," she said. She swallowed. "Very chewy lentils."

"Ungrateful wretch," he said. "I should . . . I should . . ."

"What should you do?" Toba said, laughing.

He got up from his chair. "I don't know. Eat it anyway; I don't care how it tastes."

Toba dutifully ate a bite, and then two, and then three, finding the food tasted more like itself and less like lentils the more she ate. "It really isn't bad," she said. "My grandmother's food always tastes too salty to me." Elena never salted anything, but Toba swore she could taste the salt leftover from koshering meat, to say nothing of cheese, which she despised.

He snorted. "No worry of that here. Salt is poison to Maziks, did you not know?"

She hadn't known that at all, and wondered about the implications. Was salt as easy to obtain here as in the mortal world? Though if it were poison, perhaps not. They could not mine it or make it from seawater, in that case, and since they refused to trade with mortals it stood to reason it would simply not exist here in the way she was used to. At least she wouldn't miss it.

Barsilay rifled through her remaining few leaves of paper and eyed her nearly drained inkpot.

"You need to try harder than this," Barsilay said.

"I am trying as hard as I can," she said with her mouth full. "You're terrible teachers, both of you."

Barsilay opened his mouth to answer, snapped it shut, and said, "Hell." With a wave he disappeared, though whether he'd somehow teleported from the room or made himself invisible, Toba couldn't say, so she plucked another piece of pheasant from the tray, just as Asmel's boots announced his entrance into the room.

She smoothed her dirty hair away from her face and resumed chewing, trying not to look guilty.

"Did you make all this?" he asked. "Or did Barsilay bring it to you against my orders?"

Toba tore off some bread and handed it to him. "It's very good," she said, "once you get past the first few bites."

Ignoring the proffered food, he took the tray in one hand and tossed it into the air, where it vanished in a sea of sparks before showering lentils back down on the table. "Where is he?" he asked.

"He didn't mention where he was planning to go when he left," she said.

Asmel fumed as only a thwarted Mazik lord could fume. "I'm not sure what you're looking so smug about," he said. "He only set you back several days. We'll just have to restart the whole process."

"You mean to starve me again?"

"You'll never learn until you're made to! That much is clear. Apparently a nebulous fear of death is not enough motivation for you."

"I am motivated," she said. "I just can't do magic. The only magic I've ever done is that stupid trick with the fish, and that was an accident."

"You managed to do magic even with that wretched curse around your neck," Asmel said. "Long before that business with the fish."

"I've never done any magic," she said. "None at all."

He turned and took Toba's papers from before her, taking one stack under each hand . . . the Latin translation under the right, and under the left the Arabic.

"I was told you did these at the same time, writing with a pen in each hand."

"Yes," she said, "but that isn't magic."

"Have you ever met anyone else who could do such a thing? Because I have not."

She frowned a little. Then she said, "My grandmother can do it."

Asmel startled. "Your grandmother?"

"Yes, I saw her, once. She was translating for my grandfather when his hands were going bad. She was writing Hebrew with her left hand and Latin with her right. So it's not so unusual, is it?"

He stared at her for a long moment. "Yes," he said. "It is." He paced toward the window, frowning at this piece of information. "And then you went and stole Barsilay's shade."

"That was an accident," she said.

"I think you did it intuitively. I think there's magic in you, and it's likely been leaking out in small ways all your life. You probably made excuses for it. Called it strange luck. Or your grandmother tried to cover it up somehow, so you wouldn't realize what you'd done."

"That couldn't possibly be true," she said. "I can't even make lentils into bread; anyway, I'm very observant. If I'd been doing magic, I'd know."

He watched her a while. Finally he said, "Very well, then. Perhaps if you can't do anything with your own magic, you can do something with mine. Take this." And he conjured some sort of living light, half flame, half star, and passed it to Toba, who responded by ducking sideways behind the table. The plume of lightning rolled off Asmel's hand and left a blackened mark on the wall behind her.

Asmel frowned. "You were meant to take it," he said.

"It was *fire*."

"It wasn't hot," he said very slowly.

She rose and indicated the scorch mark on the stone behind her. "It burned the wall!"

"You are not a wall," he said. "Try again."

This time, she reached out with her eyes closed, and felt something make contact with her palm. He hadn't lied—it felt exactly the same temperature as her skin, but it sizzled a bit, like cooking onions, which unnerved her in case what was sizzling was her flesh. Ensuring her palm was not somehow being cooked, she prodded the light with a finger, causing it to change shape. "What is it?" she asked.

"A bit of raw magic," he said. "See what you can do with it."

She took her eyes off the magic to look at Asmel, who was watching her with his head tilted slightly to one side.

"What *can* I do with it?" she asked.

"Make it grow, to start. Change its shape or color."

She stared at him. "How do I do that?" she asked.

"I've told you exactly how: you use your will. There's nothing more than that, I promise."

Toba stared at the star in her hands. Asmel said, "Do *anything* with it. Make it a kitten; just do something."

"It would help if you told me how," she said, and then watched helplessly as the magic in her hands evaporated into the air.

"Hold it!" he ordered. "At least keep it there."

"I can't," she said, as the magic fizzled sadly into nothing. Toba dropped her hands. "I don't know how!"

"I'm not asking you to do anything that should require instruction!" he snapped. "Any child should be able to do what I've asked of you, from the cradle. No one is *taught* this level of magic. You may as well ask me how to breathe."

"Well, I'm sorry," she said hotly. "*I'm sorry* I'm so much weaker than you."

"Your self-pity won't save you," he said. "Stop acting like an infant."

Toba balled her hands into fists and made to storm from the room. "Don't you dare," he said. "Where are you going, that you think your problems won't follow?"

"I'm going to have a bath," she said. "And if no one will help me, I'll bathe in the fountain!"

✦ ✦ ✦

ANTONIO TURNED TO ELENA, horrified, while Naftaly screamed from within the coffin. "Quiet him," he said. "Give him more of the drug."

The servants, at Katarina's urging, were already prying the top back off the coffin with extinguished torches as makeshift crowbars. Elena, shaking with shock, pulled the bottle of amapola from her pocket. There was no time to measure another dose, and for that matter, the boy shouldn't *need* another dose. She'd calculated the amount according to her estimate of his weight and added twenty extra percent to be sure.

He couldn't be so much larger than she'd guessed. And she was rather worried that if she overdosed him again, he might actually die this time.

Just a sip, she thought, ought to quiet him before the guards noticed the commotion. The women of their party had taken up wailing to cover the screams, but now that the coffin was open, his shouts were at full volume, and were louder than they ought to have been; she found herself wanting to clap her hand over her good ear. "Shut him up," Antonio snapped. "Or we're all dead!"

But when Elena approached him, Naftaly snapped out a hand and slapped the bottle from her grip, where it smashed on the ground. "Witch!" he cried; half a scream and half a sob. "Damned witch, I trusted you!"

"Quiet," Elena urged softly, "you must be quiet or you'll be killed. I'll explain—"

"You'll explain nothing!" He tried to pull himself out of the coffin but was too weak to do more than rise a few inches.

Katarina said, "The guards are coming, I hear them." To the servants, she said, "Unhitch the horses."

Antonio approached, a substantial rock clutched in his right hand. "What can you mean to do?" Elena asked, gripping his arm.

"I'm going to quiet him," he said, trying to push past her.

"You might well kill him!"

"If we don't quiet him, he'll die anyway."

By then, Naftaly's screams had subsided into loud sobs. Antonio wrestled himself free and went at Naftaly again. Elena pulled her arm back and struck Antonio a blow on the jaw, knocking him flat on his back.

Antonio looked at her in shock from the ground. Katarina had climbed onto the back of one of the draft horses with the help of her servants. "Flee to the hills," Katarina told them. "If they catch you, tell them we forced you." To Antonio, she said, "Live without your fortune or die here."

Antonio made his decision quickly. He climbed onto the back of the other horse, and together, they rode away at a gallop, while the servants fled into the hills.

"Stop weeping," Elena ordered, pulling Naftaly up to sit in the coffin. "Get up. Get up or I'm leaving you."

"I'll go nowhere with you," he said, struggling to rise.

But Elena was already pulling him out of the coffin by the shoulders. When Naftaly was clearly too weak to walk, she slung his arm around her neck and dragged him.

"Witch," he croaked.

"Shut up," she said crossly. There was no cover on the chaparral, besides a spare handful of trees that were too spindly to conceal anyone.

A great melee grew up behind them; Elena dropped Naftaly into a dried-out shrub and knelt beside him. A fire had erupted in the vicinity of the wagon they'd left behind moments before, and it was surrounded by the guards from the gate.

"Why would they burn the wagon?" Naftaly whispered.

"They wouldn't," Elena said. "They're trying to put it out."

And indeed, the guards were beating the growing flames with sticks and branches, to little avail, and one of them ran back toward the gate to find help or start a bucket brigade, which would not possibly work at this distance. The ground was dry, and it was near enough to the side of the road to spread to the dry grass. Eventually, if it was not put out, it would spread back to the walls.

"One of the servants?" Naftaly asked. It was a good bit of luck; the guards were more intent on putting out the blaze than searching the area. But it couldn't have been luck; someone had started this fire.

"They fled before we did," Elena said. "It wasn't them." It should have been her, she thought. It was a good contingency, burning the wagon. She wished she'd thought of it, instead of running pell-mell into a desiccated shrub.

The branches of the shrub crackled, and Elena threw a protective arm over Naftaly, only to realize the person crouching on his other side was not a guard, but the old woman. "This bush," she said, "is about to go up like a torch. Give me the boy, and we'll be on our way." She reached out for Naftaly's arm and slung it over her shoulder; he was too weak either to help or to resist.

"Do us both a favor," she told Elena. "Stay here and burn."

NINETEEN

ASMEL LEFT TOBA alone after that.

Barsilay assumed her useless magic lessons and took to feeding her impossible quantities of food several times a day; she'd had to ask the shade to let out her dresses twice, though, if she were honest, she'd still only progressed from *alarmingly frail* to *very thin*. Still, she was delighted that when she sat in a hard chair, her hip bones no longer rode the wood, as if she'd been given the gift of a permanent cushion.

"I think you've grown an inch," Barsilay said one afternoon, sizing her up as she stood to take her lunch tray from his hands. "You used to come up to my clavicle, and today you're nearly to my shoulder."

"You're wearing different boots," she said, settling herself down to eat. "The ones yesterday were taller."

He glanced down at his feet. "Do you think so? They weren't meant to be."

"These definitely have less of a heel."

"Hm," he said. "Well. Do you prefer these, or the others?"

"Are you asking for sartorial advice from me?"

He sighed. "Heaven forbid you be useful for something."

"The ones yesterday were ridiculous," she said, palming a trio of olives into her mouth. Her manners had deteriorated precipitously; if she was going to consume the quantities of food required by Barsilay, she could only do so by stuffing her mouth like a chipmunk. "I was worried you might turn your ankle."

He frowned, lifting his boot to examine the heel, and Toba went back to eating. For the first time in her life, she felt solid—less willowy reed and more sturdy oak. Barsilay took her wrist between thumb and forefinger and gave it an appreciative squeeze. She smacked his hand away. "Please don't make me feel more like a holiday chicken than I already do."

"Now there's an idea," he said. "We could just eat you. It would simplify things, and I could go back to a normal state of affairs."

"You wouldn't dare," she said.

"You think I'm above eating a mortal?"

"I think you're far too vain," she said. "I'd make you enormously fat."

"Well," he said, watching her eat with renewed vigor. "You certainly would."

\+ + + + + +

TOBA'S INSOMNIA DID not improve. Mostly, she lay awake at night thinking of her grandparents and hoping they were in Pengoa by now, and settled. She hoped there was a courtyard at her uncle's house where her grandfather could sit in the sun, and some friends to study with. She missed her own courtyard, with the mismatched cobbles, and the orange trees, and the corner where Toba had played alone while avoiding the neighborhood children who loomed like tiny monsters outside the gate, waiting to push her into a puddle or tie her to a horse-post by her hair. She'd had a set of carved wooden animals that one of her grandfather's students had made for her. She'd played with those often and for hours.

Only sometimes, when she remembered them, they weren't wood. They were soft, like clay, and they'd moved on their own. She'd long supposed she was remembering some childish fantasy. It was too silly a thing to think on too long, or to bring up with Barsilay.

Still, she tried to remember playing with her animals, and in those memories, the cold, ever-present weight of the amulet had not been there. She remembered mud, the feel of it on her hands, slick and wet, and a burning desire for companionship that cut her keenly; it seemed she'd felt it all her life. She supposed Barsilay was better than the neighbor children who had made her childhood hell, but only because he never acted on his threats, and even Asmel had given up trying to keep her hungry when she'd pushed back. Still, she'd taken to conserving her translation to a few sentences a day, because she was running out of paper, and she didn't know what it would mean to her contracts with the Maziks when she stopped working completely. Barsilay was giving her food because it was in his interest to do so. Giving her paper was another matter; if she defaulted, she'd be in his debt. If she didn't learn to do magic soon, she'd find herself belonging to both of them.

She wondered if Asmel was right about her having done magic before, and she thought again of playing in the mud.

\+ + + + + +

ASMEL FOUND TOBA in the garden some hours later.

She was on the ground, covered in mud, having taken water from the fountain and mixed it with soil, making a mess that lay in great clods before her. She expected Asmel to comment on her state of filth. Instead, he said, "That's interesting."

Before her were several mud animals, roughly as tall as her longest finger, all moving independently. A wolf climbed onto her slipper, leaving a dirty mark there. "I have no idea how I'm doing this," she said quietly.

Asmel watched the scene for a moment before saying, "They just appeared?"

"No, I made them," she said. "But I'm not sure how they went from being mud to being alive." She turned to him. "But they aren't alive, really, are they?"

"They're as alive as your fish, or Barsilay's shade. You felt compelled to create them?"

"I don't know why," she said. "I have a dim memory of having done this before, but I can't say when. I was small then. I think maybe it was before I was given the amulet."

The mud wolf approached Asmel's gleaming boot. Before he could leave mud on it, Asmel sent it reeling back with a gesture.

"That was rude," she said. "He's only being friendly."

He dropped to a knee beside her and watched the animals frolic a bit. "What is that?" he asked, indicating the figure that looked like a great bird, only its legs were too long and its knees bent backward.

"Only something fanciful," she said.

"Tell me its name."

"It's a Ziz," she said. "I know it's foolishness; you don't have to tell me."

But Asmel only nodded. "Where have you seen one before?"

He was still looking at the animals, not at her, and the moon was bright on his hair and in his eyes; it was waxing again. He absently rubbed at the mark on his left palm with his thumb. She'd concluded, finally, that it was the exact same mark on both hands. "I haven't," she said. "I've only heard the fairy stories; you know, a giant bird that blocks out the sun and after the messiah comes the wise men will sit together and eat him, and he'll taste like roast chicken or figs or cake." She made a face. "I always hated that part. But you aren't saying such a thing is real?"

"Of course they're real," he said. "They all belong to the King. Save this one." He took a handful of mud from the pile and shaped it into something resembling a horse, then set it to run next to the other animals. "See what you can do with that. Can you make it larger?"

Cocking her head slightly to the left, Toba watched as the horse grew a fraction bigger. "You did that," she said. "I hadn't even tried yet. You couldn't even wait for me to try?"

"I didn't," he said. "You did that yourself. Now, give it a mane."

She reached out to take a pinch of mud, but he stayed her hands. "Not that way."

She frowned and tried to imagine a mane growing. Nothing happened.

"All right," he said after a moment. "I'll do it."

A mane of flowing clay sprouted from the tiny horse, who tossed it delightedly like a happy dog, leaving wet splatters around it. Asmel smiled.

"You're very smug," she said.

"That was you, again."

"It wasn't," she said. "I know it wasn't."

"You can't feel the magic leaving you?"

"I feel nothing."

He frowned. "I don't know what that means. But you plainly have magic. It must be that some unconscious part of your mind believes you are mortal, and weak. That part of your mind is holding you back."

"I'm not holding myself back," she said. "The fish were an accident, and I'm not sure how I made these animals."

"Hm," he said. Then: "Let's try this." He took her by the wrist and made a wave of his other hand, and she felt a jerk and then saw, with no small amount of vertigo, that they were on top of the alcalá. Nearby was the dome of Asmel's study. It was indeed visible from the outside, at least from close up.

Toba made a squawk of protest and clung to Asmel's arm. "What do you plan to do?" she shrieked.

"Only this," he said, and lifted Toba in his arms, so quickly that she could not even think to protest, and, while she sputtered in surprise, threw her off the roof.

+ + · + + + +

IT WAS WIDELY known in the streets of Rimon that if a woman was cursed with a violent husband, the person to see was Elena Peres.

She could not *cure* your husband, of course; that was a lost cause, but she could ease the way a bit. If you knew your husband was likely to raise his hand to you when he was drunk, you simply slipped a little of Elena's special concoction into his wine and he went to sleep instead. By the time he woke, he was too groggy to think of hitting you.

The downside to this, of course, was that one might overdo Elena's remedy, and then you'd find yourself with a sot of a husband who could not work enough to pay the rent, but even that was a small price to pay for not being beaten senseless on the regular.

It was a sideline she'd inherited, along with her ample figure and her keen mind, from her mother, though she hadn't pushed the business in earnest until after Toba's birth, when money had become a desperate concern. Once they'd spent their savings ensuring that Toba was first legitimate and second alive, the Pereses had found themselves in need of more of an income than Alasar could provide teaching languages. It turned out there was a high demand for Elena's services, and she went out—under the pretext of writing letters for the ladies of the town—and peddled her sedatives, advising her clients to start with a weak formulation and then work up to more only if necessary. Her name was whispered from sister to sister, across mikvehs and in church services, and even in the private gardens of the Arab nobles, where husbands were less likely to turn to drink, but were still husbands nonetheless, and therefore sometimes needed pacifying.

So Elena had a fair bit of experience dosing men. Usually a few hours' sleep was enough to take the wind out of anyone, and she could guess at a glance a man's weight—based on his height, his girth, and whether he was prone to muscle or fat. She knew she hadn't underdosed

Naftaly; on the contrary, she'd been very worried she'd given him too much, which meant he'd somehow burned the amapola off much faster than he should have.

She'd only known one other person who burned off amapola so quickly—so quickly, in fact, that it barely worked for more than an hour—and that person was Toba.

The old woman attempted to haul Naftaly to his feet, strain etched on her face.

"Give him to me," Elena said. "You can't lift him."

"I won't give him to you, you devil cow!"

"Shall we cut him in half?" Elena shot back, taking him back from the old woman. He was no great weight for her, only she had nowhere to go besides into the hills.

Seeming to concede her inability to escape with the boy, the old woman let him go. "Where had you intended to go, in this ingenious plan of yours?"

"The inn," Elena said. "But we can't go there now; the guards all know my face."

"They don't know mine," the old woman pointed out. "I can move him, now that he's upright. Why don't I take him, and you can go find a ditch to die in?"

"You have enough money to stay at the inn? And for the wagon to Merja, and the ship?"

The old woman's mouth made a very sour thin line. "I won't believe you have so much, either. Antonio deSantos won't pay you now, even if you could find him again, which I very much doubt."

With her free hand, Elena drew a small purse from the bodice of her dress and calmly displayed it. "I assigned myself a small down payment," she said. "In case of emergencies."

The old woman said, "Is there anyone you won't wrong?"

"It was a reasonable course of action," Elena said.

"You're wicked and foolish," the old woman said. "It's an unforgivable combination." To the boy, she added, "It might be a good time for you to have a vision of something useful, like a secret shepherd's hut."

Elena startled at this statement, but Naftaly said nothing. "Save your breath," she told the old woman, "for climbing."

TWENTY

TOBA FOUND HERSELF hurtling face-first toward the earth, and tried to call up some magic—maybe a conjuring of something soft to land on, would be helpful—but she was as hopeless as ever, and a second later she hit the ground with a force she thought would break every bone in her body.

She lay there, panting and cataloging her many pains for a few seconds before cracking her eyelids open. Asmel was just then lighting on the ground next to her, floating down feet first as if he were a very large bird.

"What is the matter with you?" she spat.

"Hm," he said again. "Well. That's *very* interesting."

Finding that, in fact, her bones were not broken, she forced herself to sit up. "Why did you . . . how did you—" she stopped and looked at Asmel again. There was a shimmering about him, on either side, and Toba realized that he had wings. Wings of air.

"You have wings," she said.

"At the moment," he replied. He lifted a hand and the wings went up like wisps of smoke.

"I don't have wings," she said.

"That's abundantly clear," he replied. "You do have something else, though."

"A headache?" she said. "Several broken ribs? Is that what I have?" She struggled to her feet, dusting her backside. "You starve me, you hurl me off the roof. If your next plan is to light me afire, I'll save you the trouble—it won't help."

He pointed to something a little ways away. Someone. The someone sat up. It was Toba.

"What is that?" Toba asked.

"You," Asmel said flatly.

The other Toba said, "What have you done to me?" To Toba, she said, "Who are you?"

"I'm . . . I'm . . . what? What is this?" She pointed an accusing finger at the second Toba. "Get rid of that, please, I'm not done yelling at you yet."

"I can't," he said. "She's not an illusion, and I didn't make her." He patted a large stone, causing the center to sink in, making it look like an enormous upholstered chair, and sat on it. "Only you would conjure a buchuk instead of wings when falling from a great height."

"A buchuk?" she said. "You're saying I've twinned myself?"

"You're the buchuk," the other Toba said. She made a releasing gesture at her, which the first Toba thought was very rude. Nothing happened, anyway.

"If you're wondering which of you is the real one—"

"I'm not," Toba said.

"Be quiet," the other Toba said.

"The answer is that I can't say—you are identical in all respects. She is your twin. The only way for an outside party to tell which of you is the clone is to end the flow of magic that sustains the alternate."

He waited. Nothing happened.

"You really don't know which of you is the original?" he asked.

When neither answered, he got up from his granite chair and approached them, first one Toba, and then the other. He drew out the arm of the second, revealing a substantial rent in her sleeve where she'd landed badly. "You are the original," he said. "She split off just before you hit the ground, which is why your fall was harder."

The first Toba made a releasing gesture. She did it again. She closed her eyes and tried to concentrate. Still nothing.

"She's still here," she said. "And don't tell me to swallow her. The fish were bad enough."

"It's taking a great deal of magic to keep her alive," he said. "You'll exhaust yourself eventually, and when you pass out, she'll go. Probably."

"I'd rather it didn't come to that," she said. "Isn't there something quicker?"

He rubbed at his chin, and then approached the second Toba. He reached out and took a lock of her hair in his hand, and before she could object, cut it off. Glancing back at Toba, he said, "Of all the things. I'm afraid there's nothing quicker."

Toba put her hand to her own hair, and discovered, with some dismay, that a substantial chunk was missing. The second Toba examined the blunt ends of her own hair and demanded, "How dare you?"

"For as long as she's here," he said, "she's effectively you. You see how dangerous this is. If she breaks an arm, yours breaks in the same spot. If she dies, well, you understand."

This sounded very bad to Toba indeed. "So it's worse than the fish."

He reached out and tugged on the second Toba's hair. The first yelped and put her hand to her scalp. "It's much worse," he said. The first Toba thought of kicking him in the shin. The second Toba did it, but not nearly as hard as she wanted to.

The Tobas exchanged a glance. "So does that mean," the first said, "that if you tell her something, I'll know it? Is it as if I can be in two places at once?"

"It's a limited bit of magic," he said. "Hard to maintain over a distance, unless you are very, very strong, and even at close range it will exhaust you quickly. What were you thinking?"

"When you threw me to my death?" She peered at her scraped elbow; it wasn't really much of an injury, and the skin was already knitting back together. If she had broken a bone, she wondered if that would have healed itself as quickly. She decided not to bring it up; lest Asmel decide to test that, too. "I wasn't really thinking anything. I was trying to summon help."

"Just *help*?"

"I'd like to see you come up with a more coherent thought when the ground is hurtling toward your face," she said sourly. "What are we going to do with her?"

"I could finish the translation," the second Toba put in. "While you continue being useless at magic."

Toba frowned. She actually enjoyed doing the translation. And anyway, if the second Toba did all the work she'd been contracted for, she'd be the one getting paid, at the end. And if she ceased to exist before that, where would the money go? "I have a better idea," she said. "The library is a shambles."

"It is not," Asmel said.

"It is," the second Toba agreed. "There's no organization at all; I don't know how you ever find anything." She nodded. "I can sort the books for you, some way, while you continue throwing her off buildings, or whatever else you have planned."

"I don't expect you to persist for more than another day," he said. "I see no reason for any of this, but if it pleases you, I won't forbid it."

So the Tobot—both of them—went back to the library. "We shall have to find something to call you," Asmel told them.

"I'm Toba," the second Toba said. "I won't be called otherwise."

"Fine then," the first said. "We'll call you Toba Bet. Will that do?"

"I suppose," Toba Bet replied. "I'm going to sort these by place of origin, I think that makes most sense. I'll start by drawing a map of the shelves, if you can spare me some paper."

"You know I haven't any extra."

"Yes, but—"

Barsilay came in bearing Toba's lunch, and seeing the two of them, stopped in his tracks. "Just what we need," he muttered, then: "Which of you is eating this lamb?"

Toba Bet glanced over at Toba, and Toba realized she had a vague sense of what the other woman was thinking, and it was this: *If I am only to exist for the next day, then I'm at liberty to do whatever I like.* She smiled. Toba said, "Please don't—"

But Toba Bet was already stalking toward Barsilay. "I'll take it," she said sweetly, and then she took the tray from Barsilay's hands and upended the entire affair over the top of his very surprised head.

✦ ✦ ✦

NAFTALY REGAINED THE use of his legs a few minutes later, and he and the women made their way quickly into the hills, until the old woman had fallen so far behind they were forced to stop for the night. The guards, Naftaly decided, must have followed the horses. Or else, in possession of the deSantos fortune, they were not inclined to do the labor of chasing them down. He hoped Katarina had escaped, at least until it dawned on him that she'd known Elena had been planning to drug him, and had failed to warn him.

He decided that he disliked Elena a great deal.

However, she was the only one of the three with any money. They slept in the wild that night, beside a fire they made from dry brush gathered by Elena, lit with a flint and the short knife the old woman had taken off some poor sot back in Eliossana.

Naftaly felt remarkably recovered when he woke the next morning, the last traces of Elena's death-miming tincture having burned their way out of his system. He cracked his eyes as the old woman kicked dirt into the remaining embers of their fire, and slowly sat up. Elena was not nearby.

"She's looking for water," the old woman said. "Though I told her not to bother; neither of us will drink anything she brings."

Naftaly grunted an agreeable syllable. "Are you better now?" she went on. "We could make a run for it while she's gone. I doubt she'd be able to catch up to us."

"Where would we go?" he asked. "Did you manage to pick her pocket last night while she slept?"

"I planned to, but I don't think she *did* sleep," she grumbled. "There's something not right about that woman."

"You mean because she poisoned us both?"

"It's more than that," she said. "There's something about her that's *wrong*, do you feel it?" She sat down heavily on the fallen tree Naftaly leaned against. "A woman her age shouldn't be able to stay up all night, least of all after running for her life and climbing a mountain."

"Didn't you stay up all night? Or how else do you know she didn't sleep?"

"Well," she said. "Not entirely."

"Then perhaps she slept when you did."

"When I woke this morning, she was in the exact position she'd been in last night, down to the wrinkles in her skirts. I'm telling you, there's something unnatural about her."

Elena appeared up the rise of the hill a moment later, carrying a clay pot balanced on her ample hip. "I've found water," she said. "There's a stream not far from here."

Naftaly did not ask where she'd found the pot. He thought he was probably better off not knowing. Elena set it on the ground between Naftaly and the old woman, who did not attempt to drink from it.

"You're dehydrated, and you're old," Elena said. "You should drink before we begin." When neither moved, she added, "For heaven's sake," cupped her hands, dipped them into the water, and drank several gulps herself. "There, does that satisfy you?"

"You could be immune to whatever you've put in it," the old woman said. "I've heard of such things."

"Fine," Elena said, hitching up her stockings. She reached into her pocket and pulled out the purse she'd got from Antonio, tossing it to Naftaly. "I'll not hold you hostage. Go south. Find a ship, if one will have you. But first, I will ask you this: do you ever dream of people you know?"

The old woman said, "What nonsense is this?"

But Naftaly looked at Elena for a long moment before replying, "I dream of people I know sometimes."

"Sometimes," she said. "Not often, I'd wager, and I'd also wager you dreamed of either your mother or father, but not both. Which was it?"

Naftaly felt as if the amapola might be taking hold again. He said, "My father."

"And do you really not know why?"

Naftaly said, "You have those dreams too. You visit that place, too."

"Not me," she said. "But my mother did."

"Stop listening to her," the old woman said. "She's trying to confuse you again. Go on now!" she snapped at Elena. "Go running off into the mountains by yourself, you'll get no sympathy from us."

Elena looked at Naftaly for a long moment before saying, "You said the woods were north of here, just beside the road?" Naftaly nodded, and she turned her back on them and began walking north.

"What was she carrying on about dreams for? Is she mad?"

Naftaly was fairly sure she wasn't mad, but seeing as his mouth was dry as ashes, he drank as much water as his hollow stomach could hold. When, after a few minutes, he hadn't died or been rendered insensible, the old woman followed suit.

"I have to follow her," Naftaly said, getting to his feet.

He offered the old woman a hand and pulled her up. She said, "For what purpose? We have money now."

Naftaly did not know how to explain his lifetime of trying to wrestle answers from his father, who never shared anything beyond admonitions to keep things quiet. Despite his father's exhortations, he *had* asked others about the dreams during his childhood—a few times, before he'd learned not to bother—with an off-hand remark here or there, probing for crumbs of recognition in his friends or neighbors. He never received anything beyond blank stares and a bit of recoil once Naftaly had accidentally identified himself as strange. Likewise, he'd poked about in books, when he'd come across them, but he'd never found any information at all.

But Elena knew about the dreams. She knew what they meant, and she could tell him, and more than likely he'd never have another chance to learn.

"The money will still be in my pocket in an hour," he said. "I need to speak to her."

Naftaly helped the grumbling old woman back to the road and scanned for other travelers: the Inquisition looking for them, Jews headed south, or bandits looking for an easy mark. Satisfying himself there was no one around, he offered the old woman his arm to lean on, which she did, heavily.

"Are you all right?" he asked, because she seemed to be limping a bit on the left.

"You try sleeping on the ground when you're my age," she said. "See how it feels. Didn't the witch say she was going north?"

She had, only Naftaly saw right away what the old woman meant; Elena was nowhere in sight.

"She must have walked past the top of that hill," he said, knowing it made no sense; the hill had to have been more than a mile ahead, toward the horizon, and Elena had only started minutes before them.

It was hours later when they caught up to her, glaring at a spot on the ground toward the side of the road. Upon inspection, Naftaly could see that it was the mark the old woman had made with a handful of white stones, to indicate where they'd come out of the woods. Only there was no sign of any wood—of any great trees at all—anywhere in sight.

"I don't understand," Naftaly said. "This is definitely where we were. Where is the forest?"

"Perhaps it's some sort of illusion," Elena said slowly.

The old woman said, "What illusion could disappear a forest? This was more than three trees in a row."

"It's moved again," Naftaly said. "Like it did that night. We didn't walk out the wrong side; it moved."

"Forests," said the old woman, "do not move."

Elena said, "This one did." She sat down heavily in the dirt. "I can't leave."

The old woman waved a hand expansively at the nothing in front of them. "You propose spending the next week traipsing the countryside playing hide-and-seek with a wood? There is nothing here!"

"No, there's no finding it that way, I think. It will require asking the Maziks where they've put it."

"The Maziks," the old woman scoffed. "And how do you propose to ask them anything?"

"I can't," Elena said. "But the boy can."

Naftaly said, "What do you mean?"

"I've already given you half the money from Antonio. If you do this for me, if you help me find the gate again, I will give you the rest. There's enough there for you to get a ship anywhere in the world and more besides."

"And what will you do, when he has all the money?" the old woman asked.

"I'll make do," Elena said.

"How is it you think I can speak to a Mazik?" Naftaly asked. "I've never so much as met one."

"The place you dream of each night is the Mazik dream-world. Every person you have ever dreamed of is a Mazik, or part. Ask one of them."

Naftaly thought about this revelation. If he dreamed inside a Mazik dream-world, the implication had to be that he himself was part-Mazik, and his father had been. Was that why they had the book? Naftaly quickly patted his coat to make sure it hadn't been taken while he'd been unconscious—he felt a surge of guilt that he hadn't bothered checking before. It was there.

Did the other Maziks have those strange eyes, even when they were awake?

Did this make him a bad person? He didn't think so.

"My father knew," he said. "I think. Only I think he was ashamed."

"It isn't anything to be ashamed of," Elena said. "It only *is*. The gate you saw connects the Mazik world with ours every full moon, and that was where Toba went."

He held out his burned hand. "The last Mazik I dreamt of gave me this."

She bent to examine his hand. "Hm," she said. "Well, don't ask that one."

TWENTY-ONE

"I'VE RECEIVED AN invitation to court tonight," Asmel said, tossing a scroll onto the library table, which Toba could see was covered in glittering golden writing which she still could not read. This irritated her as much as anything else she'd endured, but her requests for lessons in written Mazik had all been met with incredulity. "No one will kill you," Barsilay had said, "for being illiterate." And then he'd muttered something about her inability to prioritize, her lack of focus, and the sad state of her figure.

That morning, Barsilay had been attempting to parlay Toba's mud-animal skills into something more useful; for the past several hours, she'd been trying to create a pen that could write by itself. Her efforts had been met with no success at all. She was very sweaty, extremely tired, and in possession of one entirely non-sentient reed pen.

Toba Bet had begun her task by using up most of Toba's remaining paper making lists and drawing a map, and then, when she realized she'd missed several shelves—a second map. The far end of the table was covered with stacks of books she'd pulled down. Toba had a vague notion of what she was trying to accomplish, but mainly she was working very hard to block her thoughts out, because they were distracting her from what she was doing. From within the shelves, they could hear the sound of her singing some bawdy song she'd made up to entertain herself. She'd developed a fondness for the word "bollocks," and where it did not rhyme, she simply forced it through.

"I never appreciated how inhibited you are," Barsilay said to Toba. To Asmel, he said, "You can't mean to take her to court."

Asmel merely took in the scene . . . girl, pen, books, miserable heir, and the food that Toba now always had in arm's reach, and shook his head. "The other is still here?"

"Indeed," Barsilay said. "And she's worse than this one. Can we please kill the spare? I didn't agree to feed two."

"I hear you," Toba Bet called, halting her song. Then: "He's ashamed to admit that I'm the one he prefers."

"No you are not," he muttered. To Asmel, he said, "You must leave her here. It would be a disaster."

"You know I can't," he said, more to Toba than to Barsilay. His tone, since the creation of Toba's buchuk, had altered; less angry and more . . . Toba was not sure what it was more of. Perplexed, she guessed. Puzzled. He seemed to have come to the conclusion that her lack of magic really was, as she'd maintained, outside of her control. She was not a bad pupil; rather, she was a strange creature that didn't seem to follow the rules he took for granted. He simply didn't understand how she worked, and he'd decided this was not her fault.

"The Infanta will be in attendance," Asmel went on, "and she's already told everyone I have a girl here. If I don't bring her, La Cacería will be at the door tomorrow."

"Can't you simply turn down the invitation?" Toba asked. "Say you're busy or unwell?"

"One does not turn down an invitation from the King," Asmel said.

From within the shelves, Toba Bet sang, "Bollocks to the King!"

Ignoring this, Toba said, "So it's a summons."

"Yes," he agreed. "It's a summons. For tonight. They know you're here, so both of us will have to go, and you will have to rise to the occasion. Can you?"

Toba took the challenge full on the chin and said, "No."

+ + + + + +

TOBA'S GOWN WAS so sheer she could feel the air moving through the fabric.

Barsilay had insisted this was, in fact, a very modest dress. Maziks in general did not go in much for modesty, he'd told her, and the two of them had argued a great deal about the height of the neckline. He'd finally agreed for more coverage, mainly because he'd decided it was best to cover her arms and her clavicle, both of which still showed signs of unusual slimness. He'd also forced the issue of lifts in her slippers, giving her an extra inch of height which Toba thought hardly made a difference, and a few extra swirls of fabric around her backside to give the illusion of robustness in that area.

"I'm small and thin," she told him. "No outfit will convince anyone otherwise."

"You're small and thin for a human," he told her. "For a Mazik, you look positively blighted. If only you'd eaten more."

"I ate what you gave me," she shot back.

"There was an entire leg of today's pheasant left over!"

"No one could eat a whole pheasant!" she said. "And anyway, it was lentils, and no one ever got fat eating lentils."

"You ungrateful creature," Barsilay said, and dramatically swirled from the room, where he met Asmel in the doorway. "She won't pass," he told him.

Asmel gave no indication that he'd heard, but walked into the room, where the shade was finishing plaiting Toba's hair with tiny blue flowers. He stared at her for a moment, looking concerned.

"Well?" she said, finally. "This wasn't my idea, by the way. I have no desire to meet your court."

Asmel sighed. "It's your court as well," he reminded her, "and if I don't present you, it will look more suspicious. But Barsilay's not wrong."

"I can't be other than I am," she said. "Unless you want me to walk on stilts and pad my shift more than Barsilay's already done, this is what we're stuck with."

"I have given this some thought," he said. "I'm tasking Barsilay with starting a rumor about you."

"A rumor? You're going to tell everyone I had some horrible childhood disease that left me a runt?"

"Maziks do not suffer disease," he said. "No. We'll let on that you were on the receiving end of some curse while your mother was carrying you."

"Who would have cursed a pregnant woman?"

"Many people," he said. "It's a story with two advantages. First, it's not so far from the truth. And second, it's dramatic enough both to capture the court's imagination and garner their pity. They'll wonder about you, but they'll be too polite to ask about it directly, and perhaps they won't pry for further explanations."

"Or different explanations," she said. "Won't they ask who my mother was? Or my father?"

"I've given you a pedigree," he said. "You are Barsilay's cousin, recently arrived from P'ri Hadar. Your grandmothers were sisters. Your father was no one of consequence."

"Meaning I'm a bastard," she said.

"All the best lies have a bit of truth," he said. "I suggest you remember that; it might save your life someday."

\+ + + + + + +

IT WAS STILL daylight when Toba accompanied Asmel to the palace of the Mazik King. Barsilay had gone ahead earlier, presumably to begin stoking the fires of rumor, so it was only the two of them alone in a coach made of blond wood, pulled by six blond horses.

Toba had seen Asmel raise the coach out of a few stray timbers. She didn't know where the horses had come from, but they were odd . . . from the shoulders down, they resembled any normal horse Toba had ever seen, but their heads were the heads of large goats, with short horns, and square-pupiled eyes which were far too close together, on the front of the animal's face, like an owl, or a person. She'd thought at first they *were* just strange goats, but when she'd approached they'd whinnied rather than bleated. Toba wasn't sure if it was better to categorize an animal based on its speech rather than its appearance, but Asmel had called them horses, so she decided it must be.

Earlier, Toba had taken the sapphire from her amulet and had the shade string it on a silver chain by some invisible tether that made it appear to float beneath her throat. She fingered the stone absently; since the destruction of the amulet, it no longer felt cold, but warm, and while the amulet had blighted her, the stone itself was so familiar it gave her comfort. Anyway, Asmel had told her sapphires were not naturally occuring in the Mazik world; that all corundum gems on this side of the gate were red, and blue stones were rare and imported. Toba thought an exotic gem made her look more like a lady, and less like a scrawny girl in a padded dress.

In the coach, Asmel sat on a blue silk cushion and made no attempt at conversation.

"Is it very far?" she asked.

He looked up from the window, where he'd been focusing his attention. "The King keeps his summer palace north of the city," he said. "We have only to take the road around. It won't be long." Giving her his full attention, he added, "I am trying to determine what you need to know of Relam, when you meet him."

"The King? Why should I know anything of him at all?"

"To avoid sinking yourself at first introduction," he said. "Relam has a bit of a delicate ego."

"Sounds like a bad characteristic in a king."

"Extremely," Asmel agreed. "Here are two significant facts you must bear in mind: the first is that Relam is a usurper. And the second is that it's death to mention this."

"Is that all?" she said.

"I'll make this brief: The Pomegranate Throne is only a recent invention, created by Relam after the death of the old Empire. All Maziks had one queen, once, and she ruled from the city of Luz."

Toba said, "But surely you don't mean the same Luz from the fairy stories."

Asmel turned to her in surprise. "You've heard of the city of Luz?"

"Only the tales I heard as a child," she said. "It's where they used to make the tekhelet dye. There's a wall, and the Angel of Death can't go inside, so everyone lives to a hundred and twenty, and then walks outside to die."

Asmel said, "That part *was* a fairy story. Well, there was a wall; that part was true, and it was impossible to get inside the city unless you knew the way."

"There was a riddle," Toba recalled. "*The nut has no mouth*. There was no gate in the wall . . . you had to get there from within the hollow of a tree. That can't have been true, though—what would they have done on market days? Pulled their wagons through the trunk?"

Asmel smiled. "It was only a metaphor—the city was built in the middle of an almond forest, and the forest was enchanted so that you had to know the way in to reach the city, else you would wander for weeks until you found someone who would put you on the right path."

An almond forest. She remembered something else: "Luz is where Jacob saw the angels going up and down the ladder to Heaven."

"That was slightly more than metaphor," he said. "Luz was a gate city." He held up his hands and created an illusion in the space between them: a white-walled city on a plateau; a river running behind it, and tiny imaginary people coming and going from the main gate. "There were two cities of Luz," he said sadly. "One in the older world, and one in the newer; do you understand what I mean?"

She'd read of such things, in the arguments of the rabbis. There was not only one world; the one they inhabited was simply the youngest of several attempts at creation. "This is the older world," she said.

"Yes. Two worlds, connected by the gates and ruled by the law of the Mirror; whatever happens in the younger world—the mortal world—is reflected here, in some way even I cannot fully understand. The Queen of Luz ruled all Maziks, everywhere. After it fell, Relam won his throne through trickery and violence. Do you understand what might be important to such a man?"

Toba thought on it. "Loyalty," she said. "Or at least the illusion of it."

"Yes," he said. He gave his thin-lipped approximation of a smile. "You may show your cheek to me, but do not do so here—if he senses a lack of respect from you, it will be easy enough for him to make you disappear. You want him to find you pleasantly foolish and immediately forgettable."

"I shall be a mouse," she said. "And nothing more."

"There is more," he said, holding his hand out, palm up, and showing her an image of a faceless Mazik clad in blue. "This is the livery of La Cacería. If you see it, keep your distance as well as you can." He set his hand over hers without actually touching it, as if he meant to offer comfort but could not bring himself to complete the action. "Stay by my side. I will look after you."

\+ + + + + + +

THE ALCÁZAR OF the Mazik King was a marvel cut from white marble. The floor in each room held a mosaic of geometric shapes, and Toba could not say if they'd been created with real stone or by magic, since she could see no seams. The walls were adorned with stone latticework, and every few feet was a light-stone twice the size of those in Asmel's alcalá.

She and Asmel were taken down a hallway and through a peaked doorway, and then down a set of steps and into the courtyard of the King, a paved rectangle surrounded by the alcázar on three sides and empty space on the fourth, where a low wall looked out over the valley below. The floor was set with mosaics featuring the pomegranate tree that was the symbol of the crown of Rimon, with fruit the color of rubies.

At the opposite end from the door they'd walked through was a dais, up seven steps, and at the top was the Mazik King, reclining on a divan laden with embroidered cushions. Flanking him on either side were richly dressed Maziks, some plucking stringed instruments, others amusing each other with small bits of magic—conjuring golden songbirds or altering each other's faces with flourishes of bright color. Whether this was a retinue or the King's own family, Toba could not say. They were of different hues and features: the King was pale; the men she took to be his sons were darker, though she saw no woman who was obviously the Queen, and realized she'd forgotten to ask Asmel if there were one. Floating bowls of quicksilver lined the front of the dais, spinning independently and leaving stars in Toba's eyes. She wondered where Barsilay was.

Toward the back of the dais, the Infanta sat on a jeweled cushion, dressed in vibrant plum, plucking berries from a bowl. At the sight of Asmel, her face hardened. Then she saw Toba and her eyes glittered. Under the Infanta's inspection, Toba felt a bit as if she were leaving her own body, her spirit having decided to take shelter elsewhere. She willed herself to look as unremarkable as possible.

"Asmel, my friend," the King said, extending his hand, which Asmel warily took and kissed. Dark circles under his eyes left him looking decidedly fatigued. "You never come to see us anymore."

Asmel drew into himself, a motion so subtle that Toba might have missed it if she hadn't been watching closely, and she wondered whether the issue was that Asmel hated the King, feared him, or both. She watched his glance light on a younger man seated next to the King: the man from Asmel's private garden, the one she'd seen from out her window the day after she'd arrived. His seat was second-highest to the King's, and Toba thought with some surprise that he must be the crown prince. It was he who had pressed Asmel to marry Oneca and make himself a stronger ally.

Interesting, she thought. Asmel did not seem to hate *him*.

Asmel said, "I'm afraid I've been busy tending to my ward."

The King laughed. "You've become quite a collector of them, I understand. If you're so keen on family, I'd have thought you more eager to marry." The King gave him a pointed look. "My cousin tells me you were less than pleased with her offer."

Asmel smiled tightly; the Infanta glared at him openly. "I am unworthy of her."

"That is true," the King said, while the Infanta tossed her head and pointedly turned her back. "Introduce us to your newest ward."

Toba approached, as she'd been instructed. "This is Toba," Asmel said. "Daughter of Navia."

"Second cousin to your nephew Barsilay, I've been told," the King said. "Though I thought all his people died in Luz."

"Not all," Asmel said.

"Mm. Well," said the King. "Toba. What wonders have you brought for us? Something amusing, I dare hope."

Here was the worst of it: Asmel had explained that when one was presented to the Mazik court, one made an offering of magic for the King. Usually these were great workings, designed to show off one's strength: Asmel's own adonate had been gifted his fourth great-grandfather in exchange for a reordering of the stars into a poem so beautiful the Queen had wept in delight.

Toba smoothed the padding in her dress. "My magic is not so great, Adon," she said, making the effort to broaden her vowels, hide her mortal accent. "But I will amuse you how I can."

Turning to the shade they'd brought with them—Asmel's, not Barsilay's, who still could not leave the alcalá and had been left home with the other Toba—she took a jeweled box and set it on the ground in front of her.

"Trinkets?" the King asked in a long-suffering tone.

"No, Adon," she said. "It's only a bit of earth." And she knelt down and quickly crafted a trio of lions, which roared tiny roars and attempted to climb the steps of the dais, without much success.

The King laughed. "Your ward has brought me toys, Asmel," he said.

"You requested amusement," Asmel said.

"Yes," the King said. Behind him, the two slim young men Toba presumed to be his younger sons were whispering to one another. "I did." One of the lions succeeded in climbing the first step, and the second, before falling and smashing itself back into dirt. "Ah, well, I suppose one does get tired of endless jewels and falling stars." He waved a hand. "Go and make yourself comfortable, Toba b'Navia. Asmel," said the King, "I find myself weary. A footholder, perhaps, would give me ease."

Relam smiled thinly, indicating a cushion at his feet. This would have been a grievous insult at the court of the Emir, even Toba knew that much. Coming from the Mazik King, it seemed to be something equally terrible. The crown prince looked as if it were causing him a great deal of concentration to keep his face blank; his younger brother smirked. Asmel closed his eyes a moment and gave Toba a nod.

Toba bowed, hands in front of her, as she'd been told, and turned to go, quietly sliding away from the King, who rested his slippers on Asmel's lap while Asmel's face went very still and white.

The rest of the courtyard was crowded with Maziks and she could not see Barsilay, who might have helped her. She had not asked Asmel how long they would remain, and in any case, he probably hadn't foreseen being seated at the King's feet like a dog. This was bad indeed. Toba saw a paved path under an arch, leading away from the courtyard, and carefully slipped away.

WHILE TOBA THE Original made her way through the garden of the Mazik King, Toba Bet found herself very much alone in the alcalá, with only the shade for company. She beat it at chess three times before deciding she should really be practicing her magic. She tried three times to change a lentil into an orange. She tried four times to change the color of her dress.

The other Toba had made those mud animals, and the fish, and Toba Bet herself . . . there was magic there, she just had no control of it. She couldn't change anything's form, but she could send part of her magic outside of herself, and she wondered why. Maybe there was no reason. Maybe it was just some retained skill from when Toba had been a child, before the amulet.

She decided to do an experiment, and took up the pen Barsilay had been trying to get the original Toba to animate. She succeeded in encouraging it to write a few vulgar words on the table before she lost the knack of it, but still: a victory. The elder Toba had not been able to do it, not after trying for hours. She was wearing that absurdly filmy dress and swanning about in front of Asmel's lovely eyes, but Toba Bet had used a magic pen to profane the table. So there.

It was still not as good, she told herself sourly. She tried to make the same lentil into a cake, and could not, and she tried to warm up a glass of water, and could not. She was alone, and she did not really want to go back to sorting the books, either. She could see Toba arriving at the palace inside whatever part of their mind they still shared, all those beautiful Maziks, and wished she'd been the one to go, or that Asmel had even considered such a thing.

Then she recalled the papers in the genizah in her chamber upstairs, the ones written in Hebrew, and she wondered if there might be some simple trick she could use on those.

While Toba made mud animals (of all the things) for the King, Toba Bet climbed the stairs to the room she'd chosen as her personal chamber, the shade following at her heels. As she pressed a hand to the phantom brick in the wall, revealing the space inside, she frowned a bit and asked the shade, "How is it that in all this time, neither Barsilay nor Asmel ever found these papers?" She tapped at the wall. "Did Barsilay ever come in here?"

On its slip of paper, the shade wrote, *Yes.*

"So he has seen these papers?"

No.

"He never found it?" Toba Bet was not sure how that could be; the brick was noteworthy because it attracted no dust, and she'd opened it easily enough. It was strange, but the shade wasn't useful enough to tell her more than that.

Taking a light-stone from the table, she peered inside the genizah. The page on top contained a few lines setting the time of a meeting at the moon, and then a signature: Tamar of Luz. It had been the closing of a letter.

Giving it a very stern look, she said, "I would like you to hold together and not disintegrate while I pick you up." Then carefully, she touched the edge of the paper with a fingertip, and closed her eyes, and told it very firmly that it was paper and not dust and needed to stay that way.

She held her breath and picked up the paper.

It stayed whole.

Beneath it had been another page, and Toba removed that from the genizah, too. It was another letter, written in the same Hebrew script she had to strain her eyes to read, but she *could* read it:

23 Sivan, Year 493 of the Second Age
Our Dearest Marah,

It is with great regret that we see you leave us. As our friend for three of our generations, you must understand our sense of loss. We do, however, take into our heart Tarses b'Shemhazai as your replacement envoy.

Per your earlier question: we have continued your work on combining our magic with that of your people, carried out by the few half-Maziks among our ranks. Dawid ben Aron in particular has developed quite a hand at this sort of work. He asks me to tell you that he has been working on your suggestion of transmuting objects into written words, and has thus far managed to put an entire lentil into a paragraph. He's found that Mazik speech rendered into human script seems to be most successful for this task; perhaps a working of both magics requires the use of both languages? He is trying to teach the method to some of the rest of us, as being half-Mazik he does not really need the technique as we do. So far, it mainly eludes us, though I myself managed to charm one of my eyelashes into a very well-rendered sentence for a full minute before it turned back again. I hope this will eventually be as successful as the memory spell you and I developed together in my younger days. Do those years seem so far to you? I do wonder how the passage of time affects your recollections. I was so much younger then, yet you are ever the same. And in a few years' time when I am gone, you will remain the same, still.

I will ask your Tarses to continue to pass my letters to you in Rimon, as I fear I may not see you again in Luz, either your version or mine, during what remains of my short life.

I remain your faithful friend,
Tamar of Luz

Toba Bet set the paper aside and told the book the same thing: "You are a book and not dust," and opened the cover.

This, alas, was written in Mazik. She put it back into the genizah along with the paper, and went to sit by the window and think.

The letter had been written by a mortal, in the city of Luz, and in Luz there had been half-Maziks that were not in hiding. At least some of these seemed to be working with a Mazik called Marah, who was an envoy between the mortals and Maziks—*working for whom?* Toba Bet wondered.

Marah—Barsilay had mentioned her. He'd said she would understand Toba's magic. But Asmel had said all her books were long gone. Was she gone, too? If she was a Mazik, she ought to be alive, somewhere, if Toba knew where to look.

The book vexed her, but there was little she could do about it.

She went back down to the library, to see if she could find any reference to Luz or Tamar of Luz or Dawid ben Aron.

\+ \+ \+ \+ \+ \+

THE GARDEN PATH was set in a series of patterns Toba found delightful: first a circle, then an arc shaped like a bow; triangles, squares, pentagons and so on until the shapes had eight sides and then were punctuated by a pomegranate tree before beginning the sequence again. She stepped on each in turn, passing one pomegranate, then three, then six, until she was halfway between the palace and the valley below: she could see the stone retaining wall above her, if she looked back. She wondered what might be at the bottom, if she kept going. She was far enough now that she could no longer hear the music in the courtyard, or the sounds of Mazik laughter. The path here was overgrown like it wasn't used much, and she had to push branches of flowering trees out of her way as she walked. Rounding a bend in the path, she was surprised to find a small building ahead.

Not a building, more a pergola: all four walls were open, held up by posts at each corner and latticed buttresses, and a high peaked roof the color of the leaves, which was why she hadn't noticed it before. It was surrounded by overgrown flowers the size of her palm, shaped like bells, with petals in a purple and white checkered pattern that seemed unlikely to be natural. She stopped to smell one and got a face-full of yellow pollen for her trouble. It smelled familiar, though . . . what was it? Citrus? It reminded her of Barsilay, somehow, who always smelled like very expensive perfume.

Her heeled shoes pinched and they were dusty besides, so she left them behind as she gingerly walked up the slim steps; the ceiling was held up with brightly painted beams that hadn't faded from the weather, but the cushions on the floor smelled faintly of mildew. Set between these were a half-dozen eight-sided tables with silver inlay; one of these had a chessboard atop it, the pieces still assembled in some half-finished game. She admired the set-up for a minute, noting that black was losing badly; she moved a white rook forward and took a poorly placed bishop, mating the king. The piece felt cool in her hand; carved from ivory or whatever reproduction some Mazik had imitated with magic. The rook had a swirled shape, as if someone had twisted several ivory strands like clay, shaping the tops like little domes. At the top of each was a window, and when she peered into one, she could see a person inside, as small as a grain of rice. A tiny Mazik princess.

The floor, under the cushions, was set with another mosaic, the same one she'd seen repeated in the courtyard and on the pathway of the pomegranate tree, writ larger, so that if she'd lain down, the tree would have stretched taller than she was. The branches reached out to brush the edges of the floor and were laden with ruby fruit and blossoms. The part nearest the steps featured twisting roots in dramatic curlicues.

It was a salon of some kind, though it didn't seem to have had much use lately, and Toba wondered why it had been abandoned. Toba preferred it to the upper courtyard; less spectacle and more elegance, with flowers instead of bowls of quicksilver. She could imagine playing a game of chess here, and drinking some fancy Mazik tea, and listening to birdsong. She picked up a wine-colored cushion and, finding it passably dry, took it to the edge to beat out some of the pollen settled on the surface, giving it a great whack and finding herself coated with fine yellow dust. Sputtering, she dropped the thing over the railing and wiped her face with the hem of her dress. She imagined she looked dirty and jaundiced together, and swiped at her arms before deciding it was a lost cause, and anyway, she'd been gone too long and should go back to see if Asmel had been released by the King, or if Barsilay had come back from wherever he'd been hiding, whispering dramatic tales of her lackluster origins.

She started across when her foot slipped, and, looking down, she saw that she'd somehow scuffed the surface of the mosaic. Not scuffed, she realized, upon closer inspection: she'd somehow changed it. The flower she'd stepped on had gone from red to white—and it hadn't been only the one flower. There were blotches of white between herself and the stairs, each representing some part of one of Toba's footsteps.

Turning her foot over, she expected to see remnants of red pigment on the sole, but there was nothing but her normal skin. She knelt down and dragged a finger across the image and examined it: nothing, no dust or old paint or glaze. But the colors beneath her finger had changed, as if she'd wiped steam away from a glass.

Dragging the small tables to the margins of the pergola, she tossed the pillows after, and then went back down to her hands and knees and began wiping her palms across the floor, watching in fascination as the cinnabar blossoms went white, and the pomegranates shrank down to smaller fruits the color of pale moss: an almond tree. As she kept working, she watched the color of the bark change, and in the center of the trunk, a knot changed to an open space, the center of which was a white line that ran from top to bottom, and seemed to be lit from within.

A gate, inside the almond tree: an artifact of the prior age.

She worked her way down to the roots, to find tangled within them eleven smaller trees: there, the rightmost, was the pomegranate; beside it, one she knew was fig, then olive, citrus, and some others she lacked the knowledge to identify.

Sitting back on her haunches, she looked down at her clean hands and then the tree. All this had been transformed by Relam after the fall, to show the Pomegranate and not the Almond. But if anybody could simply change it back by brushing against it, how had it remained so long?

She realized, after a moment, that uncovering the almond tree in the court of a usurper was probably a bad idea—but she'd wanted so much to see what it was, under the newer mosaic. She wondered if she could put it back, or if she should just quietly leave. And while she wondered, she found herself pulled to her feet by two enormously tall Maziks dressed in blue tunics.

While she gasped in surprise, they dragged her down the steps, and conjured a pillar of white flame that shot into the sky and melted the purple-white flowers, leaving nothing behind but the scent of burned fruit.

The Maziks holding Toba were taller even than Asmel, and their eyes were bright and faces flushed. "Stop," Toba insisted, struggling against the men who held her arms. "What are you doing?"

The man on her right inclined his head back toward the tree she'd uncovered on the floor. "Carrying out your sentence," he said.

"Sentence! For damaging the floor? That was an accident!" Well, it hadn't been, really, but it sounded better. The pillar of flame roared in her ears. She planted her heels in the ground and willed herself not to be moved.

"Damaged?" he said. "Restored, you mean."

"I don't know what you mean by that. Let me go!"

"Just toss her," the second one said. "I'm holding the flame."

"We could just do her hands," the other said, "at first."

"They might hear her in the courtyard—Relam doesn't like to hear the screaming. Just toss her."

"Fine," the first one said, and grasping her by the nape of the neck, forced her toward the pillar, which was so hot Toba could feel her skin beginning to singe.

"Stop," she said, "stop, stop, stop, I'm no one. I'm no one!" Her planted feet were sliding on the ground; she'd failed at even enough magic to hold still. "Asmel will hear of this!"

They laughed at that. "Asmel," one said in her ear, "is holding the King's feet." Her eyes burned with tears from the heat of the flame. Somewhere, in her mind, she heard the psychic whisper of the other Toba: *Scream, you idiot, it's all you have.*

She screamed. The Mazik holding her arm swore, and a hand clamped down over her mouth.

"Hurry up."

"Gentlemen," came a third voice, a new voice, "this will not do."

Toba sagged against her captor. The hand over her mouth was so large it covered her nose, too, and she struggled to breathe. Through the heat haze and her own tears, she saw Barsilay, in a silver coat that looked like he'd been sewed into it.

No, not Barsilay. The voice had been wrong, and this Mazik wore a queue of long, black hair that shone red in the dying light. As her eyes cleared, she could see the differences now; he was shorter than Barsilay, his features not quite so fine. But there was something about his expression.

"She's a Restorationist," the first man said, and indicated the floor. "See for yourself."

"Oh," he said. "This little one? I don't think so."

"Sir," the second man said, earning him a glare. "You see what she's done."

"I didn't mean to," Toba wept. "I don't even know what it is."

"Is she simple?" one of the men asked.

"Of course she is," the red Mazik said. "Were you not in the courtyard just now? She made toys for the King; you honestly believe she's capable of treason? I didn't think you were in the habit of sending simpleminded girls to an unbroken death for the great crime of disrupting a frieze."

"It was a mosaic," Toba muttered, hoping to sound foolish. Being foolish was good, if it meant not being burned.

He smiled indulgently. "Was it?"

The soldiers said, "We can't simply let her go and pretend we saw nothing."

"I see," he said. He stalked back toward the pergola, lighted the steps, and passed his hand in the air over the floor, restoring the original image. "Now can you pretend?"

When they made no answer, he said, "Alaunts should not be patrolling unsupervised. Who is your commander?"

"Sir," came the reply.

"If you leave now," he said, "I won't tell him I found you about to burn a girl without oversight. Go on," he said, in a long-suffering tone. "Hunt bigger game; this little rabbit's no meal for the likes of you." He flicked a finger at the pillar of flame, which extinguished itself.

The Mazik holding her arms released her, and Toba slumped to the ground. "Go on," he told them. "I'll tell the girl she shouldn't be meddling in what she can't understand."

One of them said, "As you say," and clipped his heels together, and the two went back down the path, in the opposite direction of the courtyard.

"There now," the red Mazik said, presenting Toba with a handkerchief as brightly embroidered as his jacket. "Dry your eyes; they've gone."

It was too splendid an item to blow her nose with, but Toba did it anyway.

"That was a bit of bad luck, your coming upon that image. I suppose you'd taken your shoes off?"

She nodded a little uncertainly.

"Only a Luzite could have revealed what was underneath, and there aren't so many of those in Rimon any longer, besides your cousin." He picked up one of the singed flowers, and watched it melt to ash in his hand. He wiped his hands clean, shaking his head. "I do apologize for calling you simpleminded. Once an Alaunt gets his teeth into something, it's a bit tricky to convince him to let go."

"It's all right," Toba said, because, as much as it rankled, it was probably better for her if the Maziks did think her simple: No one would expect her to be able to answer challenging questions, or do great works of magic. Still though: if only a Luzite could have uncovered the almond tree, it was a good bit of luck that they'd already told people she was one, as Barsilay's cousin.

Rather too good a bit of luck, she thought. Was she related to Barsilay?

No point in trying to puzzle it out in front of the man in the silver coat; she couldn't very well ask him about other Luzites in Rimon. As for being called a Restorationist: if Relam was a usurper, it only stood to reason there might still be Maziks who wanted to restore . . . something. She said, "I should return to Adon Asmel."

"Asmel is occupied." He reached out a hand and pulled her to her feet. "It will be some time before the King releases him. But I offer my own services, as he and I are friends of long standing."

"I see," Toba said, patting the pollen and ash from her skirt. "In that case, perhaps you could help me find my cousin. I have not seen him today."

"Ah," he said. "Well, if reputation is any indication, Barsilay will be in the baths. He's quite a fixture there, when he's at court. At least that's what I'm given to understand. I'm not often here myself. May I see you there?"

"To . . . to the baths?"

"Ah, you are thinking I mean the public baths . . . if he's in attendance here today, he won't have gone that far. The royal baths are within the alcázar, and not far at all. I would be most delighted to escort you there so that you may find your kinsman."

Toba had long ago learned not to trust a man who took twenty words to say what could be expressed in ten. His speech was like the embroidery on his coat—meant to distract from lack of substance beneath. Still, she did not much want to go anywhere alone, where there might be more blue-clad Maziks waiting to push her into a fire. She said, "I would find that agreeable, thank you."

He smiled, delighted, and clapped once, as a child might do. "Excellent, Lady Toba. Let's leave this derelict spot behind us and vow never to come here again."

From the mouth of a Mazik, Toba disliked the word *vow* a great deal. She nodded stiffly without answering.

"I'm so glad you agree," he said, and began back up the path toward the courtyard; only after a few moments he turned off the pavers and into the wood.

"Sir," she said.

"Don't worry, this way is only quicker," he called behind him. When she caught up, he took her hand and threaded it through his arm. "There, now you are safe, aren't you? My, you're slender. You know, your trick with the mud animals was quite a gambit. When I was presented at court, I conjured a sky full of falling stars at noon." He flashed his smile at her again, over his shoulder. "Sounds impressive, doesn't it?"

Toba nodded once.

"It would have been," he went on, pulling a branch out of the way, "except one of the stars fell into the courtyard and caught some courtesan's dress aflame."

"Really?"

He laughed. "No, not really. It only landed in the fountain. Makes a better story the other way, though, doesn't it?"

Toba smiled. It seemed the safest response.

"How did you do it? With the animals; I've not seen that done before."

"I'm afraid that's secret," she said.

"Ah," he said. "I've never been able to resist a secret." His eyes dipped to her throat and then back up. He said, "What a lovely jewel," he said. "What color do you call that?"

Toba said, "Blue."

He laughed. "What a question; of course it's blue. You have me addled, it seems. It must be your eyes. I've seldom seen eyes like yours."

Toba blinked uncomfortably. She wasn't used to flattery; but then it struck her it hadn't exactly been a complement. Were her eyes odd for a Mazik's? Wouldn't Barsilay have mentioned that?

"They're only brown, I'm afraid."

He scoffed. "Such modesty. Are you certain you and Barsilay are kin?"

She went very stiff.

"I'm only teasing. You must know what a popinjay he is, so fond of his own face I'm surprised he ever looks elsewhere. Ah. And here we are."

They'd come back to some other part of the alcázar, housed in a separate building than the one they'd walked through when she'd arrived with Asmel. This appeared to be older than the part of the palace she'd seen; the scarlet pillars at the entrance were set down into the earth, as if years of sediment had crept up around them. No one else was near.

Toba said, "Aren't you going inside to bring him out?"

"Me, bring him out? Would you deny yourself a visit to the royal baths? I can hardly believe it."

Toba shifted uneasily. "Sir, even if I did go in, I could not find my cousin, seeing as he would certainly be on the men's side."

He chuckled indulgently. "Darling," he said, and Toba wondered when she'd progressed to *darling*, or how she could retreat from it, "these are grander than the public baths, but not so large. There are no different sides for men and women."

"Then there must be different hours," she said.

"No such thing," he said. "So you see, you may go in and find him yourself."

She felt a rush of nausea. Modesty aside, she couldn't risk taking her clothes off in front of a poolful of Maziks. Her figure was too remarkable in its deficiency, even if Barsilay had already told them she'd been blighted in the womb. "I'm afraid I was often only at home in P'ri Hadar," she said. "My background did not allow for this degree of . . . sophistication."

"The lady is shy," he said. "How utterly endearing. Ah, don't be vexed with me, Lady Toba. You needn't disrobe, if that's your concern. And I can escort you. If the sight of nude men fills you with dread, you need only lean on me for protection from so many glittering phalluses."

He was mocking her. But she was meant to be too simpleminded to notice such things, and she did not want to go in alone.

But the man was still talking. "Though you may change your mind once you see what's inside. There is not a more relaxing atmosphere in all the world."

Toba was not about to strip off her dress in front of this man, not for anything, but she nodded, and followed him inside.

Toba had never been to a secular bath, though she'd read accounts of them in Latin and Arabic both. As described, nothing about the experience appealed to her. She followed the Mazik into an inner chamber, where she found the spa matron barking orders at a small army of shades; some were sent to clean, others to warm oil that had grown cold, still others to tend to a lack of towels in the caldarium. "Come," the Mazik said in her ear, and he led her through a keyhole-shaped door into a changing room where clean robes were piled on an ornate set of shelves. Toba picked one up and unfolded it; it was as filmy as silk and as translucent as the thinnest paper. "You may alter the opacity, if you wish," the Mazik said, taking his own robe and disappearing into an alcove. Toba stepped into a different one, and two shades followed her, and helped her out of her dress, which they secreted away somewhere, and proceeded to pin up her hair.

"Can you make the robe less revealing?" she whispered to one of the shades, who touched the garment and rendered it more like cloth. She exhaled as her breasts disappeared from view. This was not so bad. Truly, the robe was not much more revealing than her dress had been, aside from the fact that it was only held on by a silver belt not much sturdier than the robe itself. She stepped out, her scalp complaining from the pins in her hair, which pinched.

The Mazik was dressed in his own robe, which he had not bothered to make less transparent, and Toba resolved not to look farther south than his shoulders. What was the purpose of such a robe? It offered neither coverage nor warmth. It was like a joke, a bold wink at the viewer to gaze his fill. It was somehow, Toba thought, more indecent than being simply bare, which was at least an honest state.

The Mazik took a loose tendril of Toba's hair and slipped it beneath the pin at her temple. "There," he said. His eyes dropped down to her throat, where she still wore the jewel from her amulet. "Don't you think you had better remove that? It will be quite safe here, if you leave it with one of the shades."

Toba's hand moved to cover it. "I prefer to wear it," she said. "It is an heirloom."

"Indeed?" he said. "It's quite lovely. Only, I'd hate to see it damaged. The water is quite hot."

"I've no intention of submerging either it or myself," she said.

"Well," he said. "If you leave it, you retain the option of changing your mind."

"I seldom do. Such vicissitudes are hardly part of my character," she said, and then thought that a simpleminded homebody from abroad would probably not say *vicissitudes*.

"Boldly said, Lady Toba. Let us find your dearest cousin, shall we?"

In the next room, it seemed to be raining from the ceiling. Toba took a tentative step into the mist and found it warm; the water beaded on her skin as she walked the path to the center, where she discovered a tight spiral of steps in the center. These they followed down to a vast room with a high ceiling painted with the night sky and glowing stars, so that for a moment she thought she'd come outside by magic.

Most of the room was a bubbling bath; pillars topped with arches lined the room, separating the main bath from smaller cold pools in the corners. Toba wondered if it were a natural spring or if the Maziks were heating the water by some contraption concealed beneath the floor, and she followed her companion down the steps into the caldarium.

Barsilay was not there.

Instead, there were a few men and women, submerged to their necks in water that smelled of flowers. Steam rose from the surface, and the air was so hot Toba choked on it. She wondered how often a Mazik keeled over and drowned in this cauldron of overheated water, or maybe it only seemed so hot to her because of her human half.

"Isn't it splendid?" the Mazik said, very close to her. "Wouldn't you like to submerse yourself?"

"No," she said. "I'm sure this would be far too hot for me."

"You grow accustomed to it," he said.

"Are you sure?" she said. "It seems to be boiling."

He laughed. "It only comes bubbling from the earth." He gestured up a short flight of stairs to an upper pool Toba had not noticed; it was from this small pool that the water cascaded down into the larger bath. "See, it comes in there."

There was a woman in the upper pool, sitting with the water up to her neck, her face red and devoid of feeling. Toba said, "It must be even hotter up there, then."

"Yes," he agreed. "I imagine it is."

"Is she all right?" Toba watched the woman stare into space. "She doesn't look well."

"She's as well as she can be," he replied smoothly. "Considering who she is and what she's done."

"And who is she?" Toba asked, because she couldn't bear to leave an unanswered question alone.

"A guest of the King," he said, his voice ebullient. "In the technical sense."

It was then that Toba noticed the fine silver collar around the woman's neck. Attached to it was a chain barely broader than a strand of hair, which disappeared into the water. She was a prisoner, or else a hostage. "Her family did some rather unwholesome things during the last turning. Surely you'll have learned about this from your lord."

She wet her lips. "I'm afraid my lord hasn't much of a predilection for politics."

He smiled. The same lock of hair had crept loose from her pins, and he reached out and stroked it between his thumb and forefinger. "I suppose he hasn't. Then aren't you fortunate I can explain what he hasn't. Her house was rival for the throne, along with several others, until they behaved most dishonorably. They violated the sanctity of the baths."

"What did they do?"

The man glanced back up to the hostage, as if considering his words, or else remembering who she was before she was chained here. "It's a bit garish. I don't like to upset you."

Toba fought the urge to walk away. She wanted to know what had happened, even if it meant hearing it from this man who was making her skin twitch. "Please," she said, earning her another smile, small and unmistakably indulgent: she was a child to him.

"It happened like this," he said, reaching to stroke her hair again. "Her house knew their rivals were here, that day, in the baths: it was no secret for them to be partaking in what has always been a place free from old feuds. But her people took advantage. They salted the water. Every last Mazik in the baths died in agony."

Toba gasped a little. He continued: "She's the last member of her house, together with her brother. He sits in the baths in town, and she sits here, to ensure the water remains pure. A fair sentence from our King, would you not agree?"

Toba did not agree, but she nodded, once, because it was safer to give him what he expected. He released the lock of her hair. In a small voice, she said, "I don't see my cousin here."

"Hm," he replied. "I do wonder."

"About Barsilay?"

He tilted his head. "You are so eager for him. How close a cousin is he?"

"I beg your pardon?"

"Are you lovers?"

Toba forgot herself. "No!" she exclaimed, drawing the eyes of the other Maziks in the bath. She lowered her voice, narrowed her eyes. "Are *you*?"

He laughed. "Not at the moment," he said. "I'm most relieved, Lady Toba, to hear your affections are not engaged with him."

"Sir," she said, casting for some response, "I'm afraid I haven't even the benefit of your name."

She'd hoped that would put him on the defensive; maybe even cause him to leave, since it had taken her days to learn what to call Asmel and Barsilay, but he only replied, "Have I not told you?" he said, putting a hand to his heart. "You've charmed me into forgetting my own name. I hope you will call me Tsidon."

When she blinked at the lack of any sort of title, he added, "I'm not so fancy an Adon as your Asmel; my name will suffice. And now that I've given it to you, I shall ask if I may be bold enough to call on you one day?"

There was no way to say no. First because he'd saved her life, and second, because he was a Mazik, and he had a great deal of magic and possibly a temper, and she did not know what he would do with a rejection. He'd come very close again; the film of his robe brushed against her. She said, "I'm sure that would be . . . diverting."

"Diverting," he said. "You are quite the creature." He turned away, as if he might leave, but then turned back, stepping very close indeed, so that his face filled her view. "Since you are newly arrived from P'ri Hadar, you should know there's a tradition in Rimon: when a man and a lady first meet, they agree not to speak of their association until a second encounter. It disinvites gossip."

He was trying to convince her not to speak to Asmel or Barsilay about him. Well, let him think she intended to abide by it. Believing a neutral response to be the safest approach, she said, "I suppose that makes sense."

"Of course it does. Now, no more talk of me, or Alaunts, or almond trees. Let us enjoy the simple pleasures of the baths."

Toba nodded, and Tsidon smiled. "Then you agree," and he touched his thumb to her lips. Her tongue tingled, and she realized only then she'd consented to being bespelled. Her eyes went wide in alarm. He said, "And now it's sealed. Until next time, then, Lady Toba."

From the upper pool, she heard a splash and looked away, to see the hostage's pool filled with ripples as if she'd tried to rise. When she looked back, Tsidon had gone, leaving her only with a burning tongue. She tried to whisper the name: *Tsidon*, and found she could not. A lady trailed by a pair of shades stepped out of the bath and wafted by, skin glistening.

"I beg your pardon," Toba whispered. "But do you know the . . ." She wished to say *the man I was with*, but found she could not. She tried another way: "Did you see where . . ." She trailed off. "I find myself suddenly alone," she managed.

The woman, dark-haired with diamonds in her ears, tilted her head. "You are seeking a companion?"

"Yes," Toba said, and found she could not say more, and was quite worried the woman would think she meant she wanted *her* as a companion, with all that implied.

The woman spared Toba the briefest of glances and said, "Perhaps you can find company in the tepidarium. There will be greater numbers there." She went off through the pillars on the other side of the bath.

Relieved by the rejection, Toba's eyes went back to the hostage, whose hand was tracing shapes on the tile before her. Toba slowly climbed the seven steps to the upper pool.

The woman within was almost as thin as Toba, but her hair was elaborately braided and set with pearls, which seemed odd for a hostage until she realized Maziks would not want an ugly reminder of their vulnerability. They would want something pretty to look at while they bathed, even knowing she was a prisoner. Toba wondered how often they let her out. Creeping closer, she could see what the woman was doing with her hand; she hadn't been drawing random shapes: she'd been writing. Toba skimmed what was on the hexagonal tiles, ten characters, all in Mazik, and Toba thought for a moment she would wring Asmel's neck, or Barsilay's, or both, for not teaching her to read. The Mazik stopped writing and carefully placed her hand back in the water.

Toba stared at the shapes, which began to fill in with fresh steam. "Wait," Toba whispered. "Was that . . . was it a message?"

The woman gave no indication that she'd heard, but when a fresh batch of bathers came giggling down the stairs, she darted out a hand and wiped the tiles clean.

"I couldn't read it," Toba whispered. "Can you tell me?" But by then, the women had reached the bottom of the steps, and Toba knew she could not risk being seen talking to the hostage, especially not by the woman who had just walked into the room, trailed by half a dozen other Maziks: the Infanta Oneca.

✦ ✦ ✦

TOBA SLIPPED ON the steps, falling down the bottom three, and then skidded into the next room—the tepidarium—just as Oneca's voice reached her. She was telling a joke, apparently, because the other women in her party laughed, an obligatory laugh that was the typical response to humor from someone you feared.

Toba was surprised to find herself in a circular atrium, the center of which was a garden where Maziks were ministered to by shades rubbing scented oil into their skin and hair. How had she come outside, without going back up the stairs? She tried to see if they were at the bottom of an excavated site, but it didn't seem so. All she could see was a round portico, and then the garden, and above it, the sky.

In the center was a pool filled with swimming, lounging, nude Maziks, all of whom had turned at her entrance.

Toba had never seen so much bare flesh, and she flushed. A shade hovered in her direction carrying a flagon of oil, and she shushed it away. A second shade approached with a cup of wine, and she took it to have something to do with her trembling hands. Sipping it carefully—it tasted less of grape and more of honey—she realized among the Maziks she was nearest was Odem, mostly naked with rubies in his ears. All the other Maziks in the courtyard were arrayed toward him, even those sitting on the other side of the pool, as if hoping to catch a little of what he might be saying. One of the men at his side said, "Did Tsidon really come here?"

And one of the women whispered, "Yes, and the Prince sent him away."

"Was he angry?"

Odem turned toward the women speaking, and the others silenced themselves. His eyes then fell on Toba, and she bowed. His puzzled gaze lingered a moment and he nodded: a dismissal. Gratefully, Toba stepped back, and caught the familiar sound of Barsilay's voice.

He lay at the far end of the pool, relaxing on a chaise while a shade combed his dark, wet hair and another rubbed oil into his feet. To either side of him were Maziks being similarly attended: a woman whose hair was being braided into coils around her ears, a man arching his neck to provide his shade better access to a tender spot. All of them were listening to Barsilay, who seemed to be regaling them with a humorous story, as he finished, and they laughed appreciatively, and then he saw Toba and his face went frozen for a moment before returning to its easy smile. He beckoned her over, and she went.

"Cousin," he said. "I'd have thought you too prudish for these environs."

Toba had, of course, never laid eyes on a naked man before, and did not know where to rest her gaze. She decided to keep her eyes on the silver ring Barsilay always wore on his forefinger, at least until he moved that hand to rest on his thigh. "Oh dear," one of the other men said. "Is she well?"

"Have you even bathed?" one of the women asked. "You don't look like you've touched water since you arrived."

Toba wet her lips. "It was too hot," she said softly. Her pleading gaze met Barsilay's, hoping the dreadful man would take pity and get her out before she said something truly outrageous, or else Oneca made her way into the courtyard.

"Aw," the woman said. "The poor dear. Let's off with the robe and have a massage."

"No," Toba said quickly. "Thank you."

"Come, there's no need to be ashamed," the man said. "We are all friends, are we not?"

"I'm afraid my dear cousin has exhausted herself today," Barsilay said, rising from his couch. "Dear one," he said, as one might speak to a child, "let's find you a quiet spot to rest."

"Yes," she said, not a little testily. "I'm sure that will be helpful."

He drew her away, allowing a scowl to settle on his face once the other Maziks were behind him. "You made a spectacle of yourself here," he said. "That was poorly done, all of it."

"Would it have been better to parade myself in front of them?"

"By far!" he snapped. "You made more of a scene covered up like that than you would have showing your boney backside."

"Bad enough I had to see a dozen naked men today," she replied. "I was not about to let them see me, too."

"You are trying to appear unremarkable," he said. "When you don't do as the others, you fail. Next time you are in a room with a hundred bare-skinned Maziks, you take off your damned clothes. Your modesty doesn't serve here. And if you don't wish to see naked men, don't come to a bath, Hashem's sake."

"Are you saying there's no boundary I may set for myself?"

"Be reasonable," he said. "Recall what's at stake here. Now where is Asmel? I can't believe he allowed you to come here alone."

She didn't quite know how to phrase Asmel's humiliation, so she told him directly, while Barsilay's face went stony. "I see," he said darkly.

"So I came to find you, else I would have been alone."

Barsilay tied his hair back with a cord, set a hand on Toba's back, and steered her outside. "And how did you find me?"

Toba opened her mouth, and felt the words waft off her tongue before she could speak them. "Someone told me to find you here. Why were you here?"

"I told you, I was spreading false tales about you. This seemed the best place to do it. One likes nothing better than gnawing on a rumor in the bath, especially if it's a bit vicious."

"Don't they think it odd you would be spreading vile tales about your own kinswoman?"

"Hardly. Come; if we're lucky, some triviality has distracted the King and we can collect Asmel."

He tucked her arm into his elbow, rather as Tsidon had done, and led her up a different path in the direction of the courtyard. Toba tried to tell him about the Alaunts, and failed. She tried to tell him about coming to the baths with Tsidon and failed. "How often do you visit the baths?"

"The royal baths? When I'm called to court. The public baths, as often as I'm able. It's quite invigorating. I'll take you next time I go, if you like. Perhaps you'll meet some ladies there."

"I saw the hostage," she said.

Barsilay sighed. "It hadn't occurred to me you would notice the hostage. Most don't, anymore."

They'd stopped under a tree the likes of which Toba had never seen, heavy with glossy leaves, and laden with buds about to burst into fruit. She wondered how many seasons had passed since the hostage had been able to see the ground or the sky. What a life, day after day submerged in scalding water, listening to conversations you couldn't take part in by people who ignored you and only cared if you dropped dead because it meant they'd have to get out of the water. Watching the other Maziks enjoy their leisure while you sat silent and chained among them. She said, "Can't anyone help them?"

He laughed a little, falsely and sadly, and muttered, "Help them."

She said, "I presume from the tale I heard just now that it was La Cacería who poisoned the water, and those hostages are completely innocent of anything at all."

Barsilay lifted an eyebrow.

"And everyone knows this?"

"I couldn't say what everyone knows," he said.

"But you know. And you do nothing to help them?"

"Yes," he said sharply. "I do nothing. I've been doing nothing since long before you were born. Does that satisfy you? Are you superior now, because it occurred to you that someone ought to help them?"

She said, "There must be something that can be done."

"We could petition the King, perhaps? Maybe he's forgotten he's the one who put them there, is that it?"

"I only meant—"

"Or I could go in there and put your new friend over my shoulder, and walk back out? Certainly no one would stop me, is that what you believe? Is your imagination so lacking?"

Toba crossed her arms and looked away.

"You think I enjoy living under Relam's boot? You think I delight in watching my uncle hold his feet? You cannot know. Half the people in the bath could be Falcons and you would never even guess, 'til you were face-down in the water with a wire through your throat, or found in some back room with salt poured in your eyes, and I've seen both, and worse. Maziks burned for nothing in the street while their children clutched their knees and burned right with them; the most apolitical Maziks you've ever seen burned as Restorationists, or accused of teaching magic to humans, or sometimes they didn't even bother to make up a reason. They culled us like cattle, all to put Relam on the throne. And the rest of us can only hope his son is nobler than his father's been, and hope we don't die before we find out."

"And yet you go and frolic in the very water used to torture innocent people," Toba said.

He said, "I go to the baths because Barsilay b'Droer is a man who goes to the baths. Now leave me be."

She turned away from him, angrily pulling the pins from her hair and setting it to rights. Only then did she notice that a lock of her hair—the one Tsidon had caressed—was missing.

\+ + · + + + +

NAFTALY DREAMT OF a vast garden on the top of a hill, overlooking a valley below.

He'd decided to stay with Elena and help her. It was only one night's dreaming, he'd told the old woman, who seemed disconcerted that her companion was some part Mazik, but then shrugged and said, more than a bit grudgingly, "You're a devil, but you're a good boy, so I suppose it's all right."

It wasn't mainly for the money, however, but for what Elena might be able to tell him. Toba, she'd explained, was the child of a full Mazik, and Elena's own line contained Mazik ancestry strong enough that her mother had told her things. Everything his father had kept from him—his dreams, his visions, what they were and what they meant and who he was—might still be within his grasp: clarity, in his life, instead of secrets. Perhaps his visions weren't a sign of benign madness. And if the dream-world was real, as Elena had told him, then the people in it were accessible to him.

He just had to find a Mazik to speak to who wasn't keen on attacking him. And below him, the garden was filled with Maziks, so many his palms prickled at the sight.

All richly dressed, as he was, and speaking quietly to one another as music played from nowhere. To one side, a dais sat empty, except for a flock of tiny golden songbirds the size of large insects that flitted about, singing a song with the timbre of windchimes.

Elena had exhorted him to ask one of these fine Maziks about the gate. But there was no way to do so subtly, with so many all packed so close together. His eyes scanned the crowd for the red Mazik, but these Maziks were all dark.

This was madness. He'd only get himself killed here. *Wake up*, he told himself.

He did not wake.

He looked up to the sky, where the stars were moving too fast; he watched constellations drifting like clouds on the wind.

He decided to leave the garden; he was too afraid. He picked his way down a rocky path leading away from the Maziks until the sounds of the gathering and the birds on the hilltop no longer reached him.

Sitting on the path in front of him was a young man with a queue of dark hair, with one boot off, wearing an amused expression. "Hello, friend," he said. "Are you coming or going?"

It was the man who had pulled him inside, away from the mounted men in blue on the night his father had died—the tall Mazik with the orange eyes. "It's you," Naftaly said.

"Hm?" the Mazik said, still examining his foot. He gave no indication he recognized Naftaly; perhaps he didn't. They'd only been together a few minutes. Naftaly probably only remembered it so well because he was unused to people touching him in dreams, and this man had.

Naftaly said, "Are you hurt?"

"I've only turned my ankle," the Mazik said. "It will right itself in a moment, I think. I suppose I was being too quick in my retreat, but it's bad enough I have to attend those things awake—couldn't stand a night there, too. Paid my respects, you know. I assume you've gone already?"

Naftaly made a noise of affirmation, though he did not know what he meant. Was this a real place?

"So much is turning these days. But I suppose we all succumb eventually, don't we?" The Mazik smiled in a lopsided way that was very deliberately charming. "Everyone thinks himself the exception. Until he can't stand it any longer."

"It?"

"Life," said the Mazik. "What did you suppose we were speaking of? Reality, I guess more like."

Naftaly said, "Are you drunk?"

"I am," the Mazik said. "Quite. There was wine"—he waved a hand—"somewhere in that garden. Didn't you say you were there? Do you think about it?"

"About wine?"

"About the limits of your own immortality."

"No," Naftaly said, fairly sure he'd picked the wrong Mazik to ask about the gate. Non-murderous *and sober*, he told himself.

"I do. I wonder when it will be my turn to give into the fatigue and just . . . dream." He sighed. "Though I suppose I could be the next exception. Besides the Queen of P'ri Hadar, you know. Relic of the First Age and so forth."

"And what is her secret, do you think?"

The Mazik smiled languidly. "There are books written on the subject. Personally, I always thought she lived for spite. Her hatred of Luz has kept her fresh."

"Sustained by an endless grudge?" Naftaly asked, because it seemed wise to pretend he knew what the other man was talking about.

"Something like it. You do have to admire the commitment. They say that when she seized the throne, she threw a celebration that lasted a year."

"I suppose that's one way to earn the goodwill of your subjects."

"Yes, either you celebrated or she killed you. Wasn't much of a choice, really." The Mazik's energy appeared to flag, and he grew quiet.

Naftaly, hoping perhaps he could still steer the conversation toward the gate, said, "May I help you stand?"

"Aren't you the kind one." The Mazik slowly pulled himself to his feet without replacing his boot. "But I seem to be healing. Come, let's find somewhere away from the din. Were you looking for the menagerie? I'm not sure if it's here tonight or not, but I'd hoped to find it."

Naftaly silently followed him. Overhead, the stars continued their frantic movements; Naftaly tried not to look. It made him feel ill.

"An old friend once told me there is a grand menagerie in the human realm," Naftaly said. "At the alcázar of the Emir of Rimon. I've been thinking that I would like to see it."

"From what I've heard, the Emir of Rimon has fled across the sea." The Mazik had slowed his pace, so they walked side by side. He had an elegant profile that looked like it should have been stamped on the side of a coin, and when the starlight lit his face through the trees, his irises glowed the color of sunset. He was tall, and his shoulders were broad, and his ankle must have improved because he walked with a sauntering grace that was almost a dance. He smelled of almond and . . . something else. Orange? No; too floral. It was bergamot, with the almond.

The night air was too warm. Naftaly tugged at his earlobe. The Mazik laughed; Naftaly could not have said why.

Naftaly said, "But I can't believe he decamped with the whole affair. Would have taken an awfully large boat."

The Mazik smiled a little. "A large boat indeed. So why haven't you gone to the human realm to see it?"

"Well," he said. "It's a bit of a chore. With the gate."

"Ah," he said. "Yes, it does move on the other side. But that's really no trouble, provided you know where it will be. It's just a matter of getting a peek at the Codex and checking the date and time. You simply have to find someone with a copy."

The Maziks kept such things written down in a book? The Maziks *had* books? "Is that so?"

"Oh," the splendid Mazik said, "yes, I've done it once or twice. You know, childish exuberance and all that. You must have some friend with a copy, surely?"

"I'm afraid not," Naftaly said.

The Mazik smiled. "Well, now you have. Give me your hand."

Naftaly drew back in alarm, but the other man laughed. "Don't worry, I'm not about to maim you. How else can I show you where to go? You do wish to know, don't you?"

Reluctantly, Naftaly pulled the glove off his right hand and held it out. The Mazik took a fingertip and traced a few lines across Naftaly's palm, which glowed silver where he'd touched him. "Always navigate from Mount Sebah," the Mazik said, marking a point toward the center of Naftaly's hand with a silver circle. "Here is the river. Do you see?"

"Yes," Naftaly said.

He drew a final curve across Naftaly's palm, and Naftaly shivered at the cool touch of his finger. "Here is the path of the next moon. There: that's as much as I can give you."

Naftaly regarded the silver map on his hand. He wanted to ask if it would still be there when he woke, but didn't dare. He did, however, feel a pulling sensation on his arm. He turned sharply, but there was no one there.

"Someone trying to wake you?" the Mazik asked.

Naftaly felt another tug.

"They seem eager, don't they? Aren't you the lucky one." He leaned in close and, in Naftaly's ear, whispered, "Find me again quicker, won't you? It took so long after the last time."

Naftaly could not answer, because he'd woken to the vigorous shakes of Elena.

"I'm awake," he said. "I'm awake, stop."

"I've been shaking you for five minutes," she said. "We were worried something had happened to you—your breathing went all strange."

"I'm fine," he said, sitting up and rubbing at the back of his head. "Five minutes, really?"

"You didn't notice?"

"Not until a moment ago."

"Did you learn about the gate?" Elena asked hopefully.

The details were slipping quickly; he was already forgetting where the Mazik had drawn the moon's path. He held up his right hand; in the center of his palm were the silver lines the Mazik had drawn. "I have a map," he said, touching the markings to see if they would stay. They felt cool to his touch, and electric, like the air before a storm. "It was a gift."

THE COURSER DREAMED that night about the garden of the King, a dream so improbable it nearly made her laugh. She thought at first she'd been summoned by the Caçador for some reason or other, but he was nowhere visible in the throng of richly dressed Maziks parading among the highly scented flowers.

She could not imagine why in the world she'd come there. She couldn't have wished to; she had no use for parties or whatever else this was. She was not even dressed like the other Maziks, but in the dark clothes she always wore that were better suited to her work.

She'd just made the decision to leave and try to go somewhere else—somewhere alone, preferably—when a shadowy figure caught her eye from the roof of one of the lesser pavilions.

It was one of the Falcons, not the Peregrine herself—who knew where she was these days—but one of her lieutenants, a woman remarkable for being a Rimoni, while nearly the rest of the force was from Baobab, as was the Peregrine herself. It was odd for her to be there; minding the dream-world was normally a job of Tsidon and the Hounds. It was also odd that the Courser had noticed her, which meant she'd allowed herself to be seen deliberately, which meant she wanted the Courser to come and speak with her. The Courser circled back behind the small pavilion and leapt to the roof.

The Falcon acknowledged her with a tilt of her head, without looking away from the garden below. "Why are you here?" she asked the Courser, neither hostile nor friendly; simply cataloging information.

No point lying. "I'm not really sure," she said. "I just happened to be here."

"Responding to the King's summons, I suppose," the Falcon said.

"What summons?" the Courser asked.

"Watch a moment," the Falcon replied. Most of the Maziks appeared to be coming and going from the main pavilion across the patio from where they were concealed. "The Prince is in there," the Falcon told her. "With the King. The lesser princes are nearby, too, you'll see them in a moment."

"Why are they all going in to see the Prince?"

"Because they've been summoned, same as you," the Falcon said. "They're swearing an oath to support the crown prince when the time comes."

"Already?"

"The King knows the rumors circulate. He's trying to prevent a coup after he dies, though he swears it isn't imminent."

"Is it imminent?"

"It is," the Falcon said. "He sleeps more than wakes these days already. It is only a matter of time."

"Could he not rally?"

"I'm sure he thinks he will, but you and I know otherwise."

"If this is a summons," the Courser said. "Must I go down there, too?"

"He's not forcing people just yet," the Falcon said. "The summons is to come here only. He's decided not to force the oath itself, yet."

"That's why you're here; to see who goes and who doesn't."

The Falcon nodded. In all this conversation, her eyes had not left the scene below them. The Courser vaguely wondered how she was keeping track. Or what the Caçador would do with the information, when he learned it.

The Caçador, she knew, was hoping to convince the King to replace Odem as heir with one of the King's younger sons, who were far less ambitious and less predisposed against La Cacería. Ardón—the elder—had made a particular effort to make it known he supported La Cacería's work.

It was Ardón, she noted, who was off to the side of the rest of the party, speaking with the Lymer. That was a surprise, indeed. Most of the Maziks at court despised him. He'd killed too many of their friends.

"Is the Caçador here, too?" the Courser asked.

"He came and left very early, before most of the others arrived," she said. "The Lymer has only just appeared."

"Did he swear to the Prince?"

"He did."

Now that was odd, indeed. Why would he swear an oath to support Odem, then make a point of cozying up to his brother? Tsidon leaned in and kissed the prince on the cheek, their eyes met, and then he vanished, having woken himself.

"Hm," said the Falcon.

The Courser wondered why she was making a point of showing her all this.

The Courser's eyes swept the area again. The queue to the pavilion had thinned a bit, and she could see inside. The King sat on a dais, looking quite fatigued for a man already asleep, while the crown prince stood at his left side. A Mazik the Courser knew to be a breeder of horses stepped forward, kissed Odem's hand, and Odem kissed each of his cheeks in return.

A noise caught her ear, closer to her than the pavilion, and she saw the youngest prince engaged in very obvious foreplay with some courtier not a hundred feet from the place his brother was receiving his oaths—a show of disrespect so blatant the Courser could not quite believe it was real.

"Why is he putting on such a spectacle at his brother's oath-getting?"

The Falcon said, "A man that malleable can only be performing so because he's been told to."

The Courser wondered what was being planned here. Clearly the Caçador preferred the younger princes to Odem, but why not intervene before the oaths were granted? Before he himself had made such an oath?

The Falcon briefly tore her eyes from the garden and met the Courser's. "The Peregrine thinks well of you. You are not as friendless as you believe."

The Courser did her best not to react to this information. The Peregrine did not need friends; she had her Falcons. Unless, perhaps, she was worried there might be a split in La Cacería, and she was trying to keep the Courser from falling on the Lymer's side of it. But the Peregrine would have known that was impossible.

The Falcon asked, "Does the Caçador still call you the left hand of the new age?"

She wasn't aware that was common knowledge. The Falcon said, "The Caçador's plans are changing."

That much was obvious. If he'd been planning to replace the prince with one of the younger men, he should not have allowed the oath-getting. He should not have allowed the Lymer to be seen with the prince. And he should not have ordered the youngest prince to make a fool of himself. The Courser said, "What is he planning, then?"

"We don't know yet. But if the Caçador is replacing his best tools, you should be very careful."

TWENTY-TWO

ONE OF THE peculiar things about the destruction of her amulet was that Toba no longer menstruated.

She hadn't been afflicted with the condition often even before she'd come to the Mazik world; it was always spotty and often irregular, but now it had stopped completely. She'd been due for it since just after her arrival, and at first she thought it must be stress. But days passed, and then a week, and now she had some feeling in her bones it would not come back. She would have liked to have asked someone about it, but the idea of broaching the subject with Barsilay was mortifying, and with Asmel, unthinkable. She decided to accept it as another peculiarity of Mazikhood, like the strange eyes, or the agelessness, or the fact that their men grew no beards.

Still, she found herself longing for the comfort of the mikveh, especially now, when the touch of the Alaunts and the view of so much naked Mazik flesh left her feeling unclean. She'd hoped that the other Toba might not be bound by whatever spell he'd placed on her tongue, that *she* could tell Barsilay what had happened, but whatever spell Tsidon had cast seemed to affect them both. The mikveh always left her feeling emotionally tethered, and she craved the feeling badly. Late that night, when she was sure the men would be asleep, she asked the shade if there were any natural water sources very close to the alcalá.

Yes, it said.

"Is it close enough that you could show me?" she asked.

The shade fluttered a little before answering, *Yes.*

Deciding this was good enough, she followed the shade to what turned out to be a stream in the western shadow of the alcalá, under stars bright enough to light the area.

The stream was not deep enough to immerse herself in. Still, Toba shed her clothes, leaving her necklace with the blue stone hanging around her neck, and waded toward the center, splashing herself with the freezing water.

"That looks extremely unpleasant."

Toba splashed backward to find Barsilay—of course it would be Barsilay—throwing pebbles into the stream just above her, perched on a rock like a handsome gargoyle. She made a strangled little shriek and fell into a crouch. "How dare you follow me," she spat.

Uncurling a finger at the shade, he said, "If you don't want me to know where you are, you might reconsider taking bits of me with you." He stretched his legs out in front of him and removed his boots, one and then the other, and dipped his bare feet into the stream. "This is horrible," he said. "Why would you *bathe* in this?"

Toba did not care to explain the situation to him. "Can you leave?"

"Of course I can," he said airily, wiggling his toes, creating tiny splashes that seemed to amuse him. He'd been angry past speaking only a few hours ago. Either he'd forgotten or he was very good at pretending. "There's a salamander just there," he said, pointing his ringed finger to a space to Toba's left. "Under that rock, you can catch it if you like. Eat it, maybe. Humans are always catching things and eating them, aren't they?"

"Why would I want to eat a salamander?"

"Why are you bathing in freezing stream water, when you refused the finest bath in the city? I have no idea why you do anything."

"I would like you to leave!" she said.

"Is that what you're carrying on about?" he said. "Is it because you're naked?"

She spluttered. "Yes!" she barked.

"Huh," he said. "Well you needn't worry on that score. I've as much interest in you as you have in that salamander, and no, it isn't your gender. It's simply that you aren't my sort."

She glared at him.

"Oh, are you offended?"

Toba did not even know anymore. "I am so tired of men," she grumped. "Men in the alcalá. Men in the palace. Men in the *mikveh*—I could murder you all, and I wouldn't even be sorry."

"Little liar, you'd miss me terribly." He got up and walked over to Toba. "I came because I woke and sensed our friend there had gone outside the walls." He lifted the rock to Toba's left, picked up a glistening black salamander by the tail, and held it in the palm of his hand. "Which likely meant you were out here, too, and I was worried." He took the salamander's tail between his thumb and forefinger and placed it on Toba's shoulder. "You shouldn't be out here, it isn't safe."

Toba batted the salamander into the stream, where it quickly burrowed its way back into the mud. "Who would find me here in the dark?"

"I can think of a number of people," he said, a little more seriously. "And you wouldn't want to meet any of them in your present state, believe me."

It hadn't occurred to Toba that someone might come upon her so close to Asmel's alcalá; it seemed so isolated. Looking up at Barsilay over the tops of her bent knees, it dawned on her that she hadn't so much as heard a footstep when he'd approached, and Barsilay was never quiet. The darkness seemed suddenly less comforting than it had been.

"Bring me my clothes," she called to the shade. Only the shade flitted about uncomfortably and did not approach. "Now, if you please," she added.

"It can't go any further," Barsilay said with no small hint of amusement. "It can't go beyond the shadow of the wall."

Toba scowled at Barsilay. "Oh," he said. "You *are* angry. What will you do? That's right, you can't do anything. Not on purpose. How frustrating that must be for you."

Toba imagined Barsilay's head catching fire. When nothing happened, she splashed him with frigid water instead. He shot her an indignant look and waved a hand to evaporate the water droplets from his clothing. "This is my favorite coat," he muttered. "And you've got mud on it."

"If you would leave," she said, "I would not splash you."

"I would be happy to leave, once you're back inside," he said. "Believe it or not, I'm not here to ogle you. I'm here to prevent your head ending up on a pike, and mine alongside it. Do you want all my hard work today to be for nothing?"

"The hard work of enjoying a nude massage with your friends?"

"I never said I enjoyed it," he said.

"Give me some clothes," she seethed, "and I will go back in."

He smiled. "If that is what you wanted, you should have said so. Nicely. With a *please* and a *thank you* and, perhaps a *you're truly dashing in starlight, Barsilay, may I admire your profile?*"

"I'm waiting, you conceited troll."

"But you haven't even told me what kind of clothes you want," he said. "Some parameters—"

"Just give me a sheet to wrap myself in," she said. "I'll dress inside."

"Fine," he said, conjuring a length of white fabric and tossing it at her, where Toba had to rush to catch it before it landed in the water. "You're no fun, though."

BARSILAY FOLLOWED TOBA back inside, through the courtyard, and up to Toba's room on the second floor. While the shade gave her a simple brown dress to wear, he sat in the corner under the window, peering at a mud elephant that lay sleeping on the sill; the other animals had lost their animation the day before, but this one seemed more tenacious. She did not bother trying to send Barsilay away. At least he did her the courtesy of not watching her dress. Perhaps, she wondered, he was drawn to her out of boredom, or loneliness.

Once dressed she cleared her throat, and Barsilay glanced up at her from his spot beneath the window. “You could wear whatever you wanted, and you choose that?”

“I’m not so vain as you,” she said. “Anyway, brown doesn’t show dirt so easily.”

He smiled at the elephant. “Yes, I can see how that would be important to you. But that’s a rather large gem for a woman who claims not to be vain.”

She fingered the necklace. “It’s all I have left of my amulet.”

“The amulet that cursed you? What an odd thing to have formed an attachment to.”

The man was infuriating; if only she could have picked someone else to stand in for her cousin. Except . . . there was a chance he *was* her cousin, if they were both from Luz, and that was such a rare thing in Rimon.

Or he could be more than a cousin. She had no idea how old he was, really. Was there a resemblance between Barsilay and herself? She didn’t see it—he was too handsome, she had to admit, but still, it was possible. “Barsilay,” she said, “could you be my father?”

He barked a laugh into his fist. “Your father? No, sweet. There’s no chance of that; I don’t bed mortals, as a rule.”

“*As a rule* implies you do sometimes,” she said.

“Fine,” he said, “I don’t do it at all. There’s no purpose; you’re all too inexperienced to make it interesting. Now what brought that question on?”

She could not tell him what she’d learned from uncovering the almond tree at the palace—that she was of Luz—because Tsidon himself had told her that. Toba felt her way around the edges of Tsidon’s spell; it would have to be specific in what it forbade, otherwise it would make it too obvious that she'd been enchanted. She parted her lips and tried to skirt the restrictions. "It's only that I have some questions about the pedigree you created for me." There: she'd managed that much. The spell was very specific indeed. She could ask questions, provided they were the right ones. She continued: "I'm meant to be the daughter of your grandmother's sister, sent from Luz." She smiled: she'd said the word. "Are there other Maziks in Rimon to whom I might be related? Won't they wonder why they've never heard of me?"

"No," he said. "I have no family, here or elsewhere, save Asmel, and even he is only my uncle through marriage."

"The rest of your family perished in Luz," she said, because the King had said something like that.

"Yes," he said. "They did indeed, all besides myself and Marah. She and Asmel had no children. They were too often living apart, and Mazik women don't bear children so often as mortals."

Toba cataloged that piece of information for later pondering. She asked, "What happened to Luz? Was it conquered?"

"No," he said. "It wasn't conquered." He conjured an image of a walled city surrounded by almond trees, much as Asmel had done, then as Toba watched he conjured the sliver of light that was the Luz gate. It let out a blinding flash, and then water began to pour in, a deluge that swirled around the city until it was completely underwater—not even the turrets on the walls remained.

"It flooded through the gate?" she said. "I don't understand."

He tugged at his ear a bit before saying, "I suppose you're friendless enough I don't need to worry about you bringing this up outside the alcalá." He met her gaze. "Are you sure you wish to know? You can't accidentally repeat what I haven't told you."

"Please," she said.

"Very well. What happened in Luz was that the sages—yours, not ours—tried to destroy the gate. No one knows why," he added, pre-empting her next question. "In doing so, they damaged the firmament. The waters of the universe rushed in and did not stop rushing in until it was completely submerged." The light from the near-full moon lit half his face through the window. "What I've just shown you," he said quietly, "is the death of the last age. When the Empire fell, there were those who hoped we would return to the ancient ways, the time of the Judges. But it was not to be." Barsilay's illusion had not yet faded. In front of them stood the image of sea and sky; Toba reached out and touched it with her fingertip, wondering if it would feel wet, but at her touch the entire image fizzed away, like bubbles in a spring.

He made a second illusion: a map, that showed cities as bright points of light. Some, she recognized, others not. "That's P'ri Hadar," she said, pointing to the light in the east. "And here is Rimon." She counted eleven, all together.

"These are the remaining gate cities," Barsilay said. "All used to have a counterpart in the younger world. Once, all bore allegiance to the one queen in Luz, who ruled by divine mandate. But after the fall, most of them devolved into turmoil. Do you know what this is?" he asked, showing her an illusion of a rounded plant, pale and scaled like a dragon might be. Not a plant . . . a fungus. Toba had seen it illustrated; there were lands along the Silk Road where they were made into ink.

"It's a type of mushroom," she said.

"And you know what happens if you destroy one?" he asked. He held the sphere over his left palm and crushed it with his right; a plume of sparkling, illusory spores shot out from between his hands. "So it was when they destroyed the Queen. Monarchy became a contagion, taking root where it was able. Now, instead of one queen, we have ten kings. In Rimon, the struggle was worst and longest, between those who sought to restore the Mandate of Luz, and those who wanted to return to the Judges, and the members of the Adonate who tried to assert themselves as local kings. You can't imagine the bloodshed; houses long allied killing each other's sons in the streets. One Adon would declare himself king and then be dead the next morning. But something else rose up from the ashes of Luz—an order you will have heard of."

"You mean La Cacería."

He inclined his head. "In the beginning they had a single professed mission: to protect the gates."

"From the Sages who tore out the gate in Luz? But aren't they all dead?"

"However the gate was torn out, it could not have been done by mortal magic alone. It's believed Mazik magic was involved. The blame for what happened fell squarely on the shoulders of two parties: those Maziks who maintained relationships with mortals, and on the crown of Luz that allowed such friendships to occur. La Cacería was very popular, at first. They had many sympathizers among the Adonate of Rimon. But as the cycle continued, and a king would rise and then be dead, La Cacería made a deal with Adon Relam b'Gidon. They set him on the throne of Rimon, and in exchange, they are the sole enforcers of a law they made themselves: No Mazik shall, on pain of unbroken death, ever engage with any mortal, or show allegiance of any kind to the Line of Luz, who were responsible for the loss of their gate." Barsilay wiped the map away, and replaced it with some lines written in Mazik, the text, Toba supposed, of the law. "They generally favor the use of fire in its implementation."

Toba could not read what he'd written in the air. She said, "Which character means engage?"

"This," he said, showing her: three lines horizontal, three slashed diagonally, boxed in but only on two sides. "And I haven't mistranslated, if that's your next question."

She frowned, because it was not a word one could rightly use in a law. "It's so vague," she said. "It could mean anything."

"Ah," he said. "You noticed."

Toba exhaled. "So you've broken the law if La Cacería says you have. I assume *engaging* extends to the conceiving of children."

"Among other things. A Mazik man found fathering a child on a mortal woman would be put to death." His eyes met hers. "And the child."

"But why? It seems such a strange thing, for them to worry about babies."

"Very much so, especially since there so seldom are any babies. Mazik infants are large. It's nearly impossible for a mortal to carry one to term. There are those who think it's an expedient way for La Cacería to target their enemies: accuse them of fathering a child on a human, and kill them on the spot. But I'm beginning to think there may be more to it than that. There were half-Maziks in Luz as well, you know. Children of mortal fathers and Mazik mothers."

Toba had read as much in Marah's journal. Barsilay continued: "I never met any myself. But you know that the moon limits our ability to operate in the younger world. A Mazik on the far side of the gate after moonset would die, but a half-Mazik would be protected by their mortal blood, as you were for more than twenty years. You have a power other Maziks lack, and that alone would be reason enough for La Cacería to want you dead."

On the windowsill, the elephant gave one last breath and crumbled back into a pile of dirt. "That one held on for a while," he said. "Did you feel the magic return to you?"

Toba shook her head. "Barsilay," she said.

"Mm."

"The King hates Asmel, and you keep telling me La Cacería is watching him. If he were a Restorationist he'd already be dead, so why? Is it the books he collects? That seems an enormous risk."

"It's not the books," he said. "His rift with them predates his ... bibliophilia. And they've given him license about those, so far."

"Then why?"

Barsilay smiled grimly. "Relam wanted Asmel's support after he took power, and Asmel refused. But I suspect there's more to it that he hasn't told me."

"He's never told you? But why wouldn't he wish you to know?"

"I think he does wish me to know," Barsilay said. He sat up and dropped his feet to the floor. "I can only tell you this—the sigils he wears on his hands were not present when I first came here, and he didn't draw them on himself."

✦ ✦ ✦

WHILE TOBA SHIVERED in the stream outside the alcalá, Toba Bet found her mind consumed by the message from the baths' hostage. She'd spent the better part of an hour in the library trying to recreate it, but the letters drawn in the steam had been imprecise, and she hadn't known them, rendering the task nearly impossible. She was confident in about a third of her transcription. The rest of the letters she hoped she might recognize if she saw them again.

Even if not, she was determined that this would not happen again. Toba was already stymied enough by her poor command of magic. She wouldn't be illiterate, too. And besides that, she desperately needed to know what the Alaunts had accused her of. A Restorationist, she surmised, was someone who wanted to return to the rule of Luz. But how was that possible, when Luz was beneath the sea?

Asmel had returned from court and sequestered himself in his own chamber, and Toba Bet did not think he was likely to emerge again that night. Barsilay was occupied with her elder self. And so Asmel's study, where the Mazik books were kept, would be unattended.

Aware of Toba's argument with Barsilay in some vague sense, Toba Bet stood in the middle of Asmel's study, turning a circle. There were a great many books there, but she could not tell what any of them might contain. She suspected they were books of magic, but those wouldn't help her, nor would books of history or whatever passed for Mazik philosophy or science. She wondered if any of them were translations of human books. If she had a translation of a book she knew, she might be able to use that to make sense of the language. But to determine if any of these *were* translations, she'd need to be able to read the titles, which she could not do.

What a bother.

What she needed was a primer, but she wasn't likely to find one of those, either. She took a large volume off the shelf, chosen purely because it looked newer than the others and the printing was clearer. She opened it on the desk and stared at the blocks of text before her. "I can't even tell if it goes left or right," she muttered. Sighing, she decided to go back to the basics and took a piece of paper from Asmel's supply and began copying what she presumed to be letters, one at a time, as she saw them on the page. Several minutes later, she had a list of eighty-nine letters and no idea what any of them represented.

"That can't be right," she told herself. "There can't be that many extra sounds."

Asmel came upon her staring at the writing, stopping short in the doorway.

He'd changed from his court clothes into a robe of dove gray, his hair loose like it had been recently washed and combed. Exhaustion was etched on his face. Toba Bet wondered why he wasn't asleep. Perhaps, like her, he needed the familiarity of words on a page to soothe his nerves.

Toba Bet waited for him to rage against her for being in his private study without permission, but instead he said, "You felt like learning the early history of P'ri Hadar?"

She looked down at the book and flipped a few pages, absently. "I was trying to learn to read it. I didn't know what it was." She wondered if he'd realized yet she was the second Toba. Normally he hardly acknowledged her.

Asmel came to stand next to her, looking down at her list of letters. "Why have you copied these?"

"I wrote every unique letter," she said. "I thought perhaps—"

"It's not an alphabetic system," he said, looking up from her work. "And you've set yourself an impossible task if you mean to learn by copying the book."

"How else am I to learn? No one will teach me!"

She hadn't meant to be quite so loud, and her voice echoed in the tower room. Still, she wouldn't apologize. "If you'd taught me before, I could have understood the message in the steam."

They both startled; she, that she'd managed to blurt that out—but the hostage had written the message after Tsidon had already left. "The what?" Asmel asked, and she explained to him about the hostage, and what she'd written. She showed him the little she'd been able to reconstitute from memory.

"I thought maybe I'd recognize some of the letters, if I saw them again, but I don't. Can you make out any of what I remember?"

His fingers traced the letters. "I'm not sure what the first one is meant to be, or the last," he said. "This one is a marker for future tense. And this is *dog*."

"Dog?"

"The baths hostages are more than half-mad," he said. "Even if you could remember all she wrote, I'm not sure you could trust it. You are right, though. We've waited too long to begin teaching you to read—I expect it will take some time." He smiled wryly. "I hope this will come easier to you than magic."

Toba Bet felt a vague thrill: he hadn't realized which Toba she was. He believed her the original, and as long as the other stayed away, he would not know she was the buchuk. She wondered why that should please her so much. "That particular bar is low," she said.

"Very low," he agreed. "So by comparison, this should be quite easy for you." He took her pen and scratched a few marks onto the paper. "It's a character-based language," he explained. "Each one is an entire word. It was developed so any Mazik, anywhere, can read anything written by any other."

"There's no common tongue?"

"The written word is the common tongue," he replied.

"I supposed there are benefits to that. So how many characters are there?"

"Some fifty thousand," he said.

She looked at him incredulously. "There are human systems that are no simpler," he said.

Toba Bet had heard of these systems, languages from the Silk lands, but she'd never seen them with her own eyes. "But how can anyone know so many? I don't think I know that many words at all."

"If you learn the first three thousand," he said, "you'll know the bulk of it."

"Of course you know all fifty thousand," she grumbled.

He did not answer. "Do you wish to stop?"

"No," she said. "I won't be illiterate. Couldn't you . . . I don't know. Magic the knowledge into me?"

Asmel shook his head. "It would be unwise for me to go mucking around in your mind."

"Well then," she said. "I suppose we should begin."

✦ ✦ ✦

FORTUNATELY, READING DID come more easily to Toba Bet than magic. After the first fifty characters, she began to see patterns in them: the character for *learn* was comprised of *man* and *book* together; sky was literally *moon* and *house*; food and lentils were simply the same. "How do I know which is which?" she asked.

"You'll figure it out from the context, else it doesn't matter," he said, looking down at the column of characters. "These are not badly written. And you've learned them already?"

"I think so?" she said. "And you can say my writing is good. You needn't couch it as *not bad*."

"It's adequate," he said.

"I'll take that to mean my hand is excellent."

"No."

"Refined."

"Adequate."

"So effusive."

"Why are you so desperate for unearned compliments?"

Toba Bet was caught rather by surprise and said, honestly, "I don't know." Then, "I've never been adequate. Only very good or dismally bad." Only she realized this was the original Toba's sentiment more than her own. What Toba Bet wanted was to be told she was as worthy as her counterpart. No: more.

She rubbed at her bleary eyes; she'd been staring at Asmel's barely decipherable pages for hours, and the room was dim. "We can resume tomorrow," Asmel offered.

"I only need five minutes' rest for my eyes," she said, getting up from the bench to stretch her stiff legs. The shelf across from the work-table held several glass orbs which appeared empty inside, sitting in indentations he'd made in the wood to prevent them rolling away. She scooped one up and examined it; if there were anything inside, she could not see. "What is this?" she asked. "It looks like it's filled with air."

Coming behind her, he took it back, scowling at the object as if it were offending him personally. "It is air," he said. "Old air. This one I took a month ago." He held up the sphere in his hand. "That one was from fifty years ago, the next a hundred."

"What are you doing with baubles full of air?"

"Believe it or not, I was quite well occupied before you arrived," he said. "I was testing it. I had better instruments, once. Observe." He took a slip of paper from the table, inserted it somehow into the glass, and withdrew it again. Then he repeated the process with the other spheres. "What do you notice?"

While Toba Bet watched, the slips of paper changed color . . . the first, the oldest, stayed the same, while the others turned varying shades of pink. The newest sample produced the darkest color. "What does the color change indicate?"

"The presence of salt," he said.

"But salt doesn't dissolve in air," Toba Bet said. "Does it?"

"Not directly," he said. "Usually only at the coast, where seawater mixes with the air."

"But we're miles and miles from the sea," Toba Bet said. "Did you take those in Rimon?"

"I did," he said. "And I can't account for it, but there is more salt in the air now than fifty years ago, and more fifty years ago than fifty years before that. The quantity is almost imperceptible, else we'd all be dead, but it is there."

"What could be causing it?"

"I don't know," he said. "It would help if I knew when it started, but I only began keeping track a hundred years ago because of some off-hand remark of Barsilay's; he told me one morning the air tasted sour. I'm finding it difficult to work on this in isolation. I'd been corresponding with a colleague in Zayit, but I stopped hearing from her some time ago."

The concept of Asmel as a social creature had not occurred to Toba Bet (or to the original Toba, for that matter), but she supposed if he were a scientist—or whatever Maziks called Asmel's occupation—he would have to be. "Thank you," she said. "For teaching me. For taking time from your own work to do it."

He inclined his head and she could see the fatigue heavy in his eyes. He'd sat with her for hours, nursing his own exhaustion in silence. In Toba's tower bedroom, Barsilay had departed and her counterpart had turned her attention toward her; she felt it, like a presence in her mind. It was an uncomfortable sensation she did not care for, being analyzed by herself. *What do you mean to say to him?* the other Toba wondered.

"And for keeping me safe, too," Toba Bet went on. "I know you haven't done much else since I followed you home; I know I haven't been much of a student, I just want you to know—"

Asmel looked thoroughly uncomfortable, gave a curt nod, and turned away, retaking his seat at the table. "There's no need."

"But there is. I want you to know I am trying to be worthy of the risk you've taken."

Gruffly, he said, "My assessment of your intellect has no bearing on the value of your life." Indicating the book they'd been working from, he said, "We should either resume or go to bed."

Toba Bet sat back down on the bench and pulled the book toward herself, trying to picture Asmel as he might be, human, his hair a normal sort of brown, and his eyes a normal sort of blue, and found she couldn't do it. There was no way to divorce Asmel from his Mazik oddness. Moreover, she was glad. She would not like to see him that way, she decided.

"You will not find the answers you seek hidden in my face," he said without glancing up from the book. "Pay attention to your work."

Toba Bet looked away quickly, hot with shame. Asmel rubbed a knot out of the base of his neck, taking on a leonine air as he tilted his head, his eyes sliding shut. It struck her, rather suddenly, that she'd some time ago stopped thinking of him as a beautiful creature and more as a beautiful man. It was a disconcerting realization, and she tried to think of something else besides the shape of his lower lip or the line of his jaw. She copied a few more characters, turned the page.

"Asmel," she said, "am I much changed to you, since I arrived?"

"Changed?" he asked. "In what sense?"

"In my appearance," she said. "Apart from my eyes, I mean."

Asmel gave her his attention, closing his eyes and opening them again, as if meaning to take her in with fresh perspective. "You're stouter, if only just. Your color is much improved, and your skin and hair have lost the brittle look they had. Before, you appeared ill and badly nourished. You no longer do."

"Nothing more?" she pressed.

"What more could there be?"

She did not know, truly, why she wished to test him, to see if he could really not tell her apart from the other, but there was more. She wanted him to look at her. And she wanted to understand to what degree she was different now, without the amulet. She ran a finger through the character she'd just drawn, smudging the ink. "I am struggling to get a sense of myself," she said. "My entire life I had considered myself to be something of a delicate creature—I stumbled on a step and was lame for a week. And a few days ago I was flung off a roof and suffered nothing."

Asmel smiled a little. "I am sorry for that. I believed you would manage."

"You thought you were tossing me from the nest like a fledgling, I understand. I ask because it seems as if I'm so much changed, and yet the magic does not come."

Asmel's fine hands caressed the page between them.

"It will come. I hesitate to tell you this, lest your ego grow to an unprecedented size—"

"My ego is perfectly normal sized!"

"Your ego is enormous already," he said. "And not without cause. You are a clever woman; you are adaptable, you learn easily, and your mind is curious. However, I don't believe you've ever had to struggle before. I've known others like you. For those whom much comes easily, anything difficult is written off as impossible."

"You make it sound as if I haven't tried."

"You've struggled a bit for a few days. In no world does that qualify as trying."

She turned the page and inhaled sharply. "That one," she said, pointing at a character in the top line. "That was in the message from the hostage."

"Are you certain?"

"Yes," she said. "I'm certain: what does it mean?"

Asmel frowned a little. "It means to steal."

Twenty-Three

"I DON'T SEE how we're supposed to navigate based on a few lines drawn on your palm," the old woman said, frowning at Naftaly's hand, which she held tightly between her own. Squinting, she added, "I can't even tell what I'm looking at. And even if I could, we don't have a map of the area to check it against."

"This is the river," Naftaly said, indicating the line that ran parallel to his thumb, and then the peak-shaped mark above it. "This is Mount Sebah."

"And what is that?" Elena asked, touching the starlike object under his third finger. "Is that the gate?"

"You woke me before I could ask about that," Naftaly said. "But I assume so."

"I thought this was the gate," the old woman said, prodding a set of parallel lines toward the middle of his hand.

They all stared at Naftaly's hand. Naftaly dropped it and said, "We'll be wandering aimlessly all night. It could be twenty miles from here, for all we know. This is hopeless."

"You could try again," Elena said.

"I'm not risking my life a second time to talk to another Mazik," he said. "I was very lucky tonight."

"You may be again," Elena said.

"Do I strike you as a naturally lucky person?" he asked.

"He isn't," the old woman said. "He's really quite hopeless."

Naftaly pushed his hair out of his face and made an expansive gesture at the old woman. "There you have it."

"Do that again," Elena said.

"What? Be cynical?"

"No," she said. "With your hand."

He waved his arm in an imitation of his earlier flounce and saw a flicker of light in the distance. He turned his palm inward, and the light vanished. Trying again, he held it palm out toward the northwest.

A spot of light came from the ground far in the distance.

"Try turning a circle," the old woman said. He slowly turned a complete rotation, watching as points of light appeared as he pointed toward them. A long line was visible to the southeast. "That's the river."

He glanced down at his palm again. "If that's the river, then the point to the north must be Mount Sebah." He turned again, northeast. A light appeared in the spot he knew represented the circle on his palm. "And that . . ."

"That's the gate," Elena said.

\+ + + + + +

THEY WALKED FOR hours, checking periodically the position of the light against Naftaly's hand, until the moon set and the lines on his palm no longer glowed.

"We'd better stop here," he said. "I don't want to risk going in the wrong direction, and she's exhausted."

This last bit referred to the old woman, who had slumped to the ground and was already dozing.

"I hear a stream," Elena said. "If we go just a bit farther, we'll have fresh water, and there may be fish."

"In a mountain stream?"

"Small fish," she admitted. "But at least it's something we might eat, and we're too far from Eliossana to steal more food. Come." She prodded the old woman with her toe. "We're going just a bit farther."

"Leave me to die," the old woman grumbled, but she slowly climbed to her feet.

"The moon is full in two days," Naftaly told Elena.

"We'll make it by then," she said.

Naftaly kicked at a pebble. "You've forgotten what tomorrow night is."

"It's Friday, I know," she said. "We're walking anyway."

+ + + + + +

WHEN SHE WOKE the next morning on the pallet in her library, Toba Bet was shivering with cold; the heat had broken overnight. She cursed her counterpart upstairs in her cozy tower, attended by Barsilay's shade, who could bring her an extra blanket or a hot drink. At that very moment, in fact, Toba the First was asking it for a shawl, and it was giving her some lovely thing made of blue cloth that was warm as wool and soft as silk. She knew Toba Bet was cold, too.

You might send the shade to me, she told herself. *I could use a shawl, or some breakfast.*

We'll both be down in a moment, she replied. *I'm not dressed yet.*

Toba Bet, of course, had slept in her dress. She hadn't been to the royal baths, or even to the stream outside. *Don't bother*, she thought. *Stay cozy with your servant. I have better things to do than pamper myself.*

She stomped out of the library en route to the small, empty room she'd made into a washroom, since she couldn't well have pitchers of water near the books. There was a basin filled with cold water she washed herself with, thinking spiteful thoughts about her other self. Her mind went to the garden of the Mazik King, and the almond tree on the floor, and wondered if her foot would have revealed it as well as the first Toba's.

Of course it would, she thought. *I have as much claim on her ancestry as she does, which means I, too, am from Luz, somehow.*

What a puzzle that was. Her father came from a city drowned so long ago that most men considered it myth. Why would such a man go through the gate, take a no-account mortal lover, and then leave her behind there? He could not have loved her; he must have known a pregnancy would be likely to kill her. The last thing a Mazik would do with a mortal woman he loved was risk siring a child on her.

But then, why? By the tales told by Alasar and Elena, Penina had been clever, as Toba was, but apart from that, she seemed wholly unremarkable. She hadn't been a great beauty, and she hadn't been able to have the sort of life outside her home that would have given her attention from strange men. Truly, it made little sense.

Toba Bet's very existence seemed absurd; doubly so. She was a randomly created buchuk of a randomly sired half-Mazik.

She put her dress back on and went to Asmel's study. She would learn to read, today. She would decipher the message from the hostage, today. Before Tsidon reappeared, as he said he'd do. Whatever was in the message must have to do with him.

Within the study she found Asmel asleep, laid out on the windowsill with a book spread across his chest. One long hand lay against the spine, while the other lay curled beside him on the sill, palm-up and relaxed. She watched him take a few slow breaths before concluding he wasn't about to wake, and crept into the room.

Toba Bet wondered if he'd slept there all night, or risen early and then fallen asleep again. He didn't look rumpled, but then, he never did. Probably his clothing was all bespelled not to wrinkle. She tried to make out the title of the book on his chest . . . it was either a book about learning, or a book about other books, and she couldn't make out which. With a finger she tried to pull it away from him, to see which page he'd stopped on, but his hand was heavy against the spine and she did not think she could move it without waking him. That hand—his left—still bore ink stains from the past evening's lesson. Probably he'd not been to bed, then. His eyelashes twitched slightly, and she knew that he must be dreaming. She wondered what Asmel dreamt of. She looked down to his hand on the windowsill, at the blue sigil on his half-opened palm, to see if it was something she might recognize. His fingers curled over it, though, so she knelt beside the window, craning her neck for a view from the other direction. Still, she could not quite see. Perhaps if she moved his fingers, only slightly. She carefully hooked her fingers under his.

His voice came low and sleepy: "What are you doing?"

Abashed, she pulled her gaze from his hand to his face and her own hand back to her side. He hadn't moved so much as a hair, only now his eyes were open. "I was looking at the mark on your hand," she said honestly. "I wanted to see if it was one you'd taught me."

Without altering his expression, he turned his hand over and held it out to her, palm out, fingers spread, his eyes on her face. She looked at the sigil, and his eyes, which were the wrong shade of blue for eyes—nearly violet, in this light—and looked away. "I don't know it," she said.

He lowered his hand.

"Will you tell me what it is?"

"No." He sat up from against the wall and closed the book with a snap, holding it up briefly in illustration, and said, "I've thought of a way to help you learn to read more easily. A bit of magic I'd forgotten."

"I thought you said that was a bad idea."

"It's only a little help," he said. "I won't be touching your mind. It's merely a weak spell that creates an affinity between my voice and your ear. I'll read to you while you follow the characters with your eyes; the spell will only cement the link and help you remember."

"What must I do?"

"Nothing," he said. "Only give your permission."

"It's temporary?"

"It won't last more than an hour," he said.

Toba Bet mused on it. It would be good to have a little help. She said, "All right. Cast your spell."

He leaned toward her, until his mouth was close enough to her left ear for her to hear his breath, and he whispered something that was not quite a word and not quite a sound: it was bright and sharp, like a breath on a cold day, and Toba shivered as it went through her. She looked up to him quickly, but he had already opened the book before her, a different volume than he'd had at the window, slimmer and newer, like it had seen less use.

"You must read along for this to work," he said, because she was still looking at him. Her eyes went back to the book, and he began to recite.

It was a fairy tale; something about a Mazik prince who fell in love with a princess, whose father had declared that she would never marry, and the prince was required to overcome all sorts of impossible trials to win her hand. Toba Bet felt herself falling into a kind of trance as Asmel's voice caressed each word, and she found herself wanting to close her eyes to listen better, which she knew defeated the purpose. She leaned closer to listen, then closer still, until she was pressed against him in a way she knew should be embarrassing, but she only wanted to hear him better.

Sparing her a curious glance, he continued. She pressed herself against his side.

He moved away on the bench, and she followed him.

He slammed the book shut.

"Forgive me," he said, putting his hands on her shoulders and sliding her away. "I had no idea the spell would affect you so."

He held her firmly away from him, which was when she noticed her hand was threaded through his hair. She quickly extracted it. "I'm sorry," she breathed.

"It's not meant to be that sort of spell," he said. "I think you should go until it wears off."

"But it was *working*," she protested. "I remember everything you read. Please. Just keep going."

"I don't think so," he said.

"Then . . . can you say something else? Or can you sing? There must be Mazik songs I should know."

He pressed his lips together and stood up. "What is wrong with you?" she asked, following him as he backed away. "You want me to learn this, don't you? How can I learn if you won't speak to me? Just a few more words, and then I'll leave, I promise—"

Asmel reached down with a hand on either side of her waist and lifted her up. She dug her fingers into his forearms in anticipation, but he carried her to the door and dropped her on the other side of the threshold.

"I can't learn apart from you!" she cried, but he'd shut the door in her face. She banged against the wood. "Let me back in! I only want to listen!" From inside, she heard the sound of the door being barred. She began to sob.

From the other side of the door, a sigh. "Go back to the library. If you bring me the Ibn Sina treatise on flightless birds, I shall read it to you."

Toba Bet let out a shuddering breath. "You'll let me back in?"

"With that book. Now go find it." His words set her scrambling toward the library. It was not until several frenzied hours later that she recalled Ibn Sina had never written a treatise on flightless birds.

\+ + + + + +

TOBA THE ELDER had been this time with Barsilay, peppering him with questions about Luz that he mainly dodged, while he made her observe some changes he was considering to his wardrobe.

"Do you like the green?" he asked, modeling a silk shirt the color of grass in April.

"It clashes horribly with your eyes," she told him. "How long ago was the fall of Luz?"

"Long ago. I don't see why you think it should clash with my eyes. Green looks well on everyone, doesn't it?"

"Why ask me if you don't care what I think? So any Mazik from Luz must be very old, then."

"Are you asking my age? What about purple?" He altered the hue of the tunic. "Does that play better with my eyes?"

"Are all the men from Luz like you?"

"Charming as sunrise and beautiful as starlight? I'm afraid not. Now would you say—where are you going?"

For Toba had suddenly felt the pull of Asmel's spell on her counterpart, and the craving for his voice was nearly unendurable. "Asmel," she whispered, and then fled the room. "He doesn't look half so handsome in purple," he called after her, but she hardly heard, and the next thing she was aware of was the feel of Asmel's door, unyielding first against her hands, and then her shoulder.

Barsilay must have heard her loud complaints, as he found her moments later flinging herself against the door. "What is wrong with you?" he asked. "Why are you embarrassing yourself this way?"

"Asmel won't let me in!" she cried. She rammed the door with her body again, knowing the effort would leave a bruise. She didn't care.

"You're going to hurt yourself."

"Then tell him to open the door!"

"Have you lost your mind? What in the—ah. What have you done to yourself?"

"I did nothing! I would be fine, if only he'd speak to me."

From within, Asmel said, "Take her *out*."

At the sound of his voice, Toba clawed at the door with renewed enthusiasm.

"Oh," Barsilay said. "Oh, dear." Through the door, he called, "Is this permanent?"

"Pray it isn't," Asmel answered tightly.

Barsilay sighed heavily and tossed Toba over his shoulder, carrying her outside to the front garden while she wailed Asmel's name, until he dumped her bodily into the fountain. "Cool yourself off," he said. "You can't get to him."

Toba sat in the middle of the water, pulling wet fabric away from her skin and gasping. "Why would you do that? What is wrong with you?"

"With me? Did you see yourself trying to burrow through the door just now?"

"I only wanted to learn!"

"Learn," he said. "Really, is that what you call it?"

"He was teaching me to read! He cast a spell to help."

"Don't be absurd, you were with me for the past hour . . . ah. It was the other one. Where is she?"

"In the library, he'll let her back in! Her, and not me!" She went to get up, and he pushed her back into the water.

"Stay where you are. Believe me, you'll thank me for this later."

"I won't!" she said. "You're keeping me from . . . from . . . oh no." She felt her mind go clear, all at once.

"That was sudden," he said.

She splashed her way to the edge of the fountain and climbed out of the water. "I should apologize," she said. Barsilay gripped the back of her dress and tugged her backward as she tried to pass him. "Not yet, you won't," he said. "Do you want to embarrass yourself again?"

She stopped and looked down at her sodden dress. "No," she said, "not really." She put her hands to her cheeks. "He must despise me now."

"It's his own fault," he said. "He's the one who cast the spell, and after he refused . . ."

Toba turned to him. "Refused what?"

Barsilay chewed on his lip. "Never mind."

"You've already said," she said. "Shall I go ask Asmel what he's refused?"

He held a fist in front of his mouth. "It's nothing. Only a minor disagreement." He began to walk away.

"Don't you dare," she said. "If it was a disagreement regarding me, I have a right to know what it was!"

"You spend a good deal of time going on about what you have a right to," he said. "That concept does not exist here."

If Toba could have intentionally made a fish, she would have slapped him with it. Instead, she jumped on his back. Barsilay gave a startled cry and staggered backward under her weight, and as the backs of his knees met the edge of the fountain she took the opportunity to pull him in along with her.

"You wretched creature," he said, sputtering and wiping water out of his eyes. "You made yourself heavy."

"Stop feeding me pheasants if you don't want me heavy," she shot back. "And tell me what you and Asmel discussed."

"I'll tell you nothing," he said. Toba hurled herself on top of him, knocking him down into the water.

"You do realize I could kill you with a finger," he said, pushing her off.

"You've overused that particular threat," she said. "It won't work any longer."

He spat out a mouthful of fountain water. "He ordered me not to discuss it with you."

Tilting her head, Toba said, "Does that mean you can't?"

He pressed his lips together.

"Surely you can say something. I can see that you wish to. It's probably why you brought it up in the first place: don't think I haven't realized how you operate. You throw me some thread of information,

I pull it 'til you reveal the rest, and then you can claim I wheedled the whole thing out of you if Asmel complains. So spare us the dance, and tell me what you discussed. What was the nature of your disagreement?"

"I can't tell you that. But I can tell you what we agreed on: your magical pathways were damaged by that damned amulet. It's why you can't feel your magic or control it."

"I'd assumed as much," she said. "Asmel said they would heal on their own, in time."

He met her gaze.

"That was the disagreement," she said. "You don't think they'll heal."

He shook his head fractionally.

"Then I'm doomed," she said. She glanced back up at him quickly. "Wait now—is it that you don't think they can heal, or that you don't think they'll heal on their own? Is that it?"

He smiled grimly.

"You think I can be healed." She took hold of his sodden lapels. "Do you have some idea how to do that?"

Smiling, he said, "Yes."

TWENTY-FOUR

NAFTALY'S FINGERS WERE twitchy as he said the Shema with the hand he held over his eyes marked with a Mazik map. He felt rather like he should be apologizing for it; a magic map was probably wicked, and there was probably a law about praying with your hands marked up with one. His face was still shaved, because what little scruff he'd had before Eliossana had refused to grow back, and his head was uncovered, and his tzitzit utterly disheveled, and Elena said the challah blessing over some sort of smallish bird, because that was all the food they'd managed to scrounge in two days.

"We should go," Elena said, after they'd eaten the few morsels they had to pass around.

"I have to say Kaddish," Naftaly said. "For my father."

Elena nodded. There was no minyan, it was only Naftaly, but he figured it was better than not saying it at all. Elena and the old woman waited until he was done, and then Naftaly held out his palm and checked the position of the gate in the early moonlight.

"I can't believe we're trudging through the wilderness in the dark on Shabbat," Naftaly said. He wondered what his father would make of this. Probably he would have been aghast. Trying to find Maziks, and on Shabbat, no less—it was outrageous. It was probably his fault, too, for telling Elena the truth about his dreams. This was the sort of thing that came from opening one's mouth. He resented his father, and felt guilty for it, and missed him at the same time.

"I've had to do worse," the old woman said.

"So have I," Elena agreed.

"Of course you have," the old woman said. "I won't believe you save up your murdering and witchcraft for regular days."

Elena's mouth twitched. "I do make an effort," she said.

The map on Naftaly's palm was leading them overland, off the road. As a direct journey, it did not look far, but going straight through would often have meant walking down a cliff or into a ravine, so their path led them on a serpentine route through the hills.

It had not rained in weeks, and the grass they stepped on crackled under their feet. They'd climbed up; below them they could see the shadows of the pine forest. Sebah loomed ahead of them; the moon crossed behind it, leaving them in the dark for half an hour before a turn in their path showed them the way again.

After a while, Naftaly became aware that something had changed—the earth felt different under his feet. The terrain around them had shifted, and the air itself smelled strange, like the wind after a rain. Naftaly felt the dampness of dew on his toes.

"We must be getting closer," Elena said.

Naftaly held up his palm, which still showed the gate many miles away, a dot of light on the horizon. "Not according to this."

But the landscape had gone increasingly green only in the last few moments, giving rise to towering pines that shaded the sky. Naftaly stopped dead.

"There," he said, pointing into the distance, at a low valley filled with trees. "Pomegranates, do you see? That's where the gate will be, amid those trees. But how can we have come here so soon?" He looked at his palm again. It showed the gate some distance away.

"If the wood moves," Elena said, "your map shows us where it will be tomorrow night. We've managed to stumble onto it early."

"Well, that's good news," the old woman said. "If we stay inside it, we won't have to walk farther."

"She's right," Naftaly said. "We moved within it before. As long as we stay inside the borders, we go where it goes." He sat down in the thick grass and pulled off his left boot to examine a blister.

"But," Elena said. "No, I won't believe we'll move with it."

"Why not?" the old woman said. "The boy and I already did."

"Because if that happened, people would be forever wandering into the wood and coming out someplace else. We would have heard tales about it, especially since we know it appears near the road sometimes. We would have heard of something like this."

"Perhaps people did wander in, but they wandered out so quickly the wood hadn't traveled far," Naftaly suggested.

Elena turned to him. "Could you get out right now, if you wanted?"

Naftaly set down his stocking. The landscape had changed so much in the past few moments he couldn't say for sure which way they'd come in.

"We've been in here five seconds, and already we're lost," Elena said. "The only way we'd come out again quick enough to be where we'd entered is by enormous luck."

A howl came, then two, then too many to count.

Naftaly closed his eyes. The wolves. It hadn't occurred to him that they hadn't wandered in, like he had. If the wolves were permanent residents, it would explain why no one wandered in and back out again.

"Not good," the old woman said.

"When you were here before," Elena said, "you said they ignored you."

"They did, that time."

Another howl. "That was closer than the first," the old woman said. She looked to Elena. "Can you do some magic? Can you conceal us?"

"From men, maybe. From wolves? Certainly not." She turned to Naftaly. "Did the fellow with the map tell you anything about how to call them off?"

"Must have slipped his mind," he said.

"Shall we run away now?" the old woman said flatly.

"No point," Elena said. "We can't outrun them, and we don't know which direction will take us out of the wood, anyway."

"So you suggest that we stay and be eaten?"

"I don't think they'll eat the boy," Elena said. "I think he probably smells like a Mazik."

"You've just made that up!"

"It's a sound theory," she said. "If the dream-Mazik didn't warn you about the wolves, it must be because he thought you didn't need warning."

"Because he thought I was a Mazik," Naftaly said.

"Well, and you are."

"Not," he said, "really."

"You have the dreams," Elena said, ticking the item off on a finger. "You burn through amapola like a Mazik. You have visions."

"And you think a wolf can't tell the difference between a tenth of a Mazik and a full Mazik? They chased Toba."

"Toba was wearing the amulet," she said. "You are not. And you were in the wood with Toba that night, and they left you alone."

The old woman sat down heavily and pulled off her shoes. "What are you doing?" Naftaly demanded.

"We've decided running won't save us," she said dispassionately. "So all things being equal, I'd prefer to die without exerting myself."

More howls. Elena whispered, "Look," and she pointed to a spot behind Naftaly, where a lone gray wolf sat watching him curiously, its tongue lolling playfully out of the side of its mouth as if it were a large dog.

"Shall we make a pet of it?" the old woman mused.

It turned to her, baring its teeth.

\+ + + + + +

TOBA FOLLOWED BARSILAY into part of the alcalá she'd never been inside, up the stairs from Asmel's own rooms. "I should not be doing this," he said, more to himself than to Toba.

"Your theory," she inquired of his back, "does it account for why the mud animals are the only intentional magic I can do?"

"Partly," he said. "I think that's like some sort of muscle memory." They'd come to what must have been Barsilay's sitting room. He perched on the edge of a circular table and drew some kind of stringed instrument out of the air, then began plucking a pleasant little tune. "I learned this in Luz. I couldn't tell you the notes any longer, but I can still play it, because my fingers remember. It may be the same for you. You made those animals before, more than once, likely, and haven't forgotten how."

Barsilay continued picking out his song; after a few moments, he faltered. "Interesting. I can't remember how it ends." He waved the instrument away. "You told me you don't have the dreams," he said.

"No," Toba said. "I've never dreamt at all—you think that's significant?"

"Highly," he said. "Part-Maziks enter the dream-world, I'm sure of it. La Cacería looks for them there. So it's almost certainly not your blood that's the issue. It's damage."

She put her hand to the place where the amulet had long rested on her chest. He went on, "Most of our injuries heal quickly: bruise your shin, it will heal in five minutes; break your arm, the bone will knit in a day. This is different. You aren't healing on your own. The amulet you wore caused damage too severe: it must be corrected."

"And Asmel disagrees?"

"Asmel . . . has become overly cautious. He was not always this conservative."

"He used magic on me just now, and it went wrong."

"The business with his voice?" He waved a hand. "That was nothing; it barely lasted a few minutes. Anyway, he should have known better than to cast it on a woman who looks at him the way you do. It was a predictable outcome."

Toba clenched her fists. "Are you saying that you know how to correct what's wrong with my magic?"

He hesitated. “Occasionally, the pathways of magic develop damage over the course of a lifetime. There are ways to repair them. It’s what I was studying in Luz, before I left. What you would call medicine.”

“If you could repair them, then why wouldn’t Asmel—”

“There is,” he said, “some risk of further damage.”

Toba frowned. “How great a risk?”

“I couldn’t say,” he said. “I don’t even know how bad the damage is. But it could hardly be much worse, could it?”

“Seeing as I’m already essentially useless,” she said. He gave her a small smile. Barsilay tapped his steepled fingers against his lips. “Do you want me to try?”

“I . . . I suppose it seems wise,” she said.

“Good,” he said, his eyes brightening. “Good.” There was a lounge under the window, and he patted it. “I think it will be easier if you’re not standing: come here.”

Toba lay down, slowly, remembering what Barsilay’d said about being as interested in her as in she in a salamander, and he arranged her arms at her sides. “Stay very still,” he said, and began passing a hand an inch from her skin, starting at the top of her head and working down, pausing at the hollow of her throat, where her amulet once rested. “It’s here. I can feel it, can’t you?”

“What do you feel?” she asked.

“The flow of your magic is disturbed here,” he said. “I’m surprised you’re not in pain from it.”

“I feel no pain,” she said, and when his scowl deepened, added, “Why do you seem to think that’s worse?”

“Because you *should* feel pain from this kind of injury,” he said. He put his right hand over his left. “I’m going to touch you now.”

“Will this hurt? What do you mean to do?”

“I don’t know if there will be pain,” he said. “I’m going to force some of my own magic through the damaged vein; it may open it. Don’t move. Don’t breathe.”

"You don't know if it will hurt?" she asked, but his palm was already lowering onto her skin.

For a moment, she felt him, not as a person—or a Mazik—but she felt the circuit of Barsilay's magic, and realized she was now part of that circuit; his magic flowed into her from his left hand and back out his right. It was a warm, electric sensation. His eyes, too bright, went to hers. "You're of Luz," he said tightly. "I feel it."

Toba forgot his order not to breathe. "Don't," he said, through clenched teeth. "I'm going to do it now."

She felt a searing pain in her throat and screamed, as she'd screamed the day the Infanta had wanted to kill her.

In the library, Toba Bet screamed, too.

Barsilay's face went white. Whatever was happening was not what he'd planned for, and Toba felt him trying—and failing—to pull his hands free of her. "I can't—" he gasped, and then he grit his teeth and wrenched himself away, staggering back and struggling for air.

Asmel burst into the room; the door hit the wall so hard it splintered. "The other girl just collapsed. What's happened?" he asked, taking in Toba lying prone on the lounge, tears streaming from the corners of her eyes, and Barsilay, held up mostly by the wall a few feet away. He put a hand behind Toba's back and pulled her to a sitting position before going to put Barsilay into a chair.

"What have you done?" he rasped.

Barsilay was still panting. He swiped his forearm across his face, which was beaded with sweat. "I thought if I forced some of my own magic through—"

"Had you no care for her life?" Asmel shouted.

"Don't be absurd."

Asmel rounded on him. "You might have killed her! Did you mention that before performing your little experiment?"

Toba put a hand over her mouth. Barsilay, rubbing his burned hand, said, "What would the point have been in mentioning it? If we can't repair this, she's as good as dead anyway. The longer you keep her hidden, the more questions it invites. Your fear would have killed us all. I was giving her a chance."

Asmel said, "If you try to force magic through a weakened pathway, it's likely to burst."

"I'm the one with the training in this area, not you," Barsilay said.

"Your training," Asmel said, "was limited."

"Well, what is your grand plan, then?" Barsilay said. "Do absolutely nothing but wait for La Cacería to realize she's as magicless as a doorstop?"

"She's not," Asmel said. "She can do enough for now. The pathways may regrow, now the amulet's gone."

"You're betting her life on that? All our lives?"

"I would rather bet our lives on that," Asmel said, "than on your ability to perform a great work with untrained hands."

"Yes, yes, you keep saying she ought to be dead, yet she's not, is she?" He waved his hand at Toba. "Very much alive. Perhaps I'm not so useless as you like to think, Uncle."

"How dare you?" Toba said, getting shakily to her feet. In the library, she felt her counterpart begin to rouse, and her own dizziness made Toba stumble. "How dare you do something so dangerous without warning?" She turned to Asmel. "And how dare you . . . have opinions about my condition and not share them? I am a person! I can't conjure things out of the air. I can't fly or make a shade or turn a lentil into a lambchop, but I am a thinking, reasoning person, and I deserve to be consulted in matters pertaining to my own being." She tried to ignore the spinning of the room. She would not faint, and she would not fall. "I understand I am putting you at risk. But I am not some *dog* you found in the street."

Asmel tilted his head fractionally, in what may have been the tiniest nod toward apology. Barsilay said, "I am not sorry for any of it," and quit the room.

TWENTY-FIVE

THAT NIGHT, FOR the first time, Toba dreamt.

In the beginning she did not know it was a dream, having never experienced such a thing. She was confused as to how she'd gotten so far from the alcalá, what she was doing at a stable, and what the creatures in front of her were. There were three of these, each the size of a large horse, but there was nothing else equine about them; they were birds, essentially, covered with gold-red feathers, with elongated bodies and impossibly long legs. Their necks extended beyond the tops of their pens, and with savage beaks they pecked at golden fruits from trees that grew above them.

They were Zizim, she realized, though small ones. And Asmel was right; her clay facsimiles had been accurate. She had seen these before, somehow.

Adding to her confusion was the fact that she was singular, both herself and her buchuk together in one person, and felt as if there were too much of her inside her own mind.

She was otherwise alone. She reached out to touch the feathers of the nearest Ziz, which gave a twitter and turned its great green eye toward her curiously. "I wonder what you eat," she said, because they seemed to be playing with the fruit rather than consuming it. The creature looked like a carnivore, with that beak. It would have made for an alarmingly large one, though; it was bigger than a wolf, or even a lion. It would need to eat large quantities to sustain itself, or else very large prey. The Ziz clicked its beak. Toba decided not to think further on its diet.

Wandering away from the stables, she came across a tall man eating sweets while reclining on an embroidered blanket, and realized upon further inspection that it was the King.

"Ah," he said, with some measure of disdain. "It's you. The toymaker."

Toba bowed, but he waved it away. "There's no point," he said. Then, indicating the Zizim, he added, "One is supposed to have permission to see those. Even here."

Toba wanted to ask what that meant but did not. Instead, she offered a rushed apology, which the King sighed away. She wondered if she should leave. She wondered where all his retainers were. The King offered her a piece of some honeyed pastry. "What do you think of this?" he asked.

Toba set it in her mouth; it was decidedly stale. "It's terrible," she said honestly.

"Oh, excellent," he said, pushing himself upright. "Everything tastes like dust to me lately. It's good to know I'm not always the common factor." Then he said, "I am attempting to be alone." And then added, in a muttered voice, "I am never alone."

He waved a hand at Toba, who found herself pushed away as if by a strong wind, fast and faster, until she was being smacked on all sides by the branches of trees as she flew through them, stopping only when she hit a great oak, bouncing off and onto the ground with a grunt.

Pulling herself upright, she glanced up at the stars, and realized there was no moon overhead.

She opened her eyes and found herself returned to her bed, put her feet on the floor, and ran all the way to Asmel's quarters, where she found him scratching notes onto a piece of paper from one of several large books which had taken over his work-table. She wondered why he hadn't slept; or maybe it was still early, and her ordeal had been quicker than she'd thought.

"You should be sleeping," he said, without looking up from his work.

"I was," she said. "I . . . I was somewhere else. I don't know how I came to be there, but I went to sleep in my bed and woke up at the King's stables, and there was only one of me."

Asmel looked up sharply. "What?"

"He gave me a pastry and sent me away."

"A pastry?"

"It was stale," she said.

"The King gave you a stale pastry?"

"That's . . . yes, and then he flung me into a wood, and there were birds—"

Looking back to his books, Asmel said, "You were dreaming."

"No, I can't have been," Toba said.

"You didn't think it was strange that you intruded on the King's privacy and all he did was give you sweets?"

"I can't have been," she insisted, "because I don't *have* dreams. I never do. Barsilay said it was because of the amulet." Her hand went to the base of her throat. "Is it what he did?"

"Come here," he said, rising. Toba approached, and he set his palm over her throat, closing his eyes. She felt his magic slide out of his hand and under her skin; not unpleasant, but strange, as if she were drinking hot liquid into her flesh. "The damage is still there," he said. "It seems unchanged to me. But if you're dreaming, something must be different." He opened his eyes. "You saw the King?"

"Yes. Is that bad?"

"It's . . . unusual."

"Well, what do Maziks usually dream of? What do you dream of?"

Asmel's face colored slightly. "We do not speak of such things."

"What?"

"It's not acceptable. What one does in one's dreams is private." He shifted uncomfortably. "You do understand that our dreams are shared? That these aren't like human dreams? Our minds all travel to the same place."

Toba thought on that. "So will the King remember having seen me?"

"Yes. But he won't mention it, and neither should you. It's the height of rudeness." He sighed and sat back down. "Our lives are long and constricted. It's the one true freedom we permit ourselves." He huffed. "You would see the King, of all people, though I expect you ended up there because you wanted to see the Zizim. That's prohibited, by the way."

"He said as much. Will I be punished?"

"He already believes you're a half-wit," he said. "I don't think he'd go through the embarrassment of discussing his dreams with his guards just to censure you."

"Oh, well, there's a comfort."

"It should be," he said. "You're better off being beneath his notice, I assure you."

"You don't like him," she said.

Asmel smirked. "I suppose it is your human upbringing," he said, "that leads you to take such pleasure in stating what is so patently obvious."

Toba ignored the insult. "Why?"

"Why?" he asked. "Here is what you should know of our illustrious King. He cares for exactly two things: his own power, and his own amusement. Nothing for his people, nothing for . . . wisdom. He lives in that eyesore of an alcázar and spends his days waiting for *entertainment*."

Toba had not thought the palace an eyesore. "I thought the courtyard was lovely," she said, more to be contrary than anything else.

"Oh, certainly, with those ridiculous vats of spinning quicksilver," he said. "Do you know, before someone thought to magic the damned things they used to import humans through the gate simply to rotate the basins? All to amuse the King, who enjoyed the beams of light. We'd be better off ruled by a cat."

Toba folded her arms and turned her face away.

"Are you impressed by all that needless finery? There isn't even beauty in it; it's only meant to show wealth."

"It seems a bit convenient for you to disparage the King's habits, while being blithely ignorant of your own."

"I beg your pardon."

"You're hardly living in a hut," she pointed out. "Look at this place! You're practically alone in this giant castle. A hundred people could live here and never brush elbows, and all for two men! What use did you ever have for such a vast space?"

Asmel looked at her in stunned silence. Caustically, he said, "It was a *university*."

\+ + + + + +

TOBA WAS AFRAID to go back to sleep, and she missed her grandparents badly. The idea of dreaming was strange enough, but to have dreams that were effectively real—and could be recalled by other people—seemed acutely horrible. It was bad enough to realize you could fall on your face, shame yourself and your kin, and destroy all your future prospects in the waking world, but to realize you could do all that while sleeping, too? It seemed cruel. She wanted to go home. She wanted to lie in her small bed in Rimon, where sleeping meant you closed your eyes and woke up a few hours later, and nothing transpired in between.

Asmel had said it was taboo to mention one's dreams, so there was that. Still, she didn't think the King would forget she'd stumbled into his private repose. Instead of sleeping, she went back to her translation; she'd liberated some paper from Asmel's study, having run out of her own supply, and the shade was still refusing to make her more. She couldn't go back through the gate at the moon, but she still needed to fulfil her contract with Barsilay and she only had another day left to finish, which meant she'd be working like mad to do it. Eyeing the sheets she'd taken from Asmel, she frowned: she hadn't taken enough, but she hadn't wanted to take so much he'd notice. She would be many pages short. Toba Bet had gone off to try to bully Barsilay into giving her more paper, but thus far had been unable to find him anywhere.

Toba wondered what Asmel would do with the pages, once she'd finished. Two more books to set in his byzantine book labyrinth, what a waste. A pity it seemed to be the only thing she was good for. Toba wondered what the Rambam would have thought of a bastard, half-Mazik woman translating his work some five hundred years after he died, or if his imagination could even have conjured such a bizarre turn. Talk about perplexed.

And she was in a university, or what had once been one. She kicked herself for not asking Barsilay more pointed questions. "It's just what it looks like," he'd told her.

Asmel had refused her questions, the most pressing among them being: If this was a university, what had happened to the students?

Barsilay had not been to see her that day, and while she'd sent Toba Bet to find him, she'd found no trace, making her wonder if he was avoiding her, angry at her lack of gratitude for his work to free her magic, or else unable to face her anger at his wanton imperiling of her life.

There was no one else to ask but the shade, who seemed limited to the little knowledge that Barsilay himself possessed.

"Was this really a university?" *Yes.*

"Was Asmel an instructor there?" *Yes.*

"Was it the King who closed it?" No answer.

She thought a moment. "Was it closed by La Cacería?"

There had been no answer to that, either, which led Toba to believe that Barsilay did not know who had closed it. She was sure it was one of the two, though, if not both together.

The shade itself seemed jumpy that morning and kept flickering in and out of view. Perhaps, she thought, her bond with it was beginning to weaken.

The sun was hitting the top of the fountain outside the library window—so, midmorning—and both Tobot were lounging at the table. They'd run out of the paper stolen from Asmel and they were taking turns failing to produce additional sheets. Toba Bet was the only one of the pair to have come close, having produced a layer of fine sawdust from the surface of the table in the shape of a sheet of paper. This, though, had disintegrated when she'd touched it, and she'd been unable to duplicate the effort.

"Still better than you," she'd told Toba, rather sourly.

"Is dust better than nothing?"

"It is. I think."

"Not really. You've only succeeded in marring the table," Toba said, while Toba Bet blew the rest of the dust from the spot. The finish on the table was dulled there. "How do you suppose they're doing it? Isn't the paper made from the table?"

"I assumed so, but wouldn't that destroy the table?" Toba turned to the shade. "Do they have to keep replacing the furniture, if they're turning bits of it into other things?"

The shade failed to answer.

"Maybe it's not the table," Toba Bet suggested. "Maybe the paper is made from something else?"

"There was nothing between Barsilay's hand and the table when he made the sheets."

"Maybe it's made from his skin?" Toba Bet offered.

"That's repulsive."

"Well, it's made from something. Hang on, what if this isn't really a wood table? What if it's a giant stack of paper made to look like a table, and we're only changing it back?"

Toba began to say, *You mean like the mosaic of the almond tree in the garden*, but found her tongue firmly adhered to the roof of her mouth. "Damn," she muttered. She'd wanted to ask Asmel about it since the moment it had happened.

"Well, hang on," Toba Bet said. "Perhaps we don't need to tell him precisely what happened. Barsilay said we were of Luz, and there's nothing to prevent us from repeating *that*."

Toba scowled to herself—and a bit *at* herself—because it hadn't occurred to her that Barsilay had given her a way around the spell. "I should tell Asmel," she said.

"Or I could," Toba Bet said. "I've spent more time with him than you, recently."

"All the more reason I should do it. The voice spell may still be lingering in you."

"Then it would also be lingering in you," Toba Bet said, but then relented, because she knew it had affected her more, and she was not keen to embarrass herself again. "Fine. I will try to find Barsilay again. Perhaps he knows more than Asmel on this, anyway. He's from Luz."

The two went off in their respective directions, the shade choosing to accompany the elder Toba to Asmel's study, where she found him tinkering over his astrolabes. Toba wondered if he'd slept, or dreamt, in the hours since she'd seen him last. She wondered if he dreamt of his wife, and then thought that if Mazik dreams were effectively real, one could likely not dream of someone dead. How horribly sad, to lose someone from both realms, the waking and the dreaming.

"Is Barsilay's shade with you?" Asmel asked as she entered.

The shade had retreated into the shadows by the door, as it usually did when Asmel was around, but at this it hovered back into view. "He's just there," she said, and then added, seeing Asmel's agitation, "What's wrong?"

"Has it been behaving oddly today?"

"He's the same as always," she said, "he hovers and occasionally tidies, why?"

Asmel passed her a leaf of paper covered in Mazik writing she recognized as Barsilay's hand. It contained only a few sentences, and she was able to parse out enough to realize it had to do with herself.

"I don't understand what he's written here," she said. "What is he saying about me?"

He took back the paper, tossed it into the air, and set it alight in a tiny plume of flame. "Barsilay has concluded that your father is from Luz, he wants me to know, in the most insulting tones possible. Beyond that, he tells me he's gone to the baths to clear his mind."

"Are you distressed because he's insulted you, or because he's gone to the baths? Doesn't he go all the time?"

"I'm distressed because if he found out something this important, he should have come to me right away instead of leaving me a petulant letter."

"You were very angry," she said. "We were both very angry. Maybe he's afraid to confront us. Why were you asking about the shade? Were you worried he isn't safe?"

Asmel exhaled through his nose. "I'm worried he'll ask the wrong questions while he's cavorting in the baths. Barsilay has rather a talent for ferreting out secrets. He also has a talent for running ahead of himself. What he's realized about your father is highly significant. There are fewer than a dozen men of Luz in Rimon, and some of them are dangerous indeed." Asmel picked up a reed pen from the table and ran his fingers over the tip, thinning it, until it was the thickness of a sewing needle. "If your pathways are clear enough to dream, they're clear enough for you to do this. Put out your hand."

"Why are you—" Toba cried out, because he'd pierced her fingertip with the needle he'd made from the pen and was dabbing at the resulting blood with a white cloth.

"Be still," he said.

"You might have warned me!"

He took the cloth to his work-table and pulled out a book. "If I'd warned you about the needle, it would have hurt more. Blood seeks out its own kind." He held his hand over the cloth and jerked his fingers upward. This seemed to pull the blood out, and it hovered in a tiny sphere just in front of him. It had an odd silver cast that Toba supposed must be Asmel's magic keeping hold of it.

"What are you—"

Without taking his eyes from the blood, he said, "You're going to have to do the last part, I can't do it for you. Come closer."

Toba edged closer, until her shoulder touched his. "I won't be able to do what you ask," she said. "There's no point trying, I don't have the trick of it."

"There's no trick," he said. "Intent is all. It's your blood. You're asking where it came from."

"Is there a spell you want me to say?"

"Just ask it, and mean it." He passed the drop of blood to her outstretched palm, where it hovered. "Ask," he said.

The light caught the silver cast of the blood, and Toba wondered that she hadn't dropped it yet. She thought of her nameless father, who had given her nothing but this. She said, "Where did you come from?"

The blood spun itself into filaments fine as thread, which formed themselves into a series of Mazik characters Toba could not read.

"That is your Mazik name," Asmel said.

"Who would have given me a Mazik name?" she asked.

"You named yourself," he said. "Only human children require naming. Now try again."

"Was it meant to do more?"

"Yes. You've done well; now try again."

She said, again, "Where did you come from?"

The filaments twined back into a single mass, then spun rapidly, splitting into two pieces, one a darker, richer red than the other. The paler blood exploded into a haze of fine mist. The other half formed midair into letters Toba recognized, which read *Penina bat Elena*, and unfolded above the name to read *Elena bat Beladen*.

The name above hers, which should have been Beladen's, was written in Mazik: the palest silver imaginable.

"You've noticed," he said, watching her eyes gazing up. "You had a Mazik in your mother's line as well, very long ago. It's likely how your mother survived long enough to carry you to term." Toba's eyes scanned up; she counted perhaps ten generations. The characters that made up her name made up some earlier grandmother's, too. But there was nothing where her father's name should have been.

"I don't understand," she said. "Where is my father's line?"

Asmel set down the needle, looking displeased. "Your father must have put a ward around his name to keep your blood from calling it out."

Toba looked at a streak of blood left on the table, resisting the urge to wipe it up, and wondered about her Mazik name. What was it? Asmel knew. So far as she knew, he was the only person who did know it, which gave him a queer sort of power over her.

"If he did that," she said, "doesn't that imply that my father knows I exist?"

"It more than implies it," he said. He slammed his palm down on the table, generating a stack of paper beneath it. "He knows he has a child, and he's taken measures to ensure she can't find him." Taking a pen, he scribbled a few characters Toba could actually read: *Return now.* Making a shade of his own, he handed it the note and sent it off to the baths.

"Asmel," Toba said, "does that blood spell work in reverse? Can my father have found me the same way?"

"Very likely," he said. He ran a hand down his face, displeased.

"Would it show him my Mazik name? My father?"

"Not that, at least: to get the true name of a living Mazik, you would have to hear it from their own lips," Asmel explained. "You must understand, knowing a Mazik's true name is holding a key to his will. If I gave you a command, with your name, you would be irresistibly compelled to do as I said. Refusing would be as futile as holding your breath. This is why I'm not telling you your name. If you don't know it, you can't reveal it."

"Should I be concerned that you know it?"

He said, "On my life, I will never use or share it. But to the matter at hand: your father can't know your true name, but he may know he has a daughter called Toba bat Penina, and that is bad enough."

"Bad enough," she echoed. "Asmel, if my father knows I exist, what will he do?"

"It depends on what sort of man he is," he said. "Either way, he won't want you revealed. A good man will try to conceal you. A wicked one will try to kill you."

Twenty-Six

THE FIRST NIGHT, the Tobot had shared the same dream, as if both women had been temporarily assigned custody of the same dreaming mind.

It had been uncomfortable, this sharing. Awake, the pair was becoming increasingly aware that they weren't one person. They had two very different sets of thoughts and ideas, and the overlap between them was becoming less. So when Toba Bet dreamt that night, she was at first surprised, and then delighted to find that she was dreaming her own dream.

It took her a few minutes to realize she was alone, and she could not have said precisely how she knew she'd been split from her counterpart, only that she did know. Toba the Elder was dreaming someplace else.

Toba Bet was in the alcalá, in the hall with the broken doors. Only here, the doors were solid. Whatever had happened to them in the waking world had not come here.

She decided to look for Asmel and set off in the direction of his study. When she arrived, she found it occupied not by Asmel but by Prince Odem, who was assembling some great metal device that looked like one of Asmel's astrolabes, but with several extra gears that did not seem to do anything.

"Toymaker," he said in surprise.

"Where is—" she began, but then stopped, because Asmel had told her not to use names in the dream-world.

"Not here," he said, seeming to know what she meant. "He's never here." He tried, and failed, to insert a gear into the apparatus, resulting in several key parts of the device going off-balance and falling to the ground.

"What are you trying to do?" Toba Bet asked.

"What does it look like?"

"It looks like you're trying to make an astrolabe from random spare parts with no plans," she said.

"Oh," he said. "Good. That's precisely what I'm doing."

"Why?"

"Because I don't have the plans for this. No one does." He glanced up. "I don't suppose this is something you know about?"

"Building astrolabes?"

"That, for a start."

"No," she said. "I'm sorry."

"Oh, fine, then, just hold this." He thrust a glass disc at her, and she had to scramble not to drop it. There was a smattering of pinprick holes scattered across its face, with sharp edges that caught on her fingers. "Wouldn't it be easier to do this awake?"

He took the disc from her. "Are you joking? You know, they said you were simple, but I never believed it. What are you doing here?"

"I dreamt—"

"What are you doing *here*?" he said, spreading his hand, palm down, toward the floor. "In this place, with him. Adon Sof'rim."

Adon Sof'rim, an interesting euphemism. She knew enough Mazik now to know he called him the Lord of Books.

"Listen to me," Odem went on. "Within the year my father will have entered the endless dream. I will be king. Before that happens, I want to know what Adon Sof'rim found."

"Why not ask him?"

"Because he can't tell me! But you live with him. You've seen things he hasn't shown me, I'm sure of it."

"If you're such friends, why wouldn't he tell you whatever he can?"

"He's trying to protect me," he said. "But we're past that. I can't afford La Cacería to know things I don't. I won't rule as my father has; I need the truth."

"What truth?" she asked.

He took her by the shoulders. "The truth of the third realm," he said. "What do you know about Aravoth?"

His grip on her shoulders was too tight, and she gasped, and she woke.

+ + + + + + +

IT APPEARED THAT the wolves did think that Naftaly smelled like a Mazik, because he was the one they did not try to eat. Naftaly managed to put himself between the first wolf and the old woman, while Elena took a stick and scratched a circle of nonsense words into the ground.

"Will that ward them off?" the old woman asked, huddled behind Naftaly. A second and third wolf had joined the first. One of them was rolling on the ground like a puppy. The others were creeping ever closer, as if deciding to test whether they might take a bite out of one of the women without Naftaly noticing.

"Possibly," Elena said. "We'll have to test it."

The old woman dug her fingers into the back of Naftaly's coat. "I'm not testing it," she said. "You stand there and we'll watch."

"Fine," Elena said, and stood in the middle of the circle, extending her arms to either side. "Back away," she told Naftaly, "and see what happens." Naftaly took a few steps away, the old woman scuttling along behind him. One of the wolves approached the edge of the circle, sniffed the ground, and moved off.

The trio of wolves situated itself beyond the rim of Elena's circle, and watched, and waited. Overhead, the moon was a sliver shy of full. "I suppose now we just wait," Naftaly said.

"No," Elena said. "We sleep. Or you do, at least. I want you to try to find Toba. Tell her we're here."

"And how do I find her? I've never dreamed of her before."

"Perhaps if you think of her as you're falling asleep, that will take you to her."

"I'm not sure that's how it works," Naftaly said.

"Neither am I," she agreed. "But you may as well make the effort. You sleep. I'll watch—" She gave a pointed look at the wolves. "Our friends."

So Naftaly fell asleep that night within Elena's circle of nonsense words, his head on his folded coat and Toba's name on his lips. But when he knew himself again, he was in a closed, windowless room with a low ceiling and one other occupant.

It was a man, sitting with his back pressed against the wall, his hair hanging over his face. He was paler than the last time he'd seen him, but when he looked up, Naftaly recognized him as the man he'd seen twice before: the orange-eyed Mazik who had given him the map. After a moment he spoke.

"I suppose questioning me here allows for more creativity on your part," the Mazik said. "I suppose you may as well get on with it, but I don't possess any more information now than I did three hours ago."

Naftaly turned and saw that behind him there was no door. He and the Mazik were sealed in the room together. Naftaly said, "What?"

At his voice, the Mazik looked up with his blazing eyes. The left side of his face bore the remnants of bruises in various stages of healing, but a moment later they were gone, and Naftaly supposed they must have been shadows. "Hm," the Mazik said. "You're new."

"I'm looking for someone," Naftaly said hesitantly. His hands, he realized, were gloved. He must have dreamt them on himself, to cover the mark of the red Mazik. "Is there a way out of this room?"

The Mazik laughed drily. "Friend," he said. "If there were, do you think I would be here?"

"I think we should try to find a way out," Naftaly said, because the room seemed to him to have grown smaller. "Can you get up?"

The Mazik looked at his legs. "I don't think so," he said, and Naftaly realized that both his shins were at odd angles, as if they'd been broken.

"I don't understand," Naftaly said. "What's happened to you?"

"Took a bad step," the Mazik said. "Turned my back when I shouldn't have." He looked like he might say more, but then leaned back against the stone wall again. "Another trick," he said. "Just get on with the torture, it'll save us both some time and trouble. I suppose you're here for some kind of psychic torment? You're pretty enough." He stared at Naftaly for a moment, and then said, "I've heard your voice before, I think. They've made you from my memories, some ... figment or other."

"What? No!" Naftaly protested. "I'm no figment."

"How do I know you? It was something recent. The garden," the Mazik said, leaning his head back. "I gave you a map."

"Yes," Naftaly said. "You did."

"Did you ever find the menagerie?"

"I'm afraid not," he said. "Look, I'm not sure how I ended up in this room, but I'm not here to torture anyone. I was trying to dream my way to someone, and somehow got here instead. What is this place?"

The Mazik did not answer. After a minute, he said, "If I believed you—which I don't, mind—I would encourage you to wake up and try to dream again someplace else. You don't want to be here."

Naftaly frowned. "I've never been able to do that."

"You can't wake yourself up?"

Naftaly said, "No."

The Mazik cocked his head a little, staring intently now. He said, "Come closer."

Naftaly hesitated before taking a step forward. "What is this place?" he asked. "Is it a prison?"

"Now there's an interesting idea," the Mazik said. "If this is a prison, what would that make me?"

Naftaly said, "I don't know," and the Mazik, quick as lightning, reached out and grabbed Naftaly's left wrist in his hand.

"Stop," Naftaly hissed, but the man was stronger than Naftaly by an order of several men, and he said, "If you want me to stop, wake yourself up."

"I've just told you I can't," Naftaly said, but the man had taken hold of his glove and pulled it off, revealing the burn there, as bright red as it had been the night he'd gotten it.

"Ah," the Mazik sighed. "Ah, I see." With his other hand he traced his fingers over the back of Naftaly's scar, smoothing it three times until there was nothing left, before releasing it.

"Why did you do that?" Naftaly said, cradling his unblemished hand.

"They can add it to my list of condemnable crimes," he said, coughing. "Not that I'm likely to get a trial."

"Who are you?"

"No one important," he said. "And neither are you, or you wouldn't be here. Tell me again who you were looking for?"

"I was trying to find . . . a girl. An old friend, you could say. She's a bit lost, and I'm trying to help her get home."

"Indeed," the Mazik said, understanding something that Naftaly did not. "A girl who can write with both hands, I'd wager, slight as a sylph with a tongue sharp as salt. A friend of yours, is she?"

"I'm not sure we're speaking of the same—" Naftaly stopped, feeling a sort of shimmering awareness around him, as if he were being watched by someone he could not see. The Mazik's eyes went wide in alarm. "I'm being woken. Wake up," he said. "Wake up!" and he drew back his hand and slapped Naftaly across the face, jolting him awake and upright into Elena, who had to jerk back out of the way.

"What happened?" she asked. "Did you find Toba?"

Naftaly touched his cheek. "No," he said. "No, but I found someone else."

✦ ✦ ✦

BARSILAY BROUGHT NO breakfast the next morning. Probably he was still off sulking after his fight with Asmel, Toba thought, as she tried to make her own with a small pile of lentils the shade had retrieved from the kitchen. She'd succeeded in making one into a very beany bowl of porridge, but the others seemed to be mocking her.

Toba Bet emerged from the stacks and watched her for a moment, before saying, "Look at you, turning yourself purple."

"Shut up," said Toba. "I made the porridge."

Toba Bet tasted it and scowled. "I don't think you did." She slid one of the remaining lentils toward herself with a forefinger and set her palm over it, and did not bother hiding her smugness when it became a fat loaf of white bread. "Whatever Barsilay did," she said, "it's made things easier. I couldn't have made something so fine yesterday, so easily."

"Easily? How are you making things easily?"

"I was doing magic better before he messed around with our insides, too," Toba Bet said. "I think there's more wrong with you than just the scarring."

"More wrong with me but not you?"

"Rankles, doesn't it?" Toba Bet said. "Seeing as you're the real one and I'm just a buchuk."

Toba harrumphed. Toba Bet said, "But I think that may be why. If our magic comes from will, yours is all muddled. Half your mind is always someplace else. You still want to go home."

"Don't you?"

"I know I can't," she said. "My days are numbered and we both know it—don't look like that, you think it all the time. So what else have I got but right now? You're still thinking about our grandparents and getting back to them. You haven't given that up, not really; you were fantasizing about Grandmother's cooking just now when I came in. And what's more . . . you're very worried about bad things happening to you here."

"You're equally worried," Toba said. "I can hear everything going on inside your dratted head, too."

"I'm worried, but I've also accepted it. Your fear and your useless wishing for home are clouding your intent. You worry everything you do is a mistake. Why else do you think you can't even make bread?" Toba fumed silently, which was useless, because Toba Bet could still hear her unspoken thoughts perfectly well. To be called out by some newer incarnation of herself seemed especially hard to bear. Particularly because she was hungry, and the bread did look good.

Toba Bet tore the loaf in half and handed it over, just as Asmel made his way into the library.

He did not look pleased. His usual flat affect had been replaced with a demeanor that was either angry or alarmed; with Asmel, she did not seem able to tell the difference.

Toba Bet wondered how strong the taboo was against asking about dreams. It seemed important that she'd dreamt of Odem and his ramshackle astrolabes, and Aravoth.

Of this, she knew a little, from her long hours spent reading her grandfather's books. Aravoth was the seventh circle of heaven, the dwelling-place of Hashem himself.

She did not imagine that was what Odem had meant.

Asmel's eyebrows were drawn into a scowl. "Barsilay hasn't returned yet," he said.

"Still? Don't you have a locator spell you can use or something?"

"I tried that. It only shows me the location of his shade." His eyes went far away for a moment and he added, "Someone's coming up the road."

Toba listened, but heard nothing.

"There are riders," he said, striding from the room, with the Tobot following. "At least three, possibly more."

"Well, it must be Barsilay, and we've been worried over nothing."

"It's not him. Not unless he's borrowed a horse and an escort," he said. He took the stairs down to the courtyard, then across to the gate, where there were three smart raps on the ancient metal. Asmel set a hand to the gate. "Go back inside," he said quietly. "Both of you, now."

"Who is it?" Toba whispered. He jerked his head in the direction of the alcalá.

The Tobot made their way back across the courtyard and up the steps, but stopped short of going inside, instead kneeling behind the low wall at the top of the stairs. This would, they thought, give them enough time to get upstairs if the visitors actually ended up entering. But from Asmel's expression, they thought it was unlikely he'd let them in.

Asmel stepped back and the gate swung inward. Outside was a man, flanked by four soldiers dressed in deep blue, and behind them a pair of shades, tending to a quintet of tall, gray horses. "Adon Asmel," said the foremost Mazik cheerily, and Toba realized it was the red Mazik she'd met at court, Tsidon. "I've come to call."

"You can't *possibly* think I'm going to welcome you in," Asmel said flatly. "This is no longer a public institution."

The other man laughed. "But I was given an invitation," he said. "By your newest ward."

Asmel turned toward the place where the Tobot were hiding, fifty kinds of murder in his eyes. "Did she?" he asked in the darkest voice they'd yet heard from him.

"A sweet girl," Tsidon said. "And lovely, if you admire the delicate sort."

Asmel made no answer.

"I've always liked the delicate sort," he said.

Asmel seethed.

"At any rate, I'm here to see her, not you, so if you'll just"—Tsidon waved a hand expansively—"go and fetch her. We can sit in that charming library. Do you still keep it up? With the inlaid tables? Oh, no. No, of course. You don't have those anymore." He tsked. "Well, that was long ago, wasn't it?" He smiled thinly. "Dear Asmel, you must see me inside."

Behind him, one of the other soldiers set his hand on the hilt of his sword. Tsidon, who could not possibly have seen it, raised a hand, his eyes downcast, and said, "There's no need for that." To Asmel, he said, "Will you deny me hospitality already offered?"

Asmel looked as if he might. Toba wasn't sure what that would mean for him, but the fact that Tsidon had come with soldiers did not bode well.

One Toba nudged the other, and Toba the Elder stepped out from behind the wall. Steeling herself, she came down the stairs.

"Ah!" the Mazik said, clapping once, while Asmel silently raged at her. "And here she is."

"You may speak with her," Asmel said. "*Here.*" And he pointedly took up a position a few steps behind her.

"Surely you can leave us alone long enough to have a proper conversation?"

Asmel said, "No." And as Tsidon stepped through the gate, Asmel shut it in the faces of the remaining Maziks. When the visitor looked as if he might have objected, Asmel said, "I am sure my ward did not also offer to entertain your entourage."

Tsidon dipped his chin, in the hint of a nod. "Fair enough," and then he approached Toba, smiling. "Such a stolid man," he said. "Spends too much time with books and too little with charming ladies." He dropped the hint of a bow. "Adona Toba."

Toba felt the spell's grip slip from her tongue and mentally shook herself. Whatever he said, she would not let Tsidon do such a thing to her again. She would make no further agreements.

"Sir," she said, rather curtly, to which Tsidon put a hand to his breast.

"Don't be displeased by Asmel's reaction, dearest. I am here as your servant, and desire only to make you as happy as I am to see you once again." He indicated the nearest bench and motioned for her to sit with him.

Asmel, close enough to speak in her ear, said, "Sit. You look as if you might faint otherwise." So she did, and hoped she could avoid any accidental magic. A replaying of the fish incident would only make things worse. She adjusted her necklace to have something to do with her hands. Tsidon glanced at her bosom as she did.

"Your guardian is rather protective," Tsidon went on. "You know, I've asked about you. You seem to be shrouded in mystery."

"That seems a very romantic spin on my character," Toba replied. "Did you ever consider that I'm simply too boring to inspire gossip?"

He smiled. "Hardly. You made quite the impression at court. There was a fascinating conversation about you after you left."

Toba blanched. Tsidon saw it, and smiled. "Never fear. There was only some discussion as to how long you would be keeping your charms hidden away in Asmel's moldering alcalá."

"I've been ill," Toba said. "For some time."

"You don't look ill," he said. "Maybe you're just suffering from lack of interesting company. Asmel here . . . well, he has all the charm of a boulder. And believes himself twice as weighty."

Toba tried not to smile.

Tsidon's eyes flicked up to a point behind Toba. "My presence is grating on the good Adon—perhaps we can speak further at my own residence. Will you come and see me in the city?"

Asmel laid a heavy hand on Toba's shoulder.

Tsidon stood. "Oh dear," he said. "Look who's grown paternal. Poor father, you mustn't worry I harbor ill intent. My honor is as impeccably kept as yours."

Toba felt Asmel's hand tense on her shoulder, but he only said, "Indeed."

Tsidon offered Toba a tilt of a bow. "I look forward to receiving you, then. Ah." He pulled a small silver box from his pocket and presented it to Toba. "I think you should have this."

The box was filigreed; square and as long as her thumb, crafted of silver wires joined in some way Toba could not fathom. Toba put her hand out and then withdrew it, unsure if accepting the box carried some further implication. Was there some bargain implied?

"It is only a gift," Tsidon said, "freely given." She extended her hand again, and Tsidon set the box on her palm, turned his back on them, and retreated through the gate, flicking a hand toward the shade who stilled his horse. Together with his soldiers, he was gone in a flurry of hoofbeats.

Asmel's hand had not left Toba's shoulder. "What were you thinking?" he breathed.

She tested her tongue. "I met him at court," she said. "There were two men, two Alaunts—"

"You met Alaunts and never spoke of it?"

"I couldn't! He did something." She put her hand in front of her mouth. "A spell to keep me from talking about it. But what happened was I uncovered the almond tree in a mosaic at court, and the Alaunts witnessed it. They were going to burn me, Asmel, but then he stopped them."

"Stopped them. He probably set them on you in the first place, to trick an invitation from you." He removed his hand from Toba and ran it over his face. "The man you invited into my home," he said quietly, "is Tsidon b'Noem, also known as the Lymer. Ranked second in La Cacería only to the Caçador himself."

"The Lymer," she whispered. Toba felt the earth fall away beneath her toes as she rose from the bench. "The *dog*. The message from the hostage was about the dog meaning to steal something. She knew, and I didn't understand!"

"Calm yourself," Asmel warned her.

She strode toward the fountain, and then back again when she felt some part of herself longing for the cold water. "How can I?" she demanded. "You've just said he staged the entire scene with the Alaunts so he could come here. My eyes. He said something about my eyes being unusual. Could he tell? Do they give me away?"

Toba felt fear rising in her. Asmel took her hands in his. "Don't," he said. "You must learn to keep your magic in. Especially now. Your eyes look normal to me, like a Mazik's eyes."

"To you," she said, "what about to Tsidon?"

He said, "I don't know. There are rumors about Tsidon's vision. It's possible he sees things I can't."

"But if he suspects," she said, "why didn't he take me?"

"I don't understand his aim," he said. "I suspect either he's trying to unmask your father or protect him, and I can't say which. Open the box."

Toba had been rubbing her fingers across it absently. She pushed back the top. Inside was a silver ring, inscribed with Mazik characters and set with a silver stone that caught the light.

"This is Barsilay's," she said. "I've never seen him without it."

Asmel had paled. "He would not be without it. It's the mark of my heirship."

Toba curled the ring inside her fist, and tried to use her grandmother's logic to pick apart everything Asmel had told her and Tsidon had done.

La Cacería had Barsilay, and they wanted Asmel to know. This could only be because they wanted something to exchange for him. This was almost certainly Toba herself. Only this didn't square with what they'd decided about her father. Either La Cacería was working for her father or against him; either her father wanted her dead or concealed.

"If La Cacería wanted to use me against my father," she said, "they wouldn't do it this way. There would be no need to go to all this trouble to keep my existence from being public, if they were about to reveal it."

Asmel looked troubled but said nothing. She continued: "They're working on his behalf to conceal me. But if they wanted me concealed and safe, they wouldn't be forcing you to trade me for Barsilay."

"No."

There was only one possibility left: La Cacería was working for Toba's father. And Toba's father wanted her dead.

"What will you do?" she asked.

Asmel said, "I don't know."

Twenty-Seven

"WE NEED TO go home," Toba told Toba Bet.

The Tobot were upstairs in Toba's tower bedroom; the shade hovered nervously nearby, and the elder Toba was pacing between the closed door and the window while the younger sat on the bed, examining the spot on her hand analogous to the one Asmel had pierced on her counterpart, kneading the place between her thumb and forefinger. "La Cacería will find us there."

"La Cacería has found us *here*!" Toba countered. "Tsidon knows. He has Barsilay already, and he means Asmel to trade him for . . . one of us, at least. If we stay here, we're good as dead. On the other side of the gate, at least we have a chance. If we get far enough from the gate, how can they find us?"

"A chance to do what?" Toba Bet asked. "Wander in the wilderness 'til the wolves catch us? We have nothing! No money, no one in Rimon to help us. We'd be dead in a week even without La Cacería looking for us."

"It's still better odds than we have in this place," Toba said. "Perhaps we have one chance in a thousand if we escape. Here?" She shook her head.

"You're so sure Asmel will trade us?"

"What choice does he have? They have his heir!" Sitting down on the bed, she took the other woman's hands. "The moon is tonight. We both remember where the gate is. Let's flee. We'll find a way to survive."

Toba Bet said, "No."

"No! That's it, and with no explanation!"

There was no explanation that would suffice, because both knew the other's mind. Both were torn in equal measure. It was made worse by the duality of her personae, which allowed her the freedom to take both positions at once. She was terrified to stay, and terrified to go, and as long as she could not agree with herself, she would be right at least once.

"Weren't you just telling me that fear was weakening my will? We have something very specific to be afraid of now, and my will is strong indeed."

"Asmel wishes us safe," Toba Bet said. "If we stay, we have that goodwill. If we leave, our fate goes to chance." She turned away from herself. Outside, the full moon was beginning to ascend. "I'm going to sleep."

"You're an idiot," she told herself.

"Well," she said, "either I am or you are."

TOBA HAD DONE her first drawing when she'd been nearly a year old, a picture of a courtyard full of dancing people in outrageous costumes, both men and women, with plumes in their hair, and jewels in their ears and around their bare ankles. This was in the time before Beladen had come with the amulet. She did not do such drawings afterward.

"What is this?" Elena had asked, taking up the paper from Alasar's table; he'd fallen asleep, and Toba had pinched the sheet along with his best pen and a pot of ink. Elena was not pleased. One did not sleep while watching Toba, and she should not have been in Alasar's study at all, during the day, when anyone might stop by.

The drawing was not the scrawl of a baby, but the work of a master; the only imperfections not in the rendering but in the smudging of ink by Toba's little hands, too impatient to let a line dry before moving onto the next. "Who are these people?"

"I dreamt a party," she said. "They're dancing, see?"

Elena had seen. Toba said, "They didn't pay me any attention, so I left. No one in the dream place ever talks to me."

Elena hesitated. "And where did you go then, after you left the party?"

"To the sea. Someone told me the real sea hurts us, but the dream-sea can't."

"Didn't you just say no one there speaks to you?"

"Mostly not," Toba said. "The grown-ups don't, but sometimes I find another child, and they tell me things, like the dream-sea is safe, or how to make your hair purple and your eyes red. It hurts here but not there." Toba had taken the paper back from Elena and turned it over, and was drawing on the back. "Lots of things hurt here but not there. I don't know why."

"Dreams are that way, I expect," Elena said. "But you should still be careful."

"Why?"

Elena watched Toba make stroke after stroke with her pen, without looking up. It wasn't normal for a toddler to have such concentration: Elena's younger brothers had spent their babyhoods pulling each other's hair and wreaking havoc in the yard. It didn't help that Alasar was delighted by all this, which was probably how Toba had ended up in the study in the first place. He spoiled the child appallingly. Toba was creating what was clearly the seashore: there was the surf, and there, next to it, was a child Elena at first took to be Toba, but upon further inspection realized it could not have been: it was an infant, chubby-armed and making something from the sand.

"Who is that?" Elena asked.

"My friend," Toba said. "I like her, but she's unhappy. I will rescue her, so she can come here and live with us."

Elena's breath stilled, and she bent to examine the picture. What was the child making? A sandcastle—more a sand palace, really. "Toba—"

"She lives on the other side," she said. "Of the gate."

Elena whispered, "The gate?"

"The one in the mountains. I will go there at the next moon, and rescue her, and bring her here to live with us."

"Rescue her?"

"Her father is a wicked man. I told her my father is wicked, too, so I'll go and fetch her, and all the wicked men can stay on their side of the gate, and we'll stay on ours."

Elena stood up from the table. "You mustn't do that."

"Why?"

"You're a child. You can't go into the mountains, and you can't go through any gates. It isn't safe."

"But she needs me to come," Toba insisted. "Her father will make her kill people when she's big enough. She's told me. She will have to be wicked like he is, because he knows her name and he'll make her."

"You cannot go," Elena said. "I forbid you."

Toba tilted her tiny chin down and said, "You can't forbid me to do anything."

Elena was very dizzy, and she put her hand over her face for a moment. The child would run headlong into ruin, and she was right: Elena could not stop her. Toba knew about the gate, and she knew about the moon, and she would find her way to the Mazik realm if she was determined to do so. Only there would be no coming back with a new playmate. She would disappear into the land of wicked Maziks, and never be seen by human eyes again.

Still, the child was little more than a baby, and Elena was still her guardian. She drew herself up to her substantial height and said, "Toba, you must never leave this house. And if you do, I will have to punish you."

"Then I won't tell you I'm going! I'll sneak away, and you won't know!"

"I *will* know, Toba. And then you won't be allowed any more of your grandfather's paper, or any sweets, or any time in the garden."

"You can't! You can't do that!" And she stomped her foot, and the table trembled.

"I am your grandmother," Elena said, with more conviction than she felt. "And to keep you safe, I will do that and more."

"I hate you!"

"You may hate me all you like, so long as you are safe."

"I will hate you forever," Toba said, stomping her little foot again. "And when I'm old enough I will leave you and never see you again." With that, she ran from the room, slamming the door so hard it rattled on its hinges. Elena let herself slump a little.

Alasar was watching quietly from the corner, and she frowned at him. "If you heard all that, you might have helped," she said.

"Nothing I said would have made any difference."

"She respects you," she said.

"No. She only likes me because I don't discipline her."

"You could take a turn at that, too, you know."

He held up his gnarled hands. "Not easily," he said. "In another year, she'll be stronger than both of us, and threatening her won't work. She'll do as she likes."

"What do you suggest we do?"

"I don't know," he said, slowly pulling himself up from his chair. "Can you give her something to make her sleep without dreaming?"

"Perhaps," she said. "For a time, at least."

Alasar spread his hands on Toba's drawing and pressed his face close. "I wonder who the child is."

"Some Mazik child. How can we know?"

"I suppose we can't. But she resembles Toba. Or don't you see it?"

Elena did see it, and wondered about the child's wicked father. Perhaps every Mazik had a wicked father, she told herself. The alternative—that it might be the same man, fathering children he might later make use of—was too terrifying to ponder. She found herself thinking of all the women in her family who had died in childbirth, and wondered if any of the others may have had a Mazik lover, too. A cousin of some four or five generations removed had died that way when Toba was only a few months old; the child had died with her.

She made a decision to go and ask after the midwife who had attended that birth. But no one seemed to remember who it was.

\+ + · + + + +

EXHAUSTION WON OUT over strain, and Toba fell asleep. Once dreaming, she found herself in a tower, and in the tower was a staircase: a spiral, so she could not tell whether she was closer to the bottom or the top. It was tight, as if it had been built with very small people in mind, and the steps were too narrow for her feet, and there was no railing to hold onto if she tripped.

She decided a downward trajectory might eventually lead to the ground, and then outside, while the upward staircase likely led to some tiny tower room and she had no desire to be in one of those, so down she went.

She went down a very long way.

This did not go to the ground, she decided, but to a cellar or something else below ground, and that was even worse than a tower room. She wanted out badly. She wanted to be awake.

There was a door in the wall. The stairs continued down, but Toba decided she'd rather be anywhere than in that tower, so she went through the low doorway, and down a dim, windowless hall, and found an open door at the end of it.

Sitting within the room was a table, and many stacks of books, and a man wearing a mask shaped like the face of a bird; its beak extending a hand's length beyond the end of where his nose should have been.

He looked up from his book, or appeared to—she could not see his eyes—conjured a second chair, and leaned back. "Ah," he said. "There you are."

He slid the volume he'd been reading toward her, and she went cold, because she knew she would not be able to read Mazik well enough to fool him.

"What do you make of that?" he asked.

Tentatively, she sat, and leaned over the page.

It was not in Mazik. It was in Hebrew, and she wondered if this were a trap; if a regular Mazik would be able to read Hebrew at all. She glanced up at the beaked mask, and then back at the words, and then, because she never could resist an unfamiliar book, she began to read.

She stopped reading.

"This isn't real," she said. "It doesn't mean anything."

"Doesn't it?"

"No," she said. "It rhymes, but that's all. The words don't mean anything."

"Are you sure?" he asked.

She took her fingers from the page. She had the distinct impression this was a test. "Yes," she said. "I'm sure."

"What a bother," he said, and took the book and tossed it into the air, where it burst into flames and then was gone.

Toba pulled back in her chair, unsure which was worse: staying here, or being back on the horrible staircase.

"Do you know who I am?" he asked.

"That would be an easier question for me to answer, were you not wearing a mask," she said. "At this moment, I'm not sure if I know you or not. Your voice is not familiar."

He paused. "And now?" he asked, and this time, his voice was Asmel's.

"No," she said. "You aren't him, of that I'm positive."

"And how do you know?"

Because he was playing a game with her, and Asmel would not do that, but she said, "He would have known the Hebrew wasn't real." Then she added, "What is the point of that mask, when you could simply dream yourself a false face?"

He laughed. "What do you think the point would be?"

She thought about it. "It could only be that you want me to know that you're disguising yourself. Nothing else makes sense."

"Ah," he said. "I like you. I like you a great deal. I'm glad you've come at last."

There was none of this that sounded good to Toba, and she began to have a sinking suspicion. "What is this place?"

"Only a manifestation of some part of my mind," he said. "Not one of the more attractive ones, I'm afraid. I know it's rather dreary. Though I'm sure you're used to dreary, living with Asmel."

She went rigid at his name.

He waited for her response.

She said, "If you wanted me to know you're well acquainted with him, you needn't have done it twice," she said. "Imitating his voice was sufficient."

"You are very set on proving how clever you are," he said. "Going forward, you may want to suppress that impulse. It might be your undoing, one day. Now, try again: who am I?"

"You've just finished telling me to play the fool, and you ask me that?"

He laughed. "You are subtle. Any man would be proud to have such a child."

Toba hadn't expected him to admit to it so bluntly. So here he was, the man himself, hidden away behind a ridiculous mask like a child, playing hide-and-seek in this horrible tower. He'd told her to play the fool, to be subtle, but neither suited her at all. She said, "Proud enough to have me killed?"

The voice from the bird-mask said, "Asmel made that suggestion. But I think you're intelligent enough not to believe the very man who holds you prisoner."

"Take off your mask," she said.

"Not," he said, "today."

"Why?"

"It doesn't suit me to do so," he said. "But know this: I mean you no harm. The Lymer is extracting you from your prison, nothing more."

"Why threaten my friend, then?"

"Your friend," he said. "Now that was unguarded."

Toba cursed herself. He said, "Threatening your friend is the only way to force Asmel to let you go. But rest assured, it's Asmel who wants you dead, not I."

Toba said, "Why?"

He replied, "Vengeance. But what I am proposing to him is a trade: his heir, for mine."

Toba said, "You do see that you've given me no reason to trust you."

"I realize that," he conceded. "But there are two possibilities you should consider: Either I am telling the truth, and Asmel means you harm. Or Asmel is the one telling the truth, and *I* mean you harm, and he intends to give you to me anyway."

"He hasn't said he means to—"

"He will, you will see. He will offer you to the Lymer, I've already seen it. You will accept him. And you will be glad, that day, that I value you enough to keep you safe. Now," he said, raising his hand to her. "Wake up."

He reached across the table and set his palm on the crown of her head, and Toba sat up in her bed, tangled in her sheets and as cold as if it were winter. The other Toba was in the doorway, haloed by the lightstones in the hall. Through the window, the moon was full.

Toba threw back her covers and got up. Toba Bet said, "You must not trust him."

But Toba was beyond reason. She was going to die, she had a sense of it welling from her gut: she knew. Either Asmel would trade her for Barsilay because he felt he had no choice, or else he would hold her back, and that man—her father—would come for her anyway.

"Don't," whispered Toba Bet, because Toba had begun to shake violently.

Toba by then had lost the feeling in her hands and her feet, and she collapsed, face down on the floor in front of the window, the other girl beside her, and then, from her back spurted a flock of birds, which flew out through the window.

\+ + + + + +

THE DAY NAFTALY spent resting in Elena's magic circle was the most rest he'd had since he'd left Rimon, even if it did mean lying on the rocky ground.

Several hours had passed since sunset, since moonrise, when from the floor of the valley, a shooting star had risen into the sky, leaving a streak of light in its wake. The wolves had let out a chorus of howls and then dashed off, perhaps welcoming a visit from their masters, or perhaps because they'd sighted easier prey than Naftaly's friends. He hoped it was not human.

"She'll come," Elena had said. "I feel it."

The pomegranate trees shone silver from the light of the gate, all of them heavy with fruit. He wished he felt it would be safe to eat, but thought it was not worth the risk that came with eating from a magic tree. After the wolves had gone, the old woman walked out of Elena's circle to weigh one of the dangling pomegranates in her hand.

"I wouldn't," Elena said, which was good enough to cure Naftaly of his desire to eat one.

Toba had not come, and dawn was not far off. Naftaly approached the sliver of the gate. He expected the air around it to feel different somehow; warmer, maybe, but it felt completely normal. As he drew closer, the old woman said, "What do you intend to do?"

Naftaly walked a circle around the gate; it appeared to exist from all angles. He wondered if it mattered how one approached it. Probably, it would be better to come from the direction of the pines, as Toba had done. He said, "If she's on the other side, perhaps she's afraid to come through. For all she knows, there's no one waiting here for her."

"But what if you go through and can't get back for some reason?" the old woman said.

He slipped his fingers through the blade of light but felt nothing. "If I don't see her right away, I'll come back; I don't mean to go far."

Elena nodded. "You should go, then. Before the moon gets any lower."

Steeling himself, Naftaly stepped through the gate.

For a long moment, he felt himself suspended in what felt like water that wasn't wet, as if there were such a thing. Then he came through the other side. Everything looked the same; the wood, the landscape. The pomegranates.

Less so, the cadre of fifty mounted Maziks before him, led by the man with the red-black braid who smiled slowly, triumphantly, and said, "The hart has come to me."

TWENTY-EIGHT

"DOES HE SPEAK?" one of the Mazik soldiers asked, giving Naftaly a queer look. "Is there something wrong with him?"

The red Mazik's lip curled up a hair. "Just take him," he said. He pointed at Naftaly and said, "Stay still." To one of his men, he snapped, "Check him for books, not that he likely has any."

Naftaly found himself unable to move, frozen by the Mazik's spell, and the Maziks began to advance until one of their horses shied.

The mounted Mazik got his nightmare-horse under control with the use of a hand sign. "Someone's there," he said, indicating a hill to the west.

"There's no one there," the red Mazik said, irritated, but then there came a noise, a shriek like an injured bird, and a sky-full of larks went sailing by in a flurry of wings. They came so near the gate Naftaly thought they'd pass through, but at the last moment they banked and doubled back.

The red Mazik brought his own horse closer, then, with a swift movement, gripped Naftaly by the back of his shirt and hoisted him across his saddle. Naftaly's book pressed into his ribs through his coat. The Mazik snapped, "Catch them. I want them traced," and two of the others created nets from the air and threw them skyward, failing to bring anything down.

"I want to know whose birds those are," he said. "Keep trying." He dismounted, leaving Naftaly across the horse's shoulders.

Naftaly still felt himself very much paralyzed; his arms and legs were numb as wood. But the muscles in his torso were less dead. Maybe, he thought, the Mazik had spared those to ensure he would still be able to breathe. This meant that while he couldn't move, precisely, he could lean. He wasn't sure that being on the ground was better than being slung across the horse, but at least it was a step in the right direction, if he did get the feeling back in his legs. Very slowly—until gravity took over—he slid down the side of the horse, landing in a heap by its front hooves. He looked up at the animal, and their eyes met—not one eye, as one could normally only look a horse in one eye at a time, but both. The horse looked far too much like a person, and Naftaly wished he had not looked it in the face.

The horse shuffled its feet uneasily, and Naftaly realized his mistake; now, instead of just worrying about the Maziks, he had to worry about being trampled. The horse was unshod, and its hooves appeared sharp. On the dry ground, it left marks in the shape of a Vav.

"The nets are going through them," Naftaly heard someone say.

"Then make *better* nets."

Naftaly lay on the ground willing his legs to move. The birds continued to shriek overhead, and the red Mazik was growing increasingly angry—Naftaly heard what sounded like him striking one of the other Maziks—and in the flurry of wings, one of the birds dropped a tail-feather near his face. It shimmered in the dying moonlight, a color halfway between a plum and the night sky, and Naftaly brushed his cheek against it, and his nose, and then—and he did not know why he did this, some strange instinct, he would later think—he took it between his lips and into his mouth, where it ceased to be a feather at all.

He felt a surge of warmth spread down his throat as he swallowed, and felt sensation creep into his limbs. While the soldiers continued trying to catch the bespelled larks, Naftaly picked his way back toward the gate and eased his way through, just as he heard the alarm go up at his escape.

"Go after him!" he heard the red Mazik shout, but the only answer was the protest: "But the moon—" and then Naftaly could hear no more, because he was back in the clearing with the old woman and Elena, who leapt to her feet just as he called, "They're coming, and they have horses."

✦ ✦ ✦

TOBA BET LOOPED the first Toba's arm around her shoulder and half dragged her down the stairs to Asmel's study. She saw through the eyes of the birds that they were making their way to the gate. She didn't know what it would mean if they actually passed through, but she did not think it would be good for either of them if so much of her magic went through the gate independently.

She found Asmel poring over his books; he looked thoroughly annoyed at being interrupted. "She's lost control of her magic," Toba Bet told him, because the older Toba was mostly unconscious. Asmel came and put her on the chaise.

"What happened?"

"She was overcome by fear," she told him. "There were birds, and they've fled."

"They've fled?" Asmel shook his head.

"Yes, and there were a lot. Is there something you can do? They've gone all the way to the gate, but now they're panicking because—oh."

Asmel had set his hand across Toba's eyes and pressed some magic into her mind. Toba Bet felt it, was aware of it, and had to sit down. Since there was no chaise for her, she thumped down on the floor instead. "What did you do?"

"Why are you still awake?" he said. "That should have affected you, too."

"I'm not sure," she said, fluttering her hands by her face, because she did feel worse for whatever he'd done. She'd have liked to have been asleep, but she thought it was more important to stay awake. "But the birds have gone. Will she be very weak, then? Since they didn't return to her?"

"She will be weak," Asmel said. "You could remedy that by dispelling yourself."

Toba Bet drew back. "Dispelling myself?"

"My reigning theory," he said, "is that her magic is as inadequate as it is because she's wasting so much maintaining you."

"Wasting it! She was weak as a kitten before I ever showed up."

"Yes, I know, but she might have had a chance to improve if not for you."

Toba Bet got a bit unsteadily to her feet, because she did not want to defend her right to exist while looking like a lump on the floor. "So you're saying I ought to kill myself."

"Of course not," he said. "That implies you are alive."

"Am I not?" Toba Bet asked. "Why are you insistent that I am lesser? You yourself said she and I were identical in all respects."

"You are like an image in a mirror," he said.

"I'm not! An image is . . . nothing! A two-dimensional copy; that's no analogy at all!"

"Fine, then. Not an image. A . . . a tool. You are an instrument, created by Toba, and when whatever part of her is holding on to you decides to let go, you will cease to exist."

"So it's my mortality, then? Is a person worth less because she'll live a shorter life?"

"You have no interest in my honest opinion, and I have no interest in continuing this conversation," Asmel said, turning back to his books.

Toba Bet put herself between Asmel and his desk. "Well, I have! Is an old man worth less than a child, since he has less time left?"

"That is a mortal line of thinking," he said. "Stop pressing me. You won't like my answer."

Toba Bet wanted to tear her own hair out. "So that's it, then? Do you view all mortals as tools? Worthless but for what they might do for you?"

"No! Do you not see? You are not even a mortal. You are what amounts to a very well-made shade." He pointed a finger at Barsilay's shade in the corner. "Is that Barsilay? It knows what he knows. It thinks, it acts, it even communicates now, since Toba taught it to write. Shall I hold it in the same esteem as Barsilay himself? Do you? Perhaps we shouldn't think of saving Barsilay at all, since we have this one instead: isn't it just as good?"

Toba Bet was trying very hard not to cry. "I am not a shade," she said. "I'm not."

"You are a buchuk," he said, turning his back on her a second time. "A very good one. Perhaps the finest one ever made. But Toba made you, and at some point in the future, she will unmake you. It will be easier for you if you don't forget that."

"No," Toba Bet said tearfully. "It will be easier for you."

\+ + · + + + +

NAFTALY WAS STILL slow to move and his left leg dragged a little; there would be no outrunning the mounted Maziks, if they followed him through. "Can you conceal us?" he asked Elena. "With magic?"

"I may be able to conceal two," she said. "Three is beyond me."

"Take him," the old woman said, pushing Naftaly into Elena's arms. "I'll manage."

"But—"

"Hurry up!" she snapped, while Elena's face went from shock to resolution. Pulling him farther from the gate, she dumped Naftaly onto the ground, crouching over him.

"You should—" Elena began, but the old woman, in the midst of stomping out Elena's circle said, "I'm already doing it."

Elena chanted a tangle of words that sounded more like a nursery rhyme than a spell, and a blue cast formed over her skin, spreading to Naftaly's, and he felt a coldness settle over him. The old woman, who had finished concealing Elena's magic, grabbed a handful of twigs and set them alight, before arranging herself in front of the small fire to look as if she'd been there a while. "Not good," she muttered. "Damned Maziks everywhere, and now they have horses and probably weapons. Stupid boy never listens."

"Wait," Naftaly called. "They want books."

"Books," the old woman repeated. Elena twisted his ear to quiet him, reminding him he was meant to be stone.

Seven Maziks rode through the gate, led by the red.

"If you're looking to share the fire," the old woman told them, "you might bring a bit more wood. This is growing low."

The red Mazik dismounted and approached, fingers tapping on the pommel of his sword; with the other hand, he signaled the others to wait. "Hello, Grandmother," he said. "Are you out here all alone?" He passed a hand in the air across her shoulders and down her back, as if searching for something, and frowned when he did not find it. Elena tensed as she crouched over Naftaly, and he realized she was having to exert herself strongly to maintain whatever illusion she was using to conceal them.

"Times are difficult," the old woman said. "I'm sure you know."

"Yes," he agreed. "Yes, that's very true. Have you seen a young man out here? Dark-haired, perhaps a little thin?"

She turned her face to him, doing her best to look rheumy. "I don't see much these days," she said, indicating her eyes. "I expect I might have missed you, if you weren't so splendid."

"But perhaps you heard something?" he asked, sounding thoroughly unconvinced.

"Oh, I hear lots of things," she said. "Thought I heard a stag go by a few moments ago, made quite a racket. I think there may have been wolves chasing it."

"A stag," he said sourly. "You're lucky the wolves didn't come after you, out here alone."

She laughed merrily. "If you were a wolf, which would you rather eat? A healthy young buck or myself?"

"Yes," he said. "How fortunate for you he came along. This stag." Coming to stand behind her, he raised a hand, and Naftaly realized he meant to enchant her. To what end, he couldn't say.

"Yes, well," she said, quickly. "There's always quite a bit of excitement going on these days, what with the Inquisition in town, and all that treasure they've stolen."

He paused with his hand still raised. "Is that so?"

"Oh, yes," she said. "Anything you can imagine, gold, jewels. They're supposed to send it all along to the crown, but they only pass on a tenth and hoard the rest."

His smile flattened. "Do they?"

"I heard they've only now taken a trove off some fabric merchant down in Eliossana," she went on. "Fools. They'll keep the gold and burn the rest, that's what they usually do."

The Mazik had gone very still. "What precisely will they burn?"

The old woman looked at him sideways. "Anything flammable," she said. "I hear they have a great number of books this time."

The Mazik's eyes went to the moon, growing low on the horizon. He remounted his horse, signaling the other six to follow him.

"But, sir—" one of them protested, gesturing at the sky.

"We can't risk it," he said. "You two go back in case that bitch remembers to do her job after all. The rest of you come with me. There's little time." He spurred his horse, and the five of them galloped out of the wood at great speed, while somewhere closer, the wolves howled a chorus. The horses were so swift they were a blur before they were out of sight, and then they vanished completely. The other two rode back toward the gate. One of them mimed, "*That bitch.*" The other said, "Think he knows that's what we call him, too?" and then they laughed and were gone.

A moment later, the old woman turned to Naftaly and Elena, who had slumped on top of him and was breathing very hard, and who no longer looked anything like a rock. "I suggest we not be in this wood when they come back," she said.

Twenty-Nine

TOBA WOKE ON the couch in Asmel's library. She didn't feel as if she'd *slept*, more as if she'd ceased to exist for a few hours. The sun was high overhead through the windows; it was nearly noon. "What did you do to me?"

"Put you in a coma," Asmel said. "Briefly."

She sat up stiffly. He continued: "The theory being that you would not be able to maintain the magic of those birds, once you were deeply enough unconscious." He raised an eyebrow. "I realize you think I should have asked you first, but in the moment there wasn't time for a discussion."

She sighed and rubbed at her eyes. The second Toba sat on the edge of the windowsill, looking out at the garden. Apparently *she* hadn't been rendered comatose by whatever he'd done. She wondered about the experiment Asmel had done in cutting her hair, and wondered if it would still work, and knew that it wouldn't.

"I don't understand how you are able to maintain this level of magic," Asmel said. "I expected her to vanish when I put you out, but at the very least she should have lost consciousness."

"The birds made it all the way to the gate," Toba Bet said. To Asmel, she said, "It was guarded, and they'd caught someone. If you're interested."

Asmel looked deeply troubled. Passing a hand over his eyes, he said, "I've had a noose about my neck a thousand years. And they've chosen this moment to tighten it."

"It might help," Toba said, "if I could understand what that meant." Then: "Does this have anything to do with Aravoth?"

Asmel went very still. "Where did you hear that word?" he murmured.

"In a dream," she said. "From Odem. He said—"

"Don't tell me what he said!" Asmel snapped.

"Because he asked me about it in a dream?"

"Because it's not a subject I can discuss," he said.

Toba said, "Is this why the University was closed? Why La Cacería watches you?"

"Yes," he said. "But that's as much as I can tell you."

"Why? Who are you, really?"

"An astronomer," he said, indicating the markings on the floor: it was a sextant, she realized. "But surely you've figured that out by now."

"But that isn't why you're the enemy of La Cacería. If it was, none of this would be out in the open. So why? Why can't you simply tell me?"

Asmel's face contorted, briefly. Without speaking, he opened his jaw wide. Toba drew back a second, thinking he intended some magic, but then she took his face in her hands and looked into his mouth.

The back of Asmel's tongue bore a blue-black mark—a character—as if it had been branded.

She took his left hand in hers and turned it over—it was the same mark. "They did this to you," she said. "They put some kind of ward on your tongue, to keep you from speaking of it."

He nodded. Toba fought the urge to recoil from the horror of it. "And on your hands to keep you from writing of it."

"Yes," he rasped. He turned away. "But it's not significant to what's happening now."

"Are you sure?"

Asmel looked troubled, but gave no answer.

"There must be some other way for you to tell me," she said. "In the dream-world?"

"No," he said. "No, the sigils follow me, even there."

Her mind conjured horrible images of Asmel struggling against Maziks branding his tongue, and turned away, trying not to be sick. "If it eases your mind," he said, "I did consent to this."

Toba let her fingers explore the sigil on Asmel's palm; it was hot and burned her fingertips, and she pulled her hand away. "There must be some way around it," she said. "I won't believe there isn't."

Asmel closed his eyes and seemed to turn in on himself for a long while. "There may be," he said. "You have a great deal of magic, that much is clear from the buchuk and the larks, and I think Barsilay's treatment has unblocked it. But your magic is so unpredictable, I think we dare not risk it."

From the windowsill, Toba Bet finally brought her gaze back into the room. "My magic is not so unpredictable."

Asmel waved her off, but she said, "I've been making my own meals. I can change the color of my clothes, and I can make paper and ink."

"What else?" he asked.

"I haven't tried much else," she admitted.

Asmel nodded. He said, "Change the color of your eyes."

Toba Bet blinked rapidly a few times, and then they turned as blue as Asmel's. Toba felt consternated indeed. She could not have done it at all. "Ouch," Toba Bet said. "It feels dreadful."

"Why can she do this," Asmel asked Toba, "when you cannot? She is a buchuk. You are a Mazik. She can't have more magic than you—it isn't possible."

Miserably, Toba said, "I don't know."

Asmel sighed and rubbed at his temples. "I've examined you, and your paths are clear now, and I've seen you do very intense magic three times. I thought perhaps it was maintaining the buchuk, but that does nothing to explain why she is stronger. I think what's lacking is your will, and I don't know how to fix that."

Toba Bet said, "You said there might be a way around the sigils, if her magic were better. But mine is better."

"You are only a buchuk."

"So you keep insisting," she said crossly. "But you thought me perfectly capable when you taught me to read."

Asmel looked aghast, which only made Toba Bet angrier. "So this is what it takes for you to acknowledge me. Have you improved me, then? The way I improved the shade, since I and it are so much alike?"

He tsked. Then he said, "Your eyes are still blue."

"Yes, because you haven't told me to change them back! And they still hurt—do I need to keep this up much longer?"

He thought on this. "Are your minds still linked?"

Toba Bet spat, "Yes."

Asmel said, "Come with me." When Toba also rose, he said, "Not you. Go to the library. I don't want you outside, even in the garden. I don't want to risk anyone seeing there are two of you."

Toba Bet, her eyes gone back to brown, saw Toba's face fall, but she was already following Asmel down the tower stairs, across the courtyard, and down another set of steps she'd not seen before. "Where does this go?" she asked.

"The cellars," he said. "It's where we used to keep the work that could be harmed by daylight." He passed into an open room, holding out a light-stone on his outstretched palm. Toba Bet had to keep close to avoid bumping into the wooden tables that filled the room; except for Asmel's light, it was pitch-dark. "I hid something here, before they came."

He handed Toba Bet the light and knelt down, pulling a panel away from the wall. "This is where we kept the failed experiments, until the shades had time to burn them," he said.

Inside the wall was a bin made of thin steel; within this were shards of broken glass and metal and crumbled rocks, mixed with pieces of parchment covered in hastily scrawled notes. "Help me," Asmel said, and Toba Bet set the light in a wall sconce and helped him empty the refuse of failed magic onto the floor. At the bottom there was a half-burned book, slim, nondescript, with a plain brown cover that read, *Works of Fire.*

Asmel rubbed dust and soot from the cover. With his hand, he wiped the title away, revealing a second: *For the Sharing of Memory.*

"You never retrieved it until now?" Toba Bet asked.

"It's too dangerous a thing to have anywhere someone might find it," he said, standing. "I won't even take it upstairs now."

"It lets you share memories with another person?"

"You can see what that would mean," he said, "if La Cacería got hold of it." His face darkened. "Both parties do not have to be consenting for the spell to work."

"You're going to cast this on me?"

"No," Asmel said. "You're going to cast it on me."

✦ ✦ ✦

THE WAGON TO Merja was full of chickens, and it stank.

Elena and her companions had to walk ten miles past Eliossana to find someone who would give them three spots in a cart, to be shared with four crates of chickens, a farmer, and his daughter who was being sent off to the city to stay with relations. Elena supposed this was because she was pregnant, which she'd extrapolated from the girl's constant motion sickness and wailing about the smell, which was bad but not nearly enough to induce vomiting. Under different circumstances, Elena could have given her a tonic—something with ginger and turmeric—to ease the worst of it. The farmer was grim and glared at the others, daring them to comment on his daughter's obviously out-of-wedlock condition.

The map on Naftaly's palm was gone, faded to nothing with the setting of the moon. There would be no finding the gate a second time.

Elena had wanted to argue to stay in the wood another month, 'til the next moon, but even she knew it was childish, pointless. The gate had been guarded, and likely would be again. There was no passing through from this side.

Had Toba been captured, too, the night she'd gone through?

There was no way to tell, and no way to save her. Elena had failed. And even if Toba, by some miracle, were able to find her way back through the gate, either next month or in a year, she would find herself very much alone.

Assuming she even wanted to return. There was the matter that Toba had believed for her entire life that her father was a useless merchant who'd abandoned her; that she was naturally weak and sickly, and that her amulet protected her from evil, rather than from herself.

It was the greatest lie Elena'd ever told; would ever tell, and it was very likely that Toba was now unbound, and knew the truth, and hated her. Perhaps she would never wish to see Elena again. Perhaps she preferred to be a world apart from her, nursing her betrayal, not understanding that Elena'd had no choice.

Or Toba could be a prisoner of the Maziks, or she could be dead. Elena had failed as a mother and grandmother both.

The girl was vomiting again when Elena turned to Naftaly. "I want to ask you a favor. I want you to keep trying to find Toba, in your dreams. When you do, tell her . . . tell her I hope she forgives me."

"Forgives you?"

"For not telling her the truth." More retching from the girl. Her father ordered her to stop, as if she had a choice in the matter.

"Why didn't you tell her?" Naftaly asked. "Your own mother must have told you about your own lineage."

"Yes, but I—" Here, the farmer yelled at the girl to shut up her weeping, which caused quite an uproar from some sympathetic chickens. "It was different."

Naftaly looked at her doubtfully. "Toba," she whispered, "had to be restrained. She had a great deal of magic, and she was a child."

"So when were you going to tell her? Before she had a part-Mazik child of her own, and did not understand why it could do magic?"

"It seemed unlikely," Elena said slowly, "that she would be in that position."

"You intended to keep her unmarried," Naftaly said. "Because you were afraid."

"Yes," she said. "I was afraid. When you have an infant who lights fire to her own cradle, you are afraid."

The farmer's daughter looked up at this, stricken.

"And then the goblins took her away," the old woman said quickly. "And the princess lived happily ever after, the end." To Elena she whispered, "Have a care for your words, fool, at least when discussing your demon progeny."

"Maziks," Elena hissed back, "are not demons."

"I fail to see a significant difference," the old woman said.

"That's because you've never seen a demon. You've met a Mazik, now. How did he seem to you?"

The old woman thought. "Like a man," she admitted. "But that was cunning on his part, wasn't it?"

"It wasn't. I've met Maziks, and I've met demons, and I may tell you, they are not the same creature. A Mazik thinks. He reasons. A demon is just . . . hardly more than a bit of animated, angry magic."

The wagon hit a bump and Naftaly had to keep the old woman from bouncing into the chicken crates.

"Did you keep one for a pet?" the old woman asked. "In lieu of a cat?"

"Hardly," Elena said. "A demon tried to burn down my mother's house after my youngest brother was born. We were lucky to survive." She shuddered. "It was the ugliest thing I've ever seen."

"How did you defeat it?"

"We didn't," she said. "My mother was able to cast it from the house, but that's all. There's no *defeating* one. You can't kill one, because it isn't properly alive. Even if you cleaved it in half with a blade, you'd simply have two demons instead of one."

"I'm surprised there aren't more of them, then."

"Don't be surprised," Elena said. "Be grateful."

Naftaly turned sharply to her. "Has he a soul? If a Mazik thinks and reasons, does that mean he also has a soul?"

Elena stopped short in surprise. "I don't know. Does it matter?"

Naftaly brushed some cast-off chicken down from his sleeve. "I don't know if it matters. I'm not precisely sure what a soul is."

"Well, then it certainly doesn't matter. Why is it important to you?"

The boy did not answer.

\+ + + + + +

THE BUMPING OF the cart made Naftaly ill, his empty stomach lurching, and his head throbbing with each jostle, and worse, the constant motion was making his mind cloudy. Without thinking, he clutched at the old woman's wrinkled hand.

"Are you going to be sick?" she said. "Could you do it over the side?"

But Naftaly's eyes were rolling back into his head, and he heard the old woman mutter, "Satan's bollocks" and then he was somewhere else completely: a seaside city, with winding roads leading through close-kept buildings to the harbor, filled with ships.

Naftaly had never seen a ship of any variety, but here there seemed to be all sorts: the Sefardi merchant fleet; some others, bearing the crest of Petgal; trading ships from Burgundy and Zayit. Then there were three others—vast sailing ships, bearing a flag Naftaly had never seen before, featuring a strange emblem that for all the world looked like a pair of sewing shears.

When he woke, he found his head in Elena's ample lap, her hand on her forehead while she muttered some old housewives' incantation that would not have cured a headache if recited by anyone else. They were out of the cart, on the hard ground, and Naftaly struggled to sit up, as much to free himself of Elena's ministrations as anything. "I'm all right," he told her, when she would have made him lie back. "Why have we stopped?"

"It's nearly night," she said. "We'll enter the city in the morning. Did you . . . did you see something?"

Naftaly rubbed his temple. "I saw ships," he said. "Many ships."

"Well, that's a good sign," the old woman said. "If there were no ships in Merja, we'd be in a bad way."

"There were some that were different," he said. "They seemed important." He took a twig and drew the emblem he'd seen in the dusty earth. "Do you know it?" he asked Elena.

The old woman said, "Unless the tailors have their own fleet—"

Elena cut her off. "It's not shears, son of a tailor," she said, tracing the outline with her finger. "It's a sword with a split blade." She looked up at Naftaly. "It's the emblem of the Uliman fleet."

THIRTY

"THE ONLY WAY for you to understand," Asmel told Toba Bet, "is for you to be inside my mind."

"Didn't you tell me that mucking about in someone else's mind is a dangerous thing?" Toba Bet asked. "I might damage you, somehow, and then where would we be?"

Asmel's long fingers were curled around the book, thinner than most of Asmel's collection, probably because it contained only a single spell. He'd lit the stones that sat in the wall sconces, so there was enough light for Toba Bet to see how derelict the room was. Cobwebs tangled in every corner, a layer of dust covered the tables, and their edges bore tiny scratches, as if they'd been chewed by many generations of mice. The air itself was stale; she could taste it on the back of her tongue.

"As long as you don't try to alter anything," Asmel said, "the danger should be minimal. It was very delicately written. The Mazik who created it spent nearly a century on the wording." He passed the book to her hands.

Toba Bet ran her fingers down the cover before cracking it open. "If you had this all these years, why did you never cast the spell with Barsilay? Or with Odem?"

He pursed his mouth. "This would be too great a burden for Barsilay. And too great a risk for Odem." He paused. "Will you do it?"

Toba Bet looked down at the book spread across her lap, written in too-tight penmanship that was so different from Asmel's perfect script.

This spell was an intimacy, and she hated herself a little for wanting what was not so gladly given. She said, "I will try."

+ + + + + +

ASMEL HAD TAKEN the light-stones from their sconces and set them in a circle on the floor, to help Toba Bet in the difficult task of making out the unfamiliar writing in the ancient book. The two of them sat in the middle facing each other, knees nearly touching.

"I believed Mazik magic used no spells," Toba Bet said, across the few inches that separated her face from Asmel's.

His voice was lower than she'd heard it, softer in the small, dark space. "Magic requires a movement of consciousness. For simple matters—lentils to bread, cold water to hot—you can see already the entirety of the path; for those small works, you need no spell. For more complicated journeys, your mind can't find the way to pure intention without help. It was the mortals who taught us this."

Tamar of Luz had said something like this, in her letter. Toba Bet asked, "Is a spell syntactic, then, or semantic?"

"Both equally," he said. "Creating a new spell is exceedingly difficult. It's a rare gift, to be able to concoct one as complex as this. But you are stalling. Are you afraid you can't do it, or that you can?"

"Both equally," she said. In her hands, she held a glass bowl, empty now, which she raised to her lips as she began to read the spell, Asmel occasionally whispering a word when she stumbled. She felt it catch at her mind as she saw where the spell would take her, what it would do, how it would work. "Redruna delech," she whispered, and a thin stream of magic breathed from her lungs and pooled into the bowl, where it coalesced from vapor into a small pool of silver liquid. She held out the bowl to Asmel, who breathed his own magic to mingle with hers. "Give it my name," he said softly, and whispered a name that sent pinpricks of fire down Toba Bet's spine. She repeated it to the magic in the bowl, which lit up with the sound. "Now drink," he said. "But you must look in my eyes while you do."

Toba Bet took a breath and raised the bowl to her lips, looking up into Asmel's eyes and feeling, as if in her own gut, the extent of his fear. She drank, and as the liquid hit her throat the world condensed down to a pinprick, and she felt her body collide with the floor a split second before her consciousness realized it was living in a world behind Asmel's eyes.

+ + + + + +

THAT NIGHT, NAFTALY found himself back in the cell with the injured Mazik.

"You've come back," he said. "And after I tried so hard to get you out of here. I suppose you're too mortal to summon me a pillow or a blanket?"

"I'm afraid I don't know how," Naftaly said. "I apologize."

"Mm."

"I should thank you," Naftaly said. "For healing my hand, and for the map." For all the good it had done. Toba, now, was beyond any help.

"Don't mention that," the Mazik said. "Please. Though you might tell me who put that mark there in the first place."

"It . . . it was a tall man with red-black hair."

"Ah," he said. "Interesting. I would have thought one of the lesser hounds. You've captured the attention of the Lymer himself. You should be honored."

"Should I?"

The Mazik smiled. "I'm sure he thinks so."

Naftaly came nearer and sat down. The other man lazily turned his head to face him. "I'm still not convinced he didn't send you, by the way."

"No one sent me," Naftaly said, drawing his knees up. "I'm not really sure how I keep ending up here." He looked around at the windowless walls and wondered where the dim light in the cell was coming from. He wondered, too, where the air was coming from, though he supposed at the moment he wasn't truly breathing it, his body being on a straw mattress in a seedy inn in Merja. "This is the room you're in when you're awake?"

"This very cell," the Mazik said. "I've been cursed with not being able to leave it when I'm dreaming, and I didn't think anyone could dream their way in, either."

"How long have you been here?"

"That's the worst of it," he said. "I don't know. The light never changes. I'm not even sure if it's night now or not." He closed his eyes. "I would give much, to see the stars."

"I'm sorry," Naftaly said.

"Never mind," the Mazik replied. "You look dreadful, by the way. Have you lost weight?"

"Very likely," Naftaly said. "But at least no one's struck me in the face."

The Mazik touched his split lip, as if he'd forgotten it, and came away with a trace of blood on the pad of his thumb. In an instant, the wound was gone. "There," he said. "Don't let it trouble you."

It did trouble Naftaly. "Well," he said, after spending several moments examining the healed place on his hand. "Since you don't trust me, and I don't trust you, what do we talk about?"

"You don't trust me?" the Mazik said, putting a hand to his breast. "I'm wounded."

Naftaly would have protested, somehow, but the other man held up a hand. "You shouldn't, of course. Never give your trust to one who asks for it."

Naftaly laughed drily, and to the other man's raised eyebrow, said, "Never mind. It's good advice, is all."

"You could tell me a story," the Mazik said. "To pass the time."

Naftaly had no idea what sort of tale would interest a Mazik prisoner enough to offer comfort or entertainment.

"Or I could tell you one," the Mazik offered. "Would you like that better?"

"It sounds as if you have one in mind," Naftaly said.

"I have several," he said. "Apparently sitting alone in a cell all day tends to make a man nostalgic. I've been thinking of my boyhood home."

Naftaly tried to imagine some Mazik village where this man might look at home, but failed to come up with anything plausible. A city, he decided. He wondered if all Maziks were so sophisticated. Maybe it came of living so long; they all sounded clever and had mastered the art of smiling with only one corner of the mouth. "You grew up rich in some great city," Naftaly guessed aloud. "I'm sure it was lovely."

"You're only half-correct," he said. "I was not rich, but I did live in a great city." He traced the floor with his forefinger, running it along some invisible seam in the stones. "The greatest city in the world, 'til it fell, all glittering white walls and the scent of almond flowers in the air. Luz was the fairest city in all the worlds, and our queen was the most beautiful who ever lived."

"She was a good queen?" Naftaly asked, settling into the wall.

"She was a horror, but that isn't the tale I mean to tell you. Everyone always tells tales of great and terrible queens. I never liked those stories."

"I like the stories that begin with two brothers, and one of those is a fool," Naftaly said. "Those always seemed truer."

"Yes," the Mazik said. "Yes, in any true story, there's always a fool. In mine, too, but he had no brothers. He was an only son—an only child, and he was a great fool indeed. He was a bitter disappointment to his father, because he had no wisdom, and no ambition, and lived only to play games and make free with the other Maziks. A wastrel of the highest order, you understand. An utter disgrace to his name. So his father sent him away to the university, in the hope that his sister, the boy's aunt, might make something of his useless son."

"And did she?"

"Indeed not. He was a lost cause, and she despaired of him, though she loved him anyway. But his father would not take him back. The fool studied ten years—he thought he'd make himself a physician—but he learned nothing, and cared for nothing, and then one day he overheard something he ought not to have, in the bed of the daughter of some high Adon. The Queen meant to seize the lentil fields belonging to the Adon of Izmir, to feed her army. So the next morning, our fool pulled on his boots and went home, and told his aunt. And three days later, when the Queen sent her men to take the fields, she could not find them. They'd been concealed.

"The young fool thought little of it, until a few weeks later, when he learned something else, from the square-jawed fellow who kept the stables of the Queen: she was setting a tax on the horses, for her army. Every white horse in the empire was now the property of the Queen. So once again, he pulled on his boots, and went home and told his aunt. And when the men of the Queen went out to claim the white horses, they found none. They'd all been made black.

"And then, sometime after that, our hero was feasting with some friends when one of them—a princeling bastard of the Queen herself—boasted that the Queen was giving him the youngest daughters of every house who did not pay a tax to prevent it. And so he told his aunt, and the next day that princeling was dead.

"So the wastrel decided to see what his aunt was up to, since it seemed unlikely she could be managing all this on her own. He followed her one night, through the university, and down into a chamber underground, and when she got to the door she used her finger to draw three letters—human letters—on the wood. And a door opened *within* the door, and she stepped through, and disappeared. So the wastrel did as she had done, and the door appeared, and he found himself at the bottom of a pit, because there had been a fourth letter he had not seen. And he stayed at the bottom of that pit for seven days, until his aunt came looking for him and found him there, half-starved and out of his mind with thirst. And she upbraided him for following her, and he upbraided her for using him without his permission, and he told her he would tell the Queen who it was that had thwarted all her plans, unless she told him the meaning of the letters she'd written on the door."

"And so she told him," Naftaly said.

"Indeed she didn't," the Mazik said. "She called him an idiot and refused—she knew the threat was idle. But he persisted in testing her: he went off to see the Queen. And he was just about to turn a corner inside the palace when he found himself hanging upside-down by his heels, and his aunt was before him threatening to cut his throat. But she wouldn't, he knew, because she loved him." He shifted on the stones. "Though she should have killed him. So she told him she could not simply answer his question: to know about her order meant belonging to it, and he would have to take the same vow as all the others before him, storing his name and his own command to die, spoken in his own voice, within a stone that she would keep and use in case he were ever captured. Then she told him the letters on the door were an acronym, and stood for Molcha To'ara: the watchword of ha-Moh'to."

"And what does it mean—Molcha To'ara?"

"It means," the Mazik said, his edges growing hazy, as Naftaly's eyes began to grow dark, "Monarchy is Abomination." And then Naftaly was back in the inn.

\+ + + + + + +

ON THE DOCKS were a sea of thin, frightened Jews, who looked at Naftaly's short hair and shaved face and recoiled. The old woman found a matronly woman in a brown shawl, and said, "Why is the Uliman fleet here?"

The matron looked at her blankly, and the old woman explained, "We've only just come from Rimon; we were delayed on the road."

"The Jews from Rimon left a fortnight ago," she said. "Or so they say."

"Yes, well. We had some problems. The fleet?"

"They are here for us," she said.

"For us?"

"The Sultan sent the Admiral himself. They are allowing us to settle in the empire; I'm told the ships are for Anab."

"The Sultan. In exchange for what?"

"For ourselves," she said, with a tilt of her head. "I don't know what space they have left. You should hurry and find out. They aren't even charging passage."

"They aren't charging passage?"

But the other woman had already turned to attend to two of her children, who had started to squabble over a scrap of bread that one of them was refusing to share. The old woman tugged at Naftaly's sleeve and he followed her through the crowd. "We ought to do it," she said. "An open invitation? We ought to claim it."

Naftaly knew little of the Empire; it was a faraway place that seemed to take glee in sending crews to sink Sefardi ships whenever they could, and then shrugging and claiming the men were unaffiliated pirates when complaints were raised. There were Jews there already, he knew that much—Romaniotes mainly, and the children of merchants who'd come later. It would not be home, precisely, but it would be safe, at least as long as the current sultan lived. Still, ten or twenty years' safety was a better assurance than they'd get elsewhere.

But he knew one other thing: Elena's husband had already gone on to Pengoa.

"Elena's already lost her granddaughter," he said.

"Yes, and? Let her go to Pengoa on her own. There's no reason for us to go there, too."

"I can't send her on a ship alone!"

"That woman can care for herself," she said. "Better than you can."

They turned into the doorway of the inn where they'd left Elena resting; either the ride in the cart had weakened her, or else it was leaving the gate behind them, without hope of ever returning. That morning, her muscles had seemed lax, and they'd left her abed to try to suss out the situation at the docks.

When they returned, they found her sitting up on the edge of her cot, flexing and unflexing her left hand as if it troubled her, while her right arm hung limp. Her face, Naftaly noted, sagged slightly on the same side, and when she spoke, that side of her mouth drooped.

She said something in a language Naftaly did not know. Naftaly and the old woman exchanged a glance.

Elena gave the pair of them a consternated look and repeated herself.

"That sounded like Zayiti to me," the old woman said.

Elena said something Naftaly was fairly sure was a curse.

"Do you understand her?" the old woman asked.

"No," Naftaly said. "What's wrong with her?"

Elena said something else.

"I think she's insulting you," the old woman said. "But that might just be conjecture; she usually is." She stepped closer, examining Elena's face and pulling on her right hand, which appeared slightly palsied. "I think she's had a stroke," she said.

"Do you think she understands *us*?" Naftaly asked. Elena's eyelid drooped slightly as he stooped to examine her face more closely.

Elena reached out a trembling hand and slapped him across the cheek.

"She seems to," the old woman said.

"Will she recover?"

"I don't know," the old woman said. To Elena, she added, "Is there some remedy we could give you?"

Elena shook her head and said a word Naftaly could understand: time. Only they had none, and Elena knew it. The old woman slowly stood, and said, "I'll go down and ask them for some soup for her. She'll do better if we keep her fed." Side-eyeing Naftaly, she added, "Come with me. I'm too old to carry hot soup on the stairs."

Following her down the narrow, uneven steps, the old woman muttered, "At least we won't have to listen to her counsel anymore."

Pausing at the bottom of the steps to let a few others pass, he said, "What are you implying?"

"She can't travel alone like this, and you and I are not missing out on those Uliman ships. We'll go back out at the evening's tide, and we'll go to Anab."

"You mean to take her there against her wishes?"

"It's no more than she's done to either of us," she said. "And it's kinder than abandoning her here, which is our alternative. Listen, you'll do well in Anab, the community's much larger; there will be more opportunities for you in the east. You could go into the spice trade, I don't know."

"But Elena—"

"She can no longer choose for herself!" the old woman said.

Naftaly held his hands up helplessly. "What are we to say to her when she recovers and finds out she's been dragged to the wrong side of the sea? You think she'll thank us?"

"For keeping her alive? I don't care if she thanks us or not. Listen to me, we have an opportunity to live. Such things should not be squandered."

\+ + + + + + +

WHILE TOBA BET was attempting to peruse the darker sectors of Asmel's mind, Toba the Elder decided that she would not be idle. This was her first spare moment alone since Asmel had taught her to read—technically, he'd taught Toba Bet to read, but she'd decided not to dwell on that—and she had a specific volume in mind: the book hidden in Marah's genizah. She hoped it would contain something more about Dawid ben Aron, or Tamar of Luz, or other half-Maziks.

The shade hovered at her heels and she asked it to give her some extra light while she pulled the book onto her lap—after she used Toba Bet's reinforcement spell on it a second time, in case it had waned over the weeks. When she opened the cover, however, she could see that it was not nearly as old as the letter had been. If the letter was from before the fall, the book had been written sometime later.

It was a journal, and Toba assumed it had been created by Marah herself. It seemed to begin sometime after the fall, as the first entry read:

5 Adar, Year 2 of the Third Age

I know Tamar would not have simply destroyed the gate. She must have had some reason to do what she did. I have tried to dream my way to Dawid and the other half-Maziks, but I cannot, which means they must be dead. I despair.

Rafeq has sent his creatures into the mortal realm. There are whispers, among them, about the Ziz in P'ri Hadar. I have written to the Queen, to anyone I know there, and no one has seen it. Of course the demons could be lying. But for what purpose?

2 Tishri, Year 3 of the Third Age

If the Ziz survived, then couldn't someone else have survived, too? Isn't it also possible the gate was not destroyed, but concealed?

2 Nisan, Year 3 of the Third Age

Asmel thinks I'm going mad, but Rafeq tells me his creatures are not lying. Regardless, I have begun keeping much of my search from him. It puts him at too grave a risk, with La Cacería on the rise and this new king. This Caçador, whomever he may be, is a threat to all who would seek to undo the wrong done at Luz. Asmel is too vulnerable already; I fear his neutrality will not be enough to save him with the work he is pursuing now, and its pertinence to Aravoth. But who am I to tell him to stop?

Toba's mind and Toba Bet's were still linked enough that something was rapidly occurring to her as she read: the handwriting in Marah's journal was the same as in the memory spell. She turned the page.

I have found Dawid ben Aron.

THIRTY-ONE

ASMEL'S MIND WAS a labyrinth of thoughts; a thousand years or more of memory, which all pressed in on Toba Bet at once, and she was suddenly afraid her half-human mind might not be equal to the task of finding anything specific: she was drowning. She called out Asmel's name and hoped there was some thread of his consciousness that might be able to help her find what he wanted to show her. She felt a warm, steady presence she recognized and let it lead her.

Still, she struggled to understand what was happening. She saw not just the externals of Asmel in his study—no, not his study; another word came to mind . . . his *observatory*—but felt the tug of all the thoughts he was having in that moment: Barsilay—who Toba Bet realized was still young—refusing to work; his wife distracted by some grand project of her own; and the astrolabe he was tinkering with had two gears that would not mate; it went on, and in the background of all this, a golden thread of excitement over some discovery Toba could not understand.

He left off work on the astrolabe: there were thirteen of them laid out before him, and he'd been working with one she recognized, though it seemed to be in some earlier stage of development. His hands were still unmarked with La Cacería's silencing sigils. A pair of shades was tidying after him, replacing silver tools in the rack next to the table; one of them spoke to Asmel, in Asmel's own voice: "You were meant to leave a quarter hour ago."

"Yes, I know," Asmel replied. His eyes were on the mirror-bright disc he was fixing; in the reflection Asmel's hair was not silver but black, tied up to keep out of his way while he worked. "This was meant to be *fixed* a quarter hour ago."

"You can give the lecture without it. They'll be more impressed with punctuality than a dramatic entrance."

"Who made you so officious?" Asmel asked drily. He waved his hand at the shades, who vanished, turned on his heel, and went down the steps: spinning within him was a pure excitement that made it difficult for Toba Bet to focus. The hallway was filled with black-clad Maziks, who drew back at his approach: "Adon," they muttered. "We were just—"

"Yes, yes," he said, brushing past them. Toba Bet caught a glimpse of the garden outside, which was in full bloom. A woman ran across the patio toward him, her black hair piled in a knot on top of her head. She was, Toba Bet noted, very tall. Her eyes glittered as black as her hair, and her wide lower lip was anchored between her teeth as she ran. She was not so much beautiful as striking, and Toba Bet instantly knew that this was Marah; she felt Asmel's emotions rise to her. Marah had been his wife.

"I'm sorry," she said.

"You haven't missed it," Asmel said as she fell into step beside him. "Though perhaps you should."

"I wouldn't," she said. "Unless you don't wish me there?"

Asmel frowned. He and Marah had been married so long Toba Bet could not really comprehend it, but she did understand that for much of their marriage Marah had been in Luz while Asmel had been at the university in Rimon. Asmel loved her deeply, yet their lives had been quite separate until recently. "Your political leanings have never been secret," he said.

"You're afraid I'll taint your findings by association?" she said. "La Cacería hasn't killed me yet, Asmel. If I knew who was running it, we could make an end of the entire organization."

"I'm not in a position to make an end of anything, Marah. I'm a scientist."

"Are you going to make your little speech about scientists remaining neutral in temporal affairs to avoid bias in their work? If you looked up every now and then, you'd see the world has other problems than shifting stars."

"I don't believe it has," he said.

Her eyebrows drew down in consternation, but before she could reply they'd come to the massive oak doors—not yet cracked—that led into the great hall, and Asmel pushed them open, revealing a sea of Maziks, some seated on carved benches, others standing. Asmel stopped short; he'd not been expecting so many people, and he wasn't quite sure what to make of it. His wife patted him on the shoulder and said, "It's what you wanted," and then went to find a seat in the crowd.

Drawing a great breath, Asmel approached the lectern at the front of the room, where the raucous crowd grew only louder at his approach. Toba Bet saw him mentally go through the main points of his lecture and reeled as she understood what he was about to say, what he had discovered, what it meant.

He raised a hand to silence the crowd. "I've called you all here," he said, "to discuss a discovery that changes our understanding of the very fabrics of the heavens," he said.

"You're a fool," someone cried out from the crowd.

Asmel only smiled. "Perhaps," he said. He waved his hands and an illusion bloomed before him: two worlds, crafted of glowing magic, and between them the crossed lines of an hourglass: it was, Toba Bet realized, a manifestation of the sandless hourglass she'd seen in Asmel's observatory. "You are doubtless familiar with this model," he said. "Our realm on one side, the mortal on the other, connected by proximity and the phenomena of the gates. But with the fall of Luz, it has become apparent this model is faulty." He waved a hand, abolishing the illusion.

Here, he cast a second model, the one Toba Bet had seen him working on earlier: two worlds connected not by an hourglass, but by a cylinder with a disc set in the center.

The crowd grew loud again, and Asmel had to raise his voice to be heard. "The nature of the damage to the firmament at Luz is not consistent with the old model. When the gate was removed, the stars shifted to compensate. We anticipated that effect. What we did not anticipate was that the size of the shift was not symmetrical. If the gate consisted of a single aperture, the shift would have been the same in both realms. But the evidence is that the shift was more pronounced on our side, by a matter of six degrees—"

"Six degrees is within the margin of error for stellar measurements," someone called out.

"Not for me," Asmel said, and then went on: "Such a difference indicates there was not one tear, but two. And the only explanation for that can be—"

There was an explosion, and the Maziks in the room cried out as the doors cracked and then were flung open, revealing a squadron of blue-clad soldiers, each holding a light-stone in their right hand, and a blade in their left. At the head of their column was Tsidon, face tight with excitement. The crowd went momentarily silent. Tsidon smiled grimly, before shouting a word Asmel blocked his ears from hearing: the crowd's eyes went from horrified to closed, as they collapsed in their seats, unconscious.

He thought he'd have more time. He'd set wards on the gate to slow them down; he should have had half an hour at least, and by then, it would have been too late: his words would have been out. Instead, the now-unconscious Maziks would be unable to hear the conclusion of Asmel's remarks: that the existence of two parallel tears in the firmament indicated that a world of some kind existed between them.

What Asmel did not know was how one could access this place—for his findings proved that Aravoth was indeed a real place, a material plane one could measure and observe and study. But based on everything he'd read, everything he'd learned, what he believed was this: The third realm, the in-between, was Aravoth itself, dwelling-place of the divine. Aravoth, the source of the Mandate of Luz. The Queen claimed her right to rule had been issued from Aravoth itself—from Hashem—and for this reason she could not be overthrown. According to the law, rule was retained by the heirs of the Queen, or if there were none, it returned to the Judges.

After the fall, La Cacería had put forth that the entire mandate had been an invention of the Queen herself, used to seize power in the name of something that never existed. Aravoth, they said, was a myth, and any discussion to the contrary was treason to the new king.

And now came Asmel, with his charts and measurements and incontrovertible proof. No matter how many lies La Cacería had put forth to keep Relam on the throne, no matter how much they insisted that the Queen of Luz had invented Aravoth to claim and maintain power, the mandate could not simply be wished away. As long as Aravoth existed, as Asmel's studies proved, Relam—and all the other lesser kings—were usurpers.

Asmel cared little for the truth of the mandate; his interest was in the physicality of the place: Could one visit Aravoth? Could one speak to its inhabitants, and what wisdom might they possess? But he knew the second consideration was anathema to Relam and La Cacería both. He'd known they'd have him for this, and hoped only to reach enough minds that others would carry on when he could not.

He did know, of course, that his findings would feed the Restorationists, and he'd convinced himself it made little difference: Asmel's duty was to the truth, not to any particular faction ... and if his findings tended to undermine Relam and his Cacería lackeys, well, he could not exactly feel sorry about that, anyway. Let the legal scholars sort out the legal issues. Men like Asmel were better left to study the firmament. At least this was what he told Marah, when she pointed out the irony of his position.

Asmel's illusion became nothing more than a cloud of sparks. Tsidon said, "You've been warned."

Asmel's eyes sought out his wife, and then he realized with a start she was no longer there. Either she'd fled at the first sign of La Cacería, or she hadn't bothered to hear him speak in the first place. "You cannot silence me."

To the soldiers, Tsidon said, "Arrest everyone here."

Asmel flung out a hand, and a translucent column of magic knocked Tsidon back into the wall. Asmel turned back to the crowd, raising a hand and willing them to wake, but the soldiers stepped forward, calling down magic of their own, binding Asmel's wrists and ankles to the wall in iron collars, while a searing band of molten metal slammed down over his mouth, leaving him almost senseless with agony. Tsidon climbed back to his feet and walked toward Asmel, looming over him, his hair come loose from its queue. "I suppose we can add assaulting me to your list of crimes," he said. "But it hardly signifies, seeing as you'll be dead before the next moon." He raised his left hand over Asmel's head and, almost gleefully, knocked Asmel into temporary oblivion.

\+ + + + + +

TOBA READ AGAIN:

10 Tishri—the exact date had been smudged or lost to time—*Third Age*

I have found Dawid ben Aron. He dreamt his way to me last night. He is more than half mad now, and I had trouble making out so much he told me, beyond these essentials: The mortals received a warning that the Queen of Luz was angry about the work they had been doing, using Mazik magic together with their own. She meant to send a thousand Maziks through the gate to kill every mortal in Luz, as punishment.

This, they learned from Tarses. So Tamar and the others tore out the gate, and concealed it in a book, but as it was torn out the waters of the universe rushed in. None escaped but Dawid, who had been holding the book and took the Ziz and fled.

The gate in the book is no longer fixed, and has become something of a floating gateway that can be used to connect any two points in either world. Dawid used the book to go to Mazik P'ri Hadar, where the woman who now calls herself Queen judged him guilty for the fall and locked him away, and locked the Ziz away, and locked the book away, these fifty years. How he escaped, he could not tell me, only that he would not cross to Mazik lands again. He came here, to Rimon, and tells me I am the only person alive he trusts.

He will meet me at the next moon, in mortal Rimon. He has hidden the Ziz on Mount Sebah, and he and I will meet and find a way to mend what was broken. I only fear the interference of La Cacería.

Asmel means to give a lecture that night on his findings. I fear what that will mean for him, but if he holds La Cacería's attention for a few hours while I pass through the gate, I may yet go and come back without being captured.

I do not know how we will mend the gate. I do not know if I will survive attempting to meet with Dawid. There are so few I trust, with La Cacería sniffing around the university. Rafeq is gone, locked away with his creations, and Tarses has grown distant; he is afraid, I think. He's never mentioned the tale Dawid told me about delivering a warning to the mortals of Luz. If La Cacería discovers it was he who gave the warning, they will execute him.

It was the last entry.

Toba returned the book to the genizah, which was no genizah at all but only the space Marah had created to hide her work from La Cacería, and from Asmel, too.

\+ + + + + +

THE COURSER ADJUSTED her veil and tried to decide whether killing these soldiers would be worth the trouble it would cause her later.

But the Caçador had been very clear in his orders. Already he would be cross with her: she'd been so late in her last delivery she'd almost missed her chance entirely, but there had been mortals blocking her way to the gate, and they'd been too interesting to kill, because the wolves were not attacking them.

One of them must have been a Mazik, or part, and she wanted to see what he would do. Then the damned Lymer had made a mess of things, and she'd had to wait for everyone to clear out before giving her delivery to two smiling Alaunts who complimented her sense of timing.

She'd gone to Merja because of a rumor that the Uliman fleet was due in there, the day after tomorrow. There would be an exodus from the port, and that would create a bottleneck, and it would be a good place for her to ensure the soldiers were not skimming from the top of the take.

She didn't actually care if they were; let them put coins in their pockets if they liked. She was really there because the Lymer had heard another rumor, and that rumor had proved true: the soldiers were burning the books.

The Inquisitor would die for this eventually, but first she had to make sure nothing more was burned in Merja.

One of the soldiers took a prayer book from an old man and tossed it to the pile, which grew by the moment. She picked it up and flipped through it; it wasn't what she wanted, she was sure. The soldier gave the old man a shove to move him along.

"There's too many of the damn things," the soldier told his comrade. "Don't know how he thinks we're going to get them all sent to Mansanar."

"Don't know what he wants with the devil things in the first place," the second soldier agreed. "What's the difference if they burn them in the plaça there or here?"

"They aren't meant to be burned at all," the Courser said. "I believe that point has been made clear to you."

The second whispered to the first, "If we burn half, that's still plenty to send back, and less for us to crate and carry."

She wasn't meant to hear it; if she'd been mortal, she wouldn't have. She frowned under her veil. The Caçador had been clear to her that she wasn't to kill the soldiers, because killing the soldiers wasn't subtle.

But none of these men reported to the Caçador.

She decided on a compromise. She'd kill one, instead of two as she wanted, and she wouldn't even eat him after. She pulled a knife from her belt and threw it into the offending man's windpipe. When the other man cried out, she said, "I have other knives, and I've just as much right to kill you for listening as him for speaking. You're only alive right now because I don't want to get blood on the books."

The other man watched his comrade gurgle out the rest of his life. The Courser noted that his hand twitched in the vicinity of his sword, and under different circumstances she'd have killed him for it. She wondered if he really thought he could kill her, even with that sword. It was a good blade, too good for him; most likely, he'd either taken it off a better man or inherited it from one. It would be amusing if he actually knew what he was doing. One did grow tired of killing men who fought like children.

She considered, not for the first time, that she could simply disappear on this side of the gate. Even if she bound her powers, she'd do well here, as a mercenary or an assassin: none could match her, not among mortals. She'd never have to fear a knife in her own back. If not for the Caçador knowing her name, it would be simple to just walk away from La Cacería entirely.

Instead, she tossed the prayer book back onto the pile and told the soldier, "I'll have them send you another partner."

\+ + + + + +

NAFTALY AND THE old woman made their way to the dock for the tide the next morning, Elena limping between them. She did not ask where they were going, and Naftaly did not volunteer the information.

The old woman was right, of course; Naftaly would have a better chance to make a place for himself in Anab. Still, though. He was doing wrong by Elena, and he knew it.

There was a crowd around the Uliman ships, as people jostled each other, desperate for free passage, and Naftaly realized there might not be enough places for everyone. At the head of the queue, just before the crowd reached the docks, was a cadre of soldiers barking orders at those departing and searching their belongings. Each time they moved onto the next party, there was renewed weeping as they confiscated wedding rings, hidden coins, and the occasional small piece of jewelry. Naftaly watched as a soldier pried a thin volume out of the hands of a grandfatherly man who was slapped when he refused to let go, and then the book was tossed onto the growing pile behind the soldiers, a pair of whom were sorting it into crates.

The largest crate, by far, was full of books.

"They're taking the books," Naftaly hissed at the old woman. A figure hovered near the soldiers; from the distance, Naftaly could not tell if it was a veiled man or a woman in trousers. "That was not in the edict. There was nothing about not being able to take books. Why would they even want them?"

"To burn them? They do seem to enjoy that sort of thing," the old woman suggested.

"But why bother stealing them, only to burn them?"

"You're ascribing logic to any of this? What's it matter to you—we haven't any books."

Naftaly sighed, and carefully opened his jacket enough to show her the corner of his father's book. "Oh," she said, "you do. Well, best bid it goodbye now, I'm afraid."

"I can't," he said. "I can't let them have this."

"We have no choice," she said. "Unless you know some way to make those soldiers turn into mermaids and swim off into the sea, they're going to search us, and they're going to take it."

"You don't understand," he said. "My father ordered me never to let anything happen to this," he said.

"Your father the tailor," she said.

"Listen." He pulled her closer, though with the din no one could have made out his words, anyway. "This book has been kept in my family for ten generations, I can't let it go to be burned. It's important, I feel it."

"Better it than us," she shot back.

"It's the only thing I have left," he said. "In all the world."

"The operative word," she said, "being *thing*."

Naftaly did not know how to explain that it wasn't truly a *thing* to him at all; it was hot in his hand, like a living creature with its own pulse. His father had said it contained a curse, but it didn't feel like a curse to Naftaly. It felt like something from a dream, or a vision.

"What does it contain?" she asked. "Is it a prayer book? It's very thin."

If he admitted it contained a curse, she'd toss it on the pyre herself, so Naftaly said, "I don't know."

"You don't know!"

"He told me never to read it. Listen to me, I can't let them take this."

"It might well be someone's old grocery ledger! For heaven's sake, you're talking about risking your life over a record of what someone spent on vegetables!"

"I don't think it's a ledger," he said. They were jostled from behind and had to move several steps closer to the front of the queue, and to the guards. Elena asked him a question he could neither understand nor answer. "I won't give it to them."

"You must," the old woman insisted.

Naftaly watched them pull a siddur from the hands of a man with tears in his eyes and toss it onto the growing pile.

One of the soldiers collapsed, and all the guards in the area went still as stone. Naftaly could not see what the issue was.

"I can't," Naftaly said, slipping out from under Elena's arm, transferring her weight to the old woman, who bent her knees to better accommodate the sudden burden. The veiled figure was striding away from its post, in their direction. He and the old woman paused their argument while the veiled person passed in a flume of hot air that blew Elena's hair into her face, every set of eyes in the queue pasted to her back until she was out of sight. Elena whispered a phrase Naftaly could not understand, and made a shaky gesture meant to ward off the evil eye.

"There is nowhere else for you to go," the old woman whispered. "Don't you dare do this."

"It's my father's!" Naftaly shouted, loud enough to draw the attention of the people near him. "It is all I have left of him, and I gave him my word."

"Naftaly—"

"No," he choked. "I have broken every promise I made him. I've shaved my face. I've told all my secrets—but not this. Better I should go into the sea myself. I'm sorry."

Without turning back, he took a step out of the line, and then two, and then turned and ran, clutching the book against his breast beneath his jacket. Behind him, the old woman screamed his name, and then a curse.

Thirty-Two

IN HIS MEMORY, Asmel awoke chained to the wall in a darkened room, his hands in iron devices that immobilized each finger like a second skeleton. Tsidon sat in a chair nearby. "Ah," he said. "There you are. I was wondering when you'd open your eyes to your many crimes."

Asmel's head lolled; he was weak and having trouble focusing his vision. He wondered how long he'd been insensible, or how long it would be until he was fully conscious again. "Nothing I have done," he said, "is wrong by any definition."

"Except the legal one, I'm afraid," Tsidon said. "What you were about to propose was nothing short of sedition."

"You mean to try me for what I might have said?"

Tsidon tapped the table with his fingertips, and Asmel saw with some horror his set of astrolabes appear, together with the books containing all his notes and calculations. "You think we aren't aware of what you've been teaching? Of what you're proposing?"

Toba Bet felt something settle in Asmel's mind, a strange feeling like surrender. Tsidon continued: "The Restorationists will make a meal of what you're teaching, you know as much."

"I'm no Restorationist," Asmel said.

"Yes, you've always been so pure, haven't you?" Tsidon stood and took the astrolabe in his hands. "So much evidence," he said. "I almost wonder if you wanted to be caught."

Asmel remained silent; but in his mind, while he hadn't desired capture, he'd resigned himself to it.

"Well, then. Your trial begins tomorrow." Tsidon smiled, not a little smugly. "You might want to prepare yourself for the flames. Know that none will mourn you."

He clapped his hands, and from the other side the guard opened the cell door. Tsidon meant to exit, but first he held up a finger. "Except for your ward, that is. But I suppose he's corrupted beyond saving."

Asmel's head jerked up; he'd sent Barsilay away months ago. He shouldn't have been in Rimon at all. He was meant to be—

"I thought that might get your attention."

"Where is he?" Asmel ground out.

"Not far," Tsidon said. "Would you like to see him?"

"No," Asmel said, but he understood that he could give no answer that would remediate the situation.

Barsilay was dragged in by two solders; Toba realized with some surprise that he was still young; younger, perhaps, than Toba herself, though she did not know what that meant for a Mazik, if he took twenty years or a hundred to become a man. He looked suspiciously at Tsidon and seemed to know enough not to speak.

"Uncle," he said tightly, and that was all.

\+ + + + + + +

THE OLD WOMAN could not quite believe the fool had run off and left her, not a hundred feet from the front of the queue, and over some no-account book he'd never read. She was barely able to handle Elena's weight on her own; the woman was much larger, and the old woman had not realized quite how much Naftaly had been supporting her.

She couldn't believe, after everything, that she would be dragging this horrible cow across the ocean.

On the other hand, she'd be in Anab. She would very likely be safe there for the rest of her lifetime. Somebody in Anab would have to help all these refugees, and now she would be equal to everyone else: none of them would have any money, either. Maybe some family would have an extra bed for an old woman, in exchange for a bit of help with the children or the chores.

She'd never had children of her own; she'd been unhappy about it in her younger days, but then when the mob showed up and burned nearly every Jew in Savirra, including her third husband, her parents, and every other person she'd ever cared about, she'd been glad. If she'd had children, they'd have been burned, too, and she wasn't sure how she'd have survived that.

So she wasn't entirely unsympathetic to Elena, who'd lost sight of what was right in a desperate attempt to save her grandchild. Still, though, neither had she entirely forgiven her. The old woman was good at holding two opposing ideas in her hands at once; it was the best part, she thought, of being old.

The old woman hadn't escaped Savirra because she was clever, or good, or wise, or rich. She'd escaped because she'd been lucky. Only it hadn't felt much like luck, then, walking all the way to Rimon alone because she had no place else to go and no one to ask for help. It hadn't felt much like luck when she was able to beg for a meal and a place to sleep.

She watched as those in front of her had their things searched. Naftaly had their remaining money; they wouldn't need it for the ship, anyway, and they had no jewelry, or books, or anything else the Inquisition might have a hankering for. They stepped up, and the guard took one look at them, and wrinkled his nose—not wanting to put his hands on two old crones—and simply waved them through.

The old woman shook her head to herself. If she'd had Naftaly's book, she could have gone right through with it.

All that was left now was to get on the ship.

There were children on the dock, weeping. A matron with her own children went to them and asked what in the world was the matter.

There were three of them, and the eldest told her they'd been separated from their parents; two of them were siblings, and the third they'd just found alone. They did not know if their families had gone ahead on another ship, or what had become of them.

Elena was by then hardly able to stand, and the old woman could barely manage her at all. The matron speaking to the children did not seem to know what to do, either. "Come with us," she told them. "We'll sort it out in Anab."

From the ship, a man called out and pointed at the line of people, several back from where the old woman and Elena were standing. "What is he saying?" asked the woman behind her, and her husband replied, "He's cutting off the line there. No more space on the ship."

No one said, "Good thing we got here early," or "Thank goodness," or anything like that, because of how awful it was to even think it: thank goodness I am safe, and not one of those others at the end of the line, who will have to make other arrangements tomorrow. Luck again, unearned.

"Will they send more ships?" someone asked.

"I don't know."

The old woman and Elena moved forward. She was so tired. In Anab, she thought, perhaps there would be a sunny spot where she could sit with a cat on her lap.

The matron speaking to the abandoned children had gone back to her spot, because what could she do? Give them her spot, and send her own children to Anab alone? Leave her own children there in their place?

The oldest looked to be about ten or so; the others much younger.

The old woman thought of Naftaly, the most foolish person she'd ever met, and likely the kindest. His father had sheltered him too much, probably because he was afraid for the boy, with his visions and his Mazik dreams. It was certainly why he was such an unmitigated idiot, but it was also why he'd retained such a gentle temperament. So many she'd met believed that trials made you kinder, but really, they just wore away at your character, leaving you covered in quills and hard edges. Naftaly hadn't a hard edge anyplace. He was as uncalloused a person as she'd ever known.

He would never find a way out of Sefarad his own. Probably he would wander around with that stupid book until someone murdered him.

Elena opened her eyes, and looked at the children, and looked at the old woman, and they exchanged a glance for several moments.

The old woman adjusted Elena on her shoulder and stepped out of line. To the eldest child, she said, "Can you carry one of these others on your back?"

It was a little girl, and she nodded.

The old woman said. "Then take them and go stand in that line there."

The girl looked at her a minute, confused, and the old woman said, "Go."

\+ + + + + +

NAFTALY SAT ON his cot with his head in his hands. If he could not take a book out of Sefarad, he could not leave. The world seemed very far away to him, then, as if there were not a single square foot of space for him to safely occupy. He could spend his life running from place to place, with his shaved face and short hair, but he'd be caught eventually, one way or another.

The door opened quickly, knocking against the wall, and the old woman stepped inside, dragging Elena with her. She dumped her onto her own cot and sat down.

Naftaly gawped at her. Before he could speak, she said, "There wasn't enough space for everyone who wanted to go."

"But we were near the front of the queue!" he said. "They can't have run out of space before you got to the ships."

"They didn't," she said, rubbing the shoulder she'd been using to keep Elena upright. She sighed. "There were children left on the dock; they'd been separated from their families somewhere, I don't know. I'm old." She jerked her head toward Elena. "She's old. It wasn't right." She pulled off her shoes. "I've cheated death more than my share already."

Elena lay down and turned her face to the wall without a word. In the streets, the sounds of an argument wafted up; someone owed someone else money, or someone had made eyes at someone's wife, or someone had trod on someone's toes; Naftaly couldn't hear well enough to say, except that it was the sort of normal, everyday quarrel one heard in the street of any town. For those people, outside, life had been simple yesterday, and it would be simple tomorrow. Naftaly held his head in his hands. "I don't know what to do," he said.

The old woman breathed in and out. Then she said, "There are smugglers on the docks."

Naftaly looked up. "Smugglers of books?"

"No, you idiot," she said. "Of people. When we left the ship, I heard talk. They'll take people out by small craft, a handful of miles from here, and meet a ship farther out. People are using them to get out with what little money they have hidden away."

Naftaly looked at Elena, asleep with her weakened hand tucked against her chest. "How much do you think she understands, of what's happening?"

"I think she understands," the old woman said. "She simply can't do anything about it."

"Will she improve?"

The old woman thought on this. "I don't know. I suppose it's possible. But there's nothing we can do for her, besides keep her alive. There's no medicine for her but time, you know that."

Naftaly did know that.

"I think she's lost her hearing, too," she added. "She doesn't seem to hear on the left side."

"No, she was like that before," he said. "Didn't you notice? She always turns her right ear to you when you speak to her."

"I hadn't noticed," she said. "I think we should visit the smugglers, see what we can manage. I think I should make the arrangements. You're more likely to be taken advantage of."

Naftaly would have objected, but thought better of it. "Fine," he said. "But there's only one thing: If we're willing to pay smugglers, won't they assume we have a great deal of money? Won't they wonder why we don't just book a ship directly if we have no treasure to protect?"

"We have no other choice, if you mean to keep your book," she said, "unless you can swim very, very far." She stood. "I'm going; you'll have to manage her on your own for a bit."

He removed the thin blanket from his own cot and draped it over Elena while she slept. The old woman said, "I'll see how far our coins will get us, but there may not be much in the way of choice. Smugglers are expensive."

She did not say what Naftaly already knew; if they'd gone with the fleet, their passage would have been free, leaving them enough to settle somewhere. He'd likely doomed them all, over his father's damned book.

"I understand," he said.

THIRTY-THREE

THAT NIGHT, THE Mazik was singing in his cell when Naftaly arrived, a silly song about a lamb bought for two lentils who turns out to be a princess, but who prefers to be a sheep and stays that way until she's made into stew.

His voice was weak, but he let out a soft, breathy laugh when he came to the end, looking up to meet Naftaly's eyes. "I haven't thought of that since I was a boy."

"It goes rather dark at the end," Naftaly said. "Do Maziks often eat their princesses?"

"Only when it suits us," he said, drawing his knees up. "How goes it, my friend?"

Naftaly considered how best to answer, before saying, "I've damned myself and my entire company, all over a promise and a worthless heirloom."

"Ah," said the Mazik, nodding. "What a familiar set of troubles. Come sit with me; I think I have enough magic to get us some wine." He dragged himself across the stone floor to the opposite wall, where a crude bowl filled with water sat on the ground. He submerged the tip of his smallest finger, and the water went purple.

"I'm afraid I'm a bit tired at the moment," he said. "I can give us wine or goblets, but not both." He sipped at the bowl of wine before handing it over to Naftaly, who took a long gulp of the syrupy liquid.

"Hardly matters," Naftaly said. "Can we really get drunk here?"

"Oh yes," the Mazik said. "At least, I know I can. I'm not sure how it might work for you." He took another sip before handing back the bowl. "I suppose an experiment is in order?"

Naftaly took another swallow. "What a concept. If I drink enough, I'll wake up—is that it? Does make it a bit hard to forget my troubles."

"You're right," the Mazik said. "Better not to get too drunk, then—anyway, I'd rather you not go yet. I've had enough singing to myself for one evening."

But Naftaly found he was already feeling cloudy-minded. "That was strong," he said. "Whatever you made."

"Oh dear," the Mazik said. "You are a lightweight." He drained the rest of the bowl himself before setting it down. "You've gone all pink." He ran his thumb along the top of Naftaly's cheek. "Are you slipping away already?"

But Naftaly said, "I feel . . ." He shook his head. "Dee. Deright? Delightful. That's it. You were telling me how you became some kind of . . ." He waved a hand. "Spy? I'm not sure where you were going with the tale."

"Pretty thing," the Mazik said. "I never said that was *me*."

"Didn't you?"

"Oh no," he said. "I'm really very boring."

"That must be why you're in prison," Naftaly said, laughing. "For your criminal dullness."

"That must be it," the Mazik said. "I'm so fortunate you're here to relieve me of the monotony of my own company."

"I wish I could do more. I wish I knew how"—his breath hitched, he was feeling drunk indeed—"to help you. To find a door to this place and open it."

The Mazik said, "You do enough."

Naftaly knew that was not true. But he said, "Then tell me what happened next, in your story. To the wastrel who was not you."

"I'm afraid there's no more to tell," the Mazik said.

"I won't believe that your story ended ages ago. What happened since?"

"Ah, little one. Nothing worth recounting."

"Your eyes," Naftaly said, "are orange."

The Mazik tsked. "Oh, you are drunk."

"None of the others ever have orange eyes."

"Yes, well," he said. "That's because most of the orange-eyed Maziks were from Luz, and they're nearly all dead." He tipped up the bowl again, and finding it empty, muttered a curse and let it fall to the floor with a clatter.

"Is it because of Ha . . ."

"Ha-Moh'to, well, that's an interesting question. Yes. Yes, I suppose you could say that it was." The Mazik pressed the heel of his hand against his forehead. "More wine," he said, "would be helpful."

"What happened?"

"What happened," he breathed. "Well, what happened was that our dear wastrel found himself a member of an order comprised entirely of Second-Age Maziks, all of them a great deal older and more impressive than himself, and he felt, for the first time in his wasted life, as if he'd been given the chance to prove himself."

"I don't understand," Naftaly slurred, "Second-Age Maziks."

"The Second Age," the Mazik said, "was the time of the Judges, the time before we were yoked to the rule of kings. Before . . . do you understand how our worlds are linked? Do you know about the Mirror effect?"

Naftaly shook his heavy head. The Mazik said. "Some version of what happens in the newer realm, somehow happens in the elder. We don't know why. We don't seem able to prevent it. You know the story of Samuel, and how the people begged him for a king?"

"I'm familiar," Naftaly said. "So they ended up with King Saul."

"Right, Saul. Well, Samuel told them, *Listen, you really don't want this, a king is actually a terrible idea*, but they wouldn't listen. So they got their king. And when that happened, we got a queen. Only the difference between your kings and ours is that ours don't so easily die. Saul lasted, what, twenty years? Our queen—"

"The horror," Naftaly reminded him.

"Yes, our queen, the horror, reigned from that moment on. At any rate, the Maziks in ha-Moh'to were very old and very accomplished; scholars, and wizards, and thinkers the likes of which you can't imagine, the head of them a woman called Marah, sister to the father of a young fool who thought he could run with the greatest minds of his world. For a while, he did; he was beyond useful, because what they needed was a spy, and no one would ever suspect a man with his reputation of working for *them*. The information he collected was invaluable."

"They were trying to overthrow the Queen?"

"No," the Mazik said. "No, they believed there would be no point to it, they'd only end up with another to take her place. Better to resist, in small ways, the Queen we know, than to depose her and find ourselves with someone worse: that was their thinking. But the wastrel thought he knew better. He developed a theory—a ludicrous theory. If the Mandate of Luz was the result of the Mirror effect, then the only way to break it would be to find a way to put an end to the Mirror effect itself.

"He was shouted down, of course, and the other Maziks reminded him he was there to offer reconnaissance, not to play at being a wizard—the Mirror effect was a fundamental, unbreakable tenet of the universe. They threw him out and ordered him never to speak in council again.

"But one of the Maziks found him afterward—Tarses b'Shemhazai, son of the last Judge of Luz. He flattered the wastrel, told him the others were too old, and too conservative, and they were wrong to shout him down; he called him clever." The Mazik turned his gaze to Naftaly's. "He'd never been called clever, you see."

Naftaly saw the skin around the other man's eyes crease, and then relax.

"Tarses asked how he thought that could be arranged, to break the Mirror effect, and so that damned creature, that idiot who should have stuck to fornication and feasting, told him how he thought it might be done. He said, *If you want to stop something reflecting, you break the glass*. He told him what they ought to do . . . was destroy the Luz gate." He pressed his fist into his forehead. "And three months later, it was done."

Naftaly raised his head from the wall.

"It was the humans that tore the gate out, but Tarses was the one who convinced them; tricked them, somehow. My aunt took me away before it happened," he said. "I was in disgrace, so she brought me to her husband in Rimon. I didn't know what would happen, when I suggested it." His face contorted briefly. "Ten thousand Maziks—and ten times that many humans—died that day. All because I wanted to be called clever."

"And the other Mazik," Naftaly said. "Tarses. What did ha-Moh'to do with him?"

"Ha-Moh'to died in the fall," he said. "And as for Tarses, there was only ever one person who could implicate him, and doing so would have meant implicating myself. So in the end, my greatest sin wasn't foolishness, or braggadocio, or pride." He whispered, "It was cowardice."

Naftaly reached out and laid his hand on the other man's forearm, making him wince. Naftaly said, "Why confess all this to me now?"

"Because," the Mazik said, "I will die soon, and I want you to find my uncle, Adon Sof'rim, and when you do, I want you to tell him the truth. Tell him I lied about not being sorry for any of it." He set his hand over his eyes. "I'm sorry for all of it."

Naftaly left his hand on the Mazik's arm. "And how shall I find him?"

"You will have to dream your way to him," the Mazik said after a moment. "I can give you his face." He made a circle in the air with his forefinger, and brought about an image of a man with silver hair and a sad expression. "Will you remember it?"

"Yes," Naftaly said, though he had no idea how to dream his way to Adon Sof'rim, when he barely understood how he'd dreamed his way into the cell in the first place. "But there is one thing more: you didn't know destroying the gate would cause the fall. Did Tarses?"

The illusion of Adon Sof'rim faded away, and the Mazik drew another in its place, of a grand, white-walled city consumed by the sea. "I have wondered about that very question for the better part of an age," he said. "The truth of the matter is, I don't know whether he knew or not."

\+ + + + + + +

INSIDE TOBA BET'S vision, Asmel sat in a pit lined on all sides by fire. Above him, on one side of the pit was a semicircular table, and seated at the table he could see the silhouettes of three Cacería judges. On the other side were two shades.

This last bit surprised him: he'd expected Alaunts. That they were using shades implied they wanted fewer witnesses.

One of those at the table thumbed through the leaves of a book Asmel suspected was one of his. "He's clearly guilty," the man said. "There's little to discuss."

"Agreed." The second spread his hands out on the table. "Burn everything in the blasted place, and leave the rubble to serve as a warning."

"Hm," said the third judge. "I don't know. There's something to be said for mercy in some of these cases. A broken man may serve as more of a warning than a pile of rubble. And there is the Adonate to think of. They might object if we burn one of their own."

"It's the Adonate we're trying to warn off," one of the others replied. "I'd think you'd understand as much, Adon Caçador."

"It's a delicate balance," he said. "Asmel's not unpopular. Aside from this latest business, he's always been a neutral party. I believe him when he says he's no Restorationist."

"It doesn't matter whether he is one or not," one of the others answered. "He's supporting their cause."

"Nevertheless," the third went on. "Toss him dead at the King's feet, and we may have a problem on our hands." There was a long pause. "Have you found the wife yet?"

Tsidon's voice, from the shadows, replied, "Not yet; but there are limited places she could be if she's still alive. The Peregrine found his ward, though. Fool had fled all the way to Baobab."

"Well, that's something."

"What precisely are you proposing?" the first judge asked.

"Leave Asmel alive as a warning," the third said. "Take everything to do with this latest business; sort through it and burn anything subversive. Close the university, forbid him to teach again."

"And what's to stop him writing more on the subject?"

There was silence, while a conversation Asmel could not hear went on over his head. "He won't consent to that," the second judge said. "Not even to spare his own life."

"Not his life," the third replied. "But his heir's. Call him up if you agree."

Asmel found himself pulled out of the pit. His hands ached from their restraints, and he recognized the three men who had been discussing his fate: two men Asmel had known all his life, and the third, Tarses b'Shemhazai, ancient friend of Asmel's wife, and a colleague of long standing. It was he, Asmel realized, that the other men called Caçador.

It was he who had been arguing to spare him.

"Asmel b'Asmoda," Tarses said. "For the crimes of treason and others not mentioned, will you consent to taking the sigils of silence, in exchange for your life and the lives of your dependents?"

Asmel's hands ached from the pressure of their metal armature, but he knew that would be nothing compared to what was about to happen. "If I refuse?"

"You'll burn," Tarses said. "The university will burn, your books will burn, your wife will burn, and your ward will burn. Your ashes will never know contact with the earth, and anyone who speaks your name will be blighted as long as our King sees fit."

"Then I have no choice," Asmel said.

The Caçador approached. "Then open your mouth," he said. Asmel drew a shaky breath and complied: the branding of the sigil the worst pain he'd ever known—or would ever know. His hands, marked next, were themselves agony. Asmel lay in a collapsed heap after, shaking violently. Tarses knelt before him. "I did you a great favor today," he said in Asmel's ear. "I expect you to remember it."

Asmel could only take great gasping breaths in response. Toba Bet felt searing pain in her own tongue, in her own hands, and felt him losing consciousness again and wondered how she would pull herself out of Asmel's mind and back into her own. She tried to come back to herself, whispering the release word Asmel had taught her, but instead she found herself in the gauzy light of the dream-world, and here was Asmel again, on the beach. Some time had passed; the fire-red sigils on his hands had faded to blue-black, and his body was restored to its normal robustness. His hair, now, was silver. The sea glittered black, and he sat gazing at it with his normal bereft expression.

Toba Bet realized she was seeing him from outside, and she felt herself approach him just as she understood she looked out through her own eyes now—or at least the original Toba's. On the sand below her were seashells: a muscle, a clam, a periwinkle. She picked up the periwinkle. She liked the color.

"What are you doing here?" Asmel asked. "Don't you have your own parents to dream with?"

"No," she said. "I don't. Can I stay?"

"If you must."

Toba took in her tiny hands, her tiny body; she couldn't have been more than a few years old. "My mother is dead and my father is wicked," she heard herself tell Asmel.

"That's most unfortunate," he said.

"Does that mean I'll become wicked, too?"

He turned to her a little. "I don't see why it should. There's little in blood but iron and water. Wickedness makes no home there."

"My grandmother," she said, "is afraid of me. What are those marks on your hands?"

He turned his left hand over to look at his palm, as if the sigil had been there so long he'd nearly forgotten it. "Nothing of consequence," he said.

"Do they hurt?"

"Yes," he said, "they hurt a great deal." And Toba Bet found herself flooded with shame, that as an adult it had never occurred to her to ask.

"Here then," she said, and put the periwinkle into his hand, while he blinked in surprise. "It will make you feel better." Asmel's eyebrows darted up, but Toba Bet found herself being pulled out of the memory, through the veil of her own mind, and back to the dim cellar where she knelt on the floor opposite Asmel, who gave her a weary look.

She had an urge to go back into Asmel's memory, an almost irresistible pull, and leaned forward to search his gaze again. He screwed his eyes shut. "Don't," he said. "It's a side effect of the spell, wanting more. Don't look at me yet."

She closed her own eyes and took a few breaths until the clawing need passed. "I'm sorry," she said, when she was calm. "I'm sorry for all of it." Then: "I dreamed of you as a child."

"Yes, I know," he said. "That was not the only time."

The dreams must have stopped when her grandmother gave her the amulet, and she had no memory of even one of them. "How long have you known it was me?"

He swallowed. "I wasn't certain. But I suspected, when your dreams returned. There aren't so many Mazik children." He turned to her, his eyes hollowed out, and Toba Bet wondered if he'd remembered along with her, or just watched her live his memories from the outside. "Do you understand, now?" he asked.

Toba Bet said, "Truly, I don't."

\+ + + + + +

UNDER THE COVER of darkness, Naftaly huddled against the biting sea wind and hoped Elena was not too cold. His face was covered with a crust of salt, and every few moments he gently pressed his hand against his breast to make sure the book was not becoming wet through his jacket. He'd spent the last few pennies he could spare on a square of oilcloth which he'd used for a wrapping, but a good soak would still be the end of it. The irony was not lost on him, that he was risking his life to take several bound pieces of paper out onto the open ocean, where a wave or a storm might easily destroy them. The old woman was right, he concluded. He was stupid.

Still, he could not completely regret it. At least he was trying, instead of sending the book off to a pyre.

The tiny boat, rowed by two mangy sailors, one with more hair than teeth, the other with more smell than substance, was taking them far, to a ship that would take them to Porto, where they'd have to beg a wagon to Pengoa. They'd had limited options; most of those smuggling themselves had wealth, else they wouldn't have bothered, and Naftaly of course had none. They'd had two offers, and the other was to Barcino, which, the old woman had pointed out, did not count as being smuggled out of the country.

"It's near the border," the man had insisted.

"That still doesn't serve," she'd said.

"It's a bargain," he'd said.

"Of course it's a bargain—you're offering to shuttle us from one unsafe port to another!"

So they'd taken the passage to Porto, a day's travel from Pengoa. Elena, at least, seemed pleased by the arrangement, at least until she got a look at the rowboat they'd use to get to the ship; and then she'd said a great many words in Zayiti, none of which sounded the least bit positive.

The rowboat, after what felt like several hours, arrived at a ship anchored some distance down the coast, and they were slowly hauled up onto the deck of *La Madrugada*. Bearing most of Elena's weight on his shoulders, he followed a sailor to the hold below, which smelled like mold and salt.

"How long did they tell you the voyage would last?" he asked the old woman, who had gone uncharacteristically quiet since coming on board. "Is this ship even large enough to go through the strait?"

"I was told it was a caravel," she said. "He told me three days."

Naftaly did not know much about ships, but he was fairly sure this wasn't a caravel. He was also fairly sure that Elena would not do well after three days in this hold. Already, she'd broken into a sweat. It reminded him of the Mazik's prison . . . close air and windowless, only this rolled with the waves and stank.

Several hours later, they were hauled back up to the deck and made to stand in front of the man Naftaly presumed was the captain. His face was weathered from too much sun, and he wore a silk-lined jacket that looked as if it had been taken off a larger man.

"It seems we've yet to discuss the matter of payment," he said.

Naftaly shifted Elena's weight to the old woman to free his hands. He said, "We paid your man before we boarded in Merja."

The captain smiled. "That was the boarding payment. Perhaps you misunderstood. There is another payment for the voyage. Transporting vermin is an unpleasant activity. I expect to be properly compensated for it."

Naftaly looked at the old woman, hoping she might have something to contribute to this conversation.

She did not.

"We haven't any other money," Naftaly said. "Besides what we already paid you."

"Really," the captain said, his eyes sharp in the moonlight. "Then why were you so keen not to be stopped at the harbor?" To his men, he said, "Search them."

Naftaly struggled against groping hands and heard a roar go up from his left; apparently the old woman had bitten someone, while Elena let loose with an unintelligible tirade. He felt the moment someone found the square shape of his book and cried out when it was ripped away from him.

The captain took it in his filthy hands. "It's worth nothing to anyone but me," Naftaly said.

The captain tore off the tape that sealed the book.

Naftaly let out a strangled noise, expecting something to happen, a curse to come flying out of the pages, maybe, or the captain to be struck blind or dead.

Neither happened. The captain opened the book, no doubt hoping it contained a hidden space for gold or a diamond, and leafed through the pages. He said nothing about what might be written there, and Naftaly realized he might not even be able to tell what language it was. He tossed it aside onto the deck, where Naftaly's eyes fell on it and stuck.

"Nothing," the captain said. "Did you swallow your treasure? Which of you should I gut first?"

"If we'd gone to the trouble of swallowing something," the old woman said, "why would we have bothered with you? The soldiers weren't searching anyone's insides."

The captain stopped, his knife in hand, and said, "Why smuggle yourselves at all, then?"

She looked to Elena, who jerked her head toward Naftaly and gave a curt word, which Naftaly took as a suggestion to stall. The old woman said, "There's a bounty. On the boy. He killed someone back in Eliossana."

"Really," the captain said. He inclined his head toward one of his crew, "How far is that?"

"Two days' ride," the sailor replied. "Unless it rains."

The captain did not like this answer.

"Throw them overboard," he roared.

"What?" Naftaly cried.

"Keep the damn book," he added. "We may be able to sell it for a few coins in Porto."

Naftaly was grasped by both arms and wrestled to the railing. "Wait," he called. "Wait!"

"Bit late to bargain now," one of the sailors said in his ear. He was pushed forward and felt his feet leaving the deck, while to either side the screams of the old ladies pierced him. This was entirely his fault. He'd killed them all.

To his right, he saw that Elena had somehow gotten her good arm loose and thrown a sailor over the railing ahead of her, but it was little use; there were too many of them, and they'd soon pinned her again. The old woman went over the side, too shocked even to scream, and he heard the sickening sound of her ancient body hitting the water.

He realized he'd never asked the Mazik to teach him any spells. Why hadn't he done that? Maybe he'd have something to do now, besides dying horribly—bringing down lightning, or bewitching the captain. Or—

Naftaly's upper body was over the railing; he'd hooked his legs around the nearest sailor, but he felt his balance shift more toward sea than ship. He heard Elena call his name; that much, at least, she could still say. Then, from the crow's nest, he heard a cry, and then another, words he couldn't make out with the noise of the sailors and Elena's screams, and then another sound, one he'd only ever heard once, at the beginning of the siege: the explosion of cannon fire.

THIRTY-FOUR

THIS TIME, TSIDON came to the alcalá alone.

Toba watched from her library window as he rode up on his goat-horse and put his palm against the gate, which rang like a bell under his touch. Toba Bet, who was replacing books on the shelves in the middle of the labyrinth, called, "Can't you just leave him out there?"

To Asmel, who had just appeared in the room and stood gazing out the window, Toba said, "I haven't invited him this time. Surely you can send him away."

"Unfortunately," he said, "your invitation was not discrete."

"So I can't rescind it?"

"Not without antagonizing him."

"What difference can that make, if he means to kill me regardless?"

Asmel nodded, conceding the point. Toba began to tremble, violently. "Calm yourself," he said. "He won't kill you today."

"No," she said. "Just once you've traded me away to him."

"I've already said I won't."

"Then he'll just kill me some other way!"

Toba Bet said, "Let me speak to him this time."

Asmel looked like he might balk at this, so she added, "I can deal with Tsidon right now, which is more than she can do. Let me speak to him. I'm not afraid."

He nodded. To Toba, he said, "Stay away from the windows." Then he descended the stairs to open the gate. "Why are you so much less frightened?" he asked.

"I've been anticipating my own end for weeks. Tends to take the sting away."

Asmel stopped short on the stairs, then kept going. "Don't bother to apologize," she said. "Remember, I'm only a buchuk."

Toba Bet stood at the gate, waiting for Asmel to catch up. On the other side, she knew, was the Lymer. She wondered what he would do if Asmel kept his promise not to give her up. Come in through the window and kill her in her sleep, most likely. She wondered why he hadn't already, and thought of her father in his bird-mask, saying he meant her no harm. Toba had decided he was lying, but she'd never told Asmel of that dream. Toba Bet wondered about that a great deal.

"You seem to be without your entourage," Asmel said, upon opening the gate. "Am I to take this as a show of boldness?"

"You may take it as you like, but I hardly required one for this particular errand," Tsidon said. He dropped Toba Bet a bow. "How are you, sweet?"

Toba Bet was not in the mood to maintain this farce. "Missing my cousin," she said flatly.

Tsidon smiled.

"Has he been gone so very long? I hadn't realized. But no matter; I'm sure he'll turn up soon."

"When?" she asked. Toba, upstairs, urged her to tread with caution, and Asmel shot her a quelling look. "Today? After lunchtime, maybe?"

Tsidon seemed pleased by her testiness. "It seems today is yours to show boldness, darling girl. What I mean to say is that I'm sure he'll turn up in time for your wedding."

Toba Bet regarded him. He was smugly adjusting the cuff of one sleeve, some ridiculous Mazik-made lace that looked like it had been spun by a clever spider. She'd suspected it would come to something like this: rather than demand a direct trade of herself for Barsilay, La Cacería would offer up some exchange that would allow Asmel to pretend she wasn't about to be slaughtered like a sheep. Probably there was some

Mazik rule about not handing over one's ward to be killed, else one be turned into a pillar of salt, or something worse.

Could there be anything worse for a Mazik? Likely not.

In any case, it was a reasonable course of action for Tsidon. La Cacería got Toba, Asmel got Barsilay, and no one appeared to have publicly done anything wrong. Probably they'd even go through with the wedding, to complete the bargain, and then Toba would just mysteriously die afterward.

Sourly, Toba Bet said, "Am I to take it this is your proposal?" In truth, she'd been hoping for a bit more pomp, since this was the only proposal she ever expected to receive. Oh, well. Seemed that was too much to ask, considering.

"Such a quick girl," Tsidon said. "I see no reason for delay. I'm sure your cousin is anxious to see you settled as well."

May as well make him twist a bit, she thought. "What reason can you possibly have," she said, "to want to marry me?"

"Your eternal charms, of course," he said swiftly. "Why else does one marry?"

"I have no dowry," she said.

"I have no need of one."

"I have no lineage."

"Nor do I; we're well matched in that regard."

Glancing at Asmel, she said, "My guardian would not likely consent to it."

He chuckled softly. "I think he would, but I don't need his consent. I only need yours." He stepped closer. "Do I have it?"

"As I've told you, I'm grieving the lack of my cousin. It makes it difficult to make such a . . . ponderous choice."

"And I've told you, he'll return in time to see you married."

She stared at him. "Have I your word on that? That he will be there to dance at my wedding?"

"He'll eat cake with you on your wedding day," he said, and his mouth twitched a hair at some hidden joke. "I can't guarantee dancing. Your consent?"

Toba Bet swallowed. Tsidon said, "You may have a moment to think on it," and produced a silver box on his palm, not unlike the one that had held Barsilay's ring. Perhaps he kept a stash of them somewhere, to make dramatic threats or lackluster proposals. Tsidon opened the box, presenting her with the ring inside; gold with black insets around it in the shape of a vine. It was not so fine as her grandmother's, which still sat on the original Toba's finger. Of course the other woman would have the better piece.

He set the ring on her palm. "Put it on once you've decided to have me. I'll know when you do." Turning to Asmel, he said, "I actually did come to see you as well. I bear a message."

Asmel's eyes had not left Toba Bet. He said, "You could have sent a shade with a message."

"Hm, yes. But this one I wanted to deliver in person. You've been summoned to the Plaça del Rey at sunset. Bring your ward; she'll want to see this."

Asmel's face was the color of paste. He said, "Who?"

"It's not your prodigal nephew. This is a bit more exciting. But I'm afraid the identity of the prisoner is secret. For now." He nodded to Toba Bet. "I hope you will wear my ring soon, sweet." Straightening his coat, he swept through the gate, which closed with a clang behind him, as if the university itself were casting him out and glad to be rid of him.

She realized after he'd gone that he'd given her no option to say no.

Holding up the ring on her palm, Toba Bet asked Asmel, "Is it poisoned somehow?"

He carefully took the ring between thumb and forefinger. "Not obviously," he said, his voice shaking.

"Oh, that's fine, then. I don't mind being poisoned as long as it's subtle. What is it you've been summoned to?"

"A sentencing," he said. "La Cacería means to burn someone tonight."

✦ · ✦ ✦ ✦ ✦ ✦

NO ONE HAD noticed the approach of the second ship until it was upon them; not the crew, not the captain, and not even the lookout, who was too busy gleefully watching three Jews about to be fed to the sea. By the time Naftaly found himself dropped back to the deck by the scrambling sailors, the ship flying no colors had already pulled alongside and had fired a shot that took off the front of their prow, and thrown over half a dozen hook lines, and then they were being boarded.

Naftaly found himself abandoned at the railing, not far from Elena, whom he gathered as best he could under his arm. There was a scuffle, but the smugglers' crew had been relatively small, and after the first few men had fallen dead on the deck—the captain among them—the rest had surrendered.

A pirate with close-shorn hair had a dripping sack over his shoulder, and deposited it near Naftaly, where it regained the shape of the old woman. She squawked at her treatment and then wrapped her arms around her chilled body.

Naftaly removed his coat and put it around her shoulders, though in a minute it was just as wet as the rest of her.

The pirate captain came and stood before them; gleaming boots and a red silk kerchief and a hat made from fine wool.

Around him, the crew was bound hand and foot; those who hadn't been killed were in the stern of the ship, guarded by a trio of men with long knives. The pirate captain looked down at him and said, in heavily accented La'az Sefaradi, "These were the captives?"

"Yes," the other man said. "The woman was in the water; Mehmet pulled her out."

"They were throwing you overboard?" he said to Naftaly. "Why?"

"They were extorting us," the old woman piped in. "Or trying to."

"Hm," he said. "Tie them up with the others," he said. "Perhaps we'll get a few pennies for them in Ceuta."

"You can't mean to do with us as with the others!" she said. "We were merely passengers!"

The captain laughed. "Passengers, eh?"

"It would be the honorable thing," she said. "To leave us somewhere safe."

"Honorable," he said. "And what do Sefardis know of honor?"

Naftaly would have protested, but changed his mind. As a Sefardi, perhaps his life was worth a few pennies in Ceuta. As a Jew, it might have been less.

It was a strange thing to be both Sefardi and not in the same moment, and Naftaly couldn't quite wrap his mind around what that meant. To a pirate, he was a Sefardi. To the Sefardi, he was a Jew. To a converso, he was a liability.

And that did not even take into account the situation with his Mazik-ness, which inspired an entirely different set of problems.

His identity was completely dependent on whom he was speaking to. He began to laugh, a little at first and then more at the absurdity of it. This earned him a slap across the face from one of the pirates, whipping his head back and splitting his lip, which only made him laugh harder. The old woman hissed, "Stop that, you fool."

A fool, he thought. That bit, at least, was consistent.

Across the deck, Naftaly watched one of the pirates pick up his book, open it, and startle, before presenting it to the captain, who thumbed through it. The book was written in Hebrew; Naftaly had seen enough to know that much. The captain would likely recognize it, and after that, who knew what he might do with them.

"Whose book is this?" he demanded.

The old woman shook her head at Naftaly fractionally. Naftaly opened his mouth and closed it again. Elena cried out in Zayiti.

The captain turned sharply, and she repeated herself.

He jerked his head toward Naftaly and asked a question: Naftaly knew just enough Zayiti to make out the word *Jews*. She replied with a fierce nod.

The captain handed the book to the nearest crewman and squatted down in front of Naftaly. Grasping his hands, he pulled a dagger from his belt and cut the rope. "Well, cousin," he said. "You've had a fair bit of trouble today, haven't you?"

\+ \+ \+ \+ \+ \+

THE PLAÇA DEL Rey was laid out in lime-white stone; the alcázar lay to the east; to the north lay a marketplace; to the west was the road that led out of the city. It was filled with Maziks dressed in vivid colors, their faces painted with anxiety. From their murmurs Toba gathered that they'd all been ordered here, and that no one knew who was to be burned.

It was Toba herself who had gone, shamed by her alternate's boldness in the face of her own fear, and at Asmel's insistence.

"You must not rely on her so much," he'd told her. "She will not always be available."

"But what if more birds go bursting out of me?"

"You must control it," Asmel had said. "What if the buchuk were suddenly dispelled in the middle of the Plaça? That would be a great deal harder to explain."

They'd left Toba Bet in the alcalá, with the shade and Tsidon's ring, which sat untouched on the table. She fretted, for Toba, more for Asmel, and for the fact that she'd grown attached to the idea of herself as, if not Toba's true equal, at least someone that Asmel could not do without.

Toba and Asmel had been ushered to the front of the mob. The King sat on a raised dais, blank-faced like he might have been bored. His two younger sons sat to his left, but Odem was not visible. Nearby, a grand coach sat, unhitched from the team that had carried it into the plaça. Toba supposed the prisoner must be within; the door was guarded by two of the tallest Maziks she'd ever seen. Seeing her staring, Asmel murmured, "Don't look at them."

His hands trembled and his face was gray. "Are you ill?" she asked; he only shook his head and said, "Don't speak if you can help it."

The crowd settled. Next to the King, a man in a blue coat leaned over and whispered in his ear. The King only closed his eyes in response. The man in blue made a signal and a woman approached from within a throng of soldiers. She was short for a Mazik woman; taller than Toba, but not by much, and dressed in La Cacería blue, in a tunic and close-fitting trousers with boots to the knee. She conjured a parchment to her left hand and the crowd went silent.

"For crimes against our King, we call to account Odem b'Relam."

The crowd erupted. From the coach emerged the Mazik crown prince, pulled along by the Alaunts who had guarded him.

"The King won't allow this, will he?" asked Toba. "It's his own son!"

The woman held up a hand and continued to read. "Odem b'Relam, your crimes include the following. Unnatural associations with mortals. Fathering a mortal child. Conspiracy against the King. Ideological impairment. For all these, you will be consigned to the flames on this day of the Te'ena moon, in the summer of the reign of King Relam of Rimon, long may he dream."

The King grows weary, Odem had said. His reign was ending, Odem had not made himself La Cacería's ally, and they would not risk him gaining the throne.

The prince's eyes were glassy, and he wore a lax expression, as if he were not truly there.

"He's been enchanted, or drugged," Toba whispered. But then the guards were taking a second figure from the coach. It was a child, Toba realized, of perhaps seven years old.

"No," Toba said. "No, they can't possibly—"

But when Asmel made to respond, his face contorted and he nearly collapsed.

"Asmel," she whispered fiercely. "Her eyes."

Asmel's own eyes were rolling with pain, but he nodded. Near the dais, the woman called up a column of flame; not a pyre, but a geyser of fire that burned without fuel, beginning at the ground and stretching up to the firmament.

Toba felt a hand press into the center of her back and felt ice creep from the touch; she thought it must have been Asmel, but he was utterly still next to her, his eyes fixed on Tsidon, who stood behind them both.

Toba found herself bewitched and unable to move. In her ear, Tsidon said, "Be silent and live."

Toba found herself unable even to turn her head, so when they cast the Mazik crown prince into the flame, she saw every moment. The fire was so hot, he did not even cry out, but was instantly consumed. And a moment later, when they cast the young girl after him—her perfectly round pupils filled with terror—Toba saw that, too.

+ + + + + +

NAFTALY SLID DOWN to the floor in the bottom of the hold, his stomach rolling in time with the waves. His head ached, and his conscience panged, and he knew he'd nearly gotten two people killed that night, never mind himself, and only the rare good luck of being captured by a Jewish pirate had saved them.

All for a book which had never proved any use to anyone. He could well believe his father had never read it, but that no one, in all its years, had ever thought to slip the tape off and peek inside seemed difficult to believe indeed. Still, the book was ancient and the spine was still tight, as if it had never been read at all.

Clutching the book in his right hand, he turned it over, twice. It was warm to his touch, more so in the cool air of the hold, and the leather beneath his fingers had been rubbed smooth by the hands of innumerable ancestors who had carried the damnable thing from house to house, never asking what was inside. Claiming it contained a curse was probably only a convenient way of keeping it hidden and unread; it hadn't cursed either of the men who had just looked at it—unless you counted the captain of *La Madrugada* being stabbed by pirates, but Naftaly did not think that was the book's doing. It was some kabbalist tract, probably, but what was the point in keeping it if no one was ever to read it?

Naftaly gently cracked the cover open, making an audible snap as the leather stretched for the third time in several hundred years. There was no frontispiece, save a chart of some sort, in the shape of an hourglass, and Naftaly realized the lines of the drawing were made of impossibly small words, written in such miniscule letters that no one should have been able to read them. Even holding the book an inch from his eye, he could only make out that they *were* words, though the picture itself felt somehow alive, as if it were the source of the book's heat. Turning the page, Naftaly found a page of Hebrew characters, written in a slanted hand, and then another, and then another, page after page of blocks of text.

He sounded out the first word, and then the second, and then despaired.

Kal Most'rim. He flipped a few pages ahead, tried again, despaired again.

It was nonsense.

It was written with Hebrew characters, but the words weren't real. There were two possibilities that Naftaly could see. The first of these was that it was some language Naftaly did not know, transcribed into Hebrew characters. Asking for help in reading it, however, would mean showing the book to every person he met, violating his father's trust again and again.

The second was that it was written in some sort of code—and any key that might have existed had been lost to time.

His greatest treasure was an unreadable book.

Throwing it aside, Naftaly began to weep.

THIRTY-FIVE

THE COURSER WAS dreaming, and the Caçador was calling.

Her dreams, on the Mazik side of the gate, were generally her own. While on the human side, however, they were the only way for her to speak to her master, and so every third night while she was abroad she closed her eyes to the tug of his call.

He was in the middle of the saltless dream-sea, waist-deep in water that mirrored the whirling stars, in a fine silk shirt the water was unable to touch. The Courser crouched just behind him on a flat rock that rose above the surface, one of a grotto of granite stones worn down by the false, fresh sea. Nearby, she could hear the surf breaking on the shore. This was Tarses' place, where he preferred to dream. The Courser did not know if such a place existed in the waking world, or if this was a creation of his dreaming mind. The rock underneath her was cold, the water was cold, and in the starlight she could see a faint blue cast to Tarses' skin, the only indication that he might be uncomfortable, even in his mystically dry clothing.

The Courser was very still; he'd called her, but he seemed to be watching some invisible scene play out on the surface of the water. If she disturbed him he'd be angry. He wanted, she suspected, for her to know what he was doing. She wondered if Tsidon ever sat on this rock, with his canny eyes, or the Peregrine, with her nimble limbs, waiting for their master to acknowledge them, to flick an eye in their direction, or give some curtly delivered greeting.

He reached out and set his fingertips on the surface of the water, leaving little ripples to fan out around him, then pressed the fingertips of the same hand to his forehead. He gave a sharp little intake of breath, as if he'd meant to say something, and then changed his mind. The skin around his eyes was tense, and he rubbed the wet of the dream-sea between his thumb and forefinger, as if testing it somehow.

"There is a swiftness to the turning of the world," he said.

He was frustrated; with himself, this time. What was unusual was that he'd slipped into the feeling so much that he'd revealed it. Tarses' eyes worked better at a distance—that much she knew from their long association: he could see events playing out, but they were like phantoms that only existed in his peripheral vision. Once time had placed the events directly in front of him, the sequence that linked them was gone. It meant that his long-term plans were flawless; when they began to come to fruition, however, he made mistakes. As much as he derided the Courser for her lack of finesse, the Caçador was worse: when unexpected events fouled his impeccably laid campaigns, he was terrible at changing course. It was, the Courser thought, his greatest weakness. She treasured it.

"As you say," she replied, because he liked a response to his ruminations.

He turned away from the water, casting an eye back at the Courser. "Still no sign of it."

He meant the book. "Not yet," she said.

This displeased him. So many books already searched, and still nothing. His plan was not working. Probably he thought that was her fault. "And what of the Lymer's report?"

She shifted her weight on the rock; she wanted to stand, but that would put her head at a higher level than Tarses'. "They might have burned books in Merja, had I not been there. I don't think they will, now."

He nodded, once, and walked back toward the shore, giving himself a long robe that cascaded down from his shoulders as he exited the water. The Courser was forced to follow him; she was wearing the same boots she liked to wear waking, and she hated to get them wet. Once his feet touched the sand, the scene shifted, the sand and sea and cliffs fading and reassembling themselves into the cavernous halls of Tarses' dreaming mind, a building without windows.

She hated this place. If her mind were to create some dream-edifice, she wasn't sure what it would look like, but it would not be this claustrophobic nightmare, a warren crafted from too-small labyrinthian hallways lined with shelves that contained row after row of books that made no sense in any language—a pale reflection of Tarses' most intense craving.

She willed the water out of her boots and followed him down the stairs, and then to an oak door with an iron lock. What was the point of a locked door that existed only in Tarses' mind? The Courser had no idea. Pretension, probably. He unlocked it with a key made from his own finger, saying, "I have something for you to do."

His robe had gone from blue to black as he stood in the doorway, his hand on the latch. "Make your clothes dark," he said. "It likes bright colors, and it's better it doesn't grow too interested in you."

The Courser did as she was told. "It?"

"A tool," Tarses said. "I need you back at the next moon, but I can't trust the Inquisitor without oversight." He opened the door and stepped into the room, where at the far end was a cage, and in the cage was a dark shape the Courser could not make out.

"Tarses," the shape hissed in a voice like broken glass. "You've brought us a visitor."

The Courser wanted very badly to back out of the room, because the thing in the cage was a demon. She'd seen them before, when they'd been foolish enough to cross paths with her, but she'd never heard one speak, because so far as she knew, demons *didn't* speak. Further . . . they didn't dream.

"What is this?" she whispered, because what it *was* was something unclean, even by the Courser's standards. Her skin crawled.

"It is precisely what you believe it to be, only enhanced," the Caçador said.

"You made this?"

"I stole it," he said. "Long ago, and I've been keeping it."

"You," said the demon, "were our replacement, Courser. Didn't Tarses tell you?" The creature laughed like the hiss of a serpent. "We would have been queen, but for you."

The Courser gave up a gasp and recoiled from the cage, and Tarses turned sharply to her and snapped, "Mind your face, you fool." She schooled her features back from whatever expression they'd instinctively taken, and blanked them again. Tarses did nothing to contradict the demon. It was likely true, then. Demons could exist in both realms, and had, since always. She wondered what had been done to this creature that it could be here, in the dream-world, and what that implied. It must have Mazik blood, somehow, in some small amount. She wanted to see it better, to understand, but there was nothing to see in the cage besides writhing shadows that occasionally took the shape of a clawed foot or a wing or a long-lashed eye.

"We are like you, little bird," the demon said. "We are not bound to the moon." It laughed again. "We would have been a beautiful queen, wouldn't we, Tarses, the Empress to your Emperor?"

"Be quiet," Tarses said.

"Tarses on the Mazik throne, and us the Queen of Mortals, grand, we would have been, and terrifying, and soft as moonbeams. Would you have loved us, Tarses, when we helped you break the Mirror?"

He said, "No," and the creature chuckled.

"Of course not," they said, "you love nothing. Not even her. Never her."

"I don't understand," the Courser said. "What do you want me to do with it?"

"Not *it*!" the demon cried. "Never *it*! I have a name, child, a beautiful name, bright as diamonds!"

She looked to Tarses in shock. "Is this true?"

"It is," he said.

"Tarses," the demon said. "We are not your whore, to share our name with whomever asks."

The Caçador said, "For now, you shall be called Atalef."

"We don't wish to be called that," the demon said. "It is not beautiful."

Tarses whispered something to the demon in a voice sharp and a hair's breadth past silence, and it wailed. He'd used its name, then. The Courser, who knew the feeling of having her name used as a yoke, cringed. Tarses said, "You will take Atalef with you and introduce him to the Inquisitor."

"Take it with me," she said. "How—"

"It has no body," Tarses said. "What you see, here, is all of it."

"Take our hand," said the demon, "and we will go back with you, to Mansanar, and we will keep your books safe."

She turned to the Caçador. "You want me to set a demon loose in Mansanar? It's more likely to burn your book than the soldiers are."

"We?" the demon said. "We shall burn nothing. We are quite obedient, like you. We will do everything you ask, so Tarses will give us what he's promised."

"And what is that?" the Courser asked.

"That matter," said the Caçador, "is between us, and won't be discussed with the Courser or anyone else."

"As you like," said the demon. "We care not, so long as you give us what you owe."

"Take Atalef," Tarses said, holding up a hand. "And wake. At the next moon, return through the gate."

The Courser opened her eyes, in her tent in the wild outside Mansanar. She would not sleep in a house of humans, not for anything. Still clutching her hand was the dark shape of the demon, its shadow claws gripping her tight, even when she tried to shake it loose.

"That's enough," she said.

"But we are cold. Make us a fire?"

"I know what your ilk likes to do with fire," she said, and tossed her thin blanket at the creature.

"You trust us not," they said. "Even after Tarses has promised our best behavior. Because you trust Tarses not?"

The Courser opened the flap of the tent; it was still dark, but she could see the corona of the sun peeking over the horizon. Soon, the soldiers would be beginning their duties, which meant it would be time for her to watch them, and train the demon to watch them once she was no longer available. She did not bother to answer the question: of course she didn't trust Tarses.

"You shouldn't," the demon said. "Tarses is fickle in all things. He was our master's friend, once. Until he wasn't."

"Your master is Tarses."

"Tarses now, but before it was Rafeq. You know him not. He has been away since long before you were born. We are ever so much older than you. We have been serving Tarses so much longer."

The Courser was not interested in what this demon had been doing prior to serving Tarses or how very, very old it was. "Do you always look like that," the Courser said, slipping a mail shirt over her tunic, "or can you look like a person? Because that would be helpful, if you could do it."

"We are always our beautiful selves," the demon said. "We can't change our face as you can. But we can possess."

So that's how Tarses had meant to make this creature queen. It would possess the Queen of Rimon, and do his bidding wearing her skin.

It was not so different than how he intended to use her.

Generally speaking, Tarses did not like to inform the Courser of his plans; it went against his creed. This plan, however, he'd informed her of, because she was its very lynchpin, and it took the very fabric of creation and turned it into a tool for Tarses' machinations. He would take the Mirror—by which the world of mortals was reflected in the world of Maziks—and use it to reflect his own will. He would set the Courser, as his instrument, on the throne of mortal Rimon. She would conquer the remaining gate cities, and make a new empire.

That empire would be reflected in the Mazik realm, with Tarses at its head.

This plan, it seemed, was older than she herself. How fortunate he'd obtained a better tool. She could hardly believe he'd have left so critical an operation to a demon, even one that was enhanced. "I see," she said.

Atalef continued: "You understand, do you? Only Tarses decided replacing was better than possessing. Tarses likes to replace. He likes his tools shiny and new."

None of this was news to the Courser. Atalef was trying to lead her somewhere with this line of thought. "If you are trying to manipulate me," she said, "it won't work."

A hundred spindly arms came out of Atalef, waving tiny hands at the Courser, and then the creature constricted again. This time it made itself as smooth as a sphere, and out of the sphere came a mirror of the Courser's own face, as if it had been carved of ash. The face spoke, and her own voice came from its mouth. "You think you are safe because Tarses needs you. He will make you queen of Rimon, queen of the world, and you will rule the mortal side while Tarses rules the Maziks. He will use you to control the Mirror, and the Mazik world will be free. But *you* will be the one before the Mirror, and Tarses behind, and Tarses will not always be there to whisper songs into your ear. You must be the clever one, as clever as Tarses, cleverer than Tarses. Is your mind so nimble?"

The Courser said nothing.

Atalef said, "Is this what you hope?"

"I hope for nothing," she said.

"We don't believe you," Atalef replied. "You hope. It's why you're alive, Courser, but soon you won't be."

She crouched in front of the creature, putting her face in front of the shadow facsimile. "What are you?" she asked.

"We are Mazik."

"I don't think so," she scoffed.

"We have a name. We are Mazik," Atalef said. "What do you think a Mazik is?"

She wasn't much concerned with whether this creature was Mazik or not; she hadn't spent her formative years dodging assassination by Hounds and Alaunts to begin trusting anyone that professed loyalty to Tarses. She didn't know what the demon wanted, and she didn't particularly care. Tarses had told her to put it in a room with the Inquisitor, and so that's what she would do. Perhaps it would have some line on getting the book that had not occurred to her.

The demon said: "You fly with a tether, little bird, and your singing is not pleasing to your master's ears. What will Tarses do, when he has another caged bird to sing his song, a lark to replace his lowly nightjar?"

Atalef blinked its false eyes a few times while the Courser watched, her face blank as new paper. "Nebulous threats don't concern me," she said.

"Specificity is difficult," Atalef said, "when one's name is known by another."

Riddles and more riddles and lies, and from a demon no less. The Courser tied back her hair and pulled on her boots. "I don't have time for whatever it is you're doing. Make yourself less conspicuous. We've leaving." She strode out of the tent, and Atalef followed, making itself a serpent of smoke coiled around her left arm. "I will take you to the Inquisitor," she said. "Do you know what to do once you're inside him?"

"Of course," Atalef said. "We know our business, as you do."

"Very well," she said. "Let's get this over with."

\+ + + + + +

TOBA SPENT THE night curled into a ball in her bed, knowing that she had watched a child die, and done nothing. That there was nothing she could have done did little to ease her shame. She'd been there, and she'd seen it, and that was enough—that she'd borne witness to an atrocity. In her own mind, she was complicit. If she'd attended better to her lessons, perhaps she could have overcome Tsidon's magic. If she'd eaten more of Barsilay's food, she would have been stronger. If she hadn't simply accepted that the other Toba had better control of her magic, perhaps she would have known what to do.

If she hadn't been singing the night of the moon, she would have been in Pengoa with her grandparents.

Toba got out of bed and went to find Toba Bet.

"You are stronger than I am."

"I am," she said.

"I admit it," Toba said. "But it won't do. You are a limited piece of magic, Asmel's said so. At some point, you will fade, and I will still be here, and I have to be the one that's stronger."

Toba Bet said, "Then I suggest you do something about that. I've told you why I'm stronger. I thought you'd be stronger, too, after yesterday, only you're even more afraid than you were."

"Shouldn't I be afraid?"

"You should be angry. There's no clarity in fear, and yet you keep choosing it."

"All right," Toba said. "Then I'll be angry." She went to the observatory, where she found Asmel poring over a book. A pair of shades worked furiously behind him.

She'd slept not at all, terrified of the dream-world, where she might encounter anyone and unwittingly tell them anything. The Prince was dead. A child—a very human child—had been cast to the flames. Asmel, for the rest of the night, had been unable to speak, either due to shock, or the pain of his sigils, or both.

Toba's hands fluttered in front of her face like a pair of terrified birds, and she struggled to quiet them. "What are you doing?" she asked.

Without turning, he said, "I'm trying to send a message to the King." He flexed his stiff fingers. "It's proving to be difficult for me."

"Give it to me," she said. "I'll work on it."

"You don't write Mazik well enough," he said. He threw the pen down. "It's a waste of time, anyway. He's not going to listen to any words that come from this house."

"Not even words that exonerate his own son? I can't believe that." She perched on the edge of the table and looked over the fits and starts of Asmel's letter. Near as she could tell, he was trying to explain that, from his scientific background, he knew that a half-human child could not be born with round pupils, and whomever had given evidence against his son was a traitor.

"I have long ago lost faith in the King's ability to see reason, if he ever could," he said. He pressed his fingers against his eyes. "Odem b'Relam was our great hope for the next age. He would have made a good king. Now he's ash."

She traced the strokes of Asmel's letter, an attempt to communicate around the sigils. "Odem did not think kindly of La Cacería. Was that widely known?"

"It was," Asmel said. "Also widely known is that Ardón was making overtures to Tarses, and now the throne will be his. I imagine Tarses thinks he'll have a freer hand on the reins."

"They killed Odem because he meant to abolish La Cacería. Just as they eliminated your voice to keep you speaking about Aravoth, which would have marked Relam as a usurper. But I still don't understand what difference it makes that he is a usurper, with Luz beneath the sea. It's not as if Luz could claim power now."

Asmel shook his head.

Toba's eyes went to the shelves where Asmel's astrolabes lived: the sandless hourglass on its side, the second, set with a disk. The one she'd seen in his memories, set with a cylinder. She was thinking too much of geography and too little of what was significant. "No," she said, "no, a mandate wouldn't apply to a place, it would apply to a person. Asmel, are there any heirs from that line?"

He said, "Possibly."

Toba looked over the copies of discarded paper in front of Asmel ... it was an impossible task, she realized, because he could not even write the characters he would need to describe a half-mortal child.

"If Relam knew La Cacería murdered his son on a false charge, would he destroy them?"

"If he believed it, he might."

She took up the pen and laid Asmel's left hand on top of her own. "I have an idea," she said. "Guide my hand."

It took the better part of an hour, but together, they managed to write a letter to the King. They sealed it with wax, and one of Asmel's shades took it in its ghostly hands and flung itself from the observatory window; they watched as it became a speck on the horizon in the direction of the alcázar.

Toba Bet strode into the room and crossed her arms, leaning against the doorframe. "I know we've decided that she's the important one," she said. "But I thought you should know I've finished sorting the library."

\+ \+ · \+ \+ \+ \+

NAFTALY WAS DEPOSITED together with his companions in Porto after several unpleasant, dreamless days at sea. Elena had recovered most of her strength, if not her ability to speak La'az Sefardi, and spent much of her time conversing with the captain in Zayiti. Naftaly had little idea what they discussed, but their meetings left the captain impressed enough to offer Elena a place in his household in Ceuta to care for his six children. The old woman, for her part, thought she was a fool not to accept, and told her so, frequently and with increasingly creative swearing involved.

When he found himself alone, Naftaly pondered his book. He passed through the pages again and again, hoping to make sense of them; he even broke down and showed it to Elena to see if it were written in some language she knew, but it was incomprehensible to her, too.

And then, of course, there was the greater mystery: why did he have it?

The captain left them enough coins for a wagon to Pengoa, and then they made their way into the walls of the Judería, into streets teeming with too many bodies suffering in the stale summer air. The houses within were sandwiched together one on top of the other, and there was a general aura of unease: the quarter was not large enough to absorb all the refugees that had come here, but there was no way to expand it. Everyone had been cheek to jowl already.

"This cannot last," the old woman muttered to Naftaly.

The uncomfortable thought settled on Naftaly's back like a heavy pack, and he knew that one way or another, it wouldn't. In the lanes, he heard more La'az Sefardi than Petgalese, and the strain in those speaking was palpable.

The captain had told Naftaly that Elena's brother's name was Mosse deLeon, and so they asked on the street until they were pointed in the right direction by a group of small boys in exchange for a penny Naftaly thought they could ill afford to spend.

They knocked on the door of a thin house set back from the street by a small courtyard, and when an old man with a beard the color of seafoam answered, Elena cried out and hurled herself at him, weeping and incoherent, even in Zayiti.

"Elena!" he said, and Naftaly wondered if this were her brother or her husband; either might have elicited this reaction. But she said, "Alasar, Alasar," and he knew this must be Toba's grandfather. Over Elena's shoulder, the old man cast his confused gaze first to the old woman, then to Naftaly, and then pulled them all in off the street into a room richly decorated with wood paneling and lined with bookshelves. Elena's brother, wherever he was, was a wealthy man, and while the house looked like nothing much from the street, within it was lovely. Alasar and Elena fell to a rushed, tearful conversation in Zayiti, and a maid appeared and took Naftaly and the old woman upstairs. The house was full, she explained, except for the room used to store out-of-season linens and the dishes used for Pesach. Someone was sent out to buy two feather mattresses, and while they were gone, someone else appeared and filled a basin of water, and Naftaly began to remove, layer by layer, the grime of the road and the hills and the sea.

Before anyone reappeared with a bed, he curled up on the floor and fell asleep, only to find his Mazik singing some drunk little nursery rhyme of a song in a language Naftaly did not recognize. He looked wretched; the bones in his cheeks and jaw stuck out and a crust of tears lay in tracks down his face.

At the sight of Naftaly, he stopped mid-verse, his eyes registering surprise, and between one blink and the next his face had filled back to its normal state. "My friend," he said, and his voice broke.

"Forgive me," Naftaly said, kneeling and taking the other man's hand. "I did not dream."

The Mazik turned his face away and wiped his eyes; his hair had lost its gloss and hung in hanks around his face. "I thought you'd decided I was too wicked to forgive."

"No," Naftaly said. "No such thing. I'm sorry to have left you alone in this place. I would never abandon you."

The Mazik tried, and failed, to sit up. "You've been dreamless all these nights? Have you been ill?"

Naftaly tore the cuff from his sleeve. "What are you doing?" the Mazik asked.

"Only this," he answered, and smoothed the Mazik's hair from his face and tied it back with the strip of fabric, while the Mazik went very still. The Mazik, he'd decided, would not want to look disheveled. "There," Naftaly said, once he was satisfied. "Now I can see your eyes again."

The Mazik was very quiet, and then he said, "Your kindness humbles me." He reached out a hand to Naftaly's wrist, twisting his fingers across it until the cuff spun itself back from the threads of his shirt, and was whole again. He left his hand curled around Naftaly's wrist once it was done.

Naftaly looked away. "I wasn't ill," he said. "I was at sea, can that be why? I've never traveled on a ship."

The Mazik removed his long fingers from Naftaly's arm. "The sea! Where—no. No, don't tell me where you've gone. I don't know what the sea does to dreams. We don't travel that way, because of the salt." He coughed; it was worse than it had been.

When the coughing had passed, Naftaly said, "I expect that one night I will dream of this place and you won't be in it."

The Mazik's head fell back against the stone wall. "I'm here until I die, little one," he said.

Naftaly said, "But surely they mean to release you at some point? If they were going to execute you, they'd have done it by now."

"I am merely a finch to lure the lark," the Mazik said. "And unfortunately, I can't even warn her. We've all been such fools."

"What can you mean?"

He smiled wanly. "I know more than I should. They ask me too many questions, because they think I won't be able to repeat them. *Does Adon Sof'rim suspect who the girl's father is? Does he know what she brought with her through the gate?* I'd hoped you would have found him by now."

"I'm sorry," Naftaly said. "I don't know how I can. I can't seem to dream anywhere but here."

"You must stop wishing for me, my friend."

Naftaly's face went very hot. "That isn't why I'm here!"

"It is the only reason you're here, night after night. But you must try to find someone else now."

"I can't," he said. "I have no idea how to find anyone else. If there's some trick, I don't know it."

"There's no trick," the Mazik said. "There's only your intent. If you can't find your way to Adon Sof'rim, find the girl: you know her. And when you find her, tell her that no matter what the Lymer promises, they mustn't make any bargain to get me back."

✦ ✦ ✦

ASMEL LOOKED UP to Toba. "Shouldn't you have known about the library, without her telling you?"

"I did know," she said. "It just seemed unimportant." When Toba Bet stiffened, she said, "Sorry. We've been a bit busy."

"Oh, I'm aware. There's some sort of a coup in progress, it's all very dire."

"Can you leave?" Toba snapped.

"I'm not here for *you*," Toba Bet said. She pointed a finger in Asmel's direction. "I have done nothing but sort these books for weeks. I would like you to declare my work complete."

"What's it matter?" Toba asked.

"It matters to me," Toba Bet replied. *And you know why*, she told the other Toba. *Can you not let me have even this much?* "Please."

Asmel pushed back from the desk. "I will look at the library," he said. "If that will satisfy you."

"Thank you," she said, and turned and strode down the hall, while Asmel followed and Toba hurried after them, down the tower stairs, across the way, to the human library, in which Barsilay's shade was sorting papers from one pile to another, with no apparent purpose other than to look busy.

"I tried several different methods," Toba Bet said. "Most of these books carry no date of authorship, so there was no way to sort them chronologically, and many of them have no listed author. I tried sorting them by language, but that seemed inadequate also. So you see I've arranged them geographically." She walked briskly through the labyrinth of shelves. "The books from Rimon are on these six cases. Over there"—she pointed left—"are the books from Pengoa; Ceuta is there, P'ri Hadar—"

"Stop," Asmel said. "Why have you left these empty?"

Toba Bet returned to the empty shelves Asmel had meant. "Well," she said. "I tried to organize so that books produced in close proximity would be *shelved* in close proximity. P'ri Hadar is just there, and over there is Te'ena. So I left these open for the books from Luz. I assumed you would have some from before the flood; if I'd realized there were none, I'd have filled these shelves in and moved—"

He turned to Toba. "Why didn't you mention this, if you knew about it?"

Before Toba could answer, Toba Bet said, "You may address your question to *me*. And how was I to know it was significant, that your collection contained no books from Luz? You were the one that assembled it."

"There were several Luzite books here," he said. "More than fifty, at least. Are you saying they're *gone*?"

"I'm saying they aren't here," Toba Bet said, a bit testily. "You may have moved them to the Mazik library—I haven't been in that one lately, but she doesn't remember having seen them."

"I wouldn't have moved them," Asmel said. "There would have been no point in mixing these with the rest. Are you sure you didn't misplace them?"

"Fifty books! Of course I didn't misplace fifty books. How could I possibly—"

"It's not as if random visitors wander through—" He trailed off, and his hand moved to cover his mouth, and Toba met her own gaze from across the room.

"The Infanta was in here," Toba said. "But you knocked her unconscious, and she was always chaperoned after that. How could she have taken them?"

"She must have already sequestered them somewhere when I came in," Toba said. "Turned them into something she could easily carry out in her pocket, but that implies she believed they contained something important." She sat down heavily in one of the great oak chairs. "Did they contain something important?"

"No," he said. "But she might have suspected they did."

"What did she think—the gate. She thought you had the Luz gate just sitting in your library?" Toba Bet said.

"Perhaps," Asmel said.

"So she never intended to marry you, did she?"

"No," he said. "If she was here for those books, she's working with La Cacería." Asmel let out a gasp, his face very pale, and Toba rushed to hold him up, asking, "Is it the sigils?"

"No," he said, panting. Toba struggled to hold him up, and she scowled at Toba Bet, saying, "Move, you useless cow," until the other woman was compelled to vacate the chair and help put Asmel into it. Toba put a hand to his brow, which had dropped several degrees from its usual fiery temperature.

He slumped forward, his head in his hands. "Someone," he rasped, "has just destroyed my shade."

"Asmel," Toba said. "If the King dies and his second son comes to power, what will become of you?"

Dropping his hand, he said, "Whatever La Cacería wishes, I expect."

"Then we have only one option," Toba said. "I must marry Tsidon, so that you and Barsilay can flee."

"Why not say what you mean?" Toba Bet said darkly. "To spare yourself, you will send *me* to marry him."

THIRTY-SIX

MOSSE DELEON, IT turned out, was a banker, who worked in a consortium of local men who met routinely in an office in his house. Lately, their discussions had turned to how best to accommodate the large number of newcomers, since the borders of the Judería were fixed and there was no space for additional houses. An appeal had been made to the King. A bribe had been paid. Nothing had happened.

The following week, Elena left with Alasar to look into a job suggested by the friend of a friend. She could still speak nothing but Zayiti, but Alasar could understand her, and was slowly helping her relearn Sefardi: now she could call Naftaly an idiot in both languages with equal facility. The old woman got to work regaining the weight she'd lost on the road and at sea. Naftaly understood that he was living in an unearned place and struggled to make himself useful.

Naftaly was in a corner of Mosse's office, repairing a cushion that had begun to come apart at the seam. At his desk, Mosse himself filled a ledger with large quantities of ink. He spoke perfectly good Sefardi but generally chose not to, leaving Naftaly to understand about two-thirds of what he said, and invent the rest. Since he said little enough to him to begin with, Naftaly chose not to engage him. The cushion had been made by someone with greater skill than he, and Naftaly struggled to conceal his uneven stitches behind a bit of piping. He'd just begun knotting off his thread when the door opened and Mosse's man came in and told him the Conde of Lobata had arrived and was insisting on seeing him right then.

Naftaly rose to leave, but Mosse gestured for him to sit back down. "Stay there. Try to look wealthy and unintimidated."

Unfortunately, Naftaly had no idea how to appear as either; his borrowed clothes did not even fit correctly. He pulled on the cuffs of his too-short sleeves.

"Just sitting still would be a start," Mosse said.

The man Naftaly assumed was the Conde strode in and stood in front of Mosse's great oak desk, flanked on either side by servants who kept their eyes cast to the floor. The Conde spoke in rapid Petgalese that Naftaly could only partially make out; it seemed he wanted money, and a lot of it, and it was somehow to be made a gift for the King.

Mosse's face gave little away. He asked a question about repayment. He asked a question about repayment of some other sum of money he'd given over in the past. The Conde hurled what was clearly some kind of insult, which didn't strike Naftaly as a clever way to extract money from someone already disinclined to give it, and Mosse replied in a similar vein. The Conde's face reddened. Mosse stroked his luxuriant beard. Naftaly suspected he'd never grow such a beard as that. He wondered if it were a matter of diet. Or heredity. Or sheer force of will.

The Conde narrowed his eyes. "We tolerate you for one reason only," he said coldly, in words Naftaly could understand. "But there are others, now, who do not concern themselves with whether lending money is clean or dirty, and if you will not lend to me, perhaps they will."

"If you mean the men of Zayit," Mosse said, "I highly doubt they will lend to you twice, given your history of repayment."

"I won't need them to lend to me twice," the Conde replied.

The two men regarded each other over the desk. Naftaly wondered about the wisdom of making a man hate you while asking for a favor. He also wondered about the wisdom of saying no to a man whose boot resided on one's throat.

Mosse told the Conde he needed to consult his associates. The Conde left.

Afterward, Mosse lost his façade of calm almost at once, called his servant, and quietly asked him to summon the other bankers.

"Well," he said, addressing Naftaly for the first time in Sefardi. "What did you think of that?"

Mainly Naftaly wondered why he'd been left to witness the encounter. He said, "It's never good when a man with a title appears. What did he want?"

Mosse sighed. "Money," he said. "Why else would a man with a title come here? He'd hoped to catch me alone, the better to threaten me. He's trying to negotiate an alliance between his daughter and the Infante, but the King is angling for a larger dowry than the Conde can provide."

"Is he asking for a loan, or for a gift?" Naftaly asked.

Mosse said, "By his lips, a loan. By his actions, a gift."

"I think . . . I think you said something about him having defaulted before."

Mosse nodded curtly; his hand had gone back to smoothing that beard.

"Doesn't seem to require much consideration," Naftaly said. "Why would you want to give him more money?"

"Because of what he might do if we don't give it to him. The Conde is . . . not a kind man. Rumor is he murdered his own brother for the title."

"And no one did anything?"

"Indeed not," he said. "He has at his disposal a thousand lancers; no one wants to cross him, which is why the King is interested in the alliance in the first place. But he feels he can afford to press for more money, so he is." Mosse's servant reappeared and whispered in Mosse's ear. "They're coming," he told Naftaly. "You may finish that"—he pointed at the unfinished cushion—"elsewhere."

Naftaly took his cushion and his dismissal and went to the kitchen, where he found the old woman scarfing bread leftover from breakfast, the housekeeper foolishly having left it unattended.

She held out a piece to Naftaly, who shook his head. "You missed the excitement," he said. "There was a nobleman here."

The old woman made a very sour face. "How dreadful. Has he gone?"

"Only just."

"Wanted money?"

"Yes, a lot."

"Overspent on his mistress?"

Naftaly changed his mind and tore some bread from the old woman's loaf. "Not a mistress. A dowry," he said, and explained the Conde's predicament with the Infante while the old woman chewed thoughtfully with her remaining teeth.

"Doesn't seem like it would be good for us," she said, "to have such a man so close to the throne."

"It isn't good for anyone; that's another reason they are loath to make the loan."

"They won't give it to him, then."

"I don't think so, but Mosse's sent for the others, so he means to talk it through with them, at least. Or maybe it's only a show, to make it look like there's been a debate."

"For what purpose?" she asked.

He shook his head. "Maybe then the Conde will be less likely to try to exact retribution. I don't know. He said something about getting money from the Zayitis, but Mosse doesn't think they'll give it to him, either."

The old woman said, "It's a bad business. We're living with a snare around our necks, and it takes only the whim of a single powerful man to tighten it."

Naftaly agreed. He ate more bread. The old woman said, "We should never have come here."

Naftaly did not know how to answer, but she continued, "We could be living in the house of that pirate now, eating sweetmeats near the sea. Perhaps it's not too late."

"The invitation was for Elena," he reminded her. "To teach his children. Not for us."

"We could teach them just as well," she countered.

Naftaly laughed. "What would you teach them? To pick a pocket?"

She raised her eyebrows. "He's a *pirate*. What skills do you suppose his children need?"

"Well, there you have it," he said. "Why didn't this occur to us earlier? You can teach them to thieve, and I can teach them—"

Naftaly felt the world slip sideways, and was dimly aware of his head hitting the floor, and then he saw a harbor, and in the harbor was a ship carrying only children, all of whom were crying while the docks were filled with screaming mothers, and then he was in a building—a cathedral, somewhere he did not recognize, with vaulted ceilings and archways, filled with people, all of them kneeling, and at the front of the congregation was a bishop in his miter chanting before a couple—it was a wedding. A young man, perhaps Naftaly's own age, and a girl scarcely out of childhood sipped a chalice of wine. Her fingers trembled; his did not. Naftaly wondered if Elena's brother had relented and given the Conde the money for the dowry after all, or if he'd gotten it from the bankers of Zayit, as he'd threatened. The man Naftaly supposed must be the King of Petgal knelt just behind the couple, suppressing a grim smile that Naftaly did not like. Naftaly knew no Latin, and comprehended nothing until the vows were exchanged, and he heard the names of the betrothed.

He came to with a jolt, to find his head near the hearth, the hot air curling the hair at his temples. The old woman squatted over him, her wrinkled face examining his forehead, possibly for damage, and at the sight of his open eyes she demanded, "Pestilence? Death? Rain of locusts?"

Naftaly struggled to sit up, his head aching, probably more from the collision with the floor than the vision, and he rubbed the side of his head where he'd hit. "I saw a wedding."

"Well, that's a good deal more charming than usual," the old woman said. "Was there dancing?"

"I'm afraid not," he said. "I saw the wedding of the Petgalese Infante. To the Infanta of Sefarad."

\+ + + + + +

"I WANT TO talk to you alone," Toba Bet told Asmel. "I don't think it's too much to ask."

"What for?" said Toba. "I'll know whatever you say to each other."

Toba Bet's voice dropped precipitously. "You're sending me off to Tsidon," she said. "And you're quibbling about giving me three minutes with him?"

Toba's eyes scanned to Asmel. "I will go," she said, and then did. When she'd left, Toba Bet asked, "Can you turn off whatever link exists between us? For a few moments at least?"

He tilted his head slightly, his eyes taking her in. "I can try," he said, and stepped closer, running his hands gently from the crown of her head to the nape of her neck, leaving a chill, like a wake of ice on her scalp. "Do you hear her, still?"

"No." She made a fist, and released it, and said, "She asks me to die."

Asmel nodded, once.

"*You* ask me to die."

Asmel failed to deny this. Toba Bet said, "You think I'm expendable because I was created second; that I'm *disposable*. I tell you, I am no less a person than she is, which is how you've treated me all this time."

"I don't deny it," Asmel said gently.

"But you've decided it will be her that lives, and me that dies. It made sense before: if she'd died two weeks ago, we'd both have gone. But now, we know it's not that way any longer."

He sighed. "What would you have me say? That this is unfair?"

"Yes! I'd have you say it's unfair. That you've been wrong, all this time, for having treated me as if I'm nothing more than a shade with a face." She swiped at her eyes. "Say that you will mourn me, as you would have mourned her."

He took her hand; his eyes were on it, as if wondering if there were any difference between it and Toba's; both of them knowing there was not. He said, "I've treated you poorly."

That seemed to be all he was willing to say. She pulled her hand free and turned away. "Fine," she said. "I'll marry Tsidon, and then I'll die. But first, I'll tell you what she wouldn't: she dreamt of our father."

Asmel's eyes went startled.

Toba Bet gave him a wan smile. "He was masked; I don't know who he is. But he insisted he didn't want her dead, and he called her his heir. I expect you'll say that's unthinkable. As for why she didn't tell you, you will have to ask her."

"It is unthinkable," he said, though he looked troubled. "He was trying to persuade her to accept Tsidon; that can be the only explanation."

"Yes, but to call her his heir—it's not a very sophisticated lie, is it?"

Asmel said, "No. It's not."

"I keep wondering about it," she said. "Here are the possibilities: either he's a fool who couldn't come up with a better lie, or he thinks she's a fool who would believe such a lie. I know it's likely the second—we worked very hard to make her look like a ninny at court—but still, it troubles me. It's . . . it's the sort of lie meant to ensnare a man with an ego, and he knows she is not that. Asmel, I ask you this now, because it needs saying: is there any possibility he told the truth?"

Asmel said, "None."

She nodded. "Very well." She felt the cold cap of Asmel's spell begin to waver; pinpricks of warmth broke out across her scalp, and she said, "I said I wanted only three minutes alone with you as the price for my life, but I lied. I also claim this," and she reached out and set her hands against Asmel, and went up on her toes, and kissed his startled mouth.

She felt his breath come sharp, but it was surprise, not passion, and while he made no move to push her away, he did not kiss her back, until the end, when he set a small kiss to the corner of her mouth, and set her back on her heels, and looked at her sadly.

"I won't die for her, Asmel," she whispered. "But I will do it for you."

Toba Bet felt the last of Asmel's spell fade, leaving her aware of her counterpart, waiting outside and feeling irritated about being denied this conversation. Sensing the return of the other woman's mind, Toba came back into the room, and took in Asmel standing close to the other, and felt a sense of betrayal.

Toba Bet said, "Give me the ring."

THIRTY-SEVEN

NAFTALY EXPLAINED THE details of his vision to the old woman, who had responded with a simple pronouncement: "Fuck."

In an alliance between Sefarad and Petgal, Sefarad was the larger party, which meant they would have the higher hand in any negotiations between them. The Queen of Rimon would get what she wanted. And what she wanted, everyone knew, was to expand the Inquisition and the power of the Church.

"We have to give him the money," Naftaly said. "If we don't, the King allies with Sefarad and the Inquisition comes here. He won't get it from the Zayitis."

"What do you intend to do? You think Mosse deLeon is going to listen to the two of us?"

He rubbed soot off the side of his face from his encounter with the hearth. "When are Elena and Alasar coming back?"

"I've no idea. If he's offered a position, they may stay to set up lodgings. We could send a letter; I'm sure Mosse knows how to find them."

"We can't wait for that," Naftaly said. "It might be days until we hear back, and I was under the impression the Conde was under some pressure to come up with the money quickly."

"Well, what are you going to do? Tell him you have occasional visions, and he ought to hand over a large sum of money to the Conde based on that alone? He'll never listen to you."

"If I don't even try," he said, "then what is the point of even having the visions? If I can't do anything with what I learn, I may as well be a madman." He tried to stand, and the old woman had to catch him when he stumbled.

"You go to see him like this, that's exactly what he'll think of you," she said. "Staggering about and covered with soot, look at you."

"But—"

"It will keep an hour," she said. "You need to wash, and rest, and think about what you will say." She tucked his hand into her elbow and pulled him toward the stairs. "The one time we could use that woman's tongue, and she's not here."

Naftaly felt the chill of his vision slide away as he allowed her to lead him out of the kitchen. "I'll have to guess what she would say," he said, "and hope I will guess right."

+ + + + + +

TOBA BET TOOK the silver ring from Asmel's hand and slid it onto her finger; it went from cold to hot, and then hotter and she cried out, and then some part of the silver went liquid and broke free, swirling before her, until it became Tsidon himself. He held her ringed hand in his own and smiled down at her like the wolf at the rabbit who has not yet realized its legs are pinned.

At the first sign of Tsidon's magic, Asmel had thrown up a hand, flinging Toba the Elder from the room and slamming the doors. "I resent your intrusion," he told Tsidon, when enough of him had materialized to listen. He was not exactly the man himself: he was something between a buchuk and a shade, with form but without substance. "She agreed to marry you. She did not agree to marry you this instant."

Tsidon, or what there was of him, laughed merrily. "I'm only here to negotiate the particulars, old friend, and not with you. Little one, I'm so glad you've accepted me."

So he was here for the Mazik version of the tna'im, though there were no witnesses besides Asmel. The ring seemed to squeeze Toba Bet's forefinger, and she wondered if it would eventually shrink down until her finger was no longer attached to her hand. "I'm not sure what particulars you had in mind," she said.

"Simply the normal things," he said. "The date, the location."

"Here," Asmel said quickly. "It will be here."

Tsidon looked like he might have argued, but Toba Bet cut in, "The garden is very beautiful, don't you agree?"

"Fine," he said. "Six days from today seems enough time to prepare yourself."

"Seven," she said, more to be contrary than anything.

Tsidon frowned. "In seven days, the moon comes full. Surely in P'ri Hadar the prohibition is kept against marrying under a moon?" he said.

"I meant before the sun goes down," she said. "Clearly."

"Clearly," he said drily. "But only if the ceremony is complete before the sun sets. If there are any . . . delays . . . I will take offense. Fine; in seven days, we'll be married in Asmel's garden; I will bring guests—"

"You'll bring my cousin," she countered.

"Your cousin is so often late," he said. "I'm sure he'll arrive once the Raskem is signed."

"I find that unacceptable," she said.

"I'm sorry you feel that way. Now, there's only the small matter of your dowry—"

"I want to discuss my cousin!"

"That has already been answered—"

"And I haven't got a dowry. I've already told you as much."

"This is merely a trifle," he said. "A symbolic gesture, so tradition is fulfilled: surely you know we can't be married without an heirloom of your mother's line."

She glanced at Asmel, who looked troubled indeed. She said, "I have no such—"

"But you do," Tsidon said. "You were wearing it on your lovely throat the first time I saw you, a blue stone cut in a circle. I will have that, little one, and you may make use of it when we visit court, so that all may see my wife has a fine jewel to call her own."

Toba looked to Asmel again, who looked deeply concerned, but said nothing.

"Most men," Tsidon said, "would ask far more of you. It's only because I care for you so deeply that I ask only for a trinket. Simply say you agree, and in seven days, we'll be wed, you will see your cousin, and you will leave this dreary place behind." To Asmel he said, "Tell me, friend, is she likely to receive a better offer?"

Asmel looked away from the pair of them, and said, "No."

"There you have it," Tsidon said. "Unless you've changed your mind and don't wish your cousin to see you settled?"

Toba Bet whispered, "I agree."

Tsidon clapped his hands once, saying "Splendid!" and then he faded into a mist, and then he—or whatever part of himself he'd imbued into the ring—was gone.

Toba Bet sank onto the stone floor and clawed at the ring. "It won't come off," she said. "It won't come off!"

"It won't," Asmel said, coming to crouch beside her. "Not while you live. A Mazik engagement is unbreakable, unless both parties agree." She'd dug through the skin around the ring with her fingernails, and he pulled her hand away to keep her from doing more damage. "Where is the jewel he spoke of? I want to see it again."

Toba Bet let him hold her hand still. "Do you think this is what the hostage tried to warn me of? That he would steal the jewel?"

"The character she used didn't mean jewel," Asmel said. "I assumed you just recalled it wrong, what she wrote, but now I'm not sure. She may have used a word I don't know."

"I'll send the shade for the jewel," she said. "It's upstairs with the rest of her things."

They remained crouched on the floor, with her hand in Asmel's. Toba Bet had to work very hard to resist the urge to pull at the ring again, but Asmel's magic was already working to cool the cuts she'd made in her own skin. She said, "I wish it were today. I don't know how I will bear it all this time, waiting for my little half-life to end. I suppose I never was meant to live, though, was I?" She laughed once, softly. "I think I know why Toba made me instead of wings, when you threw her from the roof. She knew she couldn't save herself, so she made me to suffer in her place. I want to hate her for it, too, but I know what it is to want life. If I could trade places with her, I would." Her eyes filled with tears. "I can't bear this."

Asmel set his hand gently on her arm, and she leaned forward until her brow met his shoulder, and neither spoke for several minutes. Finally, she said, "Asmel, can you make me sleep a while?"

"Would that comfort you?" he asked.

"Yes, I think it would. Just for a few hours. Maybe I will dream of something beautiful."

She expected him to set his hand on her scalp, as he'd done before, or on her shoulder, as he'd done with the Infanta, but instead he set a kiss to the crown of her head, and said, "Then rest, Adona," and she closed her eyes and slept.

He set her on the pallet she slept on among the shelves. When Toba the Elder had returned, feeling greatly troubled, he said, "I suppose the only thing that remains is for me to tell you your name, so that she may sign it on your Raskem."

\+ + + + + +

IT TOOK NOT one hour but three for Naftaly to be clean and cogent enough to request an audience with Mosse, by which time the other bankers had long since come and gone.

Mosse barely glanced up at Naftaly's intrusion. "If you've come to replace the cushion, leave it and go," he said. "I've a good deal of correspondence I'm behind with."

Naftaly had forgotten the cushion, which had fallen into the ashes of the hearth when he'd collapsed and was now hopelessly stained. "I'm here to discuss the matter of the Conde," he said.

At that, Mosse looked up. "There is no matter of the Conde. We've rejected his request. As to whether the Zayitis will be foolish enough to lend to him"—he shrugged—"I couldn't say."

"They won't lend to him," he said. "You ought to do it."

"I beg your pardon?"

"There are some matters I don't think have occurred to—"

"I've been in this position for twenty years," he said. "You've been here five minutes, and you think there's something that has occurred to you and not to me? I will explain the situation to you. The Conde of Lobata wants to marry his daughter to the son of the King. The King, who is quite old, and not expected to live more than another five years at most. If he succeeds in this alliance, and if anything were to happen to the Infante . . ." Here, he sat back. "Once an heir is born, the man's positioned himself to be the next regent. He's an evil man. None of us wants him in that position, even if he did intend to pay us back, which he doesn't."

"But the alternative," Naftaly said, "is for the King to marry his son to the Infanta of Sefarad."

Mosse's mouth went slack. "You can't possibly know that," he said. "Where did you get that information?"

"Suffice it to say I *have* the information," he said. "You do understand what will happen if they marry? They will bring the Inquisition here."

"That's only a guess," he said. "I won't believe the son of a Sefardi tailor has a well-positioned friend in the court of Petgal: it's absurd."

"Senhor," he exhorted. "What if I am right?"

Mosse flung down his pen. "You are asking me to give five thousand milliarès to the devil, because there is a *chance* the King will marry his heir to the Infanta of Sefarad, and a *chance* she will use that alliance to bring the Inquisition here. Only a fool would barter for those odds."

"It isn't a chance," Naftaly said. The screaming mothers in his vision threatened to return; he could hear them as easily as if they were outside on the street. "I know it seems foolish to you, but I'm telling you, you must give him the dowry."

Mosse held up his arm, flicking his other hand against the sleeve Naftaly had worked on the day before in an attempt to be helpful to the housekeeper—the seam had begun to unravel, and he'd remade it. "They tell me you mended this," Mosse said.

Naftaly nodded hesitantly.

Mosse held his arm out straight from his side. "You are asking me to trust the future of every Jew in Petgal," he said, "to a *tailor* who cannot sew a straight seam."

"Sir," Naftaly began.

"I have given you a place here for the sake of my sister, and I have heard you out for the same reason. This is the last time I will tell you: the answer is no. We will not give a single milliarè more to the Conde de Lobata; not today, not next year, not even in fifty years, Hashem forbid he live so long. And I strongly suggest you find some other way of occupying your time than in finance or politics"—he held up his sleeve again—"or tailoring."

Naftaly watched him write a few lines, turn a page, begin again. Mosse, he knew, was a man of his word. He'd say nothing else.

The old woman was waiting outside. "You heard?" he asked.

She pursed her lips. "What will you do?"

"I will ask for help," he said. "From someone else."

✦ ✦ ✦

ASMEL HAD SEEN Toba's Mazik name written in her own blood; she'd cast the spell, and it had revealed itself, but she hadn't yet learned to read Mazik then. Regarding Toba carefully for a moment, he said: "Your name is Tsifra N'dar."

Toba felt the truth of it go through her. She closed her eyes and let it settle on her shoulders like a heavy cape—a cape of feathers. "Tsifra," she said hesitantly. "It means bird . . . and N'dar is . . ."

"Splendid. Splendid Bird." He paused before adding, "It's an unusual name. A strange name."

She looked up to him again. "Is it? How so?"

"Maziks do not call themselves after animals. It's . . . it's not quite a taboo, but I would say I've never heard of such a name. I wondered about it when I saw it."

Toba felt the rightness of the name she'd called herself, and she thought of the Mazik names above her grandmother's, remembering a few characters she'd seen and learned later. "Maybe I was called after someone."

"Maziks don't call themselves after their ancestors. You'd end up with legions of living Maziks with the same name."

"But my great-grandmother was called the same as someone else: I saw the same characters twice. Maybe Mazik naming conventions don't apply to part-humans."

But Asmel was scowling now, so she added, "Why does that trouble you?"

"Because I should have noticed such a thing," he said. "And I didn't. Can you show me?"

Pulling a pin from her hair, Toba pricked her finger and spoke to the bead of blood that welled, sending it up in a maze of names from her mother's line. "There," she said.

"She's not living," he said. "That's a true name."

"No, Beladen died ages ago." She read her Mazik name: Mikra HaSom.

I know the name, Toba translated. "That's . . . poetic, I guess."

"I would like to go farther back than this," Asmel said. "There's something . . . strange."

"Is that possible?"

"If you give it more magic," he said, "you should be able to call farther back. Do you think you can?"

"I'm not sure how," she said. "I gave it all I could already."

"I can pass you some of mine," he said. "Your pathways are strong enough now, I think." He reached out and touched her hand, pushing some small burst of fire into her palm. Toba felt it run from her arm to her lips, and she asked the blood, "Where does the silver come from?"

The blood above them burst like a flower into bloom, sending names climbing to the ceiling, smaller and smaller, until they were unreadable even to Mazik eyes.

"It would be easier to see," Toba said, "if we could winnow these down. Can you eliminate the human names?"

Asmel waved and most of the names dissipated into a red haze, leaving only the silver behind. "I did call myself after someone," she said, and then pointed higher, "and there it is again. And again. It repeats, do you see? Every . . . every six generations, there it is."

"Yes," he said. "You're right; and the ones in between repeat as well—there's a sequence, I don't . . ." Asmel's eyes had gone glassy. "*The splendid bird is concealed in the third realm, I know her name . . .*" he whispered. "There is a name," he said, "the topmost name here, I can't see what it is."

Toba squinted upward. "I can't make it out, either—is there some way to make it larger?"

"Call it down," he said quietly. "It's yours."

Toba held out her hand, palm up, and the name—not silver-cast, but silver—fell through the air, coming within a breath of her skin. These were characters she did know; the name was Ystehar Amit.

"Did you know her?" Toba asked, because it was clear that he did. She knew the answer before he replied, "Of course I knew her. She was my wife. Her common name was Marah."

+ + + + + +

WHEN NAFTALY FOUND himself with the Mazik again, he asked simply, "Have you found the girl?"

"No," Naftaly replied, and felt a pang, because he had not even tried that night, but for once his own troubles were worse than the Mazik's. "Listen, I need a great deal of money."

The Mazik, sprawled on the floor, laughed. "No pleasantries tonight? Just ask me to turn out my pockets?" He lifted his face from the stones and wiped dirt from his cheek. "I'm afraid they didn't imprison me with my purse, old friend."

"But you must know some way I can get it," he urged. "Don't you?"

The Mazik drew himself up to a sitting position against the stone wall, and panted a few times with the exertion. Naftaly felt a wash of guilt. The man was suffering, horribly. He had no business asking such a man for help. "Well," the Mazik said, "I'm not sure how it works on your side, but generally speaking there are two ways to get money: you earn it, or you steal it."

"I can do neither," Naftaly said. "Or I would have already. Can't you . . . can't you turn copper to gold, or something?"

"Ah," he said. "That's what you're asking. I could, but I'm not sure how it would help you. I could give you all the gold in the worlds, and here it would sit, in this dream. I'm sorry I can't be of help to you. I should like to repay you, somehow."

"But I've given you nothing," Naftaly objected.

"Only my sanity," the Mazik said. "I'll leave it to you whether that's nothing."

Naftaly had to look away. "You healed my hand," he said.

"Barely," he said. "The skin is whole, but the mark is still there, beneath."

"Can you see it?"

"Not, me, no. But the Lymer, he could see it. His eyes are . . . not quite normal."

Naftaly wondered about this. He said, "I saw him again. My companion made an illusion of stone. He couldn't see through it."

"Now that's impressive," the Mazik said. "Human companion?"

"Yes. Well, mostly. She doesn't dream."

"Nearly all human, then. That's an interesting bit of information. Seems you're safe from him, then. As long as she's about, at least."

"As long as I'm awake," Naftaly said.

The Mazik said, "No need to worry about that, since your dreams always seem to bring you here." He shifted against the wall; he must have been terribly uncomfortable. His hair was still tied back with Naftaly's shirt-cuff, and the Mazik touched it absently. "I've become an irresistible force to your subconscious mind. Do I occupy your waking thoughts as well?"

Naftaly felt his face coloring. The Mazik laughed. "You are too sweet," he said. "Come closer, I'll see if you have enough magic to change the money yourself." Naftaly came up to the Mazik's side. He raised a trembling hand and held it above Naftaly's clavicle, and then laughed. "I forgot, you see. That this is only a facsimile." He patted Naftaly's shoulder before dropping his hand. "This isn't an accurate representation of your actual physical form. I can't tell how much magic you have."

Naftaly looked down at his hands and wondered what his face looked like, if he was as thin in dreams as he'd grown in reality. He looked at the Mazik's face, all sharp cheekbones and sparkling eyes the color of sunset, and realized he was too handsome—and too clean—for a man who'd been imprisoned for several weeks.

"This isn't quite what you look like awake," Naftaly said.

The Mazik smiled sadly. "I imagine I look a good deal worse in my waking hours," he said. "Fortunately, I haven't seen my own face lately. In any case, I'd prefer to spare both of us the grisly details."

Naftaly balled and unballed his fist. "It's just as well. If I had any real magic, I think I'd have realized it by now."

"But you have, else you couldn't have come here. It may not be enough to create anything . . . but perhaps you have enough for an illusion."

Naftaly said, "Could I make an illusion of gold?"

"That would be simple enough," he said. "Provided you were far enough away when it wore off."

Or if it didn't wear off until the gold was safely within the King's treasury. "Can you teach me to do it?"

The Mazik's eyes danced. "Ask me again?"

"Ask you to teach me? All right, could you?"

"Once more," he said.

Was this some Mazik ritual, where he had to ask three times before he could receive help? He tried again, "Please," he said haltingly. "Could you—"

The Mazik waved him off. "You're so deliciously earnest," he said. "Forgive me for abusing you a little."

Naftaly stared at him, trying to puzzle him out. "Are you joking at my expense?"

In response, the Mazik touched the space between his own eyes with two fingers, and then touched the cuff of Naftaly's shirt, which glimmered and turned to gold all at once. Naftaly touched it hesitantly; it was as hard as real metal, and cold. "But it's only a dream," he said.

"The same technique will work in the waking world," he said. "But it won't last."

"How long?"

"For me? It wouldn't wear off 'til the moon changed. For you, it will be considerably less. I'd advise you to test it out before you get yourself into trouble. Try it now, to get the sense of it. Touch here"—he tapped the space between his eyes—"and see what you want in your mind, and touch the image with your magic."

Naftaly tried the other cuff of his own shirt, and was unsurprised when it stayed cloth beneath his fingers.

"You did not believe you could do it," the Mazik said. "Remember where you are. You don't need more than a breath of magic to do things here."

Naftaly tried again, and this time a thread of gold appeared on the cuff, spreading like a swirl of dye in a pot of water, until the entire piece glittered. He looked to the Mazik, who rewarded his effort with a slow smile. "You're better than others I know," he said. "Try more, while you're here, so you understand the way of it. It won't be so easy in the waking world."

Naftaly touched the brick in the wall behind him. After three tries, he gave up, removed his left boot and his stocking, and transformed that instead.

"You're better used to handling cloth than stones," he said. "Clever of you to realize. Here." He pulled his shirt over his head and tossed it to Naftaly. "Try something larger."

Naftaly did, and found that the golden shirt was too heavy to hold. He dropped it, narrowly missing his toes. "But," he told the Mazik. "It's cold in here, and now you have nothing to wear."

"Well, then," the Mazik said. "You must give me yours."

"Was this a trick to get me to take my clothes off?" Naftaly asked, but the Mazik's arms were covered in gooseflesh, and Naftaly could not bear the sight of him cold. On one shoulder, the Mazik bore a character Naftaly didn't recognize, in some language he could not read. He was torn between wanting to ask about it and not wanting to reveal the intensity of his attention.

He turned his back and tossed the Mazik his own shirt, closing his ears against the sound of rustling cloth behind him. Looking down at his bare feet, he realized that if they continued this game, one or the other of them would soon be naked, and Naftaly suspected it would be him. "It's nearly dawn," he said. "I'll wake soon."

"But—"

Naftaly sat up in his bed, still dressed in the nightshirt he'd gotten from Mosse's maid, in the pitch-dark room, hours from dawn. It was the first time, he realized, he'd ever managed to wake himself.

He was not entirely sure if he was pleased by this or not.

Thirty-Eight

"BUT YOUR WIFE died," Toba said. "Ages ago, Barsilay said."

Asmel had grown agitated beyond anything Toba had ever seen from him; he swore and strode to the window, where he turned his back to her and drew several great breaths, before letting out a noise that might have been a sob. "Evidently not," he said in a cracked voice.

She set a hand on his shoulder, which he shrugged off. "Don't attempt to comfort me," he said. "After La Cacería released me, I used every means I could to find her. A hundred years, I tried. She was gone. She was *nowhere*."

But she hadn't been nowhere. She'd been in Sefarad, birthing a half-mortal child with square eyes. "Asmel," Toba said. "The amulet . . . I think it was meant for Marah's child. She either made it, or had it made for her."

"She did more than that," he said. "She gave you your name. She gave all of you your names. They are a message, to me." He sat back against the windowsill. "*The splendid bird and the third* . . . Hashem. Hashem. Where the *hell* is that shade?"

Toba took a scrap of paper and began to write the word *bird* in every tongue she knew, because writing eased her mind. She always thought more clearly with a pen in her hand; she'd been that way since her grandfather had taught her her letters. She missed his unfailingly calm presence. "Try again," he would say, when she'd made a mistake. "Errors indicate you are learning, nothing more."

"The Splendid Bird," Toba mused. "What did she mean by that? Do you know?"

"You should not write what others might guess to be your name," he said, and she stopped her scribbling at once. "*The Splendid Bird* is what Old Maziks called the Ziz, who lived wild in Luz before she was lost in the fall."

Of course, Marah had mentioned the Ziz in her journal—the journal from the alcove that only Toba seemed to have been able to open.

"No," Toba said. "Marah said ... wait. Wait. I must show you." She ran swiftly up to her tower room, and retrieved Marah's journal from its alcove before returning with it to Asmel, whose eyes went wide when she gave it to him. "I found it hidden in the tower room," she said.

"And you're just showing it to me now?"

Toba was already turning the pages, to the entry where Marah mentioned the Ziz. "I was only able to read it the day before yesterday. I didn't know what it was before that." She pushed the book toward Asmel, showing him the relevant page. "She said it survived—why is that so important?"

Asmel scanned the page, along with those that came after, then gently closed the journal. "It's important because what Marah wanted—what everyone outside of La Cacería wants—is to restore the gate to the firmament. But simply possessing the gate would not have been enough to put it back. Luz is beneath the sea, and Maziks cannot travel on water, the salt makes us mad, nor can we fly so far to get there. The only way to get close enough to Luz to restore the gate is with the Ziz."

"But the King of Rimon has the Zizim. I saw them."

"The King has her chicks," he said. "And this is why he keeps them close. But now, and for some time, they are too small to be ridden. If the Ziz herself survived, that means we needn't wait for her chicks to mature, and we needn't find a way to get them from Relam."

She said, "And our names have told you where the Ziz is." Looking up from her paper, she added, "She's hidden her in Aravoth."

"Yes," he rasped, "and more than that, she's given us the Ziz's name."

Toba had seen that, too, the last name in the line. The Ziz's name was Leb Ha-Yareakh.

The shade wafted into the room, bearing the sapphire from Toba's amulet. "Set it down," he commanded, and Toba nodded so it would comply. It put it on the library table, and Asmel bent down to peer at it. "Looks ordinary enough," he said.

"It's warm," Toba said. "Touch it."

He nudged it with a finger, cautiously, and then set his hand over it, his face drawn in concentration. "Marah," he said.

"Did she make it?"

"More than that . . ." He set the stone on his palm and caressed it with his thumb. "It's her magic. I feel it. I feel it." His breath shuddered. "Extracting it, once she'd enchanted the names of her line, must have been the only way for her to live."

"She was trapped on the mortal side of the gate at moonset," Toba guessed, and he nodded. "Would she have died the instant the moon set and the gate closed?"

"Yes. She would have."

"But even without magic, couldn't she still have returned to you at the next moon? Mortals can use the gates."

"I can't speculate as to why she never returned; perhaps she was prevented, somehow. We can be sure only that she took a mortal husband, and bore a child, and died an unbroken death." He set the stone back on the table. "Every six generations, the message repeated, until the magic was used up. She didn't believe I'd give up searching for her. She thought I'd find one of her descendants and learn the truth. And if your father hadn't reawakened the line, if you hadn't followed me here, I never would have." He sighed. "I was unworthy of her, before she died and after." He slumped in his chair.

Toba reached out and touched the stone, which felt warm and familiar to her. She didn't know what it would mean to give it to Tsidon.

"Asmel," she said. "There's a second stone within, did you notice? You can see it if you hold it to the light."

He held it up toward the domed ceiling, turning it in one direction and then the other. "She's tried to make it look like a flaw in the stone."

"Can it be some kind of nucleus she's spun her magic around, like the inside of a pearl?"

"That's an interesting idea," he said. "It does look like she's made the outer one to seal the inner, somehow. It's . . . I can't tell what this is."

The shade began to flicker excitedly about Asmel. "What is wrong with it?" he demanded of Toba. "Are you telling it to harry me?"

"No," Toba said, then she asked the shade: "Do you know what this is?" On the slip of paper it carried within its translucent bosom, it wrote, *Yes*.

"Can you tell us?" Asmel demanded.

"It can't," she said. "I've never been able to counter the original restrictions Barsilay put on it; it can only say yes and no. If we give this to Tsidon—" At this, the shade began tearing the paper into pieces, smaller and then smaller, until it was dust.

Asmel looked deeply troubled by this. "Barsilay knew," he muttered. "Barsilay's seen this before, and I have not." His eyes flared. He turned back to the shade. "Is this a relic of ha-Moh'to?"

It drew a circle much larger than normal: *YES.*

He rose from his chair and looked sharply at the shade. "Barsilay," he said. "Is it a killstone?"

YES.

"What is a killstone?" Toba asked.

On the other side of Asmel, the shade began to stutter. "Asmel," Toba said, but he was already looking at it in horror. "Can you help him?"

"No," he whispered. The shade guttered, and was extinguished, and ceased.

"What does it mean?" she asked. "What does it mean that it's gone?"

But Asmel's hand was in front of his mouth and he did not answer.

\+ + · + + + +

THE COURSER HAD just removed her boots when she became aware that she was not alone in her chamber.

She'd left Atalef behind in the mortal realm in the person of the Inquisitor, and was glad to be rid of it. She didn't know where Tarses had gotten the creature, but improved or not, it was a demon, and the Courser didn't trust anything she couldn't kill.

She had a suite of rooms—a pair of linked cells, really—not far from the Caçador's own residence; the easier for him to summon her. They were not large, and they had no windows her enemies might use to sneak inside. She kept them spartan deliberately; if every item was catalogued in her mind, it was easier to tell if something had been moved, or replaced. On the round table in the center of the room there was a stone.

The stone had no significance. It was there because the Caçador had teased her about her lack of decoration. "A bow to aesthetics," he'd said, "wouldn't kill you."

She hadn't wanted to bow to aesthetics, but one did not simply discount a directive from the Caçador, so she'd gone outside and found a rock and put it in the middle of her table. It was round. And grey. It was not beautiful, nor was it reminiscent of an animal or a flower or some other pleasing shape, but when the Caçador had seen it, he'd said, "Lo, aesthetics," and he'd smiled, so she'd kept it.

On top of that rock, there was another rock.

The Courser rapped on the second rock smartly with her knuckles. "Come out," she said. "Or I'll skip you into a pond."

The stone stayed stone. "Very well," she said, and went to pick it up, at which point it was no longer a stone but a woman, smallish and dark-skinned, sitting in the middle of her table. "You're so impatient," this woman said. "Would you have really tossed me in a pond?"

"You're lucky I didn't say the sea," the Courser replied, kicking her boots into the corner. "Would have served you right, sneaking in here."

"There's no sea for miles," the second woman replied, climbing down from the table. She was known to the Courser only as the Peregrine; she supposed she had some other name, but she'd given up wondering about it. "And I only wanted to see how long it would take you to notice. How did you guess it was me?"

"The fact that you hadn't tried to stab me yet," the Courser replied.

"Ah," the Peregrine said, conjuring a chair, because the Courser's dining room had only one. "What an oversight."

"I thought you were abroad," the Courser said, because the Peregrine usually was.

"I was. I was summoned back, and I don't know why, if that's your next question. I thought *you* were abroad, babysitting the Inquisitor. Or did you already kill him?"

"Not yet," she said.

"Aw," the Peregrine said. "Shame."

"You think so?"

"I only know how you enjoy it."

The Courser glanced up. "Do you?" But the Peregrine had pulled a few lentils out of her pocket and put them on a table, and made them into the sort of grand fare she preferred. She uncorked a bottle left on the table, made a face when she sniffed it and found it to be water, and offered it a disgusted glare until it cooperated and became wine.

The Peregrine leaned forward in her chair and picked up a leg of pheasant. "We found another heir in P'ri Hadar," she said. "I thought the last one was all of them. It's very frustrating."

"How many can there possibly be?"

"It's not the number," she said. "It's the time it takes to flush them out."

"Haven't you got a chart or something?"

"Of course we have a chart! But it doesn't account for the bastards."

"Why would it need to?"

"Ah," she said. "You don't know: The Queen changed the law, probably for some Adon or other. It seems to say that bastards inherit if there are no legitimate heirs within three degrees of relation."

"Surely that wouldn't apply to the succession to the throne of Luz."

The Peregrine sipped her wine. "If it hadn't, I'd be out of heirs by now. I don't think she bothered to specify, and before any challenges could be made . . ." She lifted a finger from the rim of her glass. "Well, you know."

"Ah," the Courser said.

"You can't imagine," the Peregrine said, "how much I wish I'd never been given this task. Some of the heirs had a half-dozen mistresses a piece, and who knows who fathered their children. I used to think Tsidon had the worst of it, having to burn heretics and Restorationists, but at least once you've burned one, he's dead and you can move on to the next task. I kill one and another just pops up someplace else, in some other family I've never even heard of. Even the heirs don't know they're next in line 'til the mark shows up when the prior one dies. I've been at this so long I barely remember how to do anything else." She stuffed an outsize bite of bread into her mouth. "I haven't had more than two days' rest since that winter I spent in Baobab."

"I wouldn't let the Caçador hear you complaining."

"Perhaps I should. He'd replace me and I could dream about something else."

"Not likely he'd let you," the Courser said. She didn't think she'd ever heard the Peregrine talk so much. She was like this, sometimes, after she returned from a long time abroad. Her job was to observe, to study, and to assassinate. None of those activities led to much opportunity for conversation, and the Falconry mainly worked alone, the better not to attract attention.

The Peregrine glanced up from the food. "I did hear about Odem."

The Courser took a morsel of food from the tray. She'd heard about that, too—executed in the plaça after most of the Maziks in Rimon had sworn an oath to support him. After Tsidon himself had sworn that oath, if the Falcon had told her honestly.

The oath, most likely, had been to support Odem after Relam's death. And Relam was still, unfortunately for Odem, very much alive. The Courser wondered, though, why Relam had gone along with the execution. If Tarses had threatened him, or enchanted him somehow to make him comply.

It was clever, though, allowing the oath-getting, because it made La Cacería look less like they'd been planning the assassination all along. They'd sworn an oath; even Tsidon had. Moreover, now Tarses knew which Maziks had been first in line to support Odem. Those, she suspected, would be the first to disappear now.

And the Peregrine herself had wanted to make sure the Courser knew all this.

"I suppose you have no opinion," said the Peregrine.

The Courser did not like the direction of this conversation. "What's to have an opinion on? I'm not given to bouts of thinking."

The Peregrine made a muffled noise into her dinner. "Yes, that has always been your line, hasn't it? I suppose you have no opinion on Tsidon's marriage, either."

The Courser paused, because she hadn't known about a marriage for Tsidon, or that Tsidon was the sort of man who might *want* a marriage.

"No one's mentioned it to you?" the Peregrine said. She was amused by this, that the Courser did not know so significant a fact. "Not even the Caçador?"

"I've only just returned," she said. "What's it to me, if Tsidon marries?"

"It's not the fact of the marriage," the Peregrine said, "it's the identity of the bride."

"Don't tell me he's marrying *you*."

The Peregrine laughed. "Hardly. He's marrying the ward of Asmel b'Asmoda. The cousin of your good friend Barsilay."

That was strange indeed. "Why?"

"Apparently she's in possession of a safira. Not sure how she came by it."

The Courser sat back. A safira was nothing but a chunk of petrified magic. There was nothing you could do with it besides use it as a trophy: there was no way to get at the magic inside. Relam, the Peregrine had once told her, had a box full of safiras he'd pulled from his enemies when he'd seized power, but they served no purpose besides to fan the King's ego. She said, "Whose?"

"Damned if I know. I've only heard rumors about it, and who knows if those can be trusted. People say all sorts of things, even in the Falconry."

"Really. And what are these rumors?"

"Only that it's unusual somehow. Someone said there was something *in* it." She pointed upward, and an illusion of some object in the shape of a starburst appeared before her fingertip: the same shape the Courser had been searching for years ago in Te'ena, when she'd killed the man who'd told her about ha-Moh'to, and railed against monarchy. Tsidon had called ha-Moh'to a myth, which meant it was very real and something of concern to both himself and Tarses.

"If that's true," the Courser said, "why didn't Tarses simply send you to take it?"

The Peregrine shrugged with one shoulder. "He never asked me to take it. Interesting, isn't it?" She wiped away the rest of the food with her palm, saying, "Thank you for the venue, Courser." Then she hopped lightly up from the table and left, leaving the wall open behind her.

The Courser listened to her light footsteps go down the hallway. Artifice, she knew. The Peregrine never made audible steps. She was teasing her, most likely. Or trying to distract her.

If Asmel's ward had the sunburst stone, why hadn't Tarses sent someone to steal it?

There were only three reasons she could think of: either the Caçador thought it couldn't be stolen, he didn't trust the Peregrine with it, or it wasn't what he really wanted.

Or else it wasn't really there at all, and just a rumor. Or the Peregrine had made the entire thing up as a game.

But if it wasn't real, why bother engineering a marriage for Tsidon?

The Courser closed up the wall and scanned the room for alterations, and found none.

There would be nothing visible, though: the only reason she'd even noticed the Peregrine was that she'd wanted her to. She went to the wall over her bed and ran her hands along the stones, resting a palm on one 'til it turned liquid. Then she reached through and pulled out the book she'd taken in Mansanar. She weighed it in her hands: the heft was the same, and she opened it and found the bottle of amapola still in its place. She closed the book.

Something stayed her hand as she went to put it back, and she removed the bottle a second time, and then the cork, and sniffed the contents.

Wine.

She smashed the bottle on the ground and went back out, storming to the tower where they kept the Luzite prisoner in a different cell with no window or door.

\+ + + + + + +

NAFTALY SPENT THE morning attempting to turn cleaning rags into gold with the old woman at his side. "Are you sure you did this before?" she asked, because nothing he tried was working in the least.

"I dreamt I did it before," he said. "It was easier then." He touched the corner of a rag; nothing happened.

"You seem to have lost the knack of it."

Naftaly made a noise of agreement.

"Perhaps if you tore it into smaller bits?"

"I'll try," he said. She tore off a section and handed it over. He suffered an additional failure.

"Perhaps if you ate something," she said.

"That's your solution to everything."

"Your point being?"

"I can't eat our way out of the Inquisition," he said.

"It appears you can't magic your way out of it, either."

"I am trying," he said.

"Are you? It doesn't seem like you're doing anything. Before, this table was covered in rags. And now—" She gestured expansively at the pile. "Behold. Tell me again what your Mazik told you to do?"

"He's not *my* Mazik," Naftaly said quickly.

The old woman raised an eyebrow. "What did he tell you to do? There must be more to it than what you've shown me."

"He told me to see the cloth changing, and it would, provided my intentions were clear enough."

"That seems terribly simple," she said. "And you've tried smaller scraps. What about this?" She lifted one of the bits of fabric and pulled loose a single thread, setting it in front of him. Naftaly touched his finger to it, his forehead, and the thread again.

"All our hopes rest on you," the old woman said. "If that helps."

"It doesn't," he said through gritted teeth. He thought of a golden thread, what it would feel like under his finger, what it would feel like threaded into a needle, how it would catch the light, how it would be subtle enough to bend into a shape, like a fine wire he could mold with his intentions. Still, nothing. He sighed, heavily. Failure was an old friend; he'd have thought he'd have been well used to its company by now.

Under his fingertip, he felt a prick, and realized the golden color was not his intention, but reality. He sat back and looked at the thread.

"You've done it," the old woman said incredulously. "Is it really gold?"

"It's only an illusion," Naftaly said. "And I don't know how long it will last."

The pair of them watched the thread for a few minutes.

"It still looks gold to me," the old woman said. "But we've been staring so long, I'm not sure I would notice if it did change back. Try another?" She handed him a scrap. When he continued to struggle, she said, "Sigh dramatically; that worked before."

He did; the entire piece went gold in his fingers.

Not just intention, then, but breath. The old woman took the piece and knocked it on the table, testing its durability. The corner bent, but it stayed gold. "Perhaps we should make that a test piece," she said. "If the gold changes back before the Conde gives it to the King, it won't go well for us. There's no point magicking more until we're sure it won't be back to cloth again by tomorrow."

"How long do you think we need it to remain gold?"

"A day to summon the Conde and hand it over," she said, "and another day for him to transfer it to the King, and a day for the King's men to transfer it to the treasury, and maybe another for safety's sake, in case something goes wrong."

"Four days," he said. "Seems like a long time to sustain an illusion."

"If it changes back too early, it will be worse than if we did nothing at all. What do you think the Conde will do if he realizes we've given him scraps instead of money? We'll all be dead before the day is out."

"No," Naftaly said. "Not all of us, only me. I will go alone, then there will be no one for the Conde to blame apart from myself."

"We should have a contingency," the old woman said, "in case something goes wrong."

"There can be none," Naftaly said, feeling a sense of purpose that matched his will to turn the cloth to gold. "It's my life against the lives of every one of us in Petgal. I'll take the risk."

+ + + + + +

NAFTALY CHANGED INTO what passed for his best clothes to go before the Conde, where he introduced himself as a Sefardi banker, newly emigrated, hoping that his earlier presence in Mosse's office would lend credence to the tale.

He needn't have worried—the Conde had no memory of him, but was happy to take his money, provided he could hand it over by the end of the day: five thousand milliarès, which Naftaly went home and bespelled out of scraps of linen and, when that ran out, wool.

He wondered briefly about the ethics of this, deciding it only counted as cheating the Conde if the Conde were to pay Naftaly back, which he certainly would not do, and it would not count as cheating the King, since the King was accepting the false coins from the Conde, not from him. Essentially, he decided, he was trading nothing for nothing: a fair exchange, and in any case, the ends—keeping the Inquisition on the other side of the border—justified the means, and then some.

It would likely be years before anyone going through the King's treasury noticed the chests filled with rags, and by then, he hoped, nobody would remember where they'd come from.

So he made his illusion of wealth, and he gave it to the Conde, and the Conde gave it to the King, or so Naftaly assumed.

Naftaly slept snug in his bed that night, planning to thank his Mazik for saving him, for saving everyone, really, and wondering if he'd still be wearing Naftaly's too-small shirt in the dream-world. Perhaps, he wondered as he drifted off, his tailoring skills would be stronger there, too, as his magic had been. He could sew his Mazik a new shirt, with perfectly straight seams, made of sunset silk to match his eyes.

No, he told himself. He'd promised to dream of Toba. He'd dream of Toba first, and then, after he'd woken and rolled over and made himself more comfortable, *then* he'd dream of the Mazik, and he'd tell him he'd kept his promise, and the Mazik would be well pleased with him.

Toba bat Penina, he thought as he drifted off. *Tiny and thin with dark brown eyes. I will find you tonight.*

Only he didn't. That night, for the first time in his life, he dreamt he was in his father's house in Rimon, and no one else was there.

THIRTY-NINE

THE COURSER OPENED the wall to the Luzite's cell, stepped through, and closed it behind her, setting her light-stone in a niche she pressed into the wall with her finger, and then turning to regard the filthy man who watched her with hunted eyes.

He'd been so magnificent once. The Peregrine had told her, early in his captivity, that Tsidon had modeled himself on this man, never managing to be anything other than a pale imitation. Now, though, he was sprawled out on the stone floor in the clothes he'd been taken in, reduced to rags. His broken legs and bruises had healed from the day before, but his hair was still matted with dried blood, and he stank like an unwashed human. At the sight of her, his hand lifted to his left shoulder; he abruptly stopped, catching himself: too late, she'd seen. She must have injured a pathway there which prevented it healing; perhaps when he'd complained the joint was dislocated, and she'd responded by kicking it back into place. The move had left a bruise the color of pitch that had remained even after she'd pierced the same location with several blades, some of them heated.

"Darling," he said. "You came late today. I thought perhaps you'd found another man to occupy your affections."

She strode closer. His body was broken, she'd stopped bothering to tie him weeks ago, but still, the perfect smile remained. It irked her. He should have been a weeping mass, and she did not understand why he was not. He had no comforts to cling to; he could not even dream outside this very cell.

He said, "You don't know how I've longed for your touch." A joke, then. He should not have been capable of that, either.

She knelt over him, and he looked up warily. "I'd like to talk about something else today," she said. "I'd like to talk about ha-Moh'to."

"Ha-Moh'to," he said, and then coughed that liquid cough he had. He'd been too long away from sun and air. He was dying, piece by piece, his lungs going first. "Why soil your hands asking *me*?"

She struck him across the cheek so he would remember who she was. He spat out a tooth, which skittered across the floor. "Hope that one grows back," he muttered. She struck him with the other hand, whipping his head the other way. "I commend you for your commitment to your work," he said, not bothering to wipe the blood from his chin. "But you've forgotten to ask me a question."

She grabbed his ear and twisted until he cried out. Tears filled his eyes, but he said, "No pincers today? You must be in a hurry."

"What was ha-Moh'to?"

He laughed. Laughed! "Ask your master," he said. "Or doesn't he know you're interested?"

"Is it real? It is real, or is it a myth?"

He seemed to think on this a minute, his eyes taking her in. "Poor Courser," he said. "No one tells you anything, do they?"

She struck him another blow. "*You* do not ask questions of *me*."

He sighed a long sigh. "If you thought it was a myth, why bother asking me about it?"

She put her face very near his, meaning to ask another question, but decided on a test instead, whispering, "Monarchy is Abomination."

"An interesting aphorism, Courser. Did you come to that conclusion lately?" When she raised her hand again, he held his up in defeat. "If you know that," he said, "then you know all you need to about ha-Moh'to."

She sat back then, and weaved her fingertips in the air, made an illusion of the starburst. "What is this?" she asked.

"I don't know," he said, but he'd paled.

She fashioned a dagger from her left hand. "I will take your left eye," she said, "and then your right, and then your tongue."

"Careful," he said. "Your master will want to know what you were asking when you cut me up."

"What makes you think he hasn't ordered this discussion?"

His head listed to one side, and he stared at her in that unnerving way he had. It was easy to forget how old this one was, how much longer he'd lived than she, when he was smiling. But sometimes, like this, when his face went still, she felt a shiver—some thread of fear, that he was the one toying with her.

"Your master doesn't trust you very well, does he?"

She decided to let the insult go. He wanted her angry and hitting him, because then she would not think. "I want a list of names," she said, summoning paper. "I want to know everyone who was in ha-Moh'to."

"I'm afraid I'm incapable of making such a list."

"Were *you* in it?"

He said, "I've already admitted as much."

"Who else? Who else, that you know?"

"Subtlety doesn't suit you," he said, which earned him another cuff across the nose, snapping it. "Or are you afraid to say what you're really wondering?"

"I would think you'd be more interested in preserving your pretty face," she said.

His head listed to the side, but he said, "But you so enjoy hitting me, and it goes against my creed to leave a woman unsatisfied."

She could not take his eyes, she knew that much, so she lowered her hand and pierced it through his injured shoulder instead, stopping only once the blade made contact with the stone wall behind him.

"Was Asmel in it?"

"No," he gasped. "Asmel was never a member."

She withdrew her blade, only because she was sure he'd go unconscious otherwise, and pushed a pen into his hand, holding it over the paper. "Write," she said.

"All right," he said. "All right." And he wrote: *Tarses b'Shemhazai.* And then he collapsed.

It was, of course, the name she'd been waiting to hear, the one he'd been implying, and the one she'd been too afraid to ask about directly, in case she were being observed. With that in mind, she said, "You lie."

"So he didn't tell you," he said. "I wonder why."

"The Caçador was the one who put Relam on the throne, are you denying it? He's no issue with kingship."

The wound in his shoulder was bleeding out: a human would be dead from it by now; he nearly was. His color had washed away, and if she did nothing, he would not live. "I'm neither lying nor denying what he did."

It was no explanation. Tarses had put Relam on the throne; he meant to put himself on the throne. Was Barsilay telling her Tarses had been some other person, once? It seemed hard to believe.

It seemed expedient for Barsilay to make her believe so.

"Tell me what this is," she said, showing him the image of the starburst again.

"Could be anything," he said from the floor. She took the paper and ran her finger across the characters, smearing the ink. Was this the truth or another lie? It maddened her. She wanted him broken. She didn't want to wonder if he was lying; she wanted him begging to give her the truth.

But she couldn't afford for him to die yet, either. Reluctantly, she applied her palm to the wound and did what she could to stop the bleeding but not the pain. He said nothing, only opening and closing his lips, until her face was very near his, and then he whispered, before he went unconscious, "There was another order called ha-Nazbev. Why not ask your Peregrine what became of them?"

NAFTALY WAS HALFWAY across the quarter the afternoon before Shabbat, on his way to the shop of one Senhor Mendes, tailor, to discuss the possibility of employment when the old woman caught up with him.

He was worried for his Mazik, whom he'd not dreamt of, and the worry made his strides heavy and slow. What was the point, he wondered, of dreaming of the man if he could not help him? Perhaps if he were successful, he'd return to Mosse's and take a nap. A glass of madera might induce an afternoon dream, just long enough to check on him again. Of course the Mazik would have to be asleep also for that to work. Still, might be worth a try.

His name came from behind him. "I've been looking for you for hours. What are you doing out here?" the old woman demanded, once she'd called to him and halted his steps.

"Trying to procure a livelihood," he replied. "I can't stay in Mosse's house much longer."

"Boy—"

"I know I'm not the finest tailor in Pengoa," he said. "But I'm told this fellow's busy with all the new residents, and even if he brings me on a few hours a day, that would—"

"Stop," she said, grasping his sleeve. "I need to tell you something, and it's dire."

He stopped and pivoted toward her.

"I took some of the test pieces you made," she whispered, taking her purse from her belt. "I was going to the cobbler's this morning—"

"You were going to swindle the cobbler?"

"Look," she said, opening her purse and thrusting her hand inside. She came out with a handful of small coins . . . and scraps of fabric.

"The linen is still gold," she said. "Near as I can tell, but the wool . . ."

Naftaly stared in mute horror. They hadn't tested the wool, only the linen, and then they'd run out of that. "Do you suppose the Conde's already given it to the King?"

"The morning after you gave it to him?" she asked.

Naftaly thought he might collapse in the street. The Prince would marry the Infanta. There would be no stopping it now. "The marriage," he said.

"We can do nothing about that," she said. "You must flee. There is a chance the Conde hasn't noticed you've given him chests full of scrap cloth yet. You ought to be well away from here before he does." She put her purse into his hands. "Go to the docks. Book passage anywhere, even if it's only ten miles up the coast. You can't stay here."

Naftaly felt the familiar mantle of failure settle on his shoulders. "I can't flee," he said. "There's no point to it."

"When he finds you, he'll kill you," the old woman hissed.

Naftaly almost laughed at the ridiculousness of it all. "I agreed to take that risk."

The old woman shook his arm in frustration. "Perhaps we could try changing them back to gold again. Do you think that spell works at a distance?"

But two large men had suddenly appeared and laid hands on Naftaly, who dropped the old woman's purse as his arms were pulled back behind him. "The Conde of Lobata," one said in his ear, "would like a word."

The old woman cried, "Now see here!" but there was little she could do against the Conde's men, and they batted her away. Before they dragged him away, Naftaly managed to pull an arm free. He reached into his coat and thrust his book at the old woman. "Take this," he said, but as she reached for it the men snatched it up and took it with them.

\+ + ++ + +

TOBA BET HAD her arms crossed by the window of the observatory. Asmel had woken her some minutes prior, to see if the ring was still adhered to her finger, which it was.

"Barsilay must be alive. If Tsidon had broken the conditions of the engagement, you should be able to remove the ring. Barsilay may be so weak he can no longer sustain the shade, or he may have been moved too far from the alcalá."

"Or else Tsidon has found a way around our agreement," Toba Bet said.

"No," he said. "Tsidon said Barsilay would eat cake at your wedding. He lives."

Toba picked up the safira and held it to the light, examining the inner stone. She wondered what it would take to break the outer without destroying the second stone inside, or if it were even possible. "Asmel," Toba said. "What is a killstone?"

He took the stone from her, tracing the facets with his thumbnail. "A killstone," he said, "is a mechanism used by a group that fears discovery: a secret order, or a revolutionary faction; something of that nature. If one of your number is captured and interrogated, you activate that person's name in the killstone, and he immediately enters the endless dream. It's a countermeasure to torture."

"Sounds grand," Toba Bet pointed out, "except the person in question is dead."

"Better one dead Mazik than fifty," Asmel said. "How it works is this: Every member of such a group would speak his own name into the stone, together with the command to sleep and die. The person guarding the stone could then use it in case someone ever went unaccounted for."

"And Barsilay believes this is the killstone of ha-Moh'to," Toba said.

"Could you use it?" Toba Bet put in. "If we were able to retrieve it from inside the sapphire?"

"No, I couldn't. You would already have to know the common names and faces of whomever you wanted to kill and the command to use it. I know neither."

"Would Barsilay?"

"I couldn't say," he said. "But if Marah used her own magic to seal it, she must have suspected *someone* would know how to use it."

He summoned a leaf of paper under his hand and took his pen, using his fingers to sharpen its point, then sent the safira into the air between his eye and the window, squinting at it in the light. "We can't let La Cacería have this," he said, and then, dipping the pen into his ink, he began tracing the shape of the killstone, point by point. When he was satisfied, he peeled the shape off the paper, so that a second translucent stone hovered over his palm.

"Do you suggest we try to fool Tsidon with a fake?" Toba asked. Asmel was still fiddling with his model, making the points sharper, the color deeper. Before it had been the color of milk; now it was the color of ink. "You think you can swap him a stone made of paper, and he won't notice?"

Asmel was frowning in concentration. "I can't make out the hue," he muttered. "Inside the other stone."

"Yours is too purple," Toba Bet said. "And it's too much all the same color."

He lightened it, and it took on a mottled appearance. "No," she said. "Like this." She put her own hand, palm up, over his, and the stone became darker in the center and faded lighter in the arms of its sunburst. Content, Asmel set it down next to the other stone. Toba frowned deeply, because she would not have been able to do it.

"He won't know whether the killstone is real until he's taken it out," he said, setting the false killstone down and sitting back in his chair.

"And the outer stone?"

Asmel was staring into the middle distance. "I don't know how Marah made it," he said. "It shouldn't even be possible. I can't even fathom how . . ." He picked up the sapphire again. "Rafeq. Rafeq might know."

"Rafeq?" Toba asked, recalling the singed book cover she'd found, about the common demon.

"An old colleague," Asmel said, rising; his face had gone very grim. "And a friend of Marah's, once. I suppose I owe him a visit."

"You think he can help, somehow?"

"I think the chances are slim," he said, "but he's also the only Mazik I can ask whom I can be sure won't inform La Cacería."

"Does he owe you some favor?" Toba asked.

"The opposite," Asmel said. "Unfortunately." He opened the chest under the window and removed the charcoal cloak he'd been wearing the first night she'd seen him, and draped it over his shoulders. The rest of his clothes went dusk-colored to match.

"This sounds like a fool's errand to me," Toba said. "Surely there's some other—"

"There's not," he said. "I will need one of you to come with me."

"One of us?" Toba asked.

"The elder, I think," he said. "I don't wish to take Tsidon's ring with us. Go and dress yourself for rough terrain and meet me by the northern passage."

"Is the journey very far?" she asked.

"He's quite close," Asmel said. "Rafeq is imprisoned under Mount Sebah."

+ + + + + + +

THE CONDE OF Lobata kept a house in Pengoa, away from his estates in the south, and this was where his men took Naftaly Cresques. It was a fine house, with fine furniture laid out in fine rooms, where his fine mistress snoozed in a fine feather bed, and finely liveried servants served fine scraps to his fine hounds.

Also, there was a dungeon in the basement.

Naftaly found himself in this dungeon, his arms pulled behind him, tied around a post that supported the low ceiling. A fire burned in the corner, and Naftaly was covered in sweat from it. He thought of his Mazik in his freezing cell, and wondered which was worse. The room stank. The Conde stood before him, dressed in a silk surcoat with embroidery that doubtless took some skilled artisan many months to complete.

"So," the Conde said, in accented Sefardi. "You are a sorcerer."

"That's . . . not so."

The Conde pulled a scrap of wool from his pocket. "I watched, this morning, as this slip of fabric stopped being gold in my hand. It was very interesting. I was sure it was gold; it had the right weight, the right feel. It was cold, like gold. And then"—he snapped his fingers—"it wasn't."

Naftaly breathed the hot dampness of the air and tried to find something comforting to rest his eyes on, settling on an embroidered lion on the Conde's shoulder.

"So it seems to me," continued the Conde, "that either you are a sorcerer, or you know where I can find one." He squatted down in front of Naftaly. "And something tells me . . ." He prodded a sharp finger into Naftaly's chest. ". . . the sorcerer is you."

Naftaly did not answer.

"I'm not the Inquisition," the Conde said. "I don't care what you believe. I don't care what you think. I don't even care what you do, as long as you are doing it for me. Now, tell me, is it you that changed this? Or someone else—someone in the house of deLeon?"

Naftaly closed his eyes against the question.

"Ah," he said. "Let's simplify this for you. If you won't give me the identity of the sorcerer who changed this cloth, I will have to go in search of him. It will be an arduous process. If you could just tell me, it would mean so many fewer people I have to question."

Naftaly regarded the Conde's boots. They were very, very clean, and had recently been polished. Taken together—the quality of the house, the Conde's coat, his boots . . . it led Naftaly to wonder about the man. Specifically, he wondered how often the man made loans and then defaulted.

Naftaly ran his tongue over his cracked lip. The Conde held the piece of cloth in front of Naftaly's face. "You must understand," Naftaly said. "It won't do you any good. The cloth always changes back. It's only illusion; it isn't alchemy."

"I would very much like to see how that works," the Conde said.

Naftaly said, "No."

"No?" The Conde clicked his tongue. He lifted an object from the table, which Naftaly quickly recognized as his book. He hadn't realized they'd set it there, probably while they'd been tying him up, which had taken three men—two to pin his arms and one to hold him by the throat. The Conde leafed through the pages, right to left. "Tell me about this book," he said.

"It's a prayer book," Naftaly said.

"Really."

The two men regarded each other. Naftaly's jaw throbbed where he'd been struck; sweat ran into his eyes, and he wondered why the Conde even needed a fire, in the cellar, in summer.

Naftaly said, "I could read it to you. If you like."

The Conde laughed. "Oh, I don't think so." He clapped the book shut. "So you don't want to talk about your book, and you don't want to show me how you made that gold. I suppose we'll have to talk about something else. Your kin, perhaps? Your relationship with Mosse deLeon?"

"I have none," he said. "I was a guest in his house, that's all."

"Hmm," he said. "Indeed. He's rather a prominent fellow among your kinfolk, isn't he?"

Naftaly said, "He only runs a bank."

"Right, and you'll tell me that money isn't everything. *Learning*, you'll tell me, is all; *holiness*, or whatever passes for it among your sort; all very . . . commendable, except it isn't true."

"And what would you know about it?" Naftaly said.

The Conde inclined his head. "About holiness? Nothing. About your sort? Only that the Judería of Pengoa has too many people in it." He met Naftaly's eyes. "Too many people, in too small a space, like rabbits in a warren. Prone to all sort of disasters. Plague. Fire." He held the book by the corner, suspending it over the flame of the candle. Naftaly schooled his face to blankness. "I'm not pleased with Senhor deLeon at the moment. Nor am I pleased with you. Would you like to change that?" He held out the slip of cloth again. "Show me."

The Conde's eyes were a hazel that reminded Naftaly of the wolves in the Rimon wood. Mosse had been right, he knew, not to trust this man, not with money, and not near the throne.

"I will send a man to burn his house," he said. "How far that fire will spread is up to your god or mine. You think I don't mean it? I promise I do—unless my attention is too diverted to give that order."

The Conde went to the door and rapped three times with his knuckles. "Bring me Lopes," he said.

"Wait," Naftaly said.

The Conde returned to him. "Don't waste my time," he murmured, and held the cloth in front of Naftaly's face.

Naftaly drew a breath and blew out a stream of air against the fabric; the Conde's smile widened slowly as the spell caught and the piece went hard in his fingers.

"This is excellent," he said. "An excellent beginning to your work."

Naftaly's eyes went to the Conde, who went on: "You've put me in a very unpleasant position with the King; my daughter's dowry is nothing but rags. Word from court is that he means now to pursue the Infanta of Sefarad." Naftaly let out a huff of a sob, to which the Conde paid no heed. "I'm very angry. Very angry indeed. But don't feel too put out about it." He smiled. "You are going to spend the rest of your life making it up to me. So. Now. Let's discuss what else you can do."

Naftaly laughed bitterly. "You have now seen the sum total of all my skills. It's a magic trick. That's all."

"Oh," said the Conde, pulling a dagger from his belt. "But you are selling yourself short, my boy. You likely have many talents. Let's discover them together."

FORTY

THE PEREGRINE WAS in the mews, washing her hands in the fountain when the Courser found her.

She knew enough not to bother the other woman when she was at her ablutions; there was some lengthy ritual she performed, which seemed to vary based on whether she was coming or going, and if she'd killed someone. Just then she'd washed her left hand with her right three times and her right with her left twice, which meant she was preparing herself for a mission.

"Are you leaving again already?" the Courser asked, when she was done.

The Peregrine looked over her shoulder. "I've only just left Tarses; did he send you for me again?"

"No," she said. "I'm here for myself."

That got the Peregrine's attention. "Well," she said, striding into the building while the Courser followed. "There's a first. Only I'm afraid I haven't much time."

Two of the Peregrine's women appeared from another doorway, dressed in Falcon black, their dark hair set in identical knots at the napes of their necks, their eyes quickly taking in the Courser. Baobabis, probably, like the Peregrine herself, they wore no ornament, because they were meant to draw no attention: the black they wore in the mews would be replaced with vernacular clothing when they were out. You never knew if a woman you met might be a Falcon, which was what made them so deadly.

Between them, they bore a finely wrought saddle set with rubies: the stone of the royal house of Rimon. No others were allowed to wear them. The Courser wanted to ask what the Falcons were doing with a saddle belonging to the Crown but knew better. "Set it there," the Peregrine said, indicating the round table that took up most of the room, where the Falcons gathered for their meals when they weren't abroad.

The two women—both slight and dark, as were most of the Falcons—set the saddle down and left. "Quickly, Courser," the Peregrine said.

"I heard a tale from the Luzite," the Courser said. "It would help me to know if he's being honest or lying, before I continue."

"Indeed," the Peregrine said, setting her hand on the polished leather and wiping it in a circle. "What tale would that be?"

"He said there was an order called ha-Nazbev."

The Peregrine looked up. "That isn't a tale. That's a fact." She went back to burnishing the saddle with her fingers. "Ha-Nazbev was the Society of the Elder Crown. A cabal of Restorationists, before they were wiped out."

He'd been honest about that bit at least. And he'd known the Peregrine would know about it; another morsel to file away for further reflection. "How were they wiped out?" the Courser asked.

"They had a killstone," the Peregrine said. She pushed her hand directly into the leather, saying, "Ah," and came back out with some sort of red crystal that she tossed on the floor and smashed under her boot. "It was a complicated bit of work getting the command-word, let me tell you."

"The command-word?" the Courser asked.

The Peregrine had gone back to reaching inside the saddle; she looked a little like she was assisting in the birth of a foal, only without the mess. "The word that lets the user kill anyone whose name is in it," she said, producing and smashing another crystal. "Once you have the command-word, all you need is the common name of whomever you want to kill, and we had a list. We'd already picked off most of them, but we needed a way to get to the last few we couldn't reach."

The Courser felt a need to sit down. A killstone. Was that what she'd been sent for, all those years ago? The killstone of ha-Moh'to?

And if Barsilay were to be believed, the Caçador's name was inside it.

Only she could not afford to believe him. It was exactly the lie he was likely to tell her. She said, "What did it look like?"

The Peregrine stopped in her ministrations, the barest edge of irritation creeping into her face. "Sweet," she said, "I appreciate you've taken a sudden interest in my exploits, but what I'm doing requires several hours of intense concentration, which you are breaking."

It didn't matter, the Courser thought. So far as she knew, there was no reason one killstone should look like another. Anyway, the Peregrine knew about the sunburst stone, and it hadn't registered as significant to her.

If Barsilay were telling the truth, the stone would soon be in the hands of La Cacería, and the Caçador would not know the Courser knew what it was. He'd sent her to look for it once in Te'ena; he might well entrust its keeping to her again. He thought she was ignorant.

"Courser," said the Peregrine, before she departed. "Was the Luzite telling you the truth?"

The Courser said, "Possibly."

✦ ✦ ✦

THE NORTHERN PASSAGE was the hidden doorway by the mikveh stream, which lay in the shadow of the waxing moon.

It was to be the Tamar moon, Asmel had told her, the moon that would rise on her marriage to Tsidon. Each full moon was associated with a gate; once, there had been festivals that marked the passing of each, back when there'd been twelve gates and not eleven. Celebratory foods were eaten to mark the passing of the months, which otherwise flowed on endlessly for Maziks, who scarcely felt time at all.

Toba wondered if it would be that way for her. She didn't know what her Mazik blood would mean for her lifespan; if Marah's half-Mazik child had lived to an unusual age, family lore had forgotten it. But that child, the original Tsifra N'dar, had worn the amulet all her life. She'd never felt her Mazik blood at all.

She'd asked Asmel, once, in his observatory, if she would live forever, as he had. She'd expected him to make a comment about putting the cart before the horse: if Tarses killed her, it wouldn't matter how long she might have lived. Instead, he'd only turned and said, "I don't know how long you might live. You heal as a Mazik does, but beyond that, I can only guess."

It made the world seem small indeed, that it might be something for her to watch from the far side of immortality. It would be easy to grow complacent. What was the point of ambition, when there was always more time to be had? What was the point of La Cacería, which certainly could not hope to last forever?

Asmel appeared, the stars bright on his hair, and threw a second cloak the color of dusk around her dress, and pulled his hood up. Stepping through the invisible doorway into the darkness outside the alcalá, he followed the stream, Toba following silently behind, up, up the path to Mount Sebah.

The stream had dried to nearly a trickle, it had been so long since it had rained. Toba wondered if it were dry in the mortal realm, too; did the weather match up, as well as the landscape? She supposed it must. She found herself struggling over rocks to keep pace, and he turned and spoke to her over his shoulder. "We haven't much time," he said. "I don't want to make any part of this journey under daylight."

When she stumbled again, he took her arm and pulled her to a halt. "Show me your feet," he said.

"What?"

"Your shoes," he said. She lifted the hem of her dress, revealing a pair of tooled leather half-boots with a cunning heel, designed to make her appear taller. "I recall telling you to dress for rough terrain," he said.

"All of mine are like this," she said. "I haven't any more sensible."

"Barsilay," he sighed. "Take them off."

"But the rocks—"

"Give them to me," he said, and she slipped her feet from her boots and handed them over. The heel was concealed inside the shoes, so he set a finger to the sole, flatting one and then the other. Then he knelt at her feet and replaced them, carefully holding her ankles between his thumb and forefinger. When he rose again, Toba concealed a smile. She'd forgotten how tall he was.

"He boasted he'd made you taller," he said.

"I believe he did," she replied. "I can see the tops of your shoulders now; I couldn't before."

He put his hands on her shoulders. "I'm sorry not to have done more for you," he said.

"There are worse fates than smallness."

"There are," he said. "Can you walk a reasonable pace now?"

"I think so," she said, wiggling her toes. Her skirt was too long now, but she'd deal with that later. He started back toward the base of the mountain, and she found herself able to keep pace over the rocks much more ably now that she was closer to the ground. "Asmel," she said. "How is it your colleague ended up imprisoned under the mountain? Was it La Cacería that did it?"

"It was the King," Asmel said. "Early in his reign. It was his one action I was involved with—I gave testimony against him. Rafeq likely hasn't forgotten that."

"He's been there an awfully long time, then," she said, ducking under the branch of a tree growing out of the stream bed. "He must have done something dreadful," she said.

"Dreadful is an accurate term," he said. "He was doing experiments on demons. He was convinced he could improve them."

"What exactly does that mean? How do you improve a demon?"

"He fed them some of his own magic."

Toba halted. "What would that do?"

"It gave them some measure of intelligence," he said, "and a taste for Mazik magic. You can imagine what that might have meant."

Toba shivered in her cloak. It was enchanted to repel light: when the moon shone on it, it turned itself blacker, the effect of which was that the more light there was, the harder Asmel was to see. "Is he mad?" she asked.

"I was never sure. But you should know Rafeq was an exceptionally powerful Mazik: no wards could hold his waking body. They altered this place to trap him, and getting in will be much simpler than getting out."

They'd come very near to the base of the mountain; the sides of it appeared to be made of chunks of granite. "I want you to pay attention," he said. "You will need to do this, when we leave."

Toba said, "Me?"

"Your mortal blood will be of use here," he said. "The cage that holds Rafeq will contain a Mazik, but you should be able to slip between the bars."

"But what about you?"

"If I'm right, you should be able to carry me with you."

"If you're right? What if you're not?"

"This is the reason I brought you," he said. "Pay attention. If you can't focus your mind well enough to see how I do this, we'll be stuck inside Sebah for the rest of time." He set his hand to the granite and closed his eyes. "There is one other thing. Rafeq will probably have some interest in the killstone when he discovers it, but we must make sure he doesn't get it. We need to get it to Barsilay—he may know the command-word. I will trust you to conceal it."

"I think you would do a better job of that."

"Yes, that's why I wish you to do it. Rafeq will expect me to be the one to keep it. I will need to show it to him at first, to explain what we are doing, but once I give it back to you, make it as small as you can. Then I want you to hide it in your eye."

"In my eye?"

"You can make your own food now; this is no harder, and Marah's safira will be easier for you to manipulate, since it's her magic and you are her heir. Will it smaller, and it will obey you. Once we return, you will send the buchuk to marry Tsidon, and then you and Barsilay must take the safira and flee. Do you understand? Make your way to P'ri Hadar."

"Our way, you mean," Toba said. "The three of us together."

"Yes, of course," he said. Then, "The rock is weak enough here." He took her hand in his and together, the two of them went as misty as a shade. "Come," he said, and pulled her into the mountain.

✦ ✦ ✦

IT WAS SOME hours later when Naftaly fell unconscious.

He did not know whether it was still day or night; only that enough time had passed that the Conde had seemed to grow frustrated, and had taken to striking Naftaly in the face when he could not produce the results the Conde desired. He'd finally given up and reappeared with a sack of fabric scraps, and ordered Naftaly to change them. But Naftaly was too weak, and that failure had earned him another blow across the face, hard enough to crack the back of his head against the beam he was tied to, and when next he opened his eyes, he was in the Mazik's cell.

It occurred to him that if a hard blow could send him to the dreamworld, he ought to have goaded the Conde into hitting him earlier.

The Mazik was not in his usual place leaning against the wall. He was in the middle of the floor as if he'd been dumped there, on his back with his arms shielding his face.

Naftaly quickly knelt next to him. He could see the Mazik's arms were smeared with blood. "Are you—" Naftaly began, but he knew the Mazik was not all right. "I'm here," he said. "Can you hear me?" He tried to pull his bloody arms away, but the Mazik resisted.

"Damnable creature," the Mazik said in a voice that did not sound like his usual charming tenor at all. "Let me alone." When Naftaly persisted, he shouted, "Stop touching me, *I am not like you*!" and flung an arm out, knocking Naftaly backward.

Naftaly fell back on his hands, but with the Mazik's arm still sprawled out to the side his face was visible, swollen and bruised and bloody. His eye on that side was swollen shut.

Naftaly lay panting for a moment, and the Mazik looked up to him. "Oh, little one," he said. "I am sorry."

Naftaly crawled back toward the Mazik, and rolled him into his lap. "What's happened to you?"

"Nothing new," he said weakly. "I'm quite all right." He reached a shaky hand for Naftaly's cheek. "Has someone struck you?"

"It's nothing," Naftaly said. "Only my latest self-made disaster." He breathed a few times and pushed the Mazik's hair out of his bloody face. "I wish I could simply remain here, in this place, where everything is simple."

"What you are describing," the Mazik said, "is death."

"Am I? Perhaps I am. I am a hopeless monster of good intentions and outcomes like . . . well, I'm like the Ninth of Av. Everything I touch crumbles beneath my hands."

The Mazik wheezed, and wheezed again, and Naftaly realized he was laughing. "Forgive me," he said. "It's only that you echo my own thoughts." He loosened the collar of his shirt, pulling the neck down to expose the character on his left shoulder; the mark Naftaly had seen when he'd turned his shirt to gold. "This appeared on the third day of my incarceration. I've been concealing it as best I can, but I'm running out of tricks. There are only so many ways to convince a woman to stab you in the same place."

Naftaly went numb at the thought of someone stabbing his Mazik. He put his hand over the mark. Had they branded him? "Did they give this to you? What does it mean?"

"I suppose they did, through no intention. They killed the Mazik who bore this before me, and the one who bore it before them, and now I have it. Once this is discovered," the Mazik said, "I will not live either."

Naftaly clung to him. "Can you not remove it? As you removed the mark on my hand?"

The Mazik said, "No, my dearest friend. I'm afraid I will die from this."

Naftaly woke to a bucket of water in the face.

"Let's try again," the Conde said. "Pray you are not as useless as you've been letting on."

Naftaly felt that the greater part of himself was still back in the cell with the Mazik. His Mazik, who would die, because of a mark on his shoulder he had not earned. His Mazik whom he hadn't been clever enough to save, because his will was too weak to dream of Adon Sof'rim.

Naftaly said, "Perhaps you would prefer to take my powers for yourself?"

The Conde eyed him suspiciously. "You have already played me false once. Why would I trust you twice?"

"Because," Naftaly said, "this plan involves killing me."

Forty-One

THE CAVERN INSIDE Mount Sebah had been hollowed from the rock, the floor smoothed into a surface approximating tile, but the walls left rough. A dozen light-stones illuminated the chamber, which had a hallway on the far end leading into darkness. Along one wall were rows of cages with golden bars, stacked one atop another to the ceiling. At first Toba thought they were empty, but when she stepped closer, she could see they held something. Something dark, that seemed to continually change shape, almost like a shade.

Asmel had made them both solid again, but Toba's mind was spinning from having been inside the rock. It had felt unwholesome inside the granite. It felt unwholesome in the chamber, too.

Asmel seemed to be a little worse off from it, and was breathing hard, his hand braced on his knee. "Let's not linger."

Toba watched the shapes in the cages contract and release, like beating hearts, and then heard a sound like wings beating the air. She stepped closer. Were they birds, in the cages?

The caged things spoke to her in a single voice: "Birdling," they said, in a voice smooth as silk, "won't you give us one of your feathers? We only need one."

Asmel set his hand on Toba's shoulder and pulled her back. "Stay away," he said. "Don't speak to them."

"Asmel," they said. "We know the traitor Asmel. Betrayer. Betrayer!"

He held up a hand and the room was filled with a flash of bright light that made the things cower toward the backs of their cages. "Enough," he said. "Where is your master?"

"But we have no master," they said. "Isn't that why you locked Rafeq away, Traitor Asmel? Because of what he gave us?"

Footsteps, slow and uneven, in the hallway, and then there was a man there, his hair as white as Asmel's, his face and his eyes both as pale as milk. He was dressed in a robe the color of soot that fell straight from his shoulders to his feet, as unornamented as anything Toba had seen worn by a Mazik. His hair was tied back in a queue, the ends burned black. When he talked, his speech was slow, as if it had been a long time since he'd spoken. "Asmel," he said across a clumsy tongue. "It cannot be."

"Rafeq," Asmel said.

"You've come," he said. The hollows of his eyes were filling in, now, as if he were a skull returning to flesh. "They've sent you to free me?"

The demons in the cages began to laugh. "Fool," they said. "He wants something. Why else come, after so long?"

"Quiet," Rafeq ordered them, and then he saw Toba, hidden behind Asmel's tall form. His eyes went very bright at the sight of her, and he circled around Asmel, to get closer. "A halfling," he said, but whether he meant she was half-human or half-Toba, she could not guess. "Clever, clever, clever." He lifted a lock of her hair, running his thumb over it. "Feathers!" he said. "Ah, I see, I see."

"Rafeq," Asmel said. "I need your help."

At that, the man began to laugh. "Yes, you're weaker than last I saw you. Oh! Didn't you notice you were waning?"

Asmel looked a little startled, but Rafeq continued, "Well, perhaps you should have considered needing my help before you had me imprisoned, old friend."

"The help isn't for me," Asmel said. "It's for all of us."

"Oh, indeed," Rafeq said. "And that includes me, trapped under a million pounds of rock? How long have I been here, Asmel? I lost count so long ago, how many years have passed?"

Asmel set his mouth. Rafeq howled. "You won't even say! Well, then, what use have I, for you and yours? The rest of Mazikdom can rot for all I care."

The demons had grown agitated along with their master and were beginning to shriek and beat what passed for limbs against the bars, striking blows that sounded like glass rasping against stone. "Be silent!" Rafeq cried.

"Feed us," they said. "Feed us or we'll never be silent again!"

Horrified, Asmel said, "You aren't still feeding them?"

Rafeq cried, "What choice do I have? It's either that or madness. They're never quiet. They torment me for it; I've become a goat they milk, and if I stop . . ." He made a gurgling sound. "All I want is air and stars and not to breathe lungfuls of stone every damned day 'til I go mad. I can't even dream out of this place, did you know? Did you know what they did to me?" He grabbed Asmel by the front of his cloak. "Did you know how they cursed me, when you told them? Eternity! Eternity, Asmel, under a pillar of salt." He began to weep. "It's in the walls. I can feel it. I taste it in my throat."

There was salt, somewhere: Toba could feel it at the back of her own throat, an almost imperceptible burn, and she'd only been there a few minutes. It was the salt that kept Rafeq trapped inside the mountain. Easier out than in, Asmel had told her, and now she understood: whoever had configured the trap for Rafeq had turned the deposits so that a Mazik might slip inside, but would then be unable to get back out. She wondered what they'd used to bait it. There was nothing in the world Toba wanted so much that she'd let herself be lured inside a mountain.

"Asmel," Rafeq said. "Let me out of this place. Nothing I have done has earned me *this*."

The demons went very quiet. They were listening, Toba knew. They wanted to know what Asmel would do. He said, "Examine this," and held out the safira.

Rafeq took it between his fingertips and looked up in surprise. "Marah? Why?"

It was *why*, Toba noted, and not *how*. "Do you know how she did this?" she asked.

"How she made a safira?" he said.

"A safira?" Toba asked. "You speak as if there is more than one of these in existence."

His eyes darted between her and Asmel. "It was a punishment," he said. "Or it was meant to be, in the times before even the Judges. But it was a punishment with a benefit: it allowed a Mazik to live on the wrong side of the gate." Rafeq's eyes narrowed. "If you'd joined us, you'd know all this. She never understood you."

"Ha-Moh'to was Marah's task, not mine," Asmel said. "She understood."

"No. No, she didn't. You were her greatest disappointment."

The demons were growing restless again. Asmel said, "This is an old argument."

"Yes." Rafeq paced away, the safira still clutched in his hand. "Marah was always worried about assassination. She liked to plan for contingencies, you know how she was. She had some idea someone might try to trap her on the wrong side of the gate. Do you know what it was she was looking for?"

Asmel said, "I do."

"Then do you know how close she was to finding it? She'd spoken to the man who had the book—he trusted her implicitly. All she had to do was wait 'til the moon, and he'd have given it to her, gladly. If she failed to return, if she made this safira instead, it can only be because she was betrayed. And there's only one man who could have done that. And it's your fault."

"You're saying Tarses betrayed her—how is that my doing?"

"Because I was *here*! Because you testified against me. I know you did. There were charges only you could have made."

"What you were doing—what you're still doing—is exceptionally dangerous, Rafeq."

"Does that comfort you? If I hadn't been here, I could have helped her. Marah would still be alive. We might have restored the gate by now, but instead she died because of that choice. Because you could not bear my work."

"Your work could have killed every Mazik in Rimon!"

"And how many have died because of yours, Asmel? Still poking around in Aravoth, are you?"

Toba said, "Old arguments won't get you out from under this mountain, nor will it help us with our problems today." To Rafeq, she said, "If Asmel hadn't testified against you, Tarses would have found another way. You don't know what he's become since then."

Rafeq leaned back and rubbed at his milky eyes. "What is it you want from me?"

Asmel said, "Look closer, at the stone."

Rafeq held it up to the light. "What's it hiding, hm?" Toba could pinpoint the moment he saw, and recognized, it. "Ah," he said. "How interesting."

"You know it?"

"I know it. Ate my name, once." He glanced up. "I don't know the command-word; I can't help you use it."

"I assumed as much," Asmel said.

"So what, then? You want me to help you hide it?"

"I need to do more than conceal it," Asmel said. "Someone's looking for this safira, and I need a replica I can use to fool him."

"Ha, well, that depends on who you're trying to fool, doesn't it?"

"I need something that will pass under the nose of Tsidon b'Noem."

"Tsidon of the Eyes?" Rafeq said. "You'd be better off hiding it entirely than trying to pass off a fake to him."

"We promised it before we knew what it was," Toba said. "And if we don't give him something, a lot of people are going to die."

Rafeq took the opportunity to examine the safira again. The demons whispered, "Give it to us, Rafeq. After we've eaten it, there will be nothing for anyone to find. A better solution, yes?"

Rafeq said, "You know the price of my help. If I tell you what you wish to know, will you have your halfling take me from this place?"

Asmel said, "I will. Give me the safira back."

"Give me your word, Asmel."

"I give you my word. If you tell me what I need to know, I will free you from this prison."

Rafeq closed his eyes, absorbing the vow. He passed the safira back to Asmel and said, "Then come with me."

Turning to Toba, Asmel said, "Stay here. Know that all this is done by my own will. You and the buchuk know what to do next." Then he followed Rafeq down the hallway, leaving Toba alone with the caged demons, with a sudden weight inside her pocket that she knew must be Marah's safira.

While the demons were shrieking at Rafeq to feed them again before he left, Toba held it in her palm, willing it smaller, and when it did not immediately obey, reminding it she was Marah's heir, and the safira was her heirloom, one she'd possessed all her life, and it would do as she said.

It obeyed, shrinking in her hand like melting ice, down until it was as small as a grain of sand, before Toba pressed it into the surface of her left eye.

+ + + + + +

"IF I AM allowed to choose the manner of my death," Naftaly said, "I will tell you how to take my powers for yourself."

The Conde eyed him dubiously. "And why would you tell me that? Why would you wish to be killed?"

"What is the alternative you offer me? A lifetime of slavery and torture? What happens to my powers after I die is no concern of mine. I wish only to be killed humanely; is that not a fair trade? I will tell you a secret: that book and I are as one."

The Conde looked back toward the table where he'd left the small volume. Naftaly said, "If you knock me unconscious again, and then drown me after, or cut my throat, my magic will flee my body and take up residence in that book. Then all you must do is read it, and then all my grand powers shall belong to you."

"The grand powers that you have not shown me."

Naftaly said, "I see now that you are the stronger man. You may have them all."

The Conde walked a circle around Naftaly, taking him in. "You've been in my care less than a day. And already you beg for death?"

Naftaly said, "Yes." His mind was already in the Mazik's cell, so greatly he longed to be there. The Mazik would die, he'd told him. If Naftaly died too, they would both be there again, in that place they shared. Naftaly would tell the Mazik his name, and would learn his, and spend the rest of eternity letting it roll off his tongue, again and again.

The Conde stopped in front of Naftaly. "This is a trick. It allows you to escape somehow; I won't do it."

Naftaly let out a cry of frustration. "Heaven help me," he said. "I can't even die." And he began to beat the back of his head against the post.

"Stop that," the Conde said. "Stop that at once."

"Or you'll strike me? Cut my fingers? Hold my head underwater? Go ahead." He hit his head so hard he saw stars.

He opened his eyes to the Mazik's concerned face above his. "You're here," Naftaly said. "I'm glad."

"What is happening to you?" the Mazik demanded. "You keep appearing and leaving again."

Managing to raise a hand, he touched the Mazik's cheek. "*If only you were to me like a brother . . . then if I found you outside, I would kiss you and no one would despise me.*"

The Mazik gripped his hand. "Don't recite verses, you are frightening me."

"Don't be afraid," Naftaly said. "I am not."

"Speak plainly," the Mazik said, fisting his hands in the front of Naftaly's shirt and giving him a shake.

"I'm sorry," Naftaly said. "With any luck, I'm dying."

"No," the Mazik said. "No, you can't."

"You don't understand," Naftaly said. "The mistakes I have made are unforgivable."

The Mazik's hands were tearing a hole in Naftaly's shirt. "*I* forgive you. Stay alive."

Naftaly felt himself fade in and out again. "It doesn't matter," Naftaly said. "If I die now, I stay with you."

"You don't want that," the Mazik said.

"But I do," he said. "I so want to stay. There's no place for me anywhere else. And you can tell me the rest of your story, and all your others, and trick me out of my clothes."

"You don't want this. Anyway, you don't know how."

Naftaly said, "You've already told me the secret: my intentions only must be pure. And they are. If I stay here, I'll never make another mistake."

"That's a terrible reason—"

"It's a wonderful one," Naftaly said. He held up his hand in front of his face. "I feel strange."

The Mazik's face contorted. "Didn't you want me here?" Naftaly asked.

"Not like this. If I tell you another story, will you wake? What must I offer you?"

"What's it matter if I die? Why should I wake, when you're never there?"

"Because *life*," the Mazik said, "is worth something."

"Not mine," Naftaly said.

"If you wake, I'll tell you everything you ever wanted to know. I'll teach you as much magic as you can do, I'll—I'll tell you my name, my real one, and you can order me about; it will be delightful, you'll enjoy that."

Naftaly laughed sadly. "I'm already going," he said. "I feel it."

The Mazik said, "*I would lead you to my mother's house, she who has taught me, and give you spiced wine, the nectar of my pomegranates.* There, do I have the right of it? Give me the next verse, now, or you will break the spell."

Naftaly shook his head. "I can't remember the next verse, I'm sorry." His chest had ceased to fall and rise; yet he wasn't suffering from lack of air. What an odd sensation, not to need it.

"It isn't too late!" the Mazik shouted. "Do not wish for this!" He looked up to the ceiling and sobbed. "The story I told you, about the fall—I'll finish it. I lied. It's a good tale."

"Thought that wasn't you," Naftaly whispered.

"Of course it was me," the Mazik said. "But I didn't tell you the most important part of that tale, which was that the gate wasn't destroyed. The Sages of Luz hid it in a book. Some of us have been searching for it ever since."

Naftaly felt a stutter in his intent. "In a book?"

"Yes, and I have plenty of tales to tell about the search for it."

Naftaly whispered, "*Kal Most'rim.*"

"If it were found, it would be the most powerful object in the worlds. It could open a doorway from anywhere, to anywhere at all, in the blink of an eye. Can you imagine? Where would you go?" He turned to Naftaly. "What did you just say?"

Naftaly repeated the words. His chest gave a little spasm. "Is that Mazik?"

The Mazik's eyes were so wide, Naftaly could see the entirety of his golden irises. "How do you know those words?"

"The book," Naftaly said. "I have it. I had it."

"If you have the book," the Mazik said hurriedly, "you can escape! You can go anywhere, you can . . . you must take it to Adon Sof'rim, I will show you—" and he held a hand on Naftaly's forehead, and he saw, in his mind, an alcalá, gleaming white, and within it, a courtyard with a fountain with twelve sides, and then a woman's voice, shouting, "Wake up."

The cell was filled with frigid water, and the Mazik was gone.

Naftaly's concentration was broken, and he was back in the waking world, the Conde gripping his hair in one hand, holding him still. "This will not work," the Conde said coldly. "I am in control, do not forget."

Naftaly felt as if he might vomit; his head swam and his sight was dim along the edges. He'd been so close to death; he could feel it in his blood, somehow, like the aftereffects of amapola. What had happened to the Mazik? Had the waking world intruded on the dreaming, somehow? Naftaly hadn't known that was possible. "In control of what? Of me? You are ugly," Naftaly spat. "Your mind is ugly, your heart is ugly, and you will spend the rest of your days cursing yourself for being a pathetic, small, hateful man. Let me tell you a secret." His voice dropped to a whisper. "You could have had everything. Your grandson would have been king."

The Conde looked at him in horror, letting go of his hair and backing away. "He shall not because you played me false."

"Oh, no," Naftaly said. "It is because you played Mosse deLeon false. He would have given you the money, if you were an honest man."

"You speak to me of honesty?"

"I was trying to help you," he said. "Unfortunately, I am not a wizard."

"Then what are you?"

"Come closer and I shall tell you."

The Conde narrowed his eyes, then stepped closer, and again. He leaned down so his face was level with Naftaly's. "What are you?" he repeated.

"I am," Naftaly whispered, "a fool."

The Conde cuffed him across his face again, just hard enough to cut his lip against his tooth.

Naftaly's head rolled. The Conde said, "You've taught me a valuable lesson today. I have learned exactly how hard to hit you."

✦ ✦ ✦

MOSSE DELEON KNEW a man in Labra who lent money, who knew a man who made gold rings, who knew a man who dealt in imported books, who knew a man who taught at the university, who knew a man who tutored in Latin. That was the man Alasar and Elena were going to see, in the hope he had more students than time, and would be willing to part with some; and perhaps there were others who needed Greek, or Arabic, or some other language that Alasar could teach.

Elena would have been content to remain in her brother's house, but the closeness of the Judería made Alasar too anxious, and further, he maintained he would be easier with his own income to depend on. He met the Latin tutor; they conversed in several languages, and he was pleased with Alasar, who did have a certain reputation. He asked Alasar to become his partner, and offered to loan him the money to let a room for himself and his wife, and offered to have them stay with him for Shabbat, which they did. It was a good trip.

On the return to Mosse's Sunday morning to collect their few remaining belongings, Alasar said, sadly, "Toba would have liked Labra. It's full of students."

Elena said, "Yes. She would have." She turned to him in the wagon they shared. "She will."

"You speak as if you expect her to appear again."

"She lives," she said, though she did not care to try her husband by explaining how she knew it. "We'll see her again. I believe this."

He reached out and took her hand, his knobbed from arthritis, hers mottled from age and sun. "I'm sorry," she said, "I left you to make the passage alone."

"You did right," he said. "I'm glad you tried to find her. I'm only sorry you didn't."

"She lives," she said again. "Never fear."

Alasar looked like he may have answered, but the coach had returned them to Mosse's house, and that damnable crone was running outside, even as Elena handed Alasar down.

"Whatever it is," Elena told her, "it can wait."

The old woman scowled at Elena's perfect Zayiti. "Stop babbling," she said. "We've a crisis to attend to."

Forty-Two

TOBA WAS CURLED against the wall of the cavern furthest from the cages. In the alcalá, her counterpart was sleeping, dreaming, and she was tired enough that she might have slept, too, if it hadn't been too painful to close her eyes. She'd willed her left eye to stop watering, but that only made the irritation worse. Asmel, though, had told her to hide the safira there, and she would do as he'd asked.

The demons were restless, and they were watching her: she could feel it. "Birdling," they whispered to her, in hisses like a cat's. "Come closer, and we'll tell you what your Asmel won't. We know who your father is."

"I don't care who my father is," she said.

They laughed. "Little liar, of course you care. We'll tell you, if you open these cages. All we want is to be free. Rafeq lied to you, about us, called us demons. But we aren't demons, and haven't been so for ages."

"What are you, then?"

"We are Maziks," they said.

"I don't think so," she said.

"We are," they said. "Rafeq *made us* Maziks. Gave us *will* and then locked us up, because he was afraid the others would find out, find out we were clever, and we had magic, and we had *power*. We can smell him in your blood, your father. We know who he is. Only let us out, and we'll tell you. We can tell you so many things. Who he is. What he'll do with you."

"I don't care!"

"Foolish child! You should care! You think he'll kill you clean?"

"Stop," she said. "I'm not listening to you!"

"Enough," Rafeq snapped, holding his hand up to the cages. "Let her be."

The demons began to wail, "Traitor! Traitor Rafeq, to keep us caged!"

"It's done," Rafeq told Toba. "Come with me." While the demons continued their cries, she followed him down the darkened corridor to an inner chamber, smaller even than the first, where Asmel lay spread-eagled on the floor.

Toba rushed to his side. "What have you done to him?"

"Only told him what he wished to know," Rafeq said. In the center of Asmel's chest was a sapphire-blue stone, and while Toba watched, Asmel stirred, and his hand went to it, and he opened his eyes: his eyes, now mortal-round.

Toba recoiled from the sight. "What have you done to him?" she screamed.

"Toba," Asmel said. "I chose this."

"We came here so you would make us a false stone, not … not pull out Asmel's magic!"

"There is no false stone that would serve," Rafeq said.

"Then we should have used my magic—not his!"

"Asmel," Rafeq said impatiently. "You gave me your word."

"You can't have meant to do this," Toba said. "How will we escape, with you like this? Without your magic, we're helpless." Turning to Rafeq, she said, "How can we put it back? There must be some way to put his magic back inside him!"

"Be silent, Halfling," Rafeq snapped. "Asmel, you swore me an oath. Tell her to take me out!"

"Your bargain was not with me," Toba spat, "and I won't take you anywhere unless you undo what you have done!"

"My bargain was for my freedom, and if you don't grant it, I'll let loose those demons and let them devour us all!"

"Be calm, both of you," Asmel said.

But Rafeq was beyond such exhortations, and had begun to tear at his hair. "Get me out, Asmel," he said. "Get me away from them, you promised—take me away, where I can't hear them!"

From down the corridor: the sound of shattering glass and wind. "What's that?" Toba asked.

Rafeq's eyes were huge. He whispered, "They've broken the cages."

Asmel was on his feet, barely. "Toba," he said, "remember how I showed you. You must take him."

The wind was roaring into the room, and the demons were shrieking. "Traitor! Traitor Rafeq!"

Toba grasped Asmel by the wrist and willed them both to shadow. "Not me," he said, pulling away. "You won't have the strength to take us both past the salt."

"I'm not leaving you here!" To Rafeq, she said, "Make yourself shadow, so I can take you."

"I can't," he said, holding out his hand. "I haven't the strength any longer. You must do it. Take me, before it's too late!"

The demons were in the chamber now, circling. "You haven't the strength, Rafeq," they taunted. "What will you do now?"

"Take him," Asmel said, pulling his arm free of Toba's grasp, where it immediately went back to flesh. "Take him, else I'm foresworn!"

"He is *ours*," the demons hissed, and they lunged for Rafeq, and he screamed as they began to tear into his arms, his face. They were consuming him, eating him, and when they were done they'd have every ounce of his magic within them.

"Toba!" Asmel shouted, pressing his safira into her hand. "Take him!"

Rafeq's wrist was in her hand, but Toba was too frightened to change him; too frightened to take him into the stone, too frightened to leave Asmel. "Girl," Rafeq cried. "Take me or we all die!"

Change, she told Rafeq's body. *Change: I am your master.*

His arm went to mist inside her grip.

She didn't understand how she was able to maintain her grasp on Rafeq once he'd gone to shadow. But as the demons began to rage, she pulled him through the wall, feeling the salt abrading her like sandpaper. Rafeq, behind her, was screaming from it: if she hadn't been pulling him, he would have been unable to move, stuck in the rock, in agony, for eternity. She pulled, wanting air and light and wholesome soil under her feet.

She pulled again; he was fighting her now, wanting to go back to the chamber, but she made her fingers a vice. She pulled again. They were free.

She went back to flesh in a second, and collapsed on the dirt, while Rafeq fell nearby, his face and arms missing chunks of flesh from the demons and the surface of his skin burned from the salt. "Stars," he whispered, looking up at the sky. "Stars."

He looked back from the sky to Toba's face and said, "Your eyes." Then he whipped out a hand, which somehow passed through Toba's face, through her left eye, and as she shrieked, yanked the miniscule safira free.

Toba doubled over, a hand over her eye, which burned so badly she thought she might be sick. "Give me that," Toba panted. In Rafeq's hand, Marah's safira was returning to its normal size. "It's mine. Asmel never said you could have it."

"Asmel is dead," he said. "Or will be any moment."

"No," she said. "He hasn't any magic. The demons wouldn't bother to devour him."

"That won't stop them long. Come with me," he said. "His was a fool's plan. Even if you deceive Tsidon, you'll never escape him." He lifted his face as a breeze blew in, scenting the air like an animal. "Salt?" he murmured. "What has happened . . ."

"I have to save Asmel!" Toba made a staggering lunge for Rafeq, for the safira, but he flung her back easily, and she landed in a tangle of her own limbs on the ground, panting in pain from her eye.

The gouges in Rafeq's flesh were already beginning to fill in. "Halfling, there's no saving him now. He always intended to die in that mountain. Even if the demons spare him, he will degrade."

Struggling to get up, Toba said, "Degrade, what do you mean?"

"He can live with what he's done. It won't kill him. But his memories, who he is, will falter. He'll continue on, 'til his body wears out, but the man he was is dying already."

"How long? How long does he have?"

"'Til his mind rots? I don't know. Days. Weeks. But you'd be doing him a mercy, letting the demons finish him off before he's nothing but a shell. Let him die, Halfling. It's the only gift you have left for him."

Finally able to remove her hand from her eye, she said, "I can't."

Rafeq tilted his head as he looked at her. His pallor was giving way, under the air and stars, and she could see the beginnings of his return to the Mazik he'd once been: handsome and whole; his eyes had gone amber and were darkening quickly to the color of dark honey, his skin had gone from paper to olive. "Well, then, Halfling, there are no further debts between us. Go to your Asmel, if you insist. Go and die with him."

He leapt into the sky and vanished. He carried Marah's safira—and the killstone of ha-Moh'to—with him.

Toba would ruminate later on the scope of that particular disaster. She staggered to her feet. Her strength was mostly gone, but she set her hands against the granite. The demons might not have devoured Asmel right away. They would have known she meant to come back for him, as long as he lived. She would be the one they would want, because she had magic, and because she might have the strength to release them.

She tried to make herself mist, again, and then again, and failed, and then she was aware of her counterpart's approach. She'd woken, when Toba had been inside the mountain, and she'd understood what Asmel had done. Toba Bet said, "He never should have taken you: you're too afraid. But I'm not." And the second Toba vanished into the heart of the mountain.

\+ + + + + + +

NAFTALY LOOKED UP through a haze of hot air and blood that had run into his eyes. The Conde had been forced to take a break from his tender ministrations because of the incessant beating at the door, which no amount of shouting from the Conde's quarter could dismiss.

Naftaly was unsure how much time had passed, he was so often in and out of consciousness, going under just long enough to disorient him but not enough to dream: a particular cruelty. At some point the Conde had left, leaving him in the care of a guard who prevented him sleeping but otherwise ignored him, and then the Conde returned, freshly turned out in a clean shirt. Why he'd bothered, Naftaly couldn't say. He'd already got blood on it. He'd believed the noise at the door was a hallucination until the Conde began responding to it, irritated at having his careful work disrupted.

The Conde opened the door and roared displeasure at whomever was on the other side—two men in the Conde's livery, one rather stout, one rather short; the short one held a flagon full of liquid. "You had better have a good reason to be here," he said.

Naftaly took the opportunity to beat his head against the beam again, hitting it hard enough to start a trickle of blood down his nostril, but not hard enough to knock himself out. The shorter guard gave him a dubious look. "Is he . . . is he torturing himself?"

"Stop that," the Conde ordered, and clipped Naftaly across the shoulder with his boot.

"Sir," the short one went on. "We've brought you your evening wine. With the compliments of your wife."

He scowled. "The Condessa," the Conde said tightly, "is ten years in the grave."

"Oh," said the short one, turning to the stout one. "Fuck."

The stout one struck the Conde full-force across the face with the flagon. He staggered back against the wall, and the man struck him a second time over the head, and he was still.

The stout one turned to Naftaly. "Idiot," he spat, and though Naftaly could not recognize the voice, he knew the tone that went with it.

The shorter one was already untying Naftaly's wrists; his shoulders were so stiff he could no longer pull his arms to the front, so the guard aided him in that, too, rather painfully. "Are you badly hurt?" he asked, in a voice that had become the old woman's.

Naftaly felt too numb to answer. "I can walk," he said, because that was all that mattered, at the moment. The flagon was draining its contents onto the floor at his feet. "Were you trying to poison him, or only put him to sleep?" Naftaly asked.

"My vote was for poison," the old woman said, "but the witch said it would invite too many questions. She thought embarrassment might render him muter than death."

"What?" Naftaly asked, but Elena was busy undressing the Conde, with a look of disgust. Once she'd divested him of his clothes, she tossed them into the fire. Naftaly pulled his arms the rest of the way free of his bonds and the old woman helped him to his feet.

"Poisoned," the old woman explained, "his allies might come after Mosse. She felt he was less likely to pursue further action if he had to admit you left him naked and locked in his own cell."

Naftaly took his book off the table and tucked it beneath his shirt, while the old woman held up her hand, which had begun to look rather feminine. "Are you seeing this, you old buzzard?"

Elena, whose livery had begun to stretch over her returning bosom, said, "Not good. Come."

Naftaly was still struggling with his wits knocked loose. "I'm not sure he won't take vengeance, anyway. He already threatened to burn the quarter if I didn't cooperate."

"Damnation," the old woman said. "We'll have to take him with us. Put his clothes back on," she told Elena.

Elena said something in irritated Zayiti, before waving at the fire. The old woman said, "You think no one in this house will notice we're escaping with their naked lord?"

"We kill him," Elena suggested.

"You already said that was a bad idea."

"We cannot take naked Conde back to Mosse's!"

"We could throw him off the docks," the old woman said. "Make it look like he was killed by thugs or whores."

"How we get him to the docks?" Elena said.

"Can't you make him look like something else? A large dog, or a sack of flour?"

Elena said, "Maybe, for a few minutes. Not long enough."

Naftaly pulled out his book. *You can escape*, his Mazik had said. *Find Adon Sof'rim. A key to any door, anywhere in all the worlds.* Naftaly said, "I know where we might take him."

FORTY-THREE

TOBA BET PUSHED her way through the salt and granite and found Asmel sprawled on the floor, the demons circling over him.

"You fool," he groaned. "Why have you come back to this place?"

He hadn't noticed he was talking to a different Toba, because he was addled or because of something the demons might have done to him, or because he'd never been very good at telling them apart. He appeared unharmed. Probably Toba had been right: they'd been hoping she'd come back for him. "Give him to me," she told the demons. "He's of no use to you."

"No," they whispered. "We keep him, unless you give us back Rafeq."

"Rafeq is gone," she said. "I've released him."

They howled. "Then we will devour you, Halfling!"

"Come any closer to me, and I'll go back through that wall. This place doesn't bind me, haven't you realized? Or are you as stupid as Rafeq said?"

They hissed at her. Asmel was watching her from the ground, his round eyes blinking at her. "Leave me," he said. "I never planned to live after this. I'm of no use to you now."

"I can't leave you," she said. "My will prevents me." She took a step toward Asmel, and another.

"Come no closer," they said. "We will kill you both."

"What would the purpose of that be? Kill me, and you're still stuck here, with nothing to eat. What will happen to you when the magic runs out? Will you go back to being mindless demons?"

"We are Maziks!" they cried. "We are Maziks!"

"A Mazik would seek to strike a bargain with me," she said.

"Then give us Rafeq! Give us Rafeq, and we give you your beloved Asmel, who loves you not."

"I've already told you I can't," she said.

"Then release us, too! Release us, so that we may find him: he is bound to us."

"Toba," Asmel said softly. "You mustn't do that."

"Don't tell me what I mustn't do," she ground out. "I'm not sure if I can," she told the demons. "It's very difficult."

"You needn't make us shadow," they said. "We are such already. We need only for you to take us past the salt."

"It will hurt," she warned them.

"What is pain to us? Take us past the salt, *Toba*."

"I can only hold one of you," she said. "And that one must hold the rest."

"Fine," they said. "Fine."

"And if you let go, it's no fault of mine."

"We will not let go. You will take us past the salt, and we will let you keep your broken man, who is no Mazik now. He is less, even, than we. But you may have him, to be your pet."

"Very well," she said, and she took Asmel's hand in hers.

"Toba," Asmel said, "do you know what they will do, if you let them out? They won't be satisfied to hunt only Rafeq."

She replied by making Asmel mist and pushing him ahead of her into the wall. With her other hand, she reached back. "Well?" she said. "I'm not waiting any longer in this place."

The demons undulated, spitting and hissing, and then one of them made a shape in the approximate form of a hand, and clutched hers, its talons digging into her skin.

She pulled it behind her, into the stone. The salt did not scour Asmel as it had Rafeq, so he pushed easily through the rock, and she pulled the demon behind her.

The demon's magic was caught in the salt, and it felt the same pain that Rafeq had felt, and had not expected it to be so terrible. It began to struggle, as Rafeq had done, and pulled back toward the heart of the mountain.

She pulled again, knowing the pain would grow worse, and the struggle grew fevered, its phantom hand jerking within hers. She clamped down her hand, for one second, two, three, and then she loosened her grip.

The demon pulled its hand back, then realized what it had done, and fumbled for hers again. But she was already pushing Asmel the rest of the way out, while it groped blindly for her in the stone, and she could swear she heard it screaming for her. Whether it remained in the rock or went back to the cavern, she did not know.

She was out, Asmel with her. He fell to the ground, and it took both Tobot to hold him up, he was so frail. Gasping the cold night air, he said, "You should not have come back."

\+ + + + + + +

IT WAS AN hour before dawn, the sky beginning to brighten, and Asmel was on the windowsill in the observatory looking out at the garden, while the Tobot whispered to one another about what they might do.

His safira lay on the table; Marah's was gone, and the wedding was today.

Eventually, tiring of listening to their frantic chatter, he turned his eyes toward them, their color intact, but the shape altered, and Toba found herself mourning the loss of their strangeness. Touching the center of his chest, he shivered. "There's nothing," he said. "And I was so little before. You should not have come back for me."

"Should we have left you to die in the mountain?" Toba Bet asked.

"I expected to die," he snapped. "I did not expect to be left a shell. And I did not expect that you'd let Rafeq escape with the killstone!"

"It was your plan to conceal it in my eye. I don't know how he saw it there."

Asmel put his hand over his eyes. Toba wondered if they hurt, as hers had, when they'd changed. "I don't know either. I believed the mountain would have weakened him past the point of such things. It seems I underestimated him."

"What will he do with it?" Toba Bet asked.

"I don't know," he said.

"Well, then, maybe he was right," Toba said. "It's safer with him than with us. La Cacería doesn't know he has it, and even if they did, they don't know where he's gone."

Asmel said, "Perhaps."

"You're angry," Toba Bet said, "because we prevented you martyring yourself."

Asmel gave no argument to that. Toba said, "But if you'd died, what did you think would happen to the rest of us? How do you expect us to get Barsilay to P'ri Hadar without you?"

"Barsilay knows the way," he said.

"And if he doesn't? Who knows what they've done to him. We aren't even certain he's alive!"

"He's alive," he said, reaching for Toba Bet's hand, the one wearing Tsidon's ring. "We would know—"

"Asmel," Toba Bet cut in, turning Asmel's hand palm-up, to reveal a slate of blank skin.

He held out the other hand, which was equally unmarked.

"Your tongue?" she asked.

His eyes seemed to focus inward, and he swallowed. "I feel it no longer." Holding both his hands before him, he added, "I did not consider that would happen. Truth, for everything else. Maybe it was a good bargain, after all." He clenched and opened his hands, testing them. "What day is it?" he murmured. "Is it Thursday? I should be lecturing, if it's Thursday."

The Tobot exchanged an uneasy glance. "Asmel," one said. "Are you—"

A flash of light came through the window. All of them threw up a hand to block it, and then it was gone.

"Tsidon?" Toba asked uneasily.

Asmel turned his round eyes toward the window. "No. That was a gate."

"It's daylight," Toba Bet said. To her counterpart, she added, "He's addled." But the two approached the window and looked out, because *something* had happened.

There were three people in the courtyard, looking incredulously at the alcalá; two women dressed like men, and one man who looked like he'd recently suffered a beating. The smaller woman turned to the man and began to shake him, while the larger, who carried what looked like a sack of flour across her shoulders, trained her eyes upward, to the very window where Toba stood.

"Grandmother," she whispered, and flung herself out.

\+ \+ \+ \+ \+ \+ \+

TOBA WAS NOT sure how she got from the observatory to the courtyard, if she'd sprouted wings like Asmel or if she'd only fallen without hurting herself this time; all she knew was her only wish was to be in her grandmother's arms, and then she was.

She was real. She'd lost a little of her stoutness, but she was real, and Toba pressed her face into Elena's shoulder and she wept and her legs gave out, and the other woman's did, too, until they were both weeping on the ground, because they'd been apart, and because they were together again. Then she felt some part of the other Toba's anguish, because they were outside, and she could not go to her and risk being seen. She felt a small well of jealousy, because she wanted her grandmother's attention only for herself, and then guilt, because Toba Bet was marrying Tsidon, and Toba was not, and she was dying, and Toba was not, and she whispered to Elena, "Come inside."

The other was descending the stairs, supporting Asmel, who moved like a frail old man, and her face was wet with tears because she was the second seen, and her grandmother would not know her. But instead, Elena said, "Ah." And she came forward and took the second Toba in her embrace and said, "I see, little one, I see."

\+ + + + +

NAFTALY DID NOT see. The old woman seemingly did not, either, as she muttered, "Hashem's sake," and then the tall man with the silver hair said, "Explain to me how you came to be here."

Naftaly did not know quite how to answer, because he'd expected to meet a Mazik, and this man was clearly mortal. He said, "I need to speak to . . . to Adon Sof'rim, if he's here."

The silver man said, "I am he."

Naftaly looked at him again, looking for some sign of Mazikness. Did they not all have the eyes? He was sure they did. "Forgive me, I was given to believe the Lord of Books was—"

"I am he," the man repeated firmly. Then, more gently, he added, "My appearance is lately altered. But if you seek Asmel, you have found him."

Elena made some comment before unceremoniously dumping her sack of flour at Asmel's feet, where it revealed itself to be the Conde. The Tobot recoiled. Asmel blinked a few times before saying, "If that's meant to be some sort of tribute, I don't want it."

Elena said, "Bad man."

One of the Tobot said, "Did you . . . imagine we needed another of those?" Elena gave her some explanation in Zayiti, which might have been her telling Toba that he was likely to kill her uncle, or that he'd nearly killed Naftaly, or that she'd carried him up three flights of stairs and was not about to pick him up again.

But Naftaly was trembling, because before him was the man who could save his Mazik, if anyone could. With tentative hands he took his book from his breast and held it out to him, while Asmel's eyes went wide and he made some inarticulate noise. "I was told to give this to you."

Asmel's face was very pale, and he said, "And who told you that?"

Naftaly felt a wash of tender emotion. He said, "A Mazik with eyes like a sunset, who sits a prisoner. I—I do not know his name. I've seen him only in dreams."

Asmel took Naftaly by the shoulders. He said, "Does he live?"

Naftaly's voice shook when he said, "Yes. But not for much longer. You must save him. They mean to kill him."

Asmel turned his face away. He said, "I am saving him the only way I can." Turning to one of the Tobot, he said, "Please take the wicked nobleman and put him in a locked room."

The Toba in question regarded the naked Conde distastefully. "Fine," she said. "What's one more set of wicked male parts upon my person, in the scale of things?" She hoisted the male in question over her shoulder with more strength than Naftaly could have guessed she possessed, and said, "I'll put him at the end of the western corridor."

"Be sure to leave him some food," the other Toba said. "The last thing we need is Tsidon enquiring about the stench of moldering corpse."

The old woman leaned close to Naftaly. "And which is Tsidon?" she murmured.

Toba adjusted the Conde's weight. "My groom," she said flatly. "It's how we're going to save Barsilay."

Barsilay, Naftaly thought, testing the sound of his name in his mind. "I don't understand," he said. "How does marrying save him?"

"It's an exchange," she said. "I marry Tsidon the Lymer, and Barsilay is returned to Asmel."

"No," Naftaly said, but his mind was growing fuzzy. What had his Mazik told him about a bargain? Something. "The—the Barsilay. He said you mustn't make any bargain to get him back."

"But it's the only way we can free him," Toba said.

"They mean to kill him," Naftaly said. "They mean to kill him either way. It's a trap."

"He can't kill him," Toba said. Her voice was sounding very far away. "Tsidon gave me his word. You must understand how things work here—"

"Stop," the old woman was saying. "Sit down, boy." Her hands were on Naftaly, but he shook her off. "He means to break his word," he said. "Barsilay didn't tell me how. Only that he won't be allowed to live."

Toba said, "But what would be the point of killing him, when Tsidon shall have what he wants?"

"The mark," Naftaly said, pulling at the collar of his shirt. He was sure, somehow, that the mark was now visible on his own shoulder: it was as if he could feel it there, branded on his skin. He rent the neck when the shirt wouldn't open far enough, jerking it aside to reveal his shoulder. "It's because of the mark." Only now there was no mark, but a wound cut nearly to the bone, gaping and bleeding and agonizing, and he cried out. "Do you see?"

"What?" Toba said. "It's only skin."

"No," he said, "no," and his mind raced, and his head throbbed, and his eyes rolled back, and he was only aware of the old woman cursing and catching him just before he went into a vision.

This time, there was nothing familiar in what he saw, a landscape wholly unlike anything he knew, a great plain, and rising in the middle, completely incongruously, a mountain, and on top of the mountain a bird the size of a house, its eye the size of a wagon wheel, and Naftaly approached it and asked someone he could not see, "What will happen?" and a voice he did not know answered, "Either you will succeed, or she will eat you."

✦ ✦ ✦

NAFTALY WOKE TO Elena wafting something pungent under his nose, in a room with a glass dome for a ceiling. Asmel stood over him, with one of the Tobot; the other was absent, as was the old woman.

"I'm awake," he said weakly. "You can stop now."

Elena handed the vial back to Asmel, who put a cork in it and left it lying on what looked like a work-table, if one's work involved a great number of books and strange devices that looked like hourglasses gone wrong. She asked him a question Naftaly could not understand, and Toba said, "She asks what you saw."

"A very large bird," he said. "It was either going to eat me, or not."

"The Ziz," Asmel said. "You saw her?"

"Was it real?" he asked, sitting up with Elena's help.

"Yes," Asmel said, setting the vial away. "I need to know everything Barsilay told you."

Barsilay had told him many things, and Naftaly's head still swam from his vision. There was one bit that seemed more urgent than the rest. "He has a mark on his shoulder. He said it was why he wouldn't be allowed to live."

"A sigil?" Toba asked, but Asmel waved his hand in the air, and then again, and then looked cross when nothing happened.

Toba took a pen from the table and passed it to Asmel, who passed it in turn to Naftaly. "Show me," he said. "If you can remember."

Naftaly went to the table, and on a scrap of paper, he drew the sign he'd seen. Toba said, "I don't know this sign."

Asmel said, "Are you absolutely certain?"

"What does it mean?" Toba asked.

Asmel's voice was very low when he said, "It means that Barsilay has become the heir of Luz."

✦ ✦ ✦

THE OLD WOMAN helped Toba Bet deposit the Conde in the chamber at the end of the western corridor, locking the door and then, at the old woman's urging, locking it a second time by freezing the hinges.

"I don't understand," the old woman said. "Are you telling me you're the same person?"

Toba Bet wanted to deny this, but instead she said, "Effectively."

"And you're to marry this nasty piece of work tomorrow. While the other one flees the country with your magicless Mazik lord?"

"Yes."

"And the other Mazik—the one in prison—says this is a terrible idea, because they mean to kill him anyway."

"That is what Naftaly's said." She paused. "Oh, dear. I've just learned why. What an odd king he would make. I would almost like to see it."

"Forgive me, as I'm only lately come to this parade of horrors, but this seems to be a terrible plan you people have concocted."

"If we don't flee, we're all likely to be executed," Toba Bet said. "Essentially, everything that can go wrong for us has done so."

"Were you hurled into the sea?"

Toba Bet said, "No."

"Then not everything has gone wrong for you, and count your blessings."

"Right now, my greatest hope is that my fiancé will kill me before consummating the marriage and not after," she said.

The old woman seemed inclined to concede the point. "Have you not considered breaking the engagement?"

Toba Bet held out her right hand and demonstrated that the ring would not allow itself to be removed.

"We could take the finger," the old woman mused.

"I already tried it," she said. "The knife glanced off. It seems the ring was made to prevent such a thing."

The old woman frowned. "And what if you simply ran away?"

Toba Bet blinked rapidly a few times. She said, "I have nowhere to go."

The old woman said, "Are you daft? You have a portal inside an old book, child, you can *go* wherever you damn well please."

\+ + + + + +

THE PAIR RETURNED to the observatory, where Asmel looked even worse than he had upon waking. Elena and Toba-the-fortunate were having a rapid-fire discussion in Zayiti about gate-lore, Luz, and their ill-fated plan to wed herself to Tsidon the Lymer in exchange for Barsilay the Rake Prince of Luz. Toba Bet swallowed past a lump, because she'd come to understand that in the past quarter hour Elena had already determined that the other Toba was the real one, and she was the extraneous copy.

"I don't know why you're bothering to explain this," she told the other Toba. "It has no effect on what will happen to any of us. Our only concern should be whether there is still some chance to save Barsilay, and how we can flee from this place." She approached the table, where the book sat beside Naftaly's rendition of the Mark of Luz. "Does the book take any particular skill to use?"

Elena said, "Only to control the exit. It seems you must have some clear image of where you want to go before you read, otherwise I'm not sure where it would put you."

"Couldn't we use this to get Barsilay out? Open a gate to his cell and fetch him?"

"No," Asmel said, "we don't know where Barsilay is, so there's no way to get there."

To Naftaly, the old woman said, "They do realize we haven't understood a word of this, don't they?"

Toba explained the situation a second time, in Sefardi. "I've seen the place," Naftaly offered. "In dreams."

"It's not equivalent," Asmel said. He sat down heavily. "There's nothing left I can do; I have no more magic, even if it would help. I have no allies, no favors to trade on."

"Well, hang on," the old woman said. "You're a lord, living in a castle, dressed in silk, and you're saying no one owes you *anything*?"

Asmel's eyes cut away. He said, "No one alive or at liberty."

Toba looked up. "I owe a debt."

"I fail to see how that helps us," Elena said.

But both Tobot had risen, and the one wearing the ring said, "I owe a debt *to Barsilay.*"

FORTY-FOUR

"YOU TOLD ME once," Toba reminded Asmel, "that if I failed to finish my translation, I would be in Barsilay's service until he released me. I never finished it. If I . . . if I somehow declare my intention *never* to finish it, does that make me his? Could he use that to summon me to him, if I had some way to get there?" She held up the book, illustrating the point.

Asmel flexed his fingers, as if unaccustomed to having full use of his hands, and took the book from her. "Possibly," he said. "But how would he know to summon you?"

The boy said, "I can reach him, in the dream-world."

Asmel said, "A chance meeting would not be enough . . . you would have to be completely sure you would dream of him, and I don't think—"

"I am completely sure," Naftaly said.

Asmel regarded him for a few moments before saying, "I see. Perhaps you don't have enough Mazik blood to trigger the ward in his cell that keeps the rest of us from dreaming to him." He steepled his fingers in front of his lips. Out the window, the sun had descended past the horizon. "Where is your work?"

"In the library," Toba said, nodding to Toba Bet, who was already rushing down to claim the pages. She returned with two stacks of paper, one in Latin, one in Arabic, and set them on the table. "Must I do something with them?" Toba asked.

"Declare your intention never to finish," Asmel said. "And destroy what you've already done."

Toba Bet blanched, because she would not burn text, even if it was merely a translation and incomplete besides. Instead, she set a hand over each stack of pages and changed each into a round of unleavened bread. She ate one, and then the other. Toba could taste the blandness of them in her own mouth, when she said, "I shall not fulfill my bargain to Barsilay b'Droer. Will that do?"

"Yes," Asmel said. "That will do." He turned to Naftaly. "Time grows short; the day is dawning. Will you go to him now?"

"Now?" Naftaly asked. "I could try, but—"

To Toba Bet, Asmel said, "Do you remember how I made the Infanta sleep?"

"Yes," she said.

"Do it," he answered, and then Naftaly felt her touch on the back of his neck, and he was unconscious on the table.

\+ + · + + + +

THE COURSER THREW another bucket of water into Barsilay's face. He was very adept, she'd learned, at falling asleep instantly. If she turned her attention away from him for more than a moment, his eyes were closed. There was something there for him. That was why he hadn't broken.

He didn't bother wiping the water from his face this time. "What is it you want from me?"

She said, "I want the truth about Tarses."

"Ask him," Barsilay said. "I'm sure he's nearby."

"He can't have been in ha-Moh'to and then gone on to found La Cacería. It makes no sense."

"Not to you or me," he agreed. "I can't explain his motivations. All I can surmise is that he was false then, or he's being false now. Or both.

But what's it matter, what he did all those centuries ago? Does his hypocrisy trouble you?"

Another blow, this time more out of frustration than anything. "You really aren't Tarses' style," he said. "He must despise you."

"You are trying to anger me," she said. "So I'll strike you unconscious."

"You're already angry," he said. "I'm only tired of you now. I've told you the truth. I can't help if you don't like the taste of it."

She strode the periphery of the cell, trying to clear her mind. "What difference," Barsilay said, "can this possibly make to you?"

The Courser made a starburst above her outstretched hand. "I know what this is," she said. "And I know where it is."

"Ah," he said, closing his eyes. "The knife cuts the hand that wields it, always."

"I am not a knife," she said.

"No," he said. "You are a thinking, reasoning person."

"Do not mock me."

"It is your master that mocks you," he said. "What did he tell you it was? A pretty bauble for his collection?"

She came much nearer. "I can get it," she said.

Barsilay's orange eyes caught the dim light. "Can you?"

The Courser took him in, his canny eyes, his bruised face. He'd been trying to turn her against the Caçador for days. Might as well let him think he'd won; no point telling him he was fighting a battle that ended long ago. She said, "Do you have what I need?"

He wet his lips. "Marah trusted me like no other. But why should I give it to you, who offers nothing in return?"

"I offer you vengeance," she said.

"Vengeance and three lentils are worth the lentils," he said. "I am not like you."

"I can't release you," she said.

He only watched her, waiting. "You know they're about to kill you," she said. "Between sunset and moonrise, you'll die."

That got his attention. "So soon," he said.

"Yes, so soon. I can't release you. But if between now and then you tell me everything I wish to know, I'll let you sleep in the hour before the sun goes down. Do you think that's enough time?"

She waited for him to see what she meant, what she was offering. "If I enter the endless dream here," he said, "I'm still warded. Spending eternity in this cell doesn't seem much better than the void, does it?"

"I'll break the wards," she said.

He laughed. "You and I both know you haven't the clarity to break the wards."

She cocked her head to the left. "Perhaps. But you and I both know you aren't alone in here, either."

He gave her his unbroken smile. "Now, how could that be?"

"This is as much as I can offer you," she said. "Eternity with whomever is coming to see you, whomever is keeping your mind whole, or else the void."

He watched her a long minute. She had him; she could see it. She said, "It must be good to have a friend so dedicated to you. I wonder what you can have done to deserve it."

She put her hand to the wall and called in the Alaunt on the other side. "I'm expected by the Caçador," she said. "I'll return before sundown." She took a stone out of her pocket, made it a pail of endless water, passed it to his hands. "Don't let him sleep."

\+ + + + + + +

THE MAZIK'S CELL was empty when Naftaly opened his eyes, and the room seemed to have grown smaller. He felt a strange terror, too, that hadn't been there before. "Where are you?" he called, but wherever Barsilay was, it was not in this room, at least not asleep. He approached the wall where Barsilay usually leaned, and found it still carried the scent of almond and bergamot.

He'd been here, recently.

Naftaly knelt and breathed the air. "I did what you asked," he said. "I lived, and I've taken the book to your Adon Sof'rim."

If he waited long enough, maybe Barsilay would return. He felt the sense of him, as if he were nearby. He lowered himself into Barsilay's usual spot, and leaned his head against the wall. There, on the stone next to his cheek, was a mark.

It had been carved, *3*, in a thread of silver.

Naftaly leaned back against the wall. Three of what? He said the number out loud, and then said it again in Hebrew, and nothing happened. The third dream?

The third verse. The one Barsilay had asked him to recite.

He whispered, "*His left arm is under my head, and his right embraces me.*"

Nothing happened.

It wouldn't be the words. Mazik magic was about intent, about actions. He pressed his left hand against the spot where Barsilay rested his head against the wall.

He was rewarded with a sharp pain on his palm, as if he'd pierced himself with a needle in a thousand places at once. Pulling it back, he saw it had been marked with an hourglass. As he watched, the sand flowed from the top to the bottom. It was counting down, to something. He opened his eyes.

"Well?" Asmel asked.

"He wasn't there," Naftaly said. "But he left me this." He showed Asmel his hand, as the sand trickled through flesh and settled at the bottom. He could feel it moving inside his skin, as he recalled the woman's voice, the flood of cold water. "I think it's when he wants me to come back. I think they're preventing him sleeping."

Asmel was tracing the outline of the sand with his fingertip. "This counts down to this evening," he said. "Sunset, if I'm right."

"How would he know when they plan to let him sleep again?" Toba asked.

"They can't torture him past the time of the wedding," Asmel said. "They must have set him a deadline."

Toba took up the book, feeling its weight in her hands. "It's warm," she said.

"It's always that way," Naftaly said. "I used to think it was a living thing."

Asmel nodded, as if this made sense to him. "If we can't reach Barsilay until sunset, we'll have to rescue him during the wedding."

"But what if he decides not to meet whatever deadline they've set? They must want him to do something."

"He'd already decided to do it when he cast that spell," Asmel said. "All we can do now is wait."

ELENA DID NOT like the sound of this plan at all.

It involved risking not one Toba, but both, and she was still not entirely sure how they fit together; she'd been told that the Tobot were one and the same, but it was clear to her that they were not—two girls spoke to her, with two voices, and two minds that did not always agree. The idea that one was being sent to her death—even to save the other—rankled her. If she'd had her way, she'd have taken the book and escaped with both girls back to Pengoa, this Barsilay fellow be damned. The only thing preventing her was that she didn't believe the girls would cooperate.

She could not bear to let the elder Toba out of her sight, and while she followed her up to the small room where they would both sleep for a few hours, Elena said, "There's no reason for you to go. Send the boy; he's already opened the gate. He knows how."

"You don't understand, it must be me. I'm the one who has the bargain with Barsilay. Without that, there's no way to come to where he is. He's summoning me, and I will have the book in my grasp."

"It's madness. You aren't thinking of all the things that can go wrong."

"Grandmother," she said. "There's no one else who can do this."

"Then you ought to take someone with you. *I'll* go with you."

"It will be faster with only me." Seeing Elena's rising unease, she said, "I'll be back in the time you can hold your breath. Do not fear."

"It isn't my fear that's the problem," she said, shutting the bedroom door behind them. "It's that you believe the other carries all the risk, and that makes you safe. You are planning to set foot in some sort of—" she waved her hands—"Mazik prison."

"Mine is the safer mission by far. It's only a matter of opening the gate and stepping back through—I'll be there for a matter of seconds. As long as I have the book, I can't be captured. It's like having a key that can unlock any door."

"But you don't even know what state this Barsilay will be in when you find him! What if he can't step through the gate? What if he's injured, or unconscious?"

"Then I shall carry him," Toba said.

"And the book at the same time?"

Toba stopped and set down the pins she'd taken from her hair. "Grandmother," she said.

Elena could not look at her properly. She said, "Everything that has happened to you has been my fault. But I don't know what I might have done differently. If I hadn't put that amulet on you, you would certainly have died."

"I know," Toba said.

"If I hadn't taken you out of Rimon . . ."

"I know that, too. But you must understand, it's no longer in your power to save me. You must trust in the mind you've given me. I will rescue my friend, and I will get Asmel to P'ri Hadar, and I will find a way to mend what was broken."

Elena put her arms around Toba and embraced her, smelling the top of her sweet head. She said, "And you must understand, that I don't care about any of that."

\+ + + + + + +

TOBA LAY DOWN to rest and dreamt of herself.

The pair of them were in Asmel's garden, sitting on the bench before the fountain. "Well," Toba Bet said. "This is duller than usual."

"Safer, though," the other said.

"I'm sure. But seeing as I'm about to die anyway, I might as well have some excitement while I can."

"Really, and what would that look like?"

"Asmel in the bath," she said, "would have been a good diversion."

"Really," Toba said.

"Yes, that would have been rather nice. Instead I'm here with you."

Toba waved at the fountain. "We could make mud animals."

"Yes, that's just as much fun as Asmel naked. I'm so glad you're here."

"Don't blame me for it."

"I think I will."

They sat, watching the water splash in the fountain. "I'm sorry," Toba said.

"No you aren't. You're glad to live. I would be, too: I don't blame you for that, but don't lie about it." She smiled thinly. "Who can we be honest with, if not each other?"

"Fine, then. I'm glad to live. Does feeling that make me a bad person?"

"No," Toba Bet replied. "But you'll suffer for it, anyway."

\+ + + + + + +

"WHAT USE IS being a Mazik lord without any servants?" the old woman grumbled. "Even Mosse had people to fetch hot water, and he owned a bank. This Asmel fellow—he lives in a castle, and I should have to draw my own bath? It's shameful." She glanced over her shoulder at Naftaly. "Drag me all the way to the damned Mazik realm, and I don't even get a change of clothes and a hot meal out of it."

Naftaly was becoming more agitated by the minute. He'd asked Elena for something to make him sleep for a few hours, but she'd refused, saying, "If I give you enough to put you out, you might not be able to wake when you need to, and then where would we be?" So Naftaly had asked Toba for some wine, but she'd only turned some water into some sort of juice that had gone slightly off, and he did not think that was likely to help.

Naftaly indicated the spread left on the table before himself and the old woman by one of the Tobot . . . the one that seemed a little better with magic than the other. "What do you call this, then?"

"I call it lentils," she said, "and I say to hell with it."

"A lot of people are liable to die tonight, and you're fussed there's no chicken for your dinner," Naftaly said.

"How is that different than any other day we've had the past few months?" she grumped. "Death on the horizon, always. It grows stale, if you ask me, and everyone is always telling me I should be grateful for a crust of bread and a lousy blanket: well, I'm not. We should have proper houses, you and I, with real chicken, and clean clothes, and little children making a mess in the garden." She tossed down a piece of bread. "I'm tired of being told I should be grateful for nothing."

Naftaly thought about that. He'd never felt a desire to change diapers or have a house of his own: somehow, even his eyes had never been able to see that far. What he wanted was simpler: to be useful, to anyone. He rubbed at his shoulder. It ached, a phantom pain that hadn't completely faded with the vision.

"Well," he said, picking up a lenticular drumstick. "I suppose this way is easier on the chicken."

Forty-Five

WHEN THE COURSER returned to Barsilay at sundown she found the floor puddled. "How many times did you have to douse him?" she asked the Alaunt.

"Lost count," he said. "Are you taking over here? I'm meant to be on duty at the gate."

"Go," she said. "I don't need you." She closed the wall and came to stand before Barsilay. "It's nearly sundown," she told him.

He was drenched head-down, his wet clothes clung to his form everywhere, sticking to the angles of his broken legs. "Well?" she asked. "What will you do?"

He wet his lips. "Come closer," he said. "Unless you want me to shout it."

She came closer, leaned over him. He whispered a word in her ear. She looked at him oddly. "What does that mean?"

"Marah wouldn't risk using a Mazik word," she said. "Someone might guess it." And he whispered again a word she'd never heard before.

The Courser repeated it in her own mind, twice, three times.

"You've been helpful," she said.

"It's sundown now," he said. "I can feel it." His eyes fluttered closed, and he let out a sigh. He would sleep, now, and die.

"Not quite yet," she said, and pressed two fingers to the space between his eyes.

He opened his eyes, because she'd given him just enough discomfort to keep him from sleeping. "You gave me your word."

She took in the look of betrayal on his face. He'd believed her, truly. She felt a pang of guilt; Maziks did not break their word, as a rule, which is why they seldom gave it. She said, "I lied."

After a moment he laughed, long and hard and false. "You stupid wretch. Very well. Consign me to the void. I'll pave the way for both of us."

She said, "What do you mean?"

His eyes were running tears down his bloodied face, but still his smile never faltered. "What use do you think Tarses will have for you when he finds his idiot Courser held this under her nose and never noticed?"

Then he tore open the collar of his shirt, revealing a mark on his shoulder, the shoulder he'd goaded her into injuring every day, but which was now whole, and bore the mark of the House of Luz. He hissed, "Tarses will be the one who comes to kill me. And when he sees this, no blade-arm will be enough to save you."

+ + + + + +

TOBA BET SMOOTHED the front of the dress Naftaly had embellished, one of her Barsilay-made frocks. It was a blue silk with the high neckline that she preferred and Barsilay found appalling. "You look like . . ." he'd said, after he'd crafted it. "What are those ladies who don't marry, and they live all together and make cakes?"

"Nuns," Toba had said, all those weeks ago. "You mean nuns, and no I don't."

Naftaly had embroidered the bodice, to hide the fact that neither Toba nor Asmel was capable of creating something suitable for a wedding. The stitches were too large, but he'd created a geometric design that mirrored the walls of the alcalá, and Toba Bet thought it was really quite lovely, in its way. On her breast lay the safira that contained Asmel's magic, its weight heavy on her neck.

Asmel himself lingered behind her, his eyes back to their normal shape, for the moment, courtesy of an illusion of Naftaly's, though he warned they would not hold long.

"Marah," he'd said, when he'd seen Toba Bet, and then shaken the daze from his eyes. "Forgive me."

She'd examined her own reflection, looking for traces of the woman she'd seen in Asmel's memories, and finding none. "Am I like her?" she asked.

"No," he said. "No, you are not."

She cast her eyes away from her own face, fingering one of the pearls set in her ears. "You do not owe Tsidon loveliness," Asmel told her.

"If I'm to die," Toba Bet said, "I shall do it with my head up. Not in a sack." Her breath hitched in a little catch of emotion. "What will become of me? Will I rejoin Toba, or simply . . . cease?"

Asmel made to answer, but she said, "Do not lie to spare my feelings. I deserve the truth."

"The truth," he said, stroking his palm with his thumb. "The truth is, I don't know. I've never once heard of a buchuk who existed as long as you have."

"So either is possible," she said. "I'm not sure it makes a difference, to be honest. Either way I stop existing as myself. Although I suppose you would say that I already don't properly exist, as myself. I'm only an image in a mirror."

Asmel said, "I would not say that."

\+ \+ \+ \+ \+ \+

THE OTHERS WERE gone, all of them; the Conde, still unconscious, had been shoved through a gate back to the pomegranate grove in Rimon, where he would either be clever enough to make his way to the city, or pungent enough to make his way into the belly of the wolves. The other Toba had been sent ahead along with Elena, Naftaly, and the old woman to the hills above P'ri Hadar.

It was yet another thing Toba Bet envied her counterpart, that she'd gone clear across the sea in a blink, overlooking a city she'd never see, one of the jewels of the world, according to Alasar. It was safer for them to assemble there, far from La Cacería's reach, and from there they would rescue Barsilay.

Rescuing Asmel came last.

Asmel and Toba came up with four escape routes, depending on the locations of Tsidon's Alaunts: the passage in the northern wall that led to the mikveh stream; a concealed doorway in the observatory; the window in the kitchen; and a hidden stairway leading from the cellar.

From one of those exits, Asmel would make his way to the mikveh stream, where Naftaly would be waiting with the book to open a gate.

It was a weak plan. All of them knew it.

"Why not take him to P'ri Hadar with the others?" Elena had asked.

"If I'm not present for the wedding, everything collapses," Asmel had said. "They will expect to see me here, waiting for Barsilay. La Cacería must continue to believe that is my aim, or else they will shift their own plan. If they think there's any hope of Barsilay being rescued, they'll kill him, whether it breaks the engagement or not. He's too important to be allowed to escape."

It was, Toba had concluded unhappily, the truth.

"Don't know what you're so fussed over," the old woman had said. "Even if they catch him, we have the book, don't we? It's the key to any door. As long as we have that, none of us can be caught or held. Can we use it to see Baobab?"

"If we survive the day," Asmel had said, "you may go wherever you wish."

A knock rang out on the gate below. Toba Bet squeezed her eyes shut and shuddered. "Naftaly's asleep," she said. "They've begun." She turned toward the door, and Asmel caught her shoulders. "Toba. If you have the chance to escape, you must take it. There may yet be a doorway for you to step through."

She laughed softly. "You don't believe that any more than I do."

Asmel closed his eyes, his fingers clutching her arms, his breath shaking.

"In the void," she asked, "is there pain?

He trembled. "No pain," he said.

She nodded, swallowed, lied. "All right. Then I shall not fear it."

Toba Bet opened the alcalá gate, where Tsidon was flanked by a horde of Maziks, all of them masked; black cloths covering their faces from their eyes downward. At the sight of them, Toba Bet quailed.

"Well, my bride," Tsidon said cheerfully. "Let's be wed."

+ + + + + + +

THE SANDS IN the hourglass on Naftaly's hand were down to nothing when Toba put him asleep, and he found Barsilay in a pool of blood.

Naftaly scrambled to his side; the Mazik was barely conscious, and his breath was ragged.

"What's happened?" Naftaly said, trying to discover where the blood was coming from. Rolling Barsilay off his side, he saw with a sickening horror that his entire left arm had been severed at the shoulder.

Naftaly's hands were covered with blood; the wound was fresh. "This isn't real," he said. "This isn't really happening to you."

"I'm afraid it is," Barsilay said. "I'm sorry. I tried everything else. I wanted so badly to see you one last time, before the end. This was the only way."

Naftaly followed Barsilay's eyes downward and moved the man's collar aside. The mark should have been gone, part of the severed limb, but instead it had only moved closer to the center of his chest. "She must be very angry right now. Didn't even work."

"It's all right," Naftaly said, trying to soothe him to the point of listening. "I have the book. I went where you showed me."

"I'm glad," he said.

"No, listen to me: We've found a way to save you. You must wake. Wake up and call for Toba. She'll be able to come for you."

"I don't want her," Barsilay said. "I like you so much better."

"Listen to me! She's the one that's going to free you—I can't! Open your eyes and call for her!"

"I can't," he said. "Even if I wanted to. I've no strength."

"Barsilay!" Naftaly barked.

He cracked an eye open. "Now who told you to call me that?"

"I've told you already—I'm with your Adon Sof'rim! If you wake and call Toba, she'll come and free you."

"My friend," he said. "There isn't enough magic in the worlds to save me now. If I wake, I go to my unbroken death."

"You don't know that for certain," Naftaly said. "Please. If you wake, she'll come for you, and then you'll be under the sky."

Barsilay grimaced. "But you aren't real. You're only . . . a figment."

He put his hands on Barsilay's face. "Look at me. Look at me! I am flesh and blood, and I am trying like hell to save you."

Naftaly sat with a palm on Barsilay's chest, marking the ragged rise and fall of it, and willing it to continue. For several seconds, it halted.

Naftaly lowered his forehead to Barsilay's breast and wept. After a few moments, he felt Barsilay's fingers in his hair. His voice was little more than a rasp, and he said, "If I wake, what will you give me?"

"Anything you damn well please," Naftaly said.

Barsilay laughed a little. "Only a fool would make so terrible a bargain."

"Lucky for you, that's just what I am."

Barsilay managed to still himself a bit, and he stroked his thumb beneath Naftaly's lower lip. "Fools and brown eyes," he said, "have always been my weakness."

He vanished.

+ + + + + +

"WELL?" DEMANDED ELENA. "The boy's been asleep a quarter hour, shouldn't something have happened by now?"

"I don't know," Toba said.

"The moon will be up any minute," Elena said.

Toba translated for the old woman, who replied, "We're all aware of that."

"We should wake him," Elena said. "And flee now; this is a lost cause."

"If you wake him now, he'll never forgive you," the old woman said. "And tell her to keep her voice down."

"If you wake him now, *I'll* never forgive you," Toba said. But she'd felt a pull, somewhere within her, subtle at first, but now painful. "He's done it. Barsilay's calling for me."

"Shouldn't the boy be awake?" the old woman said again.

"Maybe my spell hasn't run its course yet," Toba said, laying the book on the ground. "I'm going. I have to go now."

"Toba," Elena said, taking her by the arm, but Toba shook her off. "Would you try to stop me again? Now?"

"Little one," Elena said.

"Look after Naftaly," Toba said. "Wake him, if you can." And she knelt on the ground and began to read, feeling the pull of Barsilay's command on the magic that ran through every part of her.

From the center of the book, the gate shot up into the heavens. With one foot, Toba stepped across the book. Then, with one foot in each place, she reached down for the book, and lifted it through.

Toba stepped through and found herself in the midst of a horror.

The smell gagged her, and if she hadn't already closed the book she'd have been tempted to flee back through the gate, but Asmel had told her to close it the second she arrived, because leaving it open for more than a moment might collapse the building.

The entire floor was coated in blood.

Without the gate there was no light, and she struggled to activate the light-stone she'd brought in her pocket.

"It was true," came a voice she knew to be Barsilay's, though it hardly sounded like him. He rasped a rattling breath that made Toba's hair stand on end. "I did not believe it."

"Can you stand?"

She was near enough to see him now, in a heap on the floor in the same clothes he'd been wearing the last time she'd seen him. His collar was caked with blood, some of it fresh; his hair hung lank over his gaunt face; he'd been tortured, and he'd been starved, and Toba saw that both his legs were broken. He'd never be able to bear his own weight.

Several feet away was a second, smaller shape on the floor: Barsilay's left arm. She struggled not to faint at the sight of it, elegant fingers curled upward toward the ceiling. His hand, that had made her so many banquets, crafted her fine dresses, set a salamander on her shoulder.

"Are you bound in some way?" she choked out, but his eyes had rolled back and he made no answer.

"Don't you dare die now," she said. She hoisted his remaining arm over her shoulder and dragged him to the center of the room, to be as far from the walls as she could manage in the tiny cell, and deposited him there. Setting the light next to the book, she began to read, her voice trembling, until the gate bolted up through the tower, which began to quake. Stones began to rain down around them.

From the corner, a shadow rose from the floor: a shade, Toba thought, and then realized it was too solid. It was a woman, stepping out of the dark, who tilted her head slightly as a bird might do. "I know you," she said, and then her arm made the shape of a sword.

The silver of the gate pierced the floor and then the ceiling: the tower would be down around their ears in a moment, if it wasn't closed.

Barsilay's eyes were open again, glassy with fear, and he whispered, "Kill me and flee."

Toba ran through every contingency she could think of in the time it took the Mazik to cross the room . . . in every case, something would have to be left, either Barsilay, the book, or herself. A stone fell close enough to the Mazik to make her jump out of the way.

Summoning the strength of her will, Toba flung Barsilay through the gate.

Before she could reach for the book, the Mazik blinked across the room and slammed it shut.

✦ ✦ ✦

TOBA BET BARELY understood her own wedding. The man who stood before her, reciting blessings in Old Mazik, wore the same mask as the rest, and Toba did not know if he was some sort of holy man or if he was simply the soldier who had drawn the short straw. A glass of wine passed between herself and Tsidon. Toba Bet sipped it, and wondered if it might be poisoned, and hoped it was.

It was not.

The only part of the ceremony Toba Bet understood was when the Mazik took the glass of wine they'd drained and changed it to a piece of parchment, covered in Mazik writing: the Raskem. Toba Bet could only read parts of it, but it was clear she looked at some kind of ketubah. The man handed Tsidon a pen. He approached the document, but then held back. "In this case," he said, "I believe the lady should sign first."

Forty-Six

THE OLD WOMAN was shaking Naftaly violently when he opened his eyes, and Elena was scowling at the place where the gate had been. On his hand, the hourglass had vanished.

"How long did I sleep?" he asked. "Where is Toba?"

"Ages," the old woman said, "and she hasn't returned yet."

He sat up with the old woman's help. The sun was down; the moon had not yet risen, but he felt the pull of it, as if it were close. It was a sensation he'd never been aware of on the mortal side, and he wondered if the moon was different here, somehow, or if he was.

A star shot into the sky beside Elena, who lunged for it just in time to catch the body that came hurtling through. If Naftaly hadn't just now seen the man, he wouldn't have recognized him from his earlier dreams: he was little more than skin and bones and blood, everywhere. While Elena struggled under his weight, the light of the gate pulled back into the earth and was gone.

"Where is Toba?" Elena was demanding, but Barsilay's eyes were closed. She repeated her question, and the old woman said, "For heaven's sake, he can't answer."

Elena lowered him to the rocky ground, and the old woman swore at the sight of him.

"Open," Elena commanded the space where the gate had been. "Open again." And then more in Zayiti. Naftaly knelt at Barsilay's injured side, where his wound was seeping blood into the ground. "Elena," he begged, "you have to do something for him."

In response, she grabbed Naftaly by the arms. "Dream. Tell the buchuk not to . . . to die. We must save *one*."

"She isn't asleep," the old woman said. "He can't."

"Try!" she wailed.

"Elena, he's dying!"

"I don't care!" she shouted, rounding on him. "I don't care if he dies!"

"You don't care about anything!" the old woman countered. "Toba is dead. Without the book, Asmel is dead, too, and the rest of us are trapped here, and you would let die the only person who might give us aid?"

"I don't care if *we* die, either," Elena said darkly.

The old woman turned to her slowly. "Would you let this man die," she said softly, her hands on Barsilay's matted hair, "for spite?"

Elena was weeping; she'd been weeping, all along, and trying to conceal it, and Naftaly reached up and clutched at her skirt. "Please," he said. He could feel Barsilay's blood seeping through his clothes. In a minute it would be too late, if it wasn't already. Below them was a city he could not see, filled with Maziks, dreaming their own dreams with their own best beloveds, in gardens or in palaces, dancing and listening to music, never knowing how lucky they were to dream freely. Under his hands, Barsilay was growing cold.

Elena scrubbed angrily at her own face. "He is Mazik," she said. "I don't know how to help him."

"Then do what you would do for a man," Naftaly said. "Maybe it will be enough."

She looked at Barsilay's unconscious form, his extreme pallor, his wound, and tsked. Finally, she turned to the old woman and said, "Make fire."

There was little to burn so high in the hills; a few scrubby twigs and the old woman's headscarf, which she used for kindling, leaving her thin white hair shining in the dark. She and Naftaly held Barsilay's prone body while Elena pressed the old woman's heated knife to his wound, but he was too insensible to react. After, they stood looking at him in the firelight, his chest barely rose, but he breathed.

"Will he live?" Naftaly asked.

"I don't know," Elena said. "He lost much blood."

Naftaly smoothed Barsilay's bloody hair off his face. "The stars are out," he said. "Don't you wish to see, old friend?" To Elena, he said, "Is there nothing more we can do?"

"For a man? No. For a Mazik?" She shrugged helplessly.

"Maybe he needs magic," the old woman suggested.

Naftaly looked up to her. "I don't know. He's made of it, isn't he?"

"Asmel pulled his out," Elena said. "He lived."

"Yes, but it weakened him, I think. He seemed old."

"He is old," Elena said, but the old woman just shook her head.

Naftaly leaned over Barsilay, whose legs were propped on Elena's satchel to keep whatever blood he had left flowing through his vital organs, which Elena had said was what you would do for an injured man, though who knew what vital organs a Mazik had.

He could not have been so different. He had a heart, Naftaly knew, because he'd felt it, and blood, because he'd seen it, and lungs, because he'd heard his breath. And he had magic, somehow, flowing inside him.

Leaning down, he put his lips to Barsilay's, and exhaled, and willed his breath to fill itself with whatever trace of magic he possessed.

Barsilay's chest rose, and he drew a great breath, and his eyes cracked open. Seeing Naftaly, he croaked, "It's you." Naftaly could only weep.

"I was so afraid," Barsilay said, "that you weren't real."

\+ + + + + + +

THE MAZIK WOMAN stepped over the book while Toba watched helplessly; the woman's boots were bloody halfway up her shins. "I suppose I should thank you for taking him, seeing as he was about to get me killed."

Toba circled around the Mazik, though the room had no door that she could see. She had little magic and little strength and no hope of help. She gestured at the blood on the floor. "Did you do all this to him?"

The woman said, "Yes."

"Why?"

"He knew things. Was it always you who dreamt of him? No, your face says not. Who, then, I wonder?"

Toba gave no answer, but did her best to maintain the distance between them. The Mazik had two hands now, rather than a hand and a blade, but the blade could be back any moment. She wouldn't need one to kill her, in any case.

"Toba b'Navia," the woman said. "I know who you are. Aren't you supposed to be marrying Tsidon?"

"I had an errand to run first," Toba replied.

"I don't understand this," the woman said. "I don't understand why he's arranged this marriage. It makes no sense. What's he want with some bastard from . . ." Something about her eyes changed. "Atalef knew. You aren't some random bastard, are you?"

Toba said, "I'm not sure what you're getting at."

The woman said, "Come here."

Toba said, "You're not serious."

On the floor, there was a pail filled with liquid. "Put your hand in this."

"Are you mad?"

"Do it, or I'll kill you." The woman stepped away from the pail. "It's only water."

Toba doubted this very much, but she did not seem to have a choice, so she dipped her fingers inside. "There," she said. "Are you satisfied?"

The woman was still watching. "Show me your hand."

Toba held it out. "It's wet," she said. "You saw me put it in." But then she realized: the water had salt mixed in.

Her eyes shot up to the Mazik's expecting triumph: she'd caught her; Toba had failed the test, revealed herself. But the other woman looked very unhappy indeed. "I know who you are," she said, sounding as if she were speaking on her way to the gallows.

"And who is that?"

Sadly, the Mazik said, "The left hand of the new age."

Toba said, "I have no intention of being the left hand of anything."

The Mazik took the pail of water and swirled her own hand in it before holding it out to Toba, skin healthy and whole. "He missed your birth—you were lucky. But in the end, you won't have a choice. He will hold your will in the palm of his hand, and there is nothing you can do about it."

"Who do you mean?"

"Your father," she said. "Our father. The Caçador of Rimon."

Toba said, "You're mistaken."

"We dreamt together so often, and then you disappeared. Don't you remember? You promised to save me from my wicked father. Your wicked father couldn't find you, but now he has, and he'll make you his heir."

Toba said, "My father wants me dead."

"Why go to all the trouble of creating you, only to kill you?" She upended the pail onto the ground, where the water mixed with the blood already on the floor. Walking toward Toba, she said, "Do you know why he chose your mother? Have you not understood, 'til now? The Caçador needed a half-mortal heir to do what he could not, to rule where he could not. But he needed a mortal with Mazik blood to carry his heir to term, so he found a line descended from a Mazik woman."

"You mean Marah?"

"He never told me her name," the woman said. "Only that he sought out her daughters, and used them, and killed them."

Toba stared at the Mazik's outstretched hand, so like her own, and understood the scope of all she'd misunderstood. Marah had created a legacy to carry on her work, to repair the fabric of the worlds. And Tarses had attempted to take that legacy and fold it into his own.

"How many?" Toba asked.

"Before us? None survived; none, and now suddenly he has two, and he has a choice. I know his plan for us. But he doesn't know you're here, and I can let you go. Give me the killstone, and we both go free."

Toba looked doubtful. "I won't use it on your friend Barsilay," the Mazik said. "I don't care if he lives or dies. Give it to me, and I can save us both."

There was no lie that would serve. "I don't have it," Toba said, and the Mazik's face contorted. "It was stolen."

"Is that a lie?" she asked.

"It's the truth."

"Then you go to Tsidon," the Mazik said. "As you've sworn to do, and you will sign your Raskem and give our father your name and your will, and you will kill me."

"Sign," Toba murmured, and then she understood everything: this woman was Marah's heir, as much as she was. The same magic ran in her veins; magic that had spanned so many generations and then died out, until Tarses revived it. "I know your name, Tsifra N'Dar."

The Mazik flinched. Toba said, "There must be another way for us. I have no wish to kill you."

"There is no other way," the Mazik said. She'd circled back to the book, which lay again at her feet, and she again made her arm a blade. "He intends you to replace me. And I don't wish to die."

As swiftly as a hawk, with whatever will she had left, Toba leapt forward and tore the last page from the book, and stuffed it into her mouth, just as the other woman cut off her head.

✦ ✦ ✦

TOBA BET TREMBLED as she drank her wine, as Tsidon pushed the veil back from her face, as he passed her the pen she would use to make the marriage final. Her fingers gripped the pen, and she dipped it into the pot of ink the color of molten gold set before her.

She closed her eyes and watched herself step through the gate, hurl Barsilay from his cell, felt the moment she understood the marriage had never been La Cacería's goal, nor had her death . . . what her father wanted was her true name, signed in her own hand. Her name, which would bind her to her father's will for as long as she lived, bound to serve the man who had ordered Asmel silenced, who had forced Marah to the void, who had drowned every mortal and Mazik in Luz.

You'll be the one to live, after all, Toba told her. *Don't waste it.*

Then Toba was dead, and she was all that remained.

She felt the moment she slipped into the void, the unmitigated terror of nonexistence, as her soul snuffed out. She would have turned away, if she could, but it was impossible. It was happening to Toba herself.

The ring on her finger loosened its grip.

Toba Bet—now Toba the Singular—stumbled, and Tsidon clicked his heels on the ground, a mark of annoyance. She was taking too long.

She felt something in her mouth. A leaf of paper.

Her eyes went to Asmel's. He would not know that Toba was dead, the Toba he preferred. He couldn't know the book had been lost, except for the one page she held behind her closed lips.

Tsidon waited, as she held the pen in her hand. "Don't you wish your cousin returned?" he murmured. In the east, the sun had dipped below the horizon. Soon, the moon would become visible.

Toba ran her thumb along the edge of the pen, and felt a shudder go through herself: the ring slipped off her finger and landed on the ground, chiming like a tiny bell, and then lay still.

In the space between one breath and the next, Toba let herself become her name; not one, but many; a hundred birds the color of air. While Tsidon shouted a curse and flung himself at the safira that had fallen from her neck, she felt her wings beat, she was a flock, a swarm, and she took Asmel in her grasp and flew into the sky.

Forty-Seven

THE CLARITY OF Toba's death spurred her on, a flurry of feathers and wings and unbidden cries from her many throats. Asmel was weak in her arms, and silent, until he became aware of Toba's intended destination. "You mustn't—" he said.

But Toba paid him no heed. She paid nothing any heed—she felt nothing but terror, and an irresistible call to the last place—the only place—she'd been safe. Beneath her, the pomegranate grove came into view, and she descended.

Through her multitude of eyes, she saw the gate open, the light shoot into the sky. She was nearly there, and she could pass through in the sky without descending farther.

An arrow pierced one of her selves and she felt pain and then the death of that other small part of herself, but it was such a small pain compared to what she'd already felt that she found she could endure it. Still, more arrows came. The gate was guarded, she saw, by some twenty Maziks; half mounted Alaunts, half kneeling bowmen, and they would capture her, if they could, or kill her, if they could not. In either case, they would kill Asmel.

She would not let them kill Asmel.

The arrows flew, and she flew closer, until she could see her multitudes reflected in the eyes of the Alaunts. Two of her selves covered Asmel's ears with their small bodies, and then she began to scream. She screamed the horror of the void, of unbroken death, and she wove her magic into the scream, such that every Mazik on the ground dropped his bow, or fell from his horse, reeling in terror, covering his ears and weeping. Those who were slow to lose consciousness died, their hearts refusing to beat in that terrified space. Those who lived were altered afterward, and were never able to hold a weapon again, or to sing, or to dance.

Toba took Asmel through the gate. She took him into the city where she'd been born, to the house she'd lived in, where she'd studied with her grandfather and her grandmother had told her stories about the faraway days of King Solomon, who kidnapped the King of the Maziks to build the Temple, only afterward he did a turnabout and turned Solomon into a beggar and sent him to wander the world so he would understand how to tell truth from illusion.

The street outside her home was empty, and she set Asmel down as gently as she could, leaving him to stand surrounded by a halo of birds and the sounds of wings. He held up a hand and one of her selves lighted on it. Already she was feeling less woman and more bird. She was free, this way, and safe, and strong enough to protect Asmel.

He said, "Can you restore yourself? I cannot help you." Already the glamour on his eyes had faded, leaving him only an improbably handsome man.

The rest of her flung aside the gate and flew into the courtyard, leaving Asmel to follow, while she lighted in the trees, and along the walls, and on the roof.

"We ought not to be here," he said.

There was laundry hanging in the courtyard. And within the house, she could see the flicker of candles. There were people living there, in her house. People who had stolen her house, her bed, whatever clothing she'd had to leave behind. They'd stolen Elena's favorite mixing spoon, and her grandfather's best reading lamp, and her extra stash of ink that she kept hidden in a drawer behind her stockings. They'd wanted these things, and they'd taken them, and now they lit candles at night, as if they suffered no pangs of conscience that would force them to sit huddled in the dark, considering the wicked things they'd done.

Alasar had told her once that all the people of Sefarad lived atop the bones of their ancestors, that if you dug down, you would find streets and buildings and houses of the Visigoths and the Romans and the Phoenicians, going back to the time when men cut their meat with bronze knives and farther still. Toba had not died in this house, but her bones were here, sure as if she had.

She felt a wave of rage pass through her, enough to overcome her terror.

Asmel said, "My mind wanes with the moon, and La Cacería will be coming. Marshal yourself. We have a great deal of work to do, and none of it is here."

\+ + + + + +

TSIFRA N'DAR, SECOND living bearer of her name, was about to have a very unpleasant conversation with the Caçador of Rimon. In the space of five minutes, she'd lost the Luz gate, his presumptive heir, and the heir of Luz himself.

Her intention was that he would learn only of one of these. She'd burned the body of Toba b'Tarses, and no one knew of the Mark of Luz but her. She supposed she had Toba to thank for it, a debt eternally unpaid.

She entered the room where her father sat, a blue jewel in his hand. He had it, the safira, the killstone, and her heart sank.

She did the required obeisance, which nauseated her as much as always, and rose, and presented him with what was left of the book.

He flipped the pages, slowly, until he came to the end. "How did you get this?"

She'd considered this long and hard. If she tried to cast all responsibility from herself, he would know she was lying: better to take a small measure of blame than none, and this part seemed safest. "One of his companions came to his rescue. A man, I didn't ask his name before I killed him."

"The body?"

"Immolated," she said, and the Caçador's eyes flashed.

"I was angry," she said. "He took the last page, before he died, and sent it away."

"And you thought his identity wouldn't be useful?"

"Forgive me," she said.

"I don't."

She cast her eyes down. This would not end well.

"All the men sent to guard the gate are dead or mad," he said.

Tsifra's eyes snapped up. She had not heard this.

"Based on the Lymer's testimony, it appears Toba killed them and escaped." He snapped the book shut. "She took Asmel with her."

She tried to school the emotion out of her face. It had been Toba she'd killed. The woman had confirmed as much. Had she killed an imposter? Or was it the imposter that had fooled Tsidon?

She would puzzle it out later, somehow.

"I'm not sure what Toba thinks she can do from that side of the gate," she said. "Asmel will die."

He held up the safira. "No," he said. "I don't think he will. This is a fake." He tossed it to her, and she caught it neatly; it hummed with power and was hot in her hands.

She was not to question him, but she did, anyway. "Are you sure? This feels—"

"It does, doesn't it? But I knew Marah, and this magic is not hers. This safira belongs to Asmel. He made it to fool Tsidon."

She wondered if Tsidon were still alive, or if Tarses had killed him when he'd realized. It was not the sort of mistake one survived in La Cacería.

"Toba has the killstone," Tarses said, holding out one hand. "I should like it back." He leaned forward in his chair. "And if Barsilay's ally took the last page of the book, Barsilay will either have it or know where it is."

She nodded. "If Asmel is in the mortal realm with no magic, he'll be easily slain," she said. "And Barsilay is not likely to be moving quickly, wherever he is. He's injured."

"The book is the priority," he said. "It's the mission I would prefer for you, but the fact remains there is no one else I can send after Asmel."

"I will go," she said, "at the next moon. It won't take long."

"They may have gone a great distance by the next moon," he warned.

Tsifra made no reply. She was very sure of her ability to find Toba, because she was in possession of another piece of information that the Caçador was not. She decided it was not in her best interest to share that secret with him; she hadn't yet decided what to do with it. The fact was that Toba b'Tarses was the child of the Caçador, and Toba b'Tarses had guessed the Courser's name—which she could only do if she carried that name herself. "I will begin my preparations," she said.

"Not just yet," he said. "First, you will attend upon me at my wedding."

"I had not realized," she said. "And . . . who will be your bride?"

He smiled. "I marry Queen Oneca of Rimon."

She hesitated. "Queen," she said.

"Relam b'Gidon rules no longer. This very night he has ridden his horse into the sea."

"And Prince Ardón?" she said, and then, too late, remembered the Peregrine's injunction to be careful asking questions.

"Both the princes slit their own throats in grief," he replied.

She bowed her head. It had begun earlier than she'd expected, and it worried her. She did not know what it meant that such long-laid plans had changed, besides the obvious conclusion: Tarses was panicking. Whether this was because his preferred heir had thwarted him, or because the killstone was out of his reach, she did not know. Tarses had changed the succession because he felt Oneca would make a better tool than Ardón. With Oneca, he could sire the next heir of Rimon.

"In that case, you've made a lovely match," she said, because it was what he would wish to hear.

"Yes," Tarses said. "Yes." And he cast his eyes toward the window, where the sun had risen on the first day of the new age. Reading his disinterest as dismissal, she slowly backed out of the room, never taking her eyes from him, because Tsifra N'dar was many things, but she was not a fool.

"Tsifra," he said, and she shuddered at the sound of her name. "You made a mistake today."

"I haven't forgotten," she said. "Father."

\+ + + + + + +

ELENA FELT AS if her spirit had left her body, leaving nothing behind but old bones. She pulled herself from the grip of gravity and stood, watching as Naftaly helped Barsilay to sit up enough to get a better view of their surroundings. The moon had just emerged and the four of them cast long shadows on the barren ground.

"Where are we?" he asked.

"North of P'ri Hadar," Naftaly said. "Asmel sent us here with the book." The old woman handed him her waterskin, and he helped Barsilay to drink. He'd need more water than they had, Elena knew. They would worry about that later. There was still the matter of his legs, but she didn't think that even she possessed the strength to set them.

"Asmel sent you here?" Barsilay asked. "Where is he?"

Elena didn't think it wise to give so much bad news to a man so nearly in the grave, but she gave it anyway, because none of the others had the will to do it. Toba was dead. Toba's buchuk was dead, and Asmel was both magicless and dead. Without the book, there was no way to save any of them. He absorbed the information with little outward reaction. Then again, he probably lacked the energy to do more than listen.

When he did speak again, Barsilay said, "I don't know what happened. But this isn't P'ri Hadar."

"You're weak and it's dark," the old woman said. "Are you sure?"

Barsilay scanned the area. "I've spent quite a lot of time in P'ri Hadar," he said. "And this isn't it." He leaned heavily on the boy and took a handful of rocks and earth and held it near his face. "It's as I thought: we're still in Rimon. You'll see Mount Sebah when the clouds clear."

"But, why would he have sent us here?"

"He must have made a mistake," the old woman said.

Barsilay said, "Asmel is incapable of such a mistake."

"Perhaps he *was*," the old woman said. "He wasn't in such a good state last we saw him."

"Have a care for the man's feelings," Naftaly said. "Please."

"It's all right," Barsilay said. "And at the moment it doesn't matter how we came to be here, in any case. Look: we're north of the city. Northeast, actually. The gate will be that way. If you start walking now, you will probably reach it before sunrise."

As the shadow of the moon passed over that part of the valley, the gate opened. "There," he said. "You see it?"

"Even if we managed to get past the guards," the old woman said, "we'd be back in Sefarad again. I'm not eager to be exiled from the place twice."

"I'm not sure you have a better option," Barsilay said. "The nearest safe city is Zayit, which is not close."

"Is that where you mean to go? All the way to Zayit?" Naftaly asked.

"There's really no other option," he said. "I can't cross the sea. I will have to go north, and you will have to go back through the gate."

"And what help will there be for you in Zayit?" the old woman asked.

Barsilay said, "I don't know. Perhaps none. But the Zayitis are no friends to La Cacería. At least they won't be waiting for me if I manage to get there."

"*If* you manage?" Naftaly said.

"My friend," Barsilay said. "You do not understand. La Cacería has the gate of Luz. They can go anywhere, instantly. If they have even the slightest inkling of where I am, I will be dead in the time it takes them to flick a few pages. There won't even be any warning."

"Then we'll have to make sure they don't develop the slightest inkling of where you are," Naftaly said. "I did not come all this way to abandon you on top of a mountain with two broken legs."

"Is this because of the mark?" the old woman asked, indicating the sigil on Barsilay's bare chest. "You're the heir to a big puddle with no people in it, is that right?"

He stared at her.

She sniffed. "Doesn't sound so impressive to me. Not sure why anyone would go to the trouble of killing you."

"Remind me, again, who you are?"

"Absolutely no one," she said. "I go with the boy, that's all."

"You must be very loyal," he said. "To have come here. But even without the mark of death upon my person, the road to Zayit is long. You are facing a journey of many weeks, in winter, and we haven't even any horses."

"Horses," the old woman said, "can be stolen."

Naftaly waited for Barsilay's next complaint. He took it as a mark of desperation that it did not come. Naftaly turned to Elena. "You'll want to return to Alasar," he said.

"If I stay here," she said, "Alasar won't know Toba is dead." She looked to Barsilay. "Will your legs heal?"

He said, "They always heal by the next day."

"And your magic? When will that return?"

He said, "That I don't know. This is as weak as I've ever been."

From the hills below them, a blue flame appeared, and then another, and then another, beginning in the center of the city and spreading out like a spiral, and up into the hills, and north, to the horizon. Barsilay swore quietly. "They've lit the signal fires."

"What does it mean?" Naftaly asked.

"It means," he said, "the King is dead."

They watched the signal fires flare and settle, in turn. The night was silent. Somewhere to the south, the shriek of an animal pierced it; some creature in a great deal of pain. Naftaly shuddered at the sound, and the old woman covered her ears.

Barsilay was struggling—and failing—to get to his feet. "I don't think we can afford to wait for my legs to heal, after all. Whatever Tarses is planning is happening now. The only thing that might save us is that we came north instead of south. We can flee without passing by the city."

To Elena, Naftaly said, "We'll have to make a litter for him."

From above, the sound of wings fluttered toward them. A bat, Elena thought crossly, and then she saw it could not be: its flight was too smooth. Barsilay held up a hand, not to warn the creature off, but to offer it a perch.

"Hello, Toba," he said.

A bird lighted on his hand; the size of a dove, but with talons like a hawk and feathers the color of dusk. In its beak, there was a folded slip of paper, which Barsilay took between two fingers, passing it off to Naftaly.

Barsilay's cracked lips broke into a smile. "Well, then, little friend. Not so dead after all."

Elena's heart caught in her chest.

"I don't suppose you can tell us what's happened," Barsilay said. Naftaly had taken the slip of paper and unfolded it, his eyes catching the blue light of the signal fires. "What did she bring?"

Naftaly said, "A beginning."

+ + + + + + +

THE FRACTION OF Toba that was with Barsilay would not last; but still she felt it, one bird among the hundred that sat perched in the courtyard of the house she'd been born inside. That tiny bit of Toba watched as her grandmother ordered Naftaly to bring branches to build a litter to carry Barsilay to Zayit, with nothing but the clothes on their backs and the single page of the gate of Luz she'd managed to save. She wondered how long she'd maintain an awareness of them. She would mourn it, when it was gone, as she'd mourned her other, older self: a loss of the multiplicity of perspectives that had made her feel stronger than her circumstances should have allowed.

It was that multiplicity—Toba as a hundred birds rather than one woman—that kept her fear in check. A hundred tiny Tobot were harder to kill than a single woman. As birds, she could fly away from harm.

From betrayal.

In that moment, all the faithlessness she'd endured sat on her feathered selves like so much filth, from her city, the entire mortal realm, which offered her no quarter. From her grandmother, who had bound her magic. From her father, who meant to steal it for himself. From her sister, who had killed her.

From Asmel, who had offered her to Tarses to save her counterpart.

Would he guard her, as he'd done the other woman, now that she was dead?

She imagined turning herself back, then, and finding the comfort she craved in Asmel's embrace, ignoring what he'd done. Ignoring the fact that he was bound to know the unbroken death she'd already experienced, and that when he did she would be left alone. Unless her father found her first, and took her will, and made her his monster.

She did not change back.

Asmel turned from the house, from Toba, and walked out through the gate, and because she did not want to be alone, she followed: a flock of sorrow following a broken Mazik down the streets of a stolen city.

Glossary

Note: ç (c-cedilla) is pronounced as in Medieval Spanish: "ts."

Adon: Lord. A title among Mazik nobles.

Alcalá: Castle.

Alcázar: Palace.

Amapola: Extract of the opium poppy.

Anusim: Jews forced to convert to another religion under extreme duress.

Atalef: Bat.

Auto-da-fé: Trial by faith. The Inquisition could use this to mean torture or burning.

Buchuk: Literally, twin.

La Cacería: Literally, the hunt. The Mazik organization charged with protecting the gates, limiting contact with the mortal world, and bolstering the rule of King Relam of Rimon.

The Caçador: The Huntsman; head of La Cacería.

Conversos: Converts, either sincere or forced.

Genizah: A graveyard for books and other documents that might contain the Divine Name. Such items are treated respectfully and not destroyed.

Infanta: Princess. Male version is Infante.

La'az Sefardi: The language spoken by Jews in Sefarad.

Mezuzah: A scroll affixed to the doorpost of a Jewish home, containing the Shema.

Mikveh: Jewish ritual bath, used by men and women for a variety of reasons.

Milliarès: The currency of Sefarad.

Mourner's Kaddish: An Aramaic prayer recited after a death. A person will recite Kaddish for eleven months following the death of a parent, and again on the anniversary of the death each year.

Nagid: Title for the head of a particular Jewish community.

Ninth of Av: In Hebrew, Tisha B'Av, a date associated with several major calamities, including the destruction of the first and second temples, the crushing of the Bar Kokhba rebellion, and the massacre at Betar. Later, this date has also been associated with more modern events that occurred near the ninth of Av, including the start of the First Crusade, and the Jewish expulsions from England, France, and Spain.

The Rambam: Also known as Moses ben Maimon or Maimonides, a Sephardi Jewish rabbi, philosopher, and physician, exiled from Spain after the Almohad conquest. He later became the personal physician of the Sultan Saladin. His most famous work is the *Guide for the Perplexed*.

Rashi: A style of Sephardi Hebrew script, originating from the fifteenth century. Named for the rabbinic commentator because it was often used in the printing of his Talmudic commentaries; also often used in printed Ladino.

Raskem: Mazik version of the Ketubah, a marriage contract.

Romaniot Jews: Greek-speaking Jews who resided in areas governed by the Byzantine Empire in the eastern Mediterranean.

The Shema: Judaism's central and most widely recited prayer.

Tekhelet dye: A blue dye used to color some of the strings in a tzizit (the number of blue strings is not widely agreed upon). The technique for making the dye was lost during the Middle Ages and tzizit have been left white since. In folklore, the mythical city of Luz is often said to have retained the knowledge of how to make tekhelet.

Tzizit: Fringed garment worn under the shirts of observant Jewish men.

Ziz: One of the three mythical giant beasts mentioned in Jewish scripture and folklore, the other two being the Leviathan and the Behemoth. The Ziz is the king of birds and is said to be able to blot out the sun with its enormous wings.

Further Reading

For those interested in Jewish folklore, the works of Howard Schwartz are extensive and diverse geographically and temporally; he also notes which folktales seem to have evolved from one another over time. Stories retold in his collections were an indispensable inspiration, notably:

"The Beggar King" (from *Elijah's Violin & Other Jewish Fairy Tales*)

"The City of Luz" (*Elijah's Violin*)

"The Demon Princess" (*Elijah's Violin*)

"King Solomon and Ashmodai" (from *Leaves from the Garden of Eden*)

"The Kiss of Death" (from *Lilith's Cave: Jewish Tales of the Supernatural*)

"The Palace Beneath the Sea" (from *Miriam's Tambourine: Jewish Folktales from Around the World*)

"The Princess Who Became the Morning Star" (*Miriam's Tambourine*)

"A Voyage to the Ends of the Earth" (*Miriam's Tambourine*)

Another source is Dan Ben-Amos's three volume *Folktales of the Jews.*

For those interested in the history of Sephardi Jews at the time of the expulsion, Jane Gerber's *The Jews of Spain*, Howard Sachar's *Farewell España*, Joseph Perez's *The Spanish Inquisition*, and Lu Ann Homza's anthology of sources *The Spanish Inquisition, 1478–1614* are all excellent.

Two other works that may be intriguing to a curious reader are Edward Kritzler's *Jewish Pirates of the Caribbean*, and David Gitlitz and Linda Kay Davidson's *A Drizzle of Honey: The Lives and Recipes of Spain's Secret Jews*.

For a better understanding of the movement and distribution of Jewish communities from the fifth through the seventeenth centuries, Haim Beinart's *Atlas of Medieval Jewish History* is invaluable.

For those interested in an elementary study of modern Ladino, Alla Markova's *Beginner's Ladino* is a helpful primer.

Acknowledgments

I owe a tremendous debt to all of the many people who helped bring *The Pomegranate Gate* into the world. First, Hannah Bowman, Lauren Bajek, and the rest of the team at Liza Dawson Associates for their support, advice, and for helping the series find two great homes.

Thanks to both of my wonderfully insightful editors, Amy Borsuk at Solaris/Rebellion and Sarah Guan at Erewhon; I've been so fortunate to work with you both. Thanks also to the rest of the team at Solaris/Rebellion: Jess Gofton, Chiara Mestieri, Sara Marchington, Lin Nagle, Sam Gretton, Gemma Sheldrake, and Micaela Alcaino; and to the team at Erewhon: Viengsamai Fetters, Martin Cahill, Kasie Griffitts, Cassandra Farrin, Kelsy Thompson, Rayne Stone, Samira Iravani, and Serena Malyon.

Special thanks to folklorist Howard Schwartz, whose compiled works of Jewish folklore have been a limitless inspiration.

Finally, thanks to my family for many years of encouragement and patience.

Staff Credits

Thank you for reading this title from Erewhon Books, publishing books that embrace the liminal and unclassifiable and championing the unusual, the uncanny, and the hard-to-define.

We are proud of the team behind The Mirror Realm Cycle by Ariel Kaplan:

Sarah Guan, Publisher
Diana Pho, Executive Editor
Viengsamai Fetters, Assistant Editor

Martin Cahill, Marketing and Publicity Manager
Kasie Griffitts, Sales Associate

Cassandra Farrin, Director
Leah Marsh, Production Editor
Kelsy Thompson, Production Editor

Alice Moye-Honeyman, Junior Designer
and the whole publishing team at Kensington Books!

Learn more about Erewhon Books and our authors at erewhonbooks.com.

Twitter: @erewhonbooks
Instagram: @erewhonbooks
Facebook: @ErewhonBooks

Read on for an excerpt from
book two in the
Mirror Realm Cycle

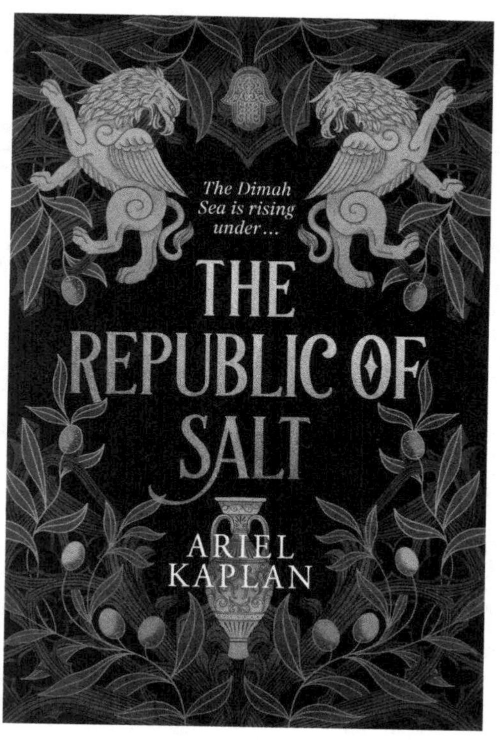

THE REPUBLIC OF SALT

Coming October 2024

Chapter One

It was three nights until the New Year, and in the mountains north of Mazik Rimon, Naftaly Cresques was laying on the ground beside two old women and a Mazik who was mostly dead. The full moon remained high in the sky, and somewhere to the south the gate to the mortal world shot like a beam of light into the sky. The autumn air left the four of them chilled, but not too chilled to sleep, or dream.

Naftaly was there entirely by accident.

He was supposed to be in P'ri Hadar; they were all meant to be in P'ri Hadar, but Asmel, the Lord of Books, had made a mistake. Only the day before he'd been forced to remove his own magic, an act which had left him weakened and with a failing memory. So when he'd opened the Gate of Luz, he'd accidentally sent Naftaly and his companions not to the Great City of the East, but only a few miles away from Asmel's alcalá in Rimon.

They'd been facing death in the alcalá. Here in the mountains, they were not much safer.

It was worse, even, than that. Naftaly's near-dead Mazik, Barsilay b'Droer, lately Naftaly's beloved and the Heir of Luz, had lost an arm and nearly bled to death on the pine-littered ground.

This was why they'd stayed the night in the mountains instead of fleeing north immediately. Elena, the younger of the old women—and in Naftaly's estimation, the cleverer—had stated rather emphatically that Barsilay, no matter his objections, could not be moved without killing him. She'd then convinced the two men and their elder woman companion to sleep a few hours, to marshal at least a little strength.

Whether Elena herself slept or not Naftaly was not sure, but as he rested his dreaming mind found itself called back into the city of Rimon, back to the garden of the King, in the shared dreamworld of the Maziks.

Only it was no longer the King's garden, Naftaly recalled, as he opened his eyes to the same courtyard he'd seen the night of the crown prince's oath-getting many weeks before. The King was dead, and his oldest son was also dead, so Naftaly assumed this must be a ceremony for the King's younger son, whose name Naftaly had never learned.

Flowers bloomed all around him, strange Mazik flowers that were silver and purple and orange the color of Barsilay's eyes. The dreamworld stars whirled overhead, and the white pergola in the courtyard seemed to glow in the pale light. The air smelled, Naftaly thought, faintly of pomegranates.

The place was full of anxious Maziks whispering to one another as they approached the courtyard, and Naftaly found himself very reluctantly carried along with the rest. He wanted badly to escape, but the Maziks were so tightly packed there was no easy way to slip out without causing a spectacle.

Naftaly assumed they had all been summoned as he had, and then he realized that Barsilay may have been summoned too, which would have been disastrous. But before he could go to look for him, all the paths into the courtyard were blocked by blue-clad Mazik guards, who moved at once to trap all the assembled Maziks inside.

From within the main pergola came a woman, very tall and dark-haired, with rubies across her forehead. To her left was a man whose orange eyes marked him as Luzite. A woman dressed in blue came and stood on the dais beside them, she put a hand to her own throat, which seemed to magnify her voice enough to be heard without shouting, though every Mazik assembled fell silent as soon as she appeared.

"The reign of Relam is over," she said. "You will give your oath to his blood and heir, the Queen of Rimon, long may she dream."

A great murmur went up, but the woman, who Naftaly supposed must be some sort of herald, continued: "The oath-getting will be not be dreaming. You will all swear your oath to our new Queen tomorrow at the royal Alcázar. Tomorrow you shall greet your Queen."

The Queen herself smiled, but only slightly. The man to her left let his eyes scan the crowd, and Naftaly was glad for once to be shorter than the people around him.

Someone near him whispered, "They say Relam rode into the sea."

Naftaly's eyes opened, and he was back in the mountains. Barsilay slept at his side; Naftaly thought of waking him, but decided the man was probably too weak to dream, and the immediate danger had passed, anyway. Elena, still sitting in the same position she'd been in earlier, said, "You had a bad dream?"

Elena, of course, knew that Naftaly's dreams were as real as most people's waking moments. A bad dream was no passing figment to be forgotten after breakfast.

"Yes," Naftaly said. "I think it was."

It was three nights until the new year, and in the mortal world Toba Bet had been a flock of birds so long she was beginning to forget what it meant to have hands.

She didn't miss them. Wings, she'd concluded, were the better choice: while hands could manipulate, wings provided escape, and escape was not a thing smartly given up.

The horror of her own death was never out of her mind. In the Mazik books Toba Bet had perused in Asmel's library, the question had been posed repeatedly: was one conscious the moment she entered the void, or did consciousness cease at that precise instant? The scope of the suffering—whether the void of non-existence was bad enough, or whether it was still worse, and you actually felt yourself inside it, however briefly—was something opined on for as long as Maziks had been writing books, which was long indeed. But the opinions put forth, no matter how well-reasoned, were merely philosophical. Or they had been, until Toba had died, and discovered the truth of the matter. Toba Bet had felt her other self—her original self, some might say her *truer* self—go into the void. The time between her death and the blotting from existence of her mind or spirit or consciousness was little more than an instant. But that instant had existed. Toba Bet had felt it, and she wasn't sure she would ever manage to stop thinking about it, like a whisper in her ear that would not quiet.

"You'd be more helpful as a person," Asmel muttered, which Toba Bet supposed was true. He'd traded his coat and splendid shoes and the ring he wore on his forefinger for simpler clothing and enough money to get them as far north as Barcino, or it would have, if Asmel had not been too much a Mazik to secure a spot in a cart.

This despite the fact that he had no magic. While his eyes were now a mortal's eyes, he remained too tall, too handsome, and his manner of speech too formal. Everyone seemed to be aware that he was in disguise, though of course none could say how—though everyone seemed to note the combination of his youthful face and silver hair. The effect was enough to make the local farmers and tradesmen and merchants too nervous to allow him to travel with them, and Asmel had been forced to use most of the money they needed for provisions and inns on a sad old horse instead. So Asmel rode and walked alternately, to save the horse's strength, and Toba Bet flew, as they put as much distance between themselves and the gate of Rimon as possible before it opened at the next moon.

Asmel had stopped to rest well off the side of the road, because Toba Bet was fairly conspicuous, and made Asmel look even less mortal as she flew around him. "I am growing weary of this," he went on, waving at Toba Bet's many bird-selves. "We're in a bad enough situation without your making it so I can't even talk to you. You know a great deal of what's happened and I am at a complete disadvantage. I don't even know if Barsilay and the elder Toba made it to P'ri Hadar or if things went badly for them." He sat down heavily and pulled his hair back from his face. "And I keep thinking that is why you won't change back, because you don't want me to know the truth."

The truth was more complicated than he'd guessed, and not only because the original Toba had died. Barsilay lived, but he was most certainly not in P'ri Hadar. Instead, he was probably in approximately the same place as Asmel and Toba Bet, only in the Mazik realm, travelling north and trying to get himself away from Rimon. Asmel would blame himself for that, Toba Bet knew. It was a fair disaster that Barsilay was still in grasping distance of the Caçador of Rimon.

They'd also lost the book containing the gate of Luz. Toba's half-sister, the Courser of Rimon, had taken it. Toba's last act, before she'd been killed, was to tear out the last page and send it to Barsilay.

Toba Bet let the part of herself that was airborne bank in a circle around Asmel, others of her were on the ground and in the trees nearby, listening carefully without responding, as she'd been doing for days while she neither ate nor slept, watching over Asmel as he ate salty mortal food and slept on the hard ground.

His eyes had gone far away as he continued his monologue. "I cannot even dream. Do you not have enough pity to tell me if my only kin still lives?"

The bird nearest flitted down to land on Asmel's shoulder, and he let out a sigh and turned to meet its eye. "If that's meant to be a comfort, it isn't." He lifted the bird in his palm and held her gently in his lap. "Whatever happened frightened you terribly. I'm sorry I couldn't protect you. I'm sorry I have no magic I can use to protect you now. But please come back to me, and I will do what I can."

Toba Bet felt his warm palm holding her small body. He said, "Shall I make you a trade, for your company? I have little left with which to bargain. What would you have, of what remains?"

Toba Bet felt wretched. He was manipulating her, of course, but he had a right to it: no matter how terrified Toba Bet was, she still had more than Asmel. She had her magic, and that meant that while Toba Bet still had a chance to escape a second trip into the void, Asmel had no other possible destination. And even if he failed to grasp the precise shape of that horror, his imagination could bring him close.

Enough, Toba Bet told herself. She had mourned herself long enough. Toba bat Penina was dead. The person who remained was Toba bat Toba, her own creation, and she would live to protect herself and Asmel for as long as she could, even if what Asmel most needed protecting from was the isolation of his own mind. Gathering herself, she drew in her breath and let her selves come together until she was a woman again, feathers smoothing to a filmy shift, not quite mortal and not quite Mazik, the product of an accidental spell. Asmel's eyes welled and he murmured, "Thank you," and he pulled Toba Bet against him. She put her own bare arms around him, trembling in the cold, and decided that hands had a use after all, and she stroked his hair while he pressed his face to her neck.

It was three nights until the new year, and three nights since the Courser of Rimon, Tsifra N'Dar, had failed to kill both the Heir of Luz and her own sister when she found herself dreaming of Atalef the Demon.

Tsifra had concluded that her sister had made a buchuk—a twin—and it was one of these versions of Toba Peres that she'd killed. What Tsifra hadn't yet determined was whether she'd killed the original or the buchuk herself. She wondered if it mattered, and had decided to table the question for later pondering: one of them, at least, was still alive, and in the mortal realm, and it would be her mission to hunt her down and return her to their father, the Caçador.

If she succeeded, this would be her last act as Courser. The Caçador would replace one sister with another he hoped was cleverer and would better suit his purposes, another half-Mazik who could carry out his will in the mortal world and help him harness the power of the Mirror. Tsifra's entire life had been spent in the pursuit of not being killed by her father or one of his agents, so much so that her awareness of her impending end left her more weary than fearful. Or so she told herself.

Tsifra did not much enjoy Atalef's company while awake let alone dreaming, and had hoped not to see him again for a very long time after having left him in Mansanar to possess the Queen's confessor. In this dream, he'd taken the shadowy shape of a cat. He paced a circle around her, growing larger until he was the size of a lion made of black shadow.

"Did your master send you?" Tsifra asked, because she could not imagine what Atalef wanted with her.

Atalef said, "No. Our master is content with our work and leaves us alone." Tsifra was glad not to be there to witness the work in question; the real confessor was bad enough even un-possessed. She wondered if anyone at court had noticed the difference.

"Whispering in the Queen's ear?" Tsifra asked. "What does the Caçador want her to do?"

"Nothing, yet," Atalef replied. "Only we aren't whispering now. We are hunting. Hunting birdlings."

"Birdlings," Tsifra repeated, because this was what Atalef called her too. "What do you mean? Are you not in Mansanar?"

"You know what we mean," Atalef murmured. He had condensed down to the size of a housecat again, and peeked at her through several dozen smoke-colored eyes. "You know precisely what we mean, Birdling."

He meant he was hunting her sister, the other Tsifra. The presently considered Tsifra did not know why they shared a name—it was not a typical thing amongst Maziks—but she suspected that her sister knew. If she found her again, she would have to ask. A problem for another day. To Atalef, she said, "I thought the Caçador was sending me on that mission."

"He changed his mind, decided not to wait," Atalef said. "The queen can whisper to herself for a bit, while we scent the air."

Tsifra did not much like the sound of that, because it meant she was redundant, and being redundant in the service of la Cacería was deadly. It was for this reason she'd killed her sister in the first place—only it turned out she'd only killed half of her. "If you're busy scenting the air, then why are you here with me?" she snapped.

"We wanted to smell you again," Atalef said. "Smell your magic. Birdlings smell different than Maziks."

"Do they," Tsifra said, and put out her hand, because the quicker he got a whiff the quicker he would leave; he was bad enough without insisting on calling her Birdling, a moniker she presumed referred to her name, Tsifra N'Dar—the Splendid Bird. She did not like to think that this demon had somehow intuited it. "Well?"

"Hm," he said. "Troublesome, indeed. There is no scent like this in Rimon. Not in the city, not in the mountains."

"Perhaps you're not smelling hard enough."

"No," he said. "She cannot be there."

"She cannot be anywhere else," Tsifra said. "She went through the gate, fifty Maziks saw her, including the Lymer." The fifty Maziks were all either dead or mad, but the Lymer had been far enough removed not to have suffered from that encounter. "The Lymer said she'd become an entire flock of birds. Can that be why?"

Atalef sat back on his haunches and changed into a shape that was decidedly not a cat. He unfurled his arms and waved his clawed shadow-hands. "It could be. It could be. If she is ten or thirty, then she is too small and too many, like us now."

"Like us? You mean like a demon?"

"Yes."

Tsifra had never experienced being a flock of birds, and wondered what it might feel like. Did Toba look out of all their eyes at once, or one at a time? She asked, "Her magic is too spread out, you mean?"

"Yes. Just so," Atalef said. "We had not considered that."

"But she can't remain like that long, can she? Won't she forget how to change back?"

"We don't know," Atalef said, which was probably true: becoming birds was not a thing that Maziks did, as a rule, making it a clever move indeed. "But if she is with the Lord of Books she will change back soon, I think. She would not want to be his pet."

Tsifra wondered about that. Was Toba not Asmel's pet already? It seemed to her that Asmel must be using Toba the way Tarses was using herself, as a tool. What other use did a Mazik have for a half-mortal?

But for all that, he'd given up his own magic before he'd given up Toba to their father.

The Courser did not like plans she could not untangle. It was too much like dealing with a second Tarses.

"But once she changes back, you'll have her."

"Oh, yes," Atalef said. "Very quickly."

And the killstone, she thought, because that was no small part of why Tarses wanted Toba; he believed she possessed the killstone of ha-Moh'to, the stone that contained Tarses's own name, and could be used against him. Atalef would give it to Tarses, because it was what he'd been ordered to do. And for all Atalef made her skin crawl, they were very much the same sort of creature: they were both Tarses's unwilling servants.

Ha-Moh'to, Tsifra had learned through much digging, had been the ancient order sworn to fight the Queen of Luz, their watchword *Monarchy is Abomination*. Their killstone contained the names of every member, and the ability to kill them instantly if only one knew the command word. Barsilay had given her a false word; whether he knew the real one Tsifra did not know.

"It's a pity," Atalef said, "we don't have the second safira."

Tsifra's mind caught on *we*, as it Atalef considered her an ally. The second safira was the one that belonged to Asmel. "What for? It's a pretty bauble. There's nothing in that one."

"Perhaps. Or perhaps it could be useful too. The Lord of Books was very wise. Our old master always told us tales of him, before he was put under the mountain—do you know why he was imprisoned?"

"No, I don't."

"He was passing too much time with us. He was doing things with us, to us, for us. So the Maziks came and locked him away, but some of us the Caçador kept for himself." Atalef faded in and out. "He had many ideas about us. What we were, what we could be for. Add a bit of Mazik magic to us and we change. Teach us and we sing, we dance, we learn. The man under the mountain thought: if we can hold a bit of magic, why not more? Why not enough for a whole Mazik?"

This was a lot of information to be freely given—it could not be freely given. She was dangerous close to conspiring with him now, only she did not know how just yet.

She could wake and end this conversation. Nothing he'd told her yet would get her into trouble.

Or she could stay and hear him out, and risk learning things she should not know. She weighed the options in her mind, and decided things could not be much worse for hearing Atalef's suggestion. If either of them managed to catch Toba, she was going to be killed anyway. She said, "How could a demon get a Mazik's full magic?" Tsifra asked.

Atalef said, "He thought we could be made into receptacles. For Safiras."

Tsifra regarded Atalef closely. He was unhappy—even without a face she could tell. "For safiras?"

"Forcing a Mazik to make a Safira, it is an old punishment. He forgets himself and goes to the void. The man under the mountain believed there was a way to put the magic into someone, somehow, as long as you were not putting it into a Mazik."

"Why not a Mazik?"

"Too much magic," Atalef said. "It would kill him. But he believed you could put it in a demon. Or a mortal. Or the person it had come out of, if they still lived. And then that whatever creature had taken the safira would have all that magic, and all those memories."

"Are you saying," Tsifra said, "that whoever gets Marah's magic put into them will have all her memories? Including the command-word of the killstone?"

"Yes," Atalef said. "We are saying so."

Here, then, was Atalef's plan, and now that she knew she could either inform Tarses or become Atalef's ally in truth. Tsifra found herself asking, "And did the man under the mountain discover how to put the magic into a demon, or a mortal?"

Atalef said, "If the safira were made into small enough pieces, it could be absorbed, he thought. Only he was never able to test it, because he was put beneath the mountain first."

What Atalef did not know what that she *did* have the second safira. Tarses had thoughtlessly given it to her for safekeeping, not believing it to be worth enough to guard himself. She whispered, "Does the Caçador know this?"

Atalef hissed back, "He does not."

Tarses only thought to keep the killstone from his enemies. He didn't realize how close he was to being able to use it himself, if he could pass Marah's magic to Atalef. He could kill Barsilay in a moment, and any other enemies who might have put their names into it.

Or Atalef could use it to kill Tarses.

Tsifra considered her next words carefully. "What precisely were you ordered to do?"

"We have three tasks," he said. "Return the other Birdling. Deliver the killstone. And kill the Lord of Books. And all three are together in one place. Once we find them, there is nothing for us to do but carry out our Master's will." Atalef made himself into a facsimile of Tarses's face, which said, "If you are clever, your order will have more empty space."

To trick Tarses into giving her vague orders . . . it was next thing to impossible. And even if she did somehow manage it, Atalef still didn't know how to absorb the safira. How did you break down an object made of ossified magic?

"The man under the mountain, how did he think a safira could be broken down? Why wasn't he able to try it?"

"What breaks down magic?" Atalef asked. "Surely you must know. Something no Mazik may ever touch. But something that *you* can. Do you know what it is?"

Tsifra startled. Could it be so simple? Atalef laughed, a sound like breaking glass.

"We will keep hunting, little birdling," Atalef said. "And we will see you when we see you, wishing for what you most desire and cannot have."

Freedom, he meant. "What we both desire," Tsifra said, but Atalef said, "No. We desire something much greater than freedom. Something you cannot understand."

"And what is that?" she asked, as Atalef began to fade.

Atalef whispered, "Unity."

Reading Guide

ERFWHON

About the Author

© ASH PHOTOGRAPHY

ARIEL KAPLAN grew up outside Washington, D.C., and spent most of her childhood reading fairy tales and mythology before settling on a deep love for Jewish folklore. She began studying the history of medieval Spain and the Convivencia while working on a Monroe Scholar project at the College of William & Mary, where she graduated with a degree in History and Religious Studies. She is the author of several books for younger readers. *The Pomegranate Gate* is her first fantasy novel.

✶ Book Discussion Questions ✶

These suggested questions are to spark conversation and enhance your reading of *The Pomegranate Gate*.

1. At one point, the old woman accuses Elena of being completely amoral. Do you think this is a fair assessment?

2. One of the main differences between Mazik and mortal magic is the relative importance of intention. What do you think about this? How important are a person's raw intentions?

3. There is a debate about whether Toba Bet, who was created by magic, is as much a person as the original Toba. Do you think she has as much a claim to personhood as the person who made her?

4. Asmel claims his academic work has always been politically neutral. Do you believe that is true, or is he overstating this? Do you think academic or scientific work is ever politically neutral? Should it be?

5. The Maziks of Ha-Moh'to worked in resistance to the Queen without trying to overthrow her because they believed a new regime might have been even worse. Do you think this was a wise course of action? Was it the most ethical course?

6. Asmel tells Toba, "There is little in blood but iron and air and water," and she should therefore not be too concerned about her father, but one of the main themes of the novel is legacy and inheritance. How can these ideas be reconciled? How important is lineage? What do we owe our ancestors, if anything?

7. The Maziks in the novel all share the same dreamspace. Toba thinks this sounds terrible, since interacting with Maziks in the dreamworld doubles her chances of social ruin. Naftaly, on the other hand, takes solace in the shared dreams, which are a respite from his feelings of isolation. Would you want to share dreams with the rest of the world? Or would it be better to keep them private?

8. Would you want to give up the serendipity of dreams you can't control if it meant never having nightmares?

9. Why do you think the Tobot are as different as they are?

10. If the characters ever manage to get to Aravoth, what do you imagine they'll find there?

11. If Elena hadn't been able to conceal Toba from her father, do you think she would become a person like the Courser?

Check Out Erewhon's Recent Titles